STORM WARNING

Also by Alice Henderson

A Solitude of Wolverines

A Blizzard of Polar Bears

A Ghost of Caribou

The Vanishing Kind

STORM WARNING

A NOVEL OF SUSPENSE

ALICE HENDERSON

WILLIAM MORROW
An Imprint of HarperCollinsPublishers

Without limiting the exclusive rights of any author, contributor or the publisher of this publication, any unauthorized use of this publication to train generative artificial intelligence (AI) technologies is expressly prohibited. HarperCollins also exercise their rights under Article 4(3) of the Digital Single Market Directive 2019/790 and expressly reserve this publication from the text and data mining exception.

This is a work of fiction. Names, characters, places, and incidents are products of the author's imagination or are used fictitiously and are not to be construed as real. Any resemblance to actual events, locales, organizations, or persons, living or dead, is entirely coincidental.

STORM WARNING. Copyright © 2026 by Alice Henderson. All rights reserved. Printed in the United States of America. No part of this book may be used or reproduced in any manner whatsoever without written permission except in the case of brief quotations embodied in critical articles and reviews. For information, address HarperCollins Publishers, 195 Broadway, New York, NY 10007. In Europe, HarperCollins Publishers, Macken House, 39/40 Mayor Street Upper, Dublin 1, D01 C9W8, Ireland.

HarperCollins books may be purchased for educational, business, or sales promotional use. For information, please email the Special Markets Department at SPsales@harpercollins.com.

hc.com

FIRST EDITION

Designed by Nancy Singer
Sea Turtle ©jenesesimre/stock.adobe.com
Map by Jason C. Patnode

Library of Congress Cataloging-in-Publication Data has been applied for.

ISBN 978-0-06-337185-9

26 27 28 29 30 LBC 5 4 3 2 1

For all the activists, scientists, and volunteers
out there who are working against all odds
to save imperiled species and
preserve their vital habitats.
You are champions.

And for Jason,
my stalwart friend, ally,
and fellow lover of wildlife and wilderness.

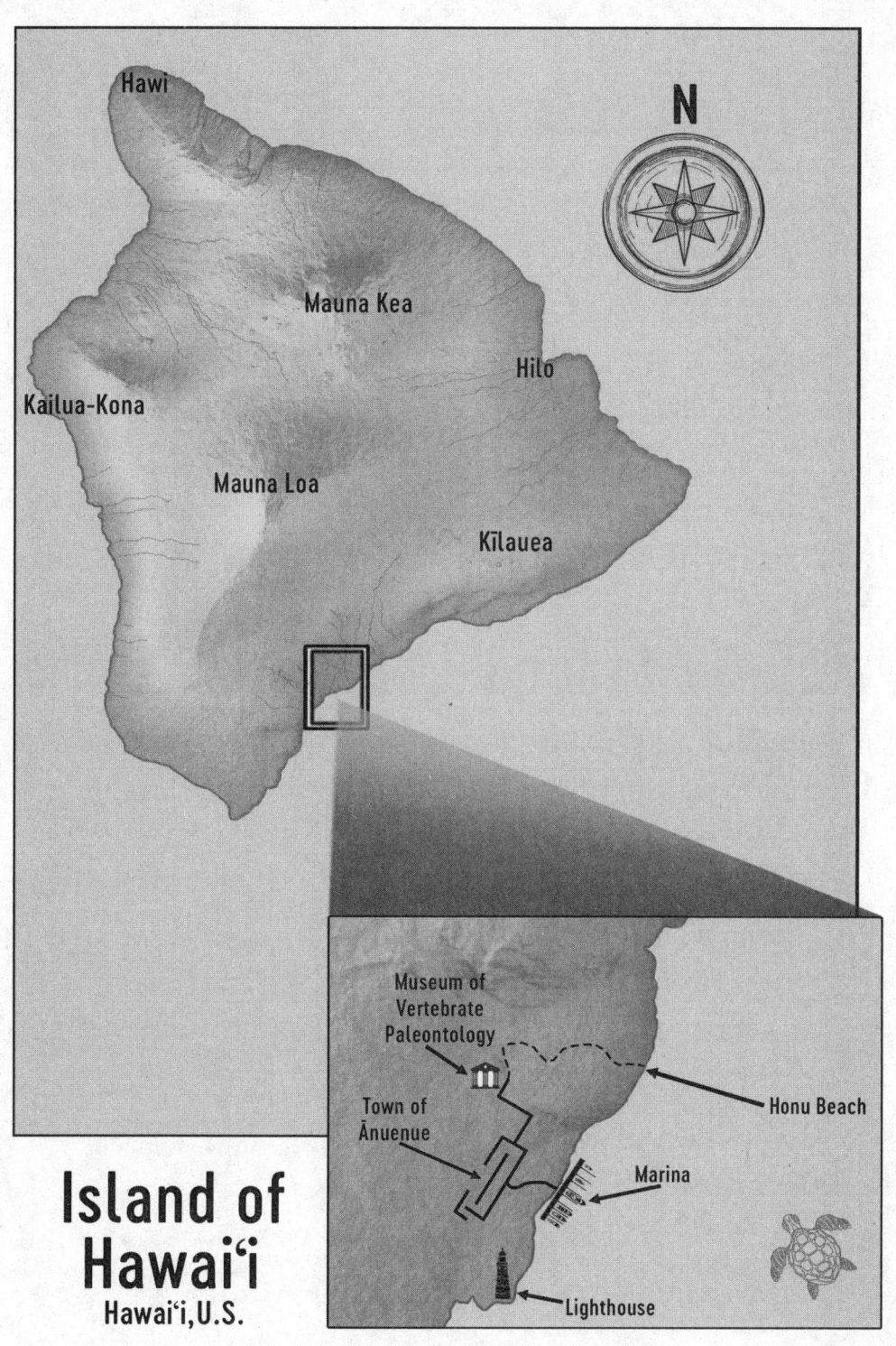

PROLOGUE

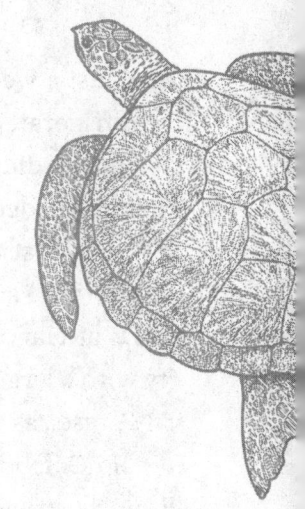

Allakaket River Gold Fields, Alaska
Two Weeks Ago

When geologist Caleb Winshaw made the find of his career, he never expected it would lead to the worst day of his life.

He and his team had been at the dig site for more than a week. A gold mining company had been working along the Allakaket River drainage, using bulldozers and excavators to remove large chunks of the permafrost, then sifting through the gravelly deposits to find gold. One of the excavator operators had dug into the side of a slope with a ripper tooth and was amazed when the full carcass of a perfectly preserved woolly mammoth had tumbled out along with chunks of silty soil and ice. His digger had nearly severed the mummy in two. He'd bounded down from the cab of the machine, calling excitedly to his coworkers.

Thankfully, they'd lost no time contacting Caleb at his private geology firm, as he was the closest researcher available. He'd instructed the gold miners to keep the mummy covered and as cold as possible, out of the sunlight. Then Caleb had jumped in his car and driven the bumpy dirt road to the site with his coworker Austin Trenor.

Caleb had been amazed when he showed up at the site and seen the massive, incredibly well-preserved mammoth, its tusks and trunk still intact, its fur still brown and fluffy. It looked like it had died just a week ago, not thousands of years ago. He knew it had to be refrigerated as soon as possible.

But he didn't have the facilities to keep it cold and run all the tests that he needed at his own lab. He was a geologist, not a paleontologist. His first thought was Dr. Nakoa Kahananui at the Museum of Vertebrate Paleontology in Hawai'i. They'd met while earning their PhDs at Harvard, and Nakoa ran a brand-new state-of-the art facility with a large, refrigerated lab and equipment to run mitochondrial DNA tests, as well as stable isotope analysis and radiocarbon dating.

So Caleb had airlifted the remains to Fairbanks via a Sikorsky S-64 Skycrane heavy-lift helicopter, then arranged for the mammoth's refrigerated transportation to Anchorage and then on to the Big Island of Hawai'i. He'd ridden with it south to Anchorage, and as he waited there to ship off the mammoth, Nigel Miller, a zoologist from a private research institute in Anchorage, had shown up.

Miller had heard about the mammoth from another gold field worker and wanted to take some small hair and tissue samples to analyze back at his own lab. Caleb knew how vital collaboration was with a find like this, so he didn't have an issue with it. They were small samples, but it still made Caleb nervous because he wasn't sure how much experience Miller had with this sort of thing.

After the mummy had been transported, Caleb returned to the gold field with Austin and Carla Siqiniq, a paleontology postdoc from the University of Alaska Fairbanks. Caleb wanted to study the site where the mammoth was found. Together they'd determined that a landslide had buried the mammoth approximately thirty-two thousand years ago. It had been a sudden event, contributing to its incredible preservation.

The side of the hill from which the mammoth had been excavated was steep and covered in silt and gravel, with large ice chunks wedged into the soil. They had to trudge through thick mud and "the mucks," what miners called the muddy mix of frozen, fine-grained silt and large chunks of plant material. At first they'd dug around the large cavity from where the mammoth had fallen, finding ancient, amazingly preserved grasses that still had their chlorophyll and were surprisingly green.

The gold mining company continued its operations, but it had been gracious enough to not touch the area where the mammoth had been found. Now Caleb stood on the steep excavated hillside, carefully going over the strata where the mammoth had lain, examining the soil and the topography to determine exactly how the creature had been buried thousands of years ago. He peered deeper into the cavity left by the carcass. Then he froze. He couldn't believe what he was seeing.

"Wait! Wait!" he yelled. "Everybody freeze!"

He held his hands out, stilling Austin and Carla, who worked nearby. His Wellingtons squished in the mud as he struggled to get closer to the scraped-out hole in the permafrost. Something was visible just inside the cavity where the mammoth had lain. He stared closer. Was it a clump of grass? A large ice wedge partially obscured a clump of fuzzy brown something. Slipping in the muck, he grabbed at a rock and hauled himself up until he was nose to the soil. Tentatively, he reached his gloved hand inside the hole. He switched on his headlamp, and the beam fell on the brownish clump. It was fur. A small, furry head, he realized. A baby mammoth.

He leaned back out of the dark hole. "There's a baby mammoth in here!" he called.

Carla and Austin scrambled up toward him, their feet sliding in the muck. They both peered inside the hole.

Caleb was staggered. This was the opportunity of a lifetime. Just like the adult mammoth, nearly every other Ice Age mummy that had ever been discovered had been accidentally dug out from the permafrost with mining equipment. Miners would pick up the remains and contact local paleontologists or geologists, who would then retrieve the mummy. Many times this meant that the mummies were accidentally damaged by the excavator ripper tooth, just as this infant's mother had been. The chance to do a careful, exacting dig of an Ice Age mummy was practically unheard of.

"We're going to need different tools," Caleb said excitedly. "Small power tools. Chisels. And we'll have to scrape away the layers of permafrost around it a little bit at a time, allowing each layer to melt before we remove the next." Only a part of the baby mammoth was visible now, just its head and shoulders. But Caleb could clearly see the slender trunk and hump of fat on its shoulders. Baby mammoths needed this extra store of fat when they were born to be able to survive their first winter. The infant was in amazing condition from what he could see, and like its mother, it looked like it had died only a week ago.

He shook his head in disbelief. He imagined the mother mammoth and baby, walking along an ancient streambed at the base of a slope. Then the landslide had let loose, burying them in moments. He felt sad for the pair, imagined the wide, grassy plains they'd foraged on together, in an ancient world filled with all manner of creatures that no longer roamed the earth: huge cave lions, short-faced bears, towering rhinoceros-like *Indricotherium,* saber-toothed tigers, and twelve-foot-tall ground sloths.

Caleb felt excitement churning in his stomach. It was an exuberant development in a dig that had so far had its share of challenges. First, they'd had to contend with the damage done to the adult. Then the original excavator operator had insisted on showing up every day to help them with the study. Caleb appreciated his enthusiasm, but unfortunately, the man had caught some kind of bug and ended up giving it to Austin. And now Caleb himself felt like he'd been fighting the infection all week, but he wouldn't let a low fever and some aches and pains keep him from the site.

And then Miller, not content with his samples, had insisted on coming to the site. He gloved and masked up, careful not to cross-contaminate with his own DNA, and took samples from the baby. Afterward, he was finicky and brusque, demanding to have his own little field station set up, which was getting in the way of the gold mining operation and not winning Caleb any fans. And Miller certainly had more funding than Caleb did—the man's private area held a small tent, some lab equipment, satellite internet—and Miller was constantly chatting away on his satellite phone from the privacy of his tent or truck, furiously taking notes and talking to far-flung colleagues around the world.

Miller also wasn't the friendliest person, either, impatient and easily irritated, and he had snapped repeatedly at the gold field employees, who weren't happy about him being constantly underfoot. They had gone on with gold extraction, wanting to make the most of the short summer, and couldn't afford to halt their small operation for what would ultimately be a monthslong excavation of the area around the pair of mammoths.

Now with the discovery of this baby, Caleb doubted Miller would leave anytime soon.

But maybe it was a good thing. The study was collaborative, after all. As a geologist, Caleb's specialty was figuring out the age of the sediment and what kind of event resulted in the mammoths getting buried.

A zoologist would know more about the biology of the mammoths, and Nakoa at the Museum of Vertebrate Paleontology in Hawai'i would be the ultimate expert. Not only did Nakoa have access to state-of-the-art equipment, but he'd processed other Ice Age mummies before, including a woolly rhino, another mammoth, and a cave lion. Caleb was excited to learn what his friend would find out.

Two days of further painstaking excavation followed, with Caleb carefully scraping away the layers of the permafrost, exposing them to the sun where they would melt. It would likely take the rest of the summer to fully expose the baby mammoth. At least Miller hadn't been too intrusive with the actual extraction of the infant. In fact, strangely, other than his initial sampling, he hadn't come up to examine the baby at all, but just remained in his tent, running soil tests. It was as if they'd reversed roles—the zoologist working on dirt and the geologist working on the mummy.

As he labored, Caleb's hand shook on the chisel. He really was starting to feel a lot worse, and his throat had grown more and more sore as the days wore on. It was getting difficult to swallow, and he knew Austin wasn't feeling too hot, either. *Damn.* Caleb definitely *had* caught the bug that was going around. But he wanted to push on.

A storm gathered in the west, dark clouds forming above the hills there. It looked like it would move right up the river valley, eventually hitting their location. Lightning flashed in the distance, and moments later he heard a distant boom of thunder.

Then he heard something else, a low hum, and paused from his work to look out to the west. He realized it was a rhythmic hum; then, as it grew closer, he could make out the beating rotors of a helicopter. It was unusual to see one out this way; aside from the Sikorsky he'd hired to transport the mammoth, he hadn't seen any air traffic at all, not even a lone bush plane.

Could be search and rescue or medevac, he thought, *trying to find some lost hiker.* As it drew closer, heading directly toward them, he wondered instead if someone might have been injured down below in the gold camp, and he'd just been too involved in the dig to notice any ruckus.

Then he saw the helicopter, but it wasn't red like a lot of medevac or SAR helicopters. It looked expensive and sleek, a dark blue helo that approached the dig site and hovered there above them. It began to descend, rotor wash hitting him suddenly and making him lose his balance on the steep, muddy slope. He tried to grab at a rock protruding from the slippery ice-filled bank, but his gloved hand slid off it, and he came careening down, landing hard on the rocky dirt below. The men operating the excavators and bulldozers paused in their work to stare at the helicopter as it landed just at the edge of the site.

"Who the devil is that?" demanded Jack Horten, the site's foreman, marching toward the helicopter as it powered down its rotors.

The sliding door on the helo jerked open and five people jumped out. Caleb felt his blood freeze. They wore black body armor and special ski masks hiding their faces, even their mouths. They all carried assault rifles. The foreman saw this and stopped immediately, backpedaling. One of the masked men came to the forefront, waving his gun at Horten to signal that he should continue to move back.

Miller emerged from his tent, saw what was happening, and froze there in the doorway.

The armed men fanned out, ordering the workers to climb down from the excavators and bulldozers. One gunman pointed up on the slope where Carla and Austin worked, motioning for them to come down. When they hesitated, the man fired his weapon into the hillside, sending up splashes of muddy silt and cracking open a large ice wedge. Carla lost her balance and came crashing down just as Caleb had, but Austin just stared down numbly. Fear filled his face, and instead of descending, he tried to scramble up the slope. He almost reached the top, where he'd be able to sprint away, when the gunman opened fire, spraying Austin with bullets. Caleb saw blood stream from a dozen holes in his colleague's back, and then Austin fell backward, sliding and bouncing down the muddy slope, landing motionless in the muck below, sightless eyes staring up at the sky.

"What in the hell!" shouted the foreman. The gunman closest to him opened fire, cutting down the man where he stood.

Trembling, Carla got to her feet, and Caleb moved toward her slowly. His mind struggled to think, to take in the situation. His mouth went dry. His feet felt rooted to the spot. There had to be a way out of this. Who were these men?

The lead gunman threw down several nylon sacks at the bulldozer driver's feet. "Fill these up," he ordered. "Fast."

The man grabbed the bags and was escorted to a safe, where he began to fill the bags with the gold they'd gathered so far that season.

But this kind of gold mining was a slow affair. Not much had been gathered yet, and Caleb thought it was a strange choice to rob such an operation. The take seemed barely worth it.

"Faster!" the man yelled. He pivoted his gun to the excavator driver. "You, help him."

The driver joined his coworker at the safe, and together they placed what gold they had into the bags. "Keep them working," the leader instructed another of the gunmen. Then he approached Caleb. Caleb's heart hammered painfully in his chest. A sour taste surged up from his stomach. He felt Carla clutching his arm tightly.

"You. What's up there?" the gunman asked, motioning to where they'd been standing when the helicopter first set down.

"It's not gold," Caleb managed to say, his throat so dry it hurt to talk.

"What were you doing up there, then?"

"It's . . . a paleontology dig site," he stammered. "A baby mammoth."

"Get it out."

"We haven't finished excavating it. It's still locked up in the permafrost."

"Get. It. Out," the man spat.

Caleb frowned, his stomach now doing flip-flops. He knew that such a well-preserved mummy could be worth quite a lot on the black market. Collectors paid millions of dollars for things like *T. rex* skeletons and triceratops skulls. A fully intact, perfectly preserved baby mammoth would be worth a fortune.

"Go up there and get it out," the man repeated.

Caleb's feet felt like concrete. His legs and arms started to go numb as his heartbeat thudded loudly in his ears. Blood rushed through his skull, almost drowning out the man's voice. "You . . . you don't understand," Caleb managed to say. "It's locked in there. I can't just pull it out."

For a second the man just stared at him. Caleb could see glinting dark brown eyes peering out from the ski mask. The man gripped the gun, and Caleb saw with a fresh wave of fear that the man's knuckles were white as he clutched the weapon.

Then the man spun suddenly and aimed his gun at the excavator driver. "You," he demanded. The man looked up, fear awash on his face. "Get back into your excavator and rip out that part of the slope." He pointed up to where the baby mammoth lay.

The man hesitated, and the gunman lifted his weapon. The driver came to life and held up his hands placatingly. "Okay. No problem." He climbed into the cab and drove the excavator to the base of the cliff. It already had its ripper tooth attached. He raised the arm and tore into the hillside.

Caleb felt sick as that whole section they'd painstakingly been excavating came crashing down, along with the baby mammoth and huge chunks of ice.

The gunman walked to where the small mammoth lay and then hooked his thumb toward the helicopter. "Get the container."

The other gunmen hurried back to the helicopter and retrieved a large metal box. They rushed it over to the baby mammoth and stowed the mummy inside. Caleb could see that the box was refrigerated, as if they'd known about the baby mammoth all along and had planned for it. The men rushed the container back to the helo, strapping it inside.

By now the bulldozer driver had finished loading up the small amount of gold in the sacks, so the gunmen placed those, too, inside the helo and then took up their posts again, guns aimed, mouths frowning and hostile.

The leader pointed at the zoologist's tent. The little man still stood framed in the tent doorway. "Destroy that equipment and any communication devices," the leader ordered.

"Now wait just a minute!" Miller stammered. "You can't do this!"

Two men shoved Miller aside and stormed into his tent. Caleb heard them smashing everything. They emerged with Miller's sat phone and threw it down in the mud, then riddled it with bullets.

"What the hell do you think you're doing? Don't you know who I am?" Miller demanded.

The leader wheeled on him and pulled the trigger on his assault rifle, letting loose a spray of bullets that cut the scientist down on the spot. He collapsed into the muck, grasping at the silt and ice, then went still.

"Everyone move together into one group," the leader ordered. He motioned for the man to climb down from the excavator cab. He joined the bulldozer driver where Caleb and Carla stood.

The leader lowered his gun and moved back toward the chopper, and for a second, Caleb's body felt a jolt of hope. Were they just going to leave now? Carla was squeezing his arm so tightly, she was starting to cut off his circulation. The bulldozer driver looked at the bodies of his boss, Austin, and the zoologist.

The leader reached the helicopter door, but then turned back. "Light 'em up," he ordered the other gunmen. They pointed their weapons at the small group.

Caleb's mind raced. Was this really happening? This couldn't be it. This couldn't be how he died. Just moments before, he'd been happily excavating a baby mammoth, for god's sake. Was this really how it was all going to end?

Then the men opened fire, and Caleb felt a course of bullets tear through him. Carla buckled, her hold on him slipping away. Bullets pinged off the excavator behind him. Searing pain erupted across his body. He collapsed into the muck, feeling a shocking mix of freezing ice water, mud, and his own warm blood.

He struggled to keep his eyes open, but his vision began to tunnel. To his horror he saw two of the gunmen approaching with cans of gasoline. As he lay struggling in the mud, he felt the fuel splash down on him. Smelled the overwhelming stench of it. And then one of the men lit a match and threw it down on the pile of twisted victims. Flames erupted around Caleb. He tried to scream as fire consumed his back, but blood bubbled up in his throat and only a strangled moan came out. Then the men opened fire again, and cold blackness enveloped him.

ONE

**Honu Beach
The Big Island, Hawaiʻi
Present Day**

Wildlife biologist Alex Carter glided through the water, swimming just above the brilliantly colored coral reef. She kicked easily with her fins, breathing through a snorkel. She drifted over a spiky brown sea cucumber as an orange-and-white-striped zebra moray eel darted out of a hole. A silver needlefish flashed in a patch of filtered sunlight. A white-spotted pufferfish moved its tiny fins to maneuver around a purple Achilles tang, the tang's orange tail giving a quick flick to propel itself out of the way. She spotted Hawaiʻi's state fish, the wonderfully named humuhumunukunukuāpuaʻa, with its lovely black and yellow stripes.

In some places the coral reef sported deep cracks, allowing her glimpses of the sandy bottom through a slice of gaping dark blue, and she realized how deep the water she swam over actually was. Then abruptly the reef ended and she found herself gliding out into the darker sea, the shadowed bottom far below. Two whitetip reef sharks circled here, gracefully powering through the water.

She turned around, sweeping over the edge of the coral reef again, and then headed back toward shore over a different section of it. Brown *Aiptasia* anemones waved their tentacles in the gentle current, and barnacles, open with their slender arms reaching out, encrusted a few rocks. A spotted eagle ray glided by, and then Alex saw a cluster of meandering and vagabond boring sponges. She hovered, searching the area carefully. A light blue unicorn fish and a yellow-and-black Moorish idol wriggled by, their fins flapping in the water. She couldn't get over the bursts of color everywhere she looked: yellows, oranges, reds, blues, and greens.

Here the reef was closer to the surface, allowing dapples of sunlight to play over its surface. And then she saw a flash of iridescent amber and brown, rising up from behind a mound of sponges. She stopped immediately, hanging back, arms waving in the warm water, watching. A rare hawksbill turtle hovered over the sponges and took a few bites of one, using its specially shaped beak, which had earned the animal its name.

Deftly the turtle plucked sponges out of tiny crevices in the coral reef. She watched as it broke off a few bites of coral, too. Some researchers thought they did this to reach more sponges, but others suspected it could be a way to get extra calcium in their diet to prepare for egg laying. Each time a turtle broke off pieces, this allowed fish to reach parts of the reef they wouldn't normally have access to and feed there.

It ate happily, artfully adjusting its flippers to stay above the bed of sponges. Alex smiled around her snorkel. But then she smiled too broadly and a little water seeped in through the edges of her snorkel. She tasted the salt water and clamped her mouth tighter, still unable to stop smiling. She looked around for other hawksbills but knew she was lucky to see just this one.

As the sunlight streamed down through the water, Alex took in the gorgeous mix of colors of its carapace: oranges, reds, yellows, with touches of black and brown. But the predominant color was a gorgeous lighter amber color, allowing it to reflect heat in the warmer waters off the coast of the Big Island. She knew that when hawksbills reached colder waters, their shells changed hue, shifting to a darker color to absorb more heat.

Alex marveled at the multicolored carapace, then spotted a location tracker attached to its shell as the turtle changed its position, and Alex knew it had to be one of the two that had already been tagged for her study. It had come ashore almost two months ago to lay eggs on the nearby beach. It had been a stroke of luck that a volunteer from the Center for Sea Turtle Restoration had been present when it happened. He alerted CSTR, and a biologist was able to come out and tag the turtle before it returned to the sea. Initially, the center had that same biologist watch over the eggs, but he had been called away to Oʻahu for a green turtle project.

The nonprofit had no other available biologists to monitor the eggs and keep them safe. The other three scientists who worked for the center were posted on different Hawaiian islands monitoring endangered green turtle nests. The center needed someone who could camp on the beach, monitor the nests, and tag any more adults with satellite trackers so that the center could get a good idea of where the turtles were migrating from.

The executive director of the center was a college friend of Ben Hathaway, the regional director of the Land Trust for Wildlife Conservation. Ben, whom Alex had worked for in the past, had recommended her.

Alex was just coming off several months of hanging out with her dad in the San Francisco Bay Area, where she'd also finished a study on how the coyote population in the Presidio was coping with living among humans.

The timing was perfect, and Alex had agreed on the spot. She'd taken a couple of days to gather gear and spend a little more time with her dad, then had flown to the Big Island. She'd set up camp on the beach where the hawksbills were coming to shore to nest. So far there were two nests: the original one, which was due to hatch any day now, and a second one that Alex had the joy of witnessing shortly after she arrived, when she'd spotted the hawksbill swimming to shore and laying and burying its eggs. She briefly caught it, dried off a portion of its shell, and attached the transmitter. In just a few minutes, the turtle was back to its normal behavior, waddling toward the surf. So now two turtles were being tracked. Alex was also greatly relieved that she didn't have to tranquilize the animal as she'd had to do with polar bears, caribou, and jaguars in the past.

She'd loved this assignment so far. After the heat and dryness of her recent job in New Mexico, it was a shock at first to arrive in this tropical clime. As soon as Alex stepped off the plane, the pleasant level of humidity struck her. A rainstorm had been brewing over the green mountains when she walked out to her rental car, and a yellow-billed cardinal, a gorgeous white-and-black bird with a vivid red head, had chirped out its call from the fronds of a loulu palm. To Alex, the call had always sounded like the cardinal was asking a question and then answering itself. She could feel tropical life all around her, in the promise of rain, in the gentle rustling of the palms on a warm breeze, in the sweet trilling of a brilliantly red 'apapane honeycreeper from a nearby branch.

And now she was here floating in the warm water, snorkeling over this incredible coral reef, taking in all the color and throngs of teeming life.

She felt blessed indeed, so grateful for the life she had built for herself, traveling from place to place to help imperiled species, each location a glimpse into the biodiversity of life.

For a few more minutes, she watched the hawksbill feeding on sponges. The fact that it was sticking around meant that it was probably going to lay a second clutch of eggs soon. To lay their eggs, most sea turtles swam far away from their foraging grounds to the beach where they were born. This could be hundreds or even thousands of miles away. They then laid several clutches of eggs about two to three weeks apart, before swimming all the way back to their foraging grounds again. There they'd eat, rest, and hang out for one to five years before repeating the trip to their natal beaches to lay more eggs.

Little was known about where these particular hawksbills spent most of their lives. Because they hadn't been known to lay eggs on this beach before, the theory was that their natal beach had been destroyed somehow, either through human development, light pollution, or sea level rise.

The center also didn't know where they were migrating from, so Alex had been excited to learn more from the satellite trackers. She did know that while most hawksbills traveled vast distances between their natal beaches and feeding grounds, the ones in Hawai'i stayed within the island chain.

The afternoon had grown late, and the water started to cool. As Alex watched the hawksbill, the late afternoon sun glinting off its shell, she started to shiver even in her rash guard. So she snapped a few pics of the turtle with her underwater camera and swam to shore.

She emerged, dripping, onto a beach of black sand with intermittent sections of old, long-cooled lava flows from ancient eruptions of Kīlauea. Activities on the beach were winding down for the day. Only two groups of people remained: a trio of surfers floating just offshore and a family of four packing up their beach chairs.

Honu Beach was a remote area on the southeast part of the island. Only a few houses had been built along its coast, and for the most part it was undeveloped and quiet.

Alex toweled off, feeling elated from the sight of the foraging hawksbill. A few hundred yards away, just down beach from the turtle nests, sat an inactive construction zone. A prominent lodging chain had begun building a new luxury hotel on the site when the first hawksbill turtle came to shore and laid eggs. The construction would have torn up that section of beach, so building was halted. The construction crew withdrew, and now the site stood silent: a crane and several bulldozers waiting for the day they could resume work, if they ever could. They'd built a breakwater and pier so that small ships could come in with building supplies, but now the dock stood empty. The footprint of the foundation had also been poured, with rebar sticking out of the concrete, but so far that was the only progress on the construction.

According to Hawaiian law, beaches were public land up to the high-tide line, so technically speaking, the hotel would not be able to own the beach itself. But even still, if the resort was built, it would bring in a lot more people. Lights and constant visitor foot traffic could drive off any future turtles from laying eggs on this beach. So currently the lodging company was tied up in litigation and the site sat vacant and silent.

Alex was grateful for the halt for the sake of the turtles.

The nearby family had their radio on, playing music softly. It shifted to a top-of-the-hour news report. "A sophisticated shipping vessel was seized at the Port of Los Angeles on suspicion of smuggling. The ship, outfitted with a special refrigerated hold, was seized on Tuesday after the crew failed to provide proper paperwork detailing their cargo manifest. When authorities boarded the ship, they found the cargo hold empty. Though the crew had initially been told to report for questioning, none showed up at the appointed time. A dragnet has failed to locate any of them, and their whereabouts are currently unknown."

Curious to hear more, Alex paused, listening. But just then the mother herded her kids toward their waiting car, picking up the radio and shutting it off.

Alex didn't like to leave the eggs for too long, so she finished toweling off and moved back toward her small camping area. When she'd first arrived in town, she'd stocked up on nonperishable food, but she'd need a volunteer to watch the nests when it came time to restock or if she needed to be gone for any considerable length of time.

The center had put out a call for volunteers, and tomorrow applicants were due to arrive on the beach for Alex to interview. She hoped she'd get some good ones, but the beach was so remote that she worried most people wouldn't want to make the trip out.

The nearest town, Ānuenue, was tiny and off the beaten path, lying a good seven miles from the beach, much of it down dirt roads. The Hawai'i Belt Road was the nearest main road, running south from Hilo, but it was still quite a distance away from this isolated location. A number of far smaller roads branched off from it, some leading to other little towns or beaches. One such road led to Ānuenue, and a pitted dirt road led from there out to this remote beach.

The small village contained just a couple of restaurants, a coffeehouse, a hardware store, a fifteen-room motel, a drugstore, a post office, a handful of gift shops, and an outfitter that rented Jet Skis, scuba and snorkeling gear, kayaks, paddleboards, and a couple of small boats. Alex herself had rented her scuba and snorkeling gear from them when she first arrived. A new museum, the Hawaiian Museum of Vertebrate Paleontology, had been built on the outskirts of the town.

And she wasn't far from a lot of spectacular sights. Before the turtle project had officially started, she'd explored Hawai'i Volcanoes National Park, and she looked forward to visiting a historical lighthouse to the south of here. Kīlauea had been erupting, sending out streams of lava. Alex had hiked on the cooling, ropy pahoehoe lava and then stayed to watch sections of the eruption glowing orange and red at night, churning white-hot pieces mixing with colder black sections. She'd been enchanted.

Now that the day had cooled off a bit, it was a perfect time to set up her equipment. UPS had delivered the necessary supplies earlier in the day. She'd stowed them all inside her rental Jeep, which was parked in a small, grassy area off the beach. The center had also lent her a life jacket and a small inflatable Zodiac boat, and this was hauled up on the shore by her tent.

She used the public shower house, rinsing off her swimsuit, and changed into a fresh pair of jeans and a long-sleeved black shirt. The island grew a bit chilly at night, so back at her tent, she donned a thin purple fleece jacket. She also grabbed her multitool, the one her father had given her years ago when she finished her PhD in wildlife biology. He'd had it engraved with "Dr. Alex Carter—Adventure Awaits," and she loved it.

Alex checked the calendar on her phone. The first batch of eggs had been laid fifty-six days ago, which meant they'd be due to hatch in about four more days, give or take. Incubation time could vary depending on temperature. The warmer the temperature, the faster the eggs incubated. But a number of instruments she was going to install would help her narrow down the time of actual hatching.

Microphones would allow her to monitor the sounds coming from the nests, and thermocouples, simple devices that measured the temperature of the sand above the nests, would give her clues about changes in temperature and let her know when hatching was imminent. When that happened, she'd have to call any volunteers she hired to the beach, to ensure all the hatchlings made it safely to the water.

She'd also ordered two security cameras that would send an alarm to her phone if any predators approached the turtle nests while she was sleeping. She worried about nests being disturbed. With hawksbills, even a nest that hadn't been messed with at all could still have only an 80 percent survival rate. She would have to be very careful and vigilant.

The family left, the area now empty except for the distant surfers and Alex. She retrieved the supplies from her Jeep and set the boxes down in the sand. She sliced them all open. Inside rested the components to build several thermocouples, a soldering iron, several multimeters, two security cameras, a microphone, and a sky quality meter, or SQM, to measure the darkness of the site.

Alex had already placed yellow caution tape in long rows at the top of the beach and just above the waterline so that people wouldn't walk on top of the nests. She didn't want to mark off exactly where the nests were with smaller areas of tape in case any poachers happened along. So now the two long stretches of yellow caution tape flapped in the wind. People could easily walk around them if they needed to, and they would add an extra layer of protection to the eggs.

First Alex went to work setting up the alarm system. On the trunk of a nearby loulu palm, she hung a camera that faced up the beach. Then, on the other side of her tent, she hung a second camera that would gaze down the beach. If any predators or poachers approached from either direction, the camera would spot them and record video and photos. On top of that, the camera system would also send an alert to her phone if it detected any movement. That way, if anyone approached at night while she was sleeping, her phone would vibrate. She'd keep it tucked inside her sleeping bag where it would be sure to wake her up.

She inserted batteries and memory cards into both cameras and then jogged up and down the beach with her phone. It alerted her each time she entered one of the cameras' fields of view. She stopped, connecting to the cameras via Bluetooth, and saw that both cameras had recorded videos of her and were working perfectly.

She stepped back, admiring her handiwork, then returned the rest of the supplies to her Jeep, keeping the sky quality meter with her for later. She'd build the thermocouples tomorrow. Returning to the shore, she gazed out at the sea, hoping more hawksbills would arrive to this protected little patch of beach.

She walked back to her tent and got out her small Sterno stove. She heated up a pot of water and made a batch of red beans and rice, then flavored it with cumin. As she ate, she gazed out at the rolling surf, watching the three remaining surfers. They talked and floated on their boards as the sky turned pink and purple after sunset.

The wind sighed in the palm fronds above her, and a warm breeze blew off the sun-warmed sand. Alex took a deep breath and really let it sink in that she was in this amazing place. She hoped she'd be able to glean important information about where these hawksbills were migrating from. She couldn't wait for the eggs to hatch, to watch the baby turtles emerge and scamper down the sand toward the waiting water.

When it got fully dark, Alex walked out onto the beach, standing at the water's edge. The waxing crescent moon would set soon, and the immense span of the dark sky opened up above her. The Milky Way arced overhead, a silvery sweep of stars so packed with light it looked like a glowing cloud. If she were on a more northerly beach, she'd probably be able to see the light dome emanating from Hilo, but out here, far on the southeast side of the island, it was incredibly dark.

She pulled out the sky quality meter and found a flat rock on the beach to place it on. She waited while it gathered information on the sky above. When it was finished, she read the result: a Bortle rating of class 2. The Bortle scale, created by the astronomer John E. Bortle, was used to judge the quality of dark sky in an area. A Bortle rating of class 1 was the darkest possible sky, one where the star-rich areas of Scorpius and Sagittarius actually cast shadows on the ground, and one could see the Triangulum Galaxy with the naked eye. An extremely light-polluted city, in which few to no stars were visible, would rate a class 8 or 9 on the Bortle scale, the worst possible skies.

Many animals needed darkness to find their way. Migratory birds used the stars to navigate. Light-polluted areas could throw them off course and into unfamiliar terrain, bringing them into collision with building glass and other threats.

Sea turtles used darkness and light as navigational clues, too. Thanks to the hotel construction being halted, this beach was darker than the ones in bigger, developed areas like Honolulu, Hilo, and Pearl City.

Movement on the beach brought her gaze up, and she saw a man and woman walking toward her, holding hands, one of them using a flashlight. As they got closer, the man eyed Alex as she picked up the SQM and entered the day's reading into her iPad. He slowed, his expression curious. "Are you the biologist?"

"Yes, that's right. Nice to meet you." She wondered how they knew about her and was curious if they'd seen the call for volunteers.

"We heard there'd be one out here." He pointed up the beach. "We live just up there. The fifth house." Then he gestured at the SQM. "What is that thing?"

"It's a sky quality meter. It rates how dark the night sky is, how many stars it can see."

"What for?" he asked.

The woman tugged at his hand, embarrassed. "C'mon, Robert. Leave her alone. She doesn't want to play twenty questions. Can't you see she's working?" She rolled her eyes at Alex. "I'm sorry, he always does this. Butting into everyone else's business."

"I'm just curious," Robert said. "I heard this was an active turtle nesting area now. But what does darkness have to do with it?"

"It's okay," Alex told the woman. "I'm happy someone's interested. Dark skies are important to turtle reproduction."

"How so?"

"When turtles hatch, they crawl toward the brightest area. Normally, that's the ocean at night, because inland will be shadowed by trees. But resorts, hotels, golf courses, and housing developments built on beachfronts throw them off. When they see those bright lights, they crawl inland instead, thinking the ocean is over there. Then they end up dying. Some are picked off by predators; others are hit by cars."

The woman frowned. "That's awful."

"I didn't know that," Robert said. "We can turn off our porch light at night if that helps."

"I'm sure it would," Alex told him.

The woman tugged on his arm again. "Let's go, Robert. Let her do her thing."

Reluctantly, he let her pull him away.

"And if you could ask your neighbors to do the same, that would be great!" Alex called after them.

"Will do!" he called back, being propelled along.

Alex watched them go, feeling amused. Often she encountered couples like that, where one was a talker and the other quiet and reserved.

She stowed her SQM in her gear and pulled out the small microphone she'd ordered, along with her earbuds. Back at the nests, she listened for any sound coming from them that would let her narrow in on the exact moment to expect hatching. For now, they were quiet.

Alex stood up, gazing out at the sea. She looked forward to tomorrow, when volunteers arrived. She hoped she'd find some good ones.

She finally retired, and had just drifted into a deep sleep, lulled by the soothing sounds of the surf, when the loud squawk of a police siren jolted her awake.

TWO

Red and blue lights flashed over Alex's tent walls. For a second, in her groggy state, she thought she was back in Boston, awakened in the middle of the night to sirens, people yelling, traffic roaring by outside her apartment window. But then she came to more fully, realizing she was still on the beach in Hawai'i. She sat up, hearing the idling of a car out by the small parking area. She crawled out of her sleeping bag, unzipped the tent, and donned her boots.

Standing up, she saw a police car parked by her Jeep. Its searchlight swept the beach, the cop still sitting inside the cruiser. Then she spotted a slender figure crouched in the dark shadows of the trees about a hundred feet away. The cruiser's searchlight spotlighted him as he gripped a tree trunk, and she clearly saw him now, an expression of terror on his umber face. He was just a young kid, maybe only fifteen or so. As soon as the spotlight fixed on him, he took off running, dashing up the beach toward her tent.

The cop jumped out of the cruiser and ran onto the beach in pursuit.

When the kid glanced back and saw how close the officer was getting, he cried, "Don't hurt me!" His voice trembled with fear.

The cop continued to give chase, hand on the butt of his gun, and Alex tried to take in the situation, to understand what was happening. The kid was clearly scared and didn't appear to be any kind of threat. She wondered why the cop was pursuing him.

The officer was huge, well over six feet with a sturdy, muscular build. She caught a glimpse of his angry, pale face as he sped by, teeth gritted, beady eyes narrowed beneath a furrowed brow. Red blotches marked his face, blood rushing to his skin's surface from exertion.

They sped past the area of the turtle eggs, then whizzed by Alex. The cop took no notice of her, quickly gaining ground and getting fairly far down the beach.

In a few long strides, the cop tackled the kid, driving him down into the sand. He wrenched the kid's hands behind his back and knelt down hard on his upper back. He whipped out a pair of cuffs and slapped them on the kid's skinny wrists.

"I didn't do anything!" the boy pleaded.

They were some distance down the beach now, but she could still hear them clearly.

"Yeah, I'll bet," the cop retorted, but he didn't get up or pull the kid to his feet. He continued to kneel on him.

"You're hurting me."

"What were you planning to do, come down here and steal this lady's equipment? I hear it's pretty expensive."

Alex frowned. She had never seen the officer before. She did know the local police had been notified of her presence and purpose on the beach. But she had no idea how he knew what kind of equipment she had or how expensive it was.

"No!" the kid wheezed. "I was just walking home."

"At this hour?" the cop yelled, kneeling harder on his skinny back.

Alex looked at the time on her phone. It was only eleven p.m. It wasn't that late. When she was a kid that age, her curfew had been one a.m.

"My aunt lives just up the beach."

The cop leaned over him, voice raised and angry. "Then why didn't you use the sidewalk out by the street?"

"I just like walking down the beach at night." When the cop

didn't respond, the boy chattered nervously. "I like the way it looks in the moonlight."

"Oh, you like moonlight, do you?" the cop guffawed, pressing a hand on the back of the boy's head. "I bet. More like you like seeing if anyone's left their back door open. See what you can steal."

"I've never stolen anything in my life," the boy protested.

"Sure," the cop scoffed. "I'll bet you're a perfect angel."

"My aunt's expecting me," the kid said weakly. He struggled to keep his mouth and nose above the sand, but the cop pressed his head back down. The fear in the teen's voice was almost choking. "She'll know this is the route I walked tonight. I walk it every day."

"Yeah, I've seen you. Probably casing houses along the way."

"I've never done that!" the boy pleaded. "I was on the way home."

"Or visiting some drug-dealing pal *on the way home*."

"I don't do drugs," the kid protested.

"Looking for someone to rob, then, *on the way home*?" the cop sneered as he repeated the phrase *on the way home*. But the officer clearly had no specific reason for stopping the teen, and the kid was terrified.

He jerked the boy's wallet from his back pocket with one hand and dug out his ID. "Jerome Callister, eh? Well, Jerome, let's see what you've got on you." He roughly dug through the rest of the kid's pockets, not finding anything but a pack of gum, which he tossed into the sand. "What'd you do?" the cop demanded. "Throw any weapons or stolen items you had in the bushes?"

"I didn't have any of those things!"

"I've seen you and your friends in town, pretending like you're just hanging out at the skate park. I doubt you're up to anything good." He leaned in close to the boy's face. "I'll teach you to run from me."

At this point, the kid actually started to cry.

Alex had heard enough. She'd fought enough bullies in her life to know one when she saw one. This guy obviously was getting off on the power of his position and had nothing whatsoever on this poor kid.

Alex approached. When she was still some distance away, she said, "Excuse me, officer?"

He whirled, his hand flying down to the butt of his gun. Alex felt a cold lump of fear flop over in her stomach. His knee ground down harder into the kid's back as he pivoted and saw her there.

She held up her hands in a placating gesture. "I'm Alex Carter. The biologist who's studying the turtles on this beach?"

"Yeah?" he asked, irritated and impatient. "What do you want?"

"I think there's been a misunderstanding here. This is one of my volunteers. I asked him to stop by here on his way home, just to make sure there weren't any poachers or dogs on the beach that could harm the eggs."

"What the fuck?" the cop cursed. "Are you serious?"

"Yes," she answered, still standing with her hands out.

At this, the cop stood up, yanking Jerome to his feet. "*This* kid?" the cop asked with disdain.

Alex nodded. "Yes. Why? Is there a problem?"

The cop's eyes darted around. He was uncomfortable, clearly caught off guard. "No . . . I just knew he was up to no good, being out here this late."

Silence hung heavily between them. Finally Alex said, "Can you uncuff him? I need to walk him through the schedule for tomorrow."

The cop stood there, deflated, like he didn't know what to do with the rest of his aggression. But she was someone he'd been told to watch out for, and he probably didn't want word of his behavior to get back to the station. Begrudgingly, he uncuffed Jerome. The boy pulled away from him, rubbing his wrists.

"I should have been notified of this," the cop said angrily. He stomped past Alex. "I expect you to send a complete list of your volunteers to the police station in the morning."

Of course the police didn't need that. Hadn't asked for that. It was a public beach. This guy was just trying to pawn off his bad behavior onto Alex's supposed oversight.

He didn't meet Alex's eyes as he walked past her. She waited until he'd reached his cruiser and pulled out of the parking area, spinning the tires and sending clods of dirt sailing through the air.

She looked back at Jerome. "You okay?"

He nodded, relief on his face. "My friends told me about that guy. I'm just here for the summer, staying with my aunt. They said that he'll stop any kid who's out alone, just looking for something to pin on you." He rubbed his wrists more and stretched his sore back where the cop had knelt on him. "We've got mean-ass cops where I'm from, too. But I wasn't expecting to meet one on a beach in Hawaiʻi."

"I hear you. Unfortunately it seems like there are people who abuse their power everywhere."

"Thanks for what you did."

"No problem. I'm glad you're all right. You going to be okay to walk home?"

Jerome turned and pointed up the beach. "Yeah. My aunt's house is just three houses up from here."

"Okay." She turned to go back to her tent, her nerves frazzled from the tense encounter. She wondered if she'd be able to go back to sleep.

"Hey," he called.

She turned back around.

"You really studying sea turtles out here?"

"I am."

"I've never seen one. I'm from Michigan. But as a kid I had sea turtles on my wallpaper in my room. Do you . . ." He hesitated.

Alex waited.

"Do you really have volunteers helping you?"

"I do."

"Need any more?" he asked.

She smiled. "Sure. Come by tomorrow and apply."

He broke into a crooked grin. It made Alex feel good after seeing that same face furrowed in terror. "All right. I will."

Jerome walked off down the beach, and Alex returned to her tent. She shucked off her boots and crawled inside, sliding into her sleeping bag. But she was too nervous to sleep. Her heart still pounded in her chest.

Then she heard a boat's motor approaching out in the dark. She tensed, wondering if poachers were trying to land on the beach. But the closer the engine came, the more she realized it was the sound of a larger craft, something too big to land on the beach. At first she thought it might pass by. It wasn't unusual, people out for an evening cruise, enjoying the starlight, doing night scuba dives.

When it sounded like it was quite near her location, the engine cut to an idle. Alex waited, listening to it, then wondered what the people were doing. She sat up and crawled out of her sleeping bag, then unzipped the tent door to peer out.

Far out from the beach, the ship had cut all its lights and just hung there, bobbing on the waves. The moonlight flashed off its hull and danced on the water, the white of waves' crests glowing as they rolled in.

She wondered if they were about to deploy a smaller launch craft, so she waited, watching. But they didn't. They could be preparing for a night dive, but the engine didn't cut out, just continued to idle.

She pulled out her binoculars and looked, but it was so distant that even with her 7x50 binoculars that let in a lot of light, she couldn't quite make much out, just the vague figures of two people moving around on deck. After a few minutes, the motor revved up again, and the boat sped off. But they didn't switch its lights back on. Alex wondered if they'd forgotten with the moon so bright. But then the lights flashed on and the boat headed farther down the coast.

She stared down the beach to where the turtle nests were, finding them undisturbed, and crept back into her sleeping bag.

THREE

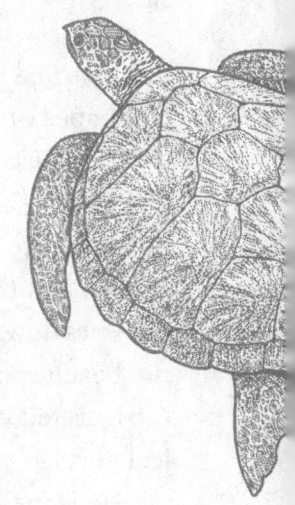

Aboard the Cargo Vessel *Sunfish*
Off the Coast of Los Angeles
Later That Night

Ship cook Artie Kuna emerged from the narrow ladder, his hand running along the cold railing. It was freezing outside, his breath pluming and the moisture hanging in the air. He stepped out into the night, seeing the expanse of stars above. He lived for these breaks, getting out of the stifling galley after a day of cooking and serving. At last, when the crew had eaten and hauled themselves off to bed or to the watch, he finally had some time to himself.

The ship was small, with a crew of only nine, but the men ate like there were twenty. He didn't know where they put it all. Some combination of hollow legs and separate dessert stomachs.

He walked across the deck, feeling the engine's hum through the soles of his boots. The deck rocked a little, but the seas were mostly calm tonight. He stepped to the edge of the railing and gripped the round metal there, leaning out over the dark waves. He breathed in the fresh sea air. As always, he'd sweated through his shirt while working over the stove.

He couldn't see any lights on the horizon, no areas of land. He'd never seen the stars as bright as they were out at sea, so much brilliance that he could barely make out many of the constellations he'd learned as a boy, as the points of light that formed the familiar shapes of Hercules and Boötes became lost amid myriad other stars. Some constellations, though, were unmistakable, and he only had to look at the brilliant golden haze that marked the center of the galaxy to spot the Teapot, nebulae curling out of its spout like smoke, and then the elegant curling tail of Scorpius. He followed the stars down to the horizon. Somewhere out there, to the east, lay the beaches of California, but the ship was headed west, carrying refrigerated vegetables, fruits, and pharmaceuticals to exotic, tropical ports.

He leaned on the rail, resting on his elbows, seeing the stars on the horizon reflected in the waters to the west. They flashed, twinkling, and he focused on them a little more closely. They were too bright. Flashing too much. Then they winked out. He blinked. They hadn't been reflections of stars in the water. They'd been something *in* the water. Pinpricks of light. He saw one flash again, then go out. He tensed, listening closely. Some noise reached him from far out there. A hum. He tried to block out the noise of the diesel engine working below, but he couldn't make out anything else other than the surging waves as the ship carved its way through the sea.

He gripped the rail, turning his head to hear better, and there it was. A smaller whine. An outboard engine. He narrowed his eyes, trying to pinpoint it in the darkness. Another light flashed, as if someone had turned on a headlamp, checked something, then quickly switched it off.

Or maybe they were trying to signal the ship. Maybe their boat had gone down, and they were trying to race for the *Sunfish,* needing to be picked up.

Artie waited for another flash of light, wondering if it was an SOS, but no further gleam came along. The whine of the outboard motor grew a little louder. It was definitely coming this way.

Artie decided he'd better alert the captain. He hurried through the narrow passageways until he reached the captain's quarters.

He knocked politely on the door but didn't hear the expected *come in*. He knocked again, wondering if the man had fallen asleep early that night. Nothing. Tentatively, he pushed on the door, finding it unlocked. He entered, the room dark beyond. Light from the passageway spilled onto the bed, which was empty.

Artie shut the door again, pondering what to do. Then he realized it was their regular poker night, which meant the captain was likely in the first mate's cabin with the ship's doctor. It was a weekly ritual.

Artie headed that way at a clip, wanting to give them the heads-up before the Zodiac arrived at the ship, possibly needing rescue. There was the possibility that they didn't need help at all—that they were pirates looking for trouble—but Artie frowned, not wanting to acknowledge this possibility.

Artie now made his way to the first mate's cabin but found it empty, too. Probably all playing in the doctor's quarters. He started in that direction, but the sudden sound of shouting froze him in his tracks.

An automatic weapon rattled above, a series of rapid bursts. He could hear men shouting, a woman, too, ordering the ship's crew about. He heard the captain's voice then, asking calmly not to hurt anyone.

"Everybody against the rail!" shouted an angry voice, a strong Australian accent punctuating the words. "Where is everyone else? I know there's nine of you."

"Asleep, I expect," Artie heard the doctor say.

Most of the crew must have been in the same place, probably the dining area, and had been rounded up quickly. He wished he'd thought to look there first.

"You two," the Australian demanded of someone. "Go down and roust them."

Artie had to see what was going on. He crept to the bottom of a ladder and peered up toward the deck. He ducked out of sight just as a man with an M4 assault rifle and a woman holding a combat shotgun appeared, framed in the doorway above. Both wore black tactical gear, knives strapped to their thighs.

Panic seized Artie. He hesitated in the passageway, not sure what to do. Then he raced for a utility closet and slipped inside, wedging himself between a mop, a broom, and a shelf of cleaning supplies. A small vent in the door allowed him a limited view of the passageway.

The two armed pirates marched to the first door, the engineer's bunk. The man had a snake tattoo on his arm, a cobra about to strike, curling up and around his elbow and then out of sight under his sleeve. He wrenched open the engineer's door, grabbing him off the bed. The man shrieked in surprise as they hauled him out.

Artie balled his fists. Damn it. He should have warned him. But he didn't have time. And the man had always slept like a hibernating bear.

"There's still two more," the man with the M4 called. They went down the passageway, swinging open doors, disappearing inside. They reached the doctor's quarters and hauled out the first mate, who had been in there, headphones on, setting up for the weekly poker match.

They marched the two crewmen down the passageway at gunpoint. The first mate had snatched off his headphones. "What the hell's going on here?" The reply was a sharp strike in the back of his head with the butt of a shotgun. He grunted, almost going down. The man with the snake tattoo shoved him forward.

The pirates walked past the utility closet, and Artie held his breath. The two crew members they'd snatched down here hadn't been aware of the gunmen's boarding. Hopefully they'd think the same of Artie, that he was sleeping in his quarters.

The assailants marched the two crew members back up the ladder.

"According to the crew manifest, there's still one more," barked the Australian, his voice echoing down the ladder.

So Artie was the last one. He had to do something. Create a distraction. Get to the radio for help. Find a weapon.

But he couldn't risk running smack into the pirates. He needed to know precisely where they were.

Leaving the closet, he crept up the ladder to take a look. He saw the other eight crew members huddled together, pressed against the ship's railing. "You watch them," the Australian ordered an intruder with a blond ponytail. "The rest of you fan out and find the last man." The Australian was impatient, angry, clearly used to things going smoothly.

Artie thought through his options. If he could get to the galley, there were knives there. Frying pans. He made a run for it, hoping he could beat the gunmen there. He sped down the passageway and into the kitchen, grabbing his biggest steak knife and a hefty frying pan. He heard steps approaching, so he darted back out and entered the passageway where the crew quarters were. For now, he slipped into the engineer's room where they'd already searched, shutting the door quietly behind him. The footsteps drew nearer, doors being thrown open.

What were these pirates' objectives? Why did they want this boat? The cargo was only frozen vegetables and fruits. No precious metals. And the pharmaceuticals they carried, from what he understood, were nothing terribly valuable—just antibiotics and some albuterol inhalers.

Boots approached the engineer's quarters. The sudden sound of a phone ringing made Artie jump. He heard someone stop outside the engineer's door. Artie scrambled under the low bunk, pulling the blankets down to cover the space where he hid.

The door flew open just as the phone stopped ringing. "Yes?" said a man's voice. "Just a minute. Let me get somewhere private."

Artie heard the door close and held his breath. It was the Australian, and he was in the room with him.

"We've taken care of the problem," the man told whoever was on the phone.

He could just hear her, a woman. "You had better," she told him. "That boat was expensive." She spoke with an English accent.

"We've made arrangements to replace it."

"I hope you're being careful. I don't want any of this tracing back to me, you hear? Burn everything if you need to. The last team did, including the witnesses. And you need to be absolutely certain you adhere to the preservation steps I've outlined for you."

"I know. You've told me enough times."

"It's vital that you follow them to the letter. I don't want any DNA contamination. Do you understand?"

"Yes. A thousand times yes. I'm not an idiot, Ms. Cromwell."

"The last team was. They completely cocked it up. Didn't follow procedure."

"I know, I know. Then they crashed over the Atlantic. You've told me. Several times."

"Damn fools. All that for nothing."

"We won't mess up the retrieval," he assured her, his voice tense, the man on the verge of losing his temper.

"I don't brook fools," she told him. "I need it. Intact. No more people snipping off samples here and there. *Intact,* do you hear me? The whole thing. You only use the special sample case under the direst emergencies. You understand?"

The Australian sighed in exasperation. "Listen here. I don't need you ordering me around like I'm some clueless toddler. You'll get what you need. Just be sure the money is ready to deliver when we do."

"You'll have your money when I'm assured it has been properly preserved."

The Australian let out a groan of annoyance. "I'm in the middle of something here. I'll call in later when there's something to report. In the meantime, stop calling me every half hour."

Artie heard a beep and assumed the man had hung up. For a few seconds he stormed angrily around the room. "Damn condescending bitch," he hissed, then threw open the door and slammed it shut behind himself.

The Australian was so angry, he hadn't thought to search the room again. He could realize that as soon as his temper cooled and be back in here in mere minutes. But Artie had no way of knowing where he was now in the passageway. He could still be right outside.

"Find him!" the Australian suddenly shouted—he *was* still right outside the door. "We can't risk him radioing for help. Check the communications room. Make sure he can't send out an SOS."

Then it hit Artie. The maintenance crawl spaces. They ran right under the floors. Hadn't the engineer picked this very room because there was a hatch in it?

Cautiously, Artie crawled out from under the bed and headed for the far corner of the room. He set down the knife and frying pan and slid aside the engineer's desk, revealing a gleaming metal hatch in the floor. He lifted it, peering down into a network of cables and pipes. The space was tiny. Smaller than he remembered. It would barely accommodate a body lying down. Grabbing his weapons again, he quickly lowered himself into the space, flattening out, then replaced the hatch. Darkness enveloped him, and he could hardly take a full breath in the cramped space. He worried about the revealed hatch above, but there was nothing he could do about moving the desk back into place.

Above him, he heard the door slam open again. Someone walked into the room. Artie scurried along on his elbows and knees, trying to get some space between him and the opening. It was awkward with the knife and frying pan. He had to push them out in front of his body.

Above him boots stomped around the room. Then they paused,

and light spilled into the narrow space. They'd found the hatch. Artie craned his neck to look back, freezing in place. His feet had cleared the edge of the opening, so all they'd see were wires and pipes. "Not here," he heard a woman say, then she slammed the hatch closed again.

Artie realized he could follow this crawl space out to the bottom of the ladder that was closest to the bridge. Then it was just a quick sprint up to the wheelhouse and the communications array. If he could somehow evade the pirates and get out an SOS . . .

He crawled faster, trying to make as little noise as possible. He passed a few more access hatches, then stopped when he estimated he'd reached the one nearest the ladder that led up to the bridge. He paused, listening, then dared to lift the hatch up a few inches. The passageway before him was clear. He rolled around, lying on his back to peek out in the other direction. It was clear there, too. They were still searching the rooms beyond. He lifted the hatch and darted out, lowering it quietly. Then he ran up the nearest ladder, peeking out onto the deck. It was clear in both directions. He sprang out and sprinted up the ladder to the bridge.

Sneaking a look inside, he found it deserted. He ran to the radio, hope springing in his chest, but he found the wires smoking and sputtering, others ripped out. The entire communications array had been cut and smashed. No VHF, MF, or satellite communications.

"Come out!" he heard the Australian yell, his voice booming across the deck from somewhere below. "Or we'll start killing the others one by one. If you cooperate, we'll lower you all into the lifeboat and set you adrift. Alive," he added.

Artie considered this offer but didn't trust him. Who's to say the pirates wouldn't just shoot them all as soon as he surrendered?

The lifeboat. Maybe he could reach it. They'd left only the one man behind to guard the crew. If he could somehow get the jump on the man, maybe they could make it to the lifeboat and roar off before these pirates knew what had happened. It was a long shot, but he had to try.

He crept to the door of the wheelhouse and stared out. The man with the snake tattoo was just vanishing down a far ladder. He didn't see anyone else.

Now was his chance. Artie sprinted down the ladder. From the rear, he quietly approached the lone man guarding his shipmates. The ship's captain spotted Artie, looked up in surprise, but Artie pressed his finger to his lips.

He gripped the frying pan tightly in one hand, coming up behind the gunman.

"Now listen here," the captain suddenly boomed in an attempt to distract the pirate. "You can't just take our ship."

The gunman took the bait, focusing on the captain and not noticing Artie as he approached.

"Yes!" chimed in the engineer, spotting Artie, too. "You know what the penalty is for piracy like this?"

Artie was just a couple feet away now, the blond pirate totally distracted. Artie lifted the frying pan and brought it down as hard as he could on the man's head. The pirate crumpled, sprawling out onto the deck, and Artie hit him again on the temple just to be sure he was out.

The rest of the crew looked at Artie with a mix of gratitude and astonishment. Artie had never done something like this in his life, and his hands shook.

"We need to get to the lifeboat," he told them, his voice quaking.

The captain grabbed the unconscious man's M4 and waved on his men. "Let's go! And quickly!"

They raced for the lifeboat. Seven of the men climbed in. Artie remained where he was, still gripping the frying pan.

"You get in, too," the captain told him.

"I'll stay behind with you. Want to be sure we all get safely off."

Together they began to lower the lifeboat. The mechanism

clanked and squealed, sounding deafening to Artie. The boat went down too slowly. He glanced back and forth, worried that any second now one of the other gunmen would emerge from a ladder.

The boat hit the water, and the first mate got ready to fire up the outboard as soon as the captain and Artie were aboard.

The captain unfurled the boarding ladder. "Down you go," he ordered Artie.

Artie didn't like the thought of going first. He and the captain went way back. He'd served on the *Sunfish* for close to ten years with the man and always found him to be fair and amiable.

"Go," the captain urged him.

Artie swung his legs over the railing and began to descend.

Then he heard the Australian shout from the deck: "You! Stop!" A burst of gunfire hailed from the captain, directly above Artie's head. Bright pops of light burned his retinas. But from his position, he couldn't see what was happening. He heard something heavy fall onto the deck, and the captain's arm flopped into view, hanging over the edge and dripping blood. Artie grabbed it, trying to pull him down, but the captain was deadweight, and he couldn't get the leverage.

The man with the snake tattoo leaned over the railing, pointing his M4 at Artie. His finger closed on the trigger. Artie let go of the ladder and plunged downward, landing just inches away from the lifeboat into the bitterly cold sea.

He heard the first mate start up the outboard motor just as a rain of bullets pierced the water's surface. Artie dove down deep, angling off to one side. He couldn't see anything in the dark, but he could feel the immense black abyss of the ocean beneath him.

Then a blinding light flashed over the water. The *Sunfish*'s searchlight. Artie looked up, seeing the outline of the lifeboat silhouetted against the brilliance. More bullets zinged down through the blue water, and now streamers of red drifted down, too.

Blood.

Artie swam more off to the side, away from the light. He couldn't hold his breath much longer. When he reached a darker patch of water, he dared to surface and sucked in a lungful of air. Treading water, he watched in horror as the man with the snake tattoo fired bursts of rounds, killing everyone on the lifeboat. Riddled now with holes, it began to sink. Then the man kicked the captain overboard. His limp body crashed hard into the waves. It floated there for a few moments before it started to sink.

His heart in his throat, Artie didn't know if the captain was still alive. He dove underwater, using powerful strokes to intercept the captain's body before it sank much more. The searchlight began fanning out, passing over the water as the pirates searched for him. Down in the depths, he made out the dim shadow of the captain's body and grabbed it. Then he swam back the way he'd come, away from the light. He surfaced beside the ship near the stern, in an area that would be difficult to see from the gunmen's vantage points.

He raised the captain's head up above the water but instantly saw that the man was dead. Bullets had pierced his temple and neck, his sightless eyes staring up toward the stars. The man's weight was pulling him down, and Artie struggled to tread water. His throat constricting painfully and tears blurring his vision, he let go, the body sinking down into the dark.

The searchlight swept the area again, and soon it would pinpoint him there. Artie dove, the sea so cold that he could barely move his limbs. He swam back in the direction they'd already searched, coming upon the sinking lifeboat. A life preserver hung on one side of it, and he grabbed it, then spotted the body of the dead engineer floating nearby, his friend's face slack and lifeless. He wore a life vest, and even though the man was dead, Artie felt racked with guilt as he stripped him of it.

Then Artie swam out into the night, away from his friends, away from the *Sunfish*, his only hope to find help.

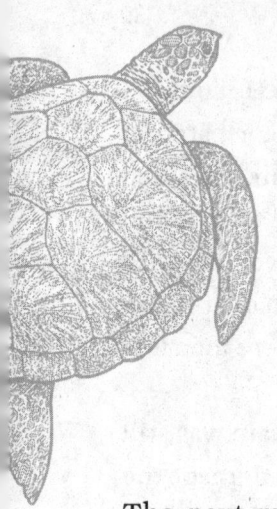

FOUR

The next morning Alex awoke feeling refreshed. The soothing sounds of the surf were truly soporific, and sleeping in a tent always gave her the best rest. She got dressed and emerged, seeing a group of early-morning surfers carrying their boards out to the water. The sun was just peeking above the horizon, painting the sea and sky in a magnificent wash of gold, pink, and red.

She stretched, breathing in the salty air. She walked over to the public shower house and took a quick rinse, then changed into some fresh clothes back at the tent. There she unfolded a small beach chair and sat down in the shade beneath the trees. She plugged her Wi-Fi router into her solar-powered Bluetti power station and loaded up the results of the two GPS transmitters they'd attached to the hawksbills.

The center had just developed a new, sleeker, less obtrusive kind of satellite tracker, and Alex and the previous biologist were the first researchers to employ them in the field. The old trackers were bulky and required a plastic bubble to be epoxied onto the turtle's shell to keep the water out. These projecting trackers could be problematic—not only could they interfere with a turtle's movement in the water, but the bulky objects could also get tangled up in fishing nets.

These new ones were nearly flat.

But getting a satellite location from a transmitter on a marine animal was a lot trickier than doing so with land animals. On land, GPS coordinates could be uploaded to a satellite regularly. But with a creature that lived largely underwater, this wasn't possible.

The National Oceanic and Atmospheric Administration satellite that received the transmissions circled Earth once every 101 minutes and was able to receive information from any single place for only about ten minutes at a time. It could receive data at this latitude about six to eight times a day, but the turtle had to be surfacing for air when the satellite passed overhead. And even if it was on the surface, it took about three to five minutes for the satellite to lock on to the transmitter and receive data. Given that hawksbills could rest underwater for up to three hours, the chance that a pass would coincide with one surfacing for air wasn't the best odds.

Because of this, location information didn't come in nearly as regularly as it did with a land animal like the mountain caribou she'd studied in Washington State or the jaguars in New Mexico. Still, she was getting data streaming in from the tagged turtles. The last ping from one was a little bit farther north, close to shore, likely feeding off sponges at the nearby coral reef. It could be the one she'd spotted yesterday.

But the other one had strange results. She frowned, seeing that it had been hanging out in the same place for some time, just offshore from where she sat. That wasn't too unusual, especially if it was feeding on the coral reefs and hanging out in the area until it was ready to lay its next clutch of eggs. But this location data showed it hadn't moved more than a foot, and the satellite had gotten a reading every single time over its last fifteen passes. That meant the turtle had happened to be at the surface each time, which seemed unlikely.

She stood up and used her binoculars to study the water in that location, then realized with a sinking feeling that it was the same area where she'd seen the boat idling the night before. Maybe the people had just been fishing. But a darker thought crept over her.

Maybe they'd been out placing an illegal gillnet.

Alex transferred the GPS location of the turtle to her waterproof GPS unit and then stowed her Bluetti and laptop in her Jeep. After she grabbed her diving mask, snorkel, and multitool, she dragged the small, inflatable Zodiac out into the surf.

She started up the motor and followed the GPS unit's navigation screen out to the spot, arriving where the transmitter had been pinging. She cut the engine and floated there for a minute.

A strange twinkling in the water drew her gaze. She reached down and ran her hand in the waves. They caught on something: a slender gillnet, the mesh so fine that it was nearly invisible.

Damn.

Gillnets got their name because fish would run into them, unable to see the fine monofilament line, and get their heads stuck. When they tried to swim forward, the mesh moved past their gills, making them unable to back up and trapping them.

Alex knew that these illegal gillnets, or "pirate nets," as they were often called, could run hundreds of feet deep and be a hundred miles long, despite a United Nations ban on large-scale nets. And the United States still allowed gillnets in federal waters off the coast of California, where fishermen used them to catch swordfish.

The turtle was likely caught in it. And it could have long since drowned.

Alex donned her face mask and snorkel and slipped into the water, hoping she wasn't too late.

FIVE

Alex swam through the water, squinting in the bright sun flashing off the waves. Some distance away, she saw six gigantic men rowing an outrigger canoe, speeding powerfully across the waters. Other than a sailboat far out on the horizon and a fishing trawler plying nearby waters, they were the only traffic out there.

Given the regularity of the location uploads, Alex knew the turtle had to be close to the surface somewhere along the net. She swam along the fine mesh, seeing a few fish darting dangerously near the deadly webbing. And then she caught the shimmer of sunlight off a colorful shell. A hawksbill turtle struggled in the net, inextricably tangled in it.

Relief washed over her. It was still alive.

She swam to it and struggled to free it from the net. But the mesh was wound too tightly. She left the turtle and kicked powerfully, swimming back to the boat. There she grabbed the life jacket and her multitool.

Alex donned the life jacket and opened the scissors on her multitool. Then she swam out again. It was pure luck that the turtle had gotten tangled so close to the surface or it would have drowned. While a resting hawksbill could stay underwater for three hours, an active or struggling hawksbill would need to surface every forty-five minutes to an hour to breathe.

The net swayed in the waves, bringing the turtle to the surface and then submerging it again, then back to the surface. No wonder the satellite had locked on to the transmitter during the last fifteen passes.

She floated beside the turtle, gently cutting through the mesh. She didn't want to slice too close and risk injuring one of its flippers. The turtle didn't struggle much, exhausted from its ordeal.

While Alex worked to free the turtle, the fishing vessel that had been floating nearby powered steadily toward her. It kept coming, and she continually had to shift her focus from the turtle to the approaching trawler to be sure it wasn't on a collision course with her. She kept waiting for it to veer away, but it didn't. Maybe it didn't see her. But surely it could see her nearby Zodiac.

At the last minute it did turn, heading directly for her boat.

The work to free the turtle was slow going as she bobbed up and down with the waves, but finally she was able to cut the turtle free. It immediately dove down into the water, disappearing from view, swimming hurriedly away from the net.

Now she turned her attention to the fishing trawler. It had stopped beside her Zodiac. Two men walked out on deck to peer down at her. As she met their gaze, she felt a primal chill go down her back. She'd always been gifted with an ability to get a sense of people, and these were two men she wouldn't want to encounter in a dark alley late at night.

One man was scrawny and almost sickly looking, with long, greasy blond hair that framed a pale, emaciated face with sharp cheekbones. The other was portly, dressed in a white pit-stained undershirt. His neck and shoulders had been sunburned bright red, and brown hair stuck out above his ears from a balding head.

"She found it," the scrawny one said, his beady eyes drilling into her.

The bigger one leered at her, scratching his belly beneath his too-tight undershirt. "Yep."

Alex hung in the water.

Then the skinny one disappeared belowdecks and emerged a moment later carrying a long metal pole with a vicious-looking barb on one end. He leaned over the railing with it, lunging the weapon toward her Zodiac. It stabbed into one side of the boat.

"Hey!" Alex cried. "What the hell are you doing?"

He stabbed it again and again, air exploding out of it. It deflated slowly, folding in on itself, pulled down by the weight of the outboard motor.

Alex continued to tread water, momentarily stunned and not sure what to do.

With her boat sabotaged, the burly man moved back to the ship's controls. He motored closer to her, so Alex swam some distance away. But he kept pace with her. The scrawny one leaned over the gunwale with the pole and made a stab at her. She ducked out of the way.

The pilot kept turning the boat, cutting off her path to shore. And she couldn't dive under with her life jacket on. But she was also so far from shore that she didn't want to shuck it off, either.

She continued to dart back and forth, evading each jab. At the next lunge, Alex seized the end of the pole and thrust it back toward the man. It hit him in the chin, momentarily stunning him, but he held fast to it. He rammed it downward again, and this time she grabbed it and pulled it hard in its current trajectory. The man stumbled into the ship's railing, almost losing hold, but managed to brace himself against the railing and maintain his grip.

She kicked away from the boat, but it continued to motor alongside her, easily outpacing her.

The skinny man went belowdecks again and emerged this time with a boat hook. He brought it down hard and it splashed in the water beside her. She realized she was going to have to ditch the life jacket and dive down deep. As he lifted the gaff, it surged up out of the water, catching her under the chin. Her head snapped back. She felt the sting of the blow along her jaw.

He took advantage of her momentary shock and brought the hook down again, this time entangling in the straps of her life jacket. He started to shove her under. Water surged up her nose. Then he jerked her toward the boat, her body hitting the hull.

She heard a sudden booming yell: "Hey! What the hell do you think you're doing?"

The men snapped their gaze to the right, and Alex saw that the outrigger canoe had raced up to the fishing vessel and that the six massive men on board all wore angry, determined faces. The man in front was the most immense of them all, easily over six and a half feet tall, she guessed. His huge, muscular arms were covered in beautiful, elaborate tattoos. His long black hair was held back in a braid that hung all the way down to the middle of his back. Every man behind him was nearly as gigantic, muscular tattooed arms gripping their oars, long black hair held back in braids or loose, flowing in the wind.

The two men on the fishing trawler stared as the outrigger canoe pulled up beside them, both looking uncertain. She read fear in their faces.

The huge man in the front of the canoe dove into the water and swam up beside Alex. He untangled the gaff from her life jacket straps and gave it a powerful tug. It ripped out of the hands of the skinny man, who lost his balance and nearly flipped over the railing, but he caught himself at the last minute.

Immediately the skinny man withdrew. "Let's get the hell out of here!"

The huge, tattooed man swam toward the boat, but it revved high into the rpms and spun around before he could reach its ladder, narrowly missing Alex where she bobbed in the water.

Alex took note of the ship's hull identification number.

"You okay?" her rescuer asked, swimming up beside her when the trawler had powered away. His kind brown eyes twinkled in a face the color of terra cotta. She guessed he was in his mid-thirties.

"Yes, thanks to you." She squinted in the bright sunlight, looking over at the canoe. "You all sure came along at the right time."

"It's our pleasure," the man said.

She readjusted her life jacket, which had been wrenched awkwardly to one side by the gaff. "I'm Alex."

"Keola." He gestured toward the canoe. "And these are my rowing mates."

She waved at them in gratitude, feeling the fear and adrenaline flooding out of her body. "Thank you all so much!"

They all smiled, calling out in turn.

"No worries!"

"Happy to help!"

"Looked like you were holding your own, but a little help never hurts," Keola said, moving to hold on to the canoe with one hand. He reached for Alex's hand and she took his, finding it warm and calloused. He pulled her over to the canoe, too. "We couldn't figure out what those guys were doing at first. But then when we saw they were attacking you . . . well, that was it. Why were they harassing you?"

"There's an illegal gillnet just over there," she said, pointing to where she'd cut the turtle loose.

"Oh no."

"I just freed a turtle from it. I think they were the ones who put it out. They must have known I'd alert the authorities."

"Good on you." He gazed out to shore. "Can we give you a lift back to land?"

She glanced over at her sinking Zodiac, which was now barely keeping afloat. "That would be great."

Keola climbed up into the canoe and then helped Alex on board. She sat behind him, finding him so gigantic that she couldn't even see over his shoulders.

Two of the rowers grabbed the deflating Zodiac to haul it to shore. Then the rest started to row in unison, going faster and faster.

She was impressed with their speed and strength. When they got close to the beach, Keola jumped off and held his hand out to Alex.

She took it and climbed off. Together they splashed through the surf to shore.

"I can't thank you enough," she told him. "Do you know who those guys were?"

Keola shook his head. "I've never seen them before."

"I'll give the authorities their descriptions."

"So what kind of turtle did you free?"

"A hawksbill."

"Wow. That's rare."

"It is. I'm doing a study here. They've been nesting on this beach."

"Hey, I heard about that. My daughter is an absolute freak for all things sea turtles. She's always bugging me to come watch them on the beach. We saw some green turtles nesting on Oʻahu last year, and since then it's been nothing but turtles turtles turtles." He cracked a big smile.

"Well, I'm actually looking for volunteers who can watch the nests when I'm not here and help me when the hatchlings emerge."

"You're kidding me."

"Would you and your daughter be interested?"

"Uh . . . that's a yes. In fact, she's going to explode. I'll tell you that right now. Absolutely explode. Yes."

"Wonderful! The Center for Sea Turtle Restoration put out a call for volunteers for later today, around two p.m. If you and your daughter want to come by then, I can walk you through what would be required, get your schedules, stuff like that."

He reached out a massive hand. "You got it."

Alex shook it. "And thank you for everything!"

"Just glad we were out here. We're practicing for the big Queen Liliʻuokalani Canoe Race."

"You'll do amazing!" she told him.

He waded back out into the surf and climbed aboard. She called out thanks to them all again, and they waved back. Then they rowed quickly out to sea, resuming their practice.

Alex peered out at the water after them, hoping the turtle was well away. She thought of all the dangers it would encounter on its way back and forth from its feeding grounds and hoped it would survive.

Then she tugged her ruined Zodiac up on shore into the trees. She'd have to see about repairing it. She called NOAA Fisheries Enforcement, and an officer came out and took her statement. She described the men and the name and hull identification number of their boat.

Then she watched while he dispatched a boat that picked up the gillnet. Thankfully, the net was on the smaller side, and no other turtles had been caught in it. The officer reported that either the net hadn't been out that long or the poachers had recently checked it and removed other captured wildlife. Alex's stomach turned at that latter suggestion and wondered if they'd managed to catch other endangered turtles either here or at other gillnets they might have stashed around the island chain.

Though she didn't have much of an appetite, she wanted to be energized when any potential volunteers showed up to apply, so she ate a simple lunch of fruit and an energy bar. She checked the time. The center's call for help provided a two-hour window for people to show up and apply, and the hour had arrived.

SIX

While she waited for volunteers, Alex gathered supplies to make some thermocouples to monitor the temperature of the nests. She hauled the Bluetti power station to the beach and laid a towel beside it. Then she grabbed the wires, multimeters, and soldering iron she'd need to make the temperature sensors. She was just about to start building them when a car pulled up. Keola stepped out from the driver's side. An energetic little girl bounded out and joined him.

The little girl's long black hair hung in two French braids that cascaded past her shoulders. Alex guessed she was about twelve years old. They walked toward her, Keola with an affectionate hand on the girl's upper back, and Alex stood up to greet them.

The girl thrust her hand out in greeting. "Hi. Are you the biologist?"

"I am." Alex shook her small hand.

"I'm Lupesina," the girl said, "and you already know my dad. He told me about the daring sea rescue!"

"It was quite daring! And I appreciate it," Alex told her.

"We want to help you with the turtles," Lupesina announced.

Alex took an immediate liking to her. "That's wonderful."

"I want to be a marine biologist," Lupesina said excitedly. "I've read every book in the library on ocean species." She glanced around, seeing Alex's tape marking off the part of the beach that people should walk around. "Are they hatching soon?"

Alex grinned. "One nest should be."

"And they're really hawksbills?" she asked.

"They are indeed," Alex told her.

The girl's eyes went wide, and she gazed up at her father. "Oh, Daddy, they're the rarest of them all! We have to help!"

He squeezed her hand. "What would the volunteer work entail?" he asked Alex.

"For the most part, I'll be camped down here on the beach taking care of things, but occasionally I'll need to go into town for supplies and to restock my food. And during those hours, I'll need someone to come down here and keep watch over the eggs, just make sure no dogs or birds get to them, or any humans try to steal them." Alex instantly pictured the little girl confronting poachers and quickly added, "The police are aware of the situation here, so if you *did* see any poachers, you should call them and not confront them yourself."

Keola grinned, towering over her. "I dare any more poachers to come around if I'm here."

Alex chuckled. "So do I!"

The girl practically jumped up and down, barely able to contain her enthusiasm. "We can do that!"

"And, of course, when it comes time for the turtles to hatch, it'll be all hands on deck to protect them from predators as they scamper down the beach. It should happen at night, but sometimes things go wrong, and it might be during the day. In that case, we'll have to protect them from the sun as they head toward the ocean, so bring some umbrellas to shade them if that happens."

"We can do that, too!" The girl's eyes shone with excitement.

Alex squinted in the bright sunlight. "What is your availability like?"

"I own a restaurant in Ānuenue," Keola told her, "but I can get one of my employees to take over with enough advance notice."

"That should be perfect then."

The girl stared up at her with expectant eyes. "Does that mean we get the gig?"

Alex grinned. "It does."

Now the girl did jump and down.

She handed them her tablet and had them fill out basic information: their contact number, any hours or days when they wouldn't be available.

"So what kind of restaurant do you own?" Alex asked.

"I moved here from Samoa with my family when I was six. My grandmother came with us and would make us all this great Samoan food when I was growing up. She taught me when I got older and I loved it. Decided to open my own place in Ānuenue serving traditional Samoan fare like palusami and koko alaisa."

"What are those dishes like?" Alex asked.

"Palusami is taro leaves cooked in coconut cream. It's really rich. We prepare it traditionally using an umu. That's a hot-rock oven. And koko alaisa is rice, Samoan cocoa, and coconut milk."

"This all sounds delicious!"

"Panikeke are my favorite!" Lupesina chimed in. "They're these yummy deep-fried dough balls."

Keola looked down at her. "I thought paifala was your favorite."

Lupesina grinned. "Well, maybe those, too."

"Paifala?" Alex asked.

"They're these half-moon-shaped pies with a coconut crust that have sweet pineapple custard inside!" Lupesina told her.

"I am definitely coming by to eat," Alex told them.

"You should! I'll make a chef's special for you," Keola offered.

"I'd love that."

"Hey, what's all that for?" Keola asked, gesturing at the wires she'd laid out on the towel.

"I'm going to make some thermocouples."

"What are those?"

"They monitor temperature, so they'll give us clues as to when the hatchlings will emerge."

He pointed at the soldering iron she'd set out. "And you have to solder them? I can help you with those. I repair retro gaming consoles as a hobby and use a soldering iron all the time."

"Great! You got a minute now?"

"Sure," he said.

They sat down cross-legged in the sand opposite each other. Lupesina wandered off to peer at the taped-off portion of the beach.

On the towel, Alex spooled out lengths of copper and constantan wire. She plugged the soldering iron into the Bluetti to let it heat up. She held up the two types of wire. "We just solder these wires together and then construct a long probe we can stick into the sand. Then we hook up a multimeter to it to get readings."

"Cool!"

Alex began twisting the wires together and handing them off to Keola, who soldered them together and then made the long probes. Lupesina stood guard on the beach, her face determined.

They made three thermocouples in case an additional nest was laid.

Lupesina wandered back by them.

"You want to see if we can confirm that one of the nests is going to hatch in a few days?" Alex asked her.

The girl's eyes widened at the thought of hatchlings. "Yes!"

Alex stood up and handed her one of the thermocouples. "Take this and we'll gently insert the probe end into the sand above one of the nests."

They stepped over the caution tape, and Alex pointed out the location of the newer nest. They knelt down together.

"How does it work?" the girl asked.

"Temperature affects how long the eggs will incubate. The

warmer the nest, the faster the eggs will hatch. And rain can cool down a nest, slowing development."

"Whoa!"

"But as the hatchlings develop in their eggs, their metabolic heat warms up the nest even more. So it'll get hotter just before the baby turtles emerge." Alex gestured at the nest. "This nest was laid recently, so the hatchlings won't be as developed yet. Let's see what the temperature is."

Alex held the multimeter while Lupesina inserted the probe into the sand, and they noted the reading.

"Now let's move to the other nest."

They shifted their location and repeated the process. "See how much hotter this one is?" Alex asked.

Lupesina nodded.

"That means they're going to hatch in just a few days."

"Wow! You'll let us know, right? So we can be here?"

"Of course."

Keola stood up, brushing sand off his jeans, and joined them.

"Thank you both for coming out," she told them. "I'll be in touch."

"Sounds good," Keola said, and he shook her hand again.

They left, the girl bounding along happily in the sand next to her father.

Alex saw a lot of herself in the girl. She remembered the excitement she'd felt when she started volunteering at a local wildlife rehabilitation and rerelease center when she was a kid. Even though she was mainly mucking out cages, she also got to go along when they released recovered hawks, eagles, deer, and bear yearlings. She'd loved the feeling that she could actually take actions that would directly benefit other creatures. She did everything she could to help after that, doing odd jobs around the neighborhood to make money to donate to nonprofits. She circulated petitions and attended protest marches to demand the government take stronger actions against climate change and species extinction.

She went on to study wildlife biology in undergrad and graduate school, ultimately earning a PhD from the University of California, Berkeley. Since graduating, she'd taken on a number of field jobs, including studying wolverines in Montana and polar bears in the Canadian Arctic, tracking elusive mountain caribou in Washington State, and determining if jaguars were using a large parcel of protected land in New Mexico. They'd all been incredible adventures, each with their own dangers and challenges, but she'd thrived. And now here she was, on this gorgeous island in the Pacific, working with sea turtles. She felt blessed indeed.

Out here in the wilds was where she was most at home. Sometimes her solo work left her feeling a little bit lonely, but she had two amazing friends, including Zoe Lindquist, whom she'd met in college in a production of *Man of La Mancha*, when Zoe had the lead as Dulcinea and Alex played oboe in the pit orchestra. Zoe had gone on to much success and was now an A-list actor in Hollywood.

Her other dear friend was her father, a landscape painter who lived in Berkeley. She and her dad were extremely close, as he'd raised her by himself since she was young. Her mother had been a combat pilot in the Air Force, and her plane had gone down when Alex was only twelve. They'd lost her.

When her mother was alive, they'd lived in a number of exotic places, moving to Air Force bases around the world, including right here in the Hawaiian Islands on Hickam Air Force Base for a while. Every time they moved, Alex and her dad delighted in each new place. He would get them a big stack of local field guides, and they'd venture out and learn all the wildlife, mushrooms, lichen, geology, and more of the area. He'd sketch in nature journals, and Alex would comb the forest floors and beaches and deserts, reveling in every delicate wildflower or section of green moss housing water bears. She learned about geologic strata and fossils and different tree species. She followed the tracks of bears and mountain lions and deer in the mud and along the sandy banks of rivers.

But they'd been lost when her mother died. Their ceaseless moving around stopped. When Alex was accepted to UC Berkeley for college, her father came with her, buying a beautiful Craftsman house in Berkeley, where he still lived. He loved to paint the national parks and regularly was accepted into plein air festivals and artist-in-residence programs.

He was planning to visit her in a few weeks, and she couldn't wait to see him.

Alex returned to her thermocouples, but only a few minutes later she spotted a lithe man making his way down the beach, not coming from the parking area but from some location farther down the sandy stretch. At first she thought he might be a beachcomber, but he wasn't dressed like one.

She guessed he was in his late sixties or early seventies, with cropped white hair and a beige face that looked like it had seen a lot of sun over the years. He wore a brown fedora, worn jeans, and a long-sleeved plaid shirt beneath a khaki vest sporting a multitude of pockets. An old canvas satchel hung over his shoulder, and he carried what looked like a sketchbook. He kept looking up at her and smiling, and striding purposefully toward her, but then something would distract him on the beach, and he'd stop to quickly sketch it. Then he'd resume his purposeful approach, only to see something else that grabbed his interest and sketch that, too. Alex felt amused watching him and could relate. She always got distracted while hiking with so many intriguing things to look at—mushrooms, birds, lichen.

Finally he finished his journey and walked animatedly up to her. He broke out in a huge smile, his brown eyes twinkling. "Dr. Carter?"

She stood. "Yes."

"I'm Dr. Nakoa Kahananui. Lovely to meet you."

They shook hands.

"I've come to inquire about the turtles. Are you still in need of help?"

"I am indeed."

"Excellent. I'd like to help. I'm the resident paleontologist at the new Museum of Vertebrate Paleontology. But I'm semiretired these days and looking for something useful to do with my time, something that will get me out of the lab. I miss the days of working in the field"—he rubbed his back—"though I don't miss bending over the grids and doing all the tedious brush work."

"It's great to meet you." Alex had heard of the new landmark museum in town and seen pics of it online. It was newly built and was a state-of-the-art facility that housed displays of dinosaur bones, impressions of dinosaur skin, and vast painted murals depicting scenes of ancient worlds. She'd heard it had even recently acquired the mummified remains of a woolly mammoth, though it wasn't on display yet. "Paleontology is a fascinating field."

"Indeed it is." He glanced around.

She nodded at his journal. "I couldn't help but notice your sketching."

He smiled sheepishly. "It's just a hobby, really. I'm something of an amateur naturalist," he confessed. "I've lived on this island all my life. My family goes back generations here. I've been documenting the decline of the honuʻea for decades and keep a phenology journal."

Alex was familiar with the term *honuʻea*, or often just *ʻea*, the Hawaiian word for the hawksbill. And she was fascinated by phenology, the study of the times of the year when things happened in nature, like when certain bird species made their nests, when the eggs hatched, when the leaves began to change in the autumn. With climate change, everything was in flux now. Because of global warming, summers were longer. Plants bloomed earlier, and seeds appeared at different times, leaving migratory animals struggling to find food.

"I've noticed that hawksbills have been appearing at new beaches," he told her. "Between overdevelopment and the bekko trade, they're in flux."

Alex nodded grimly.

Millions of hawksbills had perished because of the bekko, or tortoiseshell, trade, as they were the only turtle species harvested for the material. They'd been aggressively hunted for their gorgeous amber and gold shells for centuries, but it grew particularly deadly in the eighteenth and nineteenth centuries, when they were nearly hunted to extinction. Eventually there weren't enough turtles left to support the trade. CITES, the Convention on International Trade in Endangered Species of Wild Fauna and Flora, banned the hunting of hawksbills in 1977, but some countries like Japan and Cuba continued to push to have these protections overturned. And plenty of hawksbills were illegally killed and harvested in places like Malaysia, the Philippines, and Indonesia, and were often exported afterward to China.

"When I was a kid in the fifties," Nakoa said, "tortoiseshell was all the rage. Eyeglass frames, combs, ashtrays, plates. It was awful. And the hawksbills nearly disappeared from our beaches. But they're starting to come back, little by little. If we can continue to help them."

One thought Alex kept returning to was that the more people realized turtles and other wildlife were worth more money in ecotourist dollars than they were in the form of food, jewelry, or decorative pieces, then the better off wildlife would be.

She gestured at his journal. "I'd love to see some of your sketches."

He shyly handed her his notebook, and she flipped through the pages, finding stunning pencil sketches of shorebirds, seashells, turtles, and mountain scenes.

"These are fabulous! You're really talented!" She flipped through more pages and then handed the journal back. "My father is an artist. A landscape painter. He's coming here in a few weeks to paint and hike the beaches and mountains."

Nakoa looked around at the sea, then the mountains in the distance. "It's an inspirational place." He gazed out at billowing white clouds gathering in the west. "So what sort of work would you be requiring?"

She went over the duties and asked about his schedule. He was affable and self-effacing, and she found him to be a great fit for the project. She had him enter his information on her tablet.

"If you like, come by the museum in the next few days and I'll give you a tour," he offered.

"I'd love that. And I'm looking forward to more talks like this."

He nodded. "As am I. Let me know whenever you need me."

Just then an older, but well-maintained, station wagon pulled into the grassy parking area. Alex and Nakoa watched as it parked next to a black SUV that had been left in the small lot the day before. She hadn't seen who'd parked the SUV there and guessed they were staying with someone in one of the nearby houses.

A woman climbed out. She walked toward Alex and Nakoa, smiling and giving a small wave. As she drew closer, Alex saw that she was likely in her late sixties, with perfectly coiffed and styled short black hair. She wore a pair of thin-framed eyeglasses, which she took off and hooked into her purple shirt as she approached. A colorful, flowing broom skirt billowed around her in the breeze, and gold bangles jangled at her wrists.

"Are you Dr. Carter?" she asked.

"Yes." Alex held out her hand, and the woman shook it.

Before she could introduce herself, she held out her hand to

Nakoa and paused. "Wait . . ." she said, really turning to stare at him in awe. "Nakoa Kahananui?"

He gaped back, equally shocked. "Dora?"

They burst into smiles and embraced each other, laughing. "I can't believe it!" the woman cried.

"Me, either!" Nakoa agreed, pulling back to take her in. He held on to her hands as they parted. "I didn't think I'd ever see you again!"

"This is unbelievable!" Dora exclaimed.

They both remembered Alex standing there. "We were childhood friends," Nakoa explained.

"My family used to summer in Ānuenue," Dora added. "It was the best time of my life! Riding our bikes around, snorkeling!"

"The tie-dye shirt parties!" Nakoa laughed. "Our hands would be orange and pink for days!"

Dora looked thoughtful. "The last time I saw you was . . ."

"The moon landing party!" they declared simultaneously.

"Then my family moved to Kaua'i, and we started summering in Princeville," Dora said sadly.

"I wrote to you," Nakoa told her.

"And I wrote to you." She looked a little wistful.

"Then I moved to Massachusetts for college, and we just . . ."

"Lost touch," Dora finished. "I moved to the mainland for grad school, too."

Nakoa grinned. "But now here you are!"

"I'm astounded! I only moved back to Hawai'i a few weeks ago. I guess I wanted to recapture some of the magic of this place."

"I'm so glad you did!"

Their happiness was contagious, and Alex found herself grinning, watching the two of them.

"So what brings you to this beach in this exact moment?" Nakoa asked, still looking incredulous.

"Sea turtles!" she exclaimed. "I heard about the call for volunteers." She paused. "And where are my manners?" She turned to Alex. "Dora McNora." She laughed self-effacingly. "I know. It rhymes. I'm a retired elementary school teacher, and believe me, the kids never ceased to get a kick out of it."

"Wonderful to meet you."

The woman's face was a very pale pink, her makeup expertly applied to accentuate deep blue eyes.

Alex thought of her own somewhat disheveled appearance, her wavy brown hair hastily pulled back in a ponytail. She almost never wore makeup, though Zoe told her enough times that a little eye shadow would really make her blue eyes stand out.

"I'm here to throw my hat into the ring for the turtle project," Dora said.

"That's great. Can you tell me a little about yourself and how you became interested in wildlife?"

"Teaching science was always my favorite part when I was an educator. I'd take the kids on field trips out to the beaches and forests, teach them about wildlife and climate change."

"That's wonderful," Alex said.

"Now that I'm retired, I find that part of my life woefully empty. I'd like to start using my free time to help with projects like this one."

"Do you have a specific interest in turtles?"

"I saw a clutch of green turtles hatch once over on O'ahu. It was the most magical experience of my life, watching all those little hatchlings hurry toward the crashing surf. Anything I can do to give them a better chance at survival is okay with me."

"That's wonderful. They certainly need our help."

Nakoa turned to Dora. "They've got a lot of predators."

"Predators?" Dora asked, looking first to Nakoa, then to Alex. "I'm not as familiar with the situation. Are they in a lot of danger from them?"

"They are, unfortunately," Alex told her. "People steal the eggs. Dogs and birds eat them. Raccoons are a huge problem in other parts of the U.S. because they're one of the few species that's able to exist alongside humans, so they stick around even when beaches get developed."

"That's interesting!" Dora said. "You don't picture raccoons eating turtle eggs."

"A lot of animals around the world love to eat them," Alex told her. "Herons, frigate birds, pelicans. Coyotes, jaguars, foxes, dingoes, feral pigs."

Dora blanched. "That's quite a list."

"Invasive mongooses and ghost crabs are predators we'll have to watch out for here," Nakoa added, "along with cats."

"Cats?" Dora asked. "As in house cats?"

"That's right," Alex told her. "Outdoor house cats and feral cats decimate wildlife. In fact, recent studies by organizations like the Smithsonian and U.S. Fish and Wildlife have revealed that cats kill as many as four billion birds and up to twenty-two billion mammals every year in the U.S. alone."

Dora's jaw dropped. "Was that billion with a *b*?"

Alex nodded.

Dora shook her head. "Well, I'm keeping my cat inside from now on."

"But, like so many wildlife species," Alex continued, "by far the biggest threat to turtle survival is humans. Turtle eggs and adults go for a pretty penny on the black market."

Dora straightened. "They won't get them while I'm around!"

She seemed perfect. Alex went over the basics of what would be required, asked her other questions about her availability and transportation. She liked all the woman's answers.

"This is fantastic." Alex handed her the tablet to enter her contact info and then shook her hand again. "Welcome aboard."

The woman broke out into a warm smile. "Thanks. I'm so pleased."

Nakoa smiled at her sheepishly. "Would you care to grab a bite to eat?"

Dora brightened. "Now?"

"Sure."

"I'd love to."

"I'm afraid I walked here," Nakoa confessed. "I don't have my car with me."

"I'll drive us into town," Dora offered.

Nakoa held out his arm, and Dora took it.

They said their goodbyes to Alex, then headed off toward Dora's station wagon, giggling shyly like they were just kids again. It made Alex's heart glad to watch them. So far she'd really lucked out with the volunteers who had shown up. In the past, when she'd worked on projects that had volunteer calls, she hadn't been so fortunate. Between mansplainers, and people who just wanted an excuse to party in the woods and drink too much beer, and people who just weren't very dedicated and dropped out after a day or two, she'd had her share of volunteers who didn't work out. She hoped the people who had come out today would stick with the project until the eggs hatched.

After Dora and Nakoa left, Alex waited for others to show up. She was actually surprised she'd gotten four people. If she ended up needing more, she could open another interview window on a different day. Or maybe one of the volunteers she'd taken on would have reliable friends they could recommend. They'd need them if more turtles laid eggs on the beach.

But for now she was set. But she still hoped Jerome would make an appearance.

Alex was packing up the thermocouples when a red compact car pulled into the small parking area. A woman climbed out, and Alex stood up to greet her, wondering if she was another volunteer. And then she caught sight of the woman's face as she drew nearer, and Alex broke out into a grin. She instantly recognized the woman—her smiling sepia face and long black braids.

Alex strode forward, arms outstretched. "No way! No freakin' way! Sasha Talbot!"

The woman grinned back, and they embraced.

"What brings you out here?"

"Heard a wildlife biologist was looking for volunteers." She laughed, and they pulled apart.

Sasha was a marine archaeologist whom Alex had first met in Hudson Bay, Canada. She hadn't seen her since their harrowing ordeal out on the icy waters. But they'd bonded and stayed in touch.

"When I heard it was you, I had to come down and see you."

Alex gripped her friend's hand warmly. "I can't believe it's really you. Are you here doing a salvage dive?"

"Sure am. Trying to find the wreck of a Fieseler F 3 Wespe, also known as a 'Wasp.' It's a really unique-looking plane. This one was bought by a wealthy banking magnate in the early thirties. He transported it to Hilo, but it vanished on his first flight, and no one knows what ever happened to him or the plane."

"Intriguing!"

"Almost nothing is known about these planes now because records were destroyed. But I'd love to find it."

"Where's your new boat?" From their last conversation, Alex learned that Sasha had just purchased a brand-new boat outfitted with side-scan sonar, a small computer lab, and an ROV.

Sasha squinted into the sun and scanned the water. Then she pointed to a distant harbor where a few boats bobbed on the waves. "Over there, down the coast a few miles."

"Found anything yet?"

"Sonar turned up some interesting shapes on the seabed. One might be the wreck I'm looking for. I made a couple preliminary dives at a few plane wrecks, just to get a better feel for what I'm looking for, but still haven't found the Wasp. The coral reefs here, though, are off the chain! I could just spend all my time exploring those."

Alex nodded. "Aren't they amazing?"

When she'd first dived here on this trip, Alex was relieved to see how healthy, vibrant, and colorful the coral reefs were. She'd dived at the Great Barrier Reef a few years before and was shocked to see the coral dead and white over many miles of ocean bed. Because of global warming and land-based runoff of pollutants, coral reefs were subjected to more diseases and were turning white and dying. Whole coral communities had perished, which reduced the available food for many species, including sea turtles.

Before turtle populations were decimated by the bekko trade and other threats, hawksbills had kept sponge populations in check. But now with so few hawksbills left, some sponges, such as *Chondrilla nucula,* were overcrowding the reefs, choking out other life that was already threatened because of global warming.

"We totally need to do a dive together," Sasha suggested.

"I'd love that." Alex brushed an errant patch of sand off her jeans. "I'm almost done here for the day. You want to grab some dinner in town?"

"Sure."

"Just give me a sec to see if any of my volunteers are available to watch the eggs for a while."

SEVEN

Just then, in a lucky stroke, she spotted Jerome walking down the beach toward them, tossing a baseball up in the air and catching it. "Jerome!" she called, waving him over.

He reached them, looking a bit uncertain. "You said to come by? That you needed volunteers?"

"Your timing is perfect," Alex told him. "This is Sasha. She's a marine archaeologist," Alex said by way of introduction.

They shook hands.

Alex went through the same process she'd done with the other volunteers, asking Jerome questions about his interests, getting his contact info and availability.

Sasha gestured at the baseball. "You play?"

"Yeah. Maybe too much. My mom wanted me to come out here for the summer. She said I needed a break, that I'd been training too hard."

"What team do you play with?"

He shrugged. "Just my high school team, but I'm being scouted by a few colleges. Mom says I'll have my pick. I'm a pitcher."

"That's awesome!" Alex said.

He grinned, breaking into a huge smile. "Right? One of them is Stanford! So I started training really hard. Mom got worried I'd mess my arm up by overdoing it, though. So here I am, in Hawai'i. Supposed to just be chilling with my aunt."

"Not a bad place to be," Sasha consoled him.

"True that!"

"So what other colleges have you on their radar?" Alex asked.

He counted them off on his fingers. "Duke, Purdue, UC Berkeley, and Northwestern."

Alex was impressed. "Wow! Those are some great choices. Berkeley is my alma mater."

"Really?"

"Yeah. I loved it there."

"My mom and I are going to go check out all the campuses later this summer."

"What are you going to study?" Sasha asked.

He put one hand on his hip, looking uncertain. "I don't know yet. But I've been thinking astronomy."

Alex nodded. "That would be cool."

"Yeah. When I was a kid, my dad gave me a telescope. We used to hang out in our backyard and look at stars. Couldn't see a whole lot. Detroit's pretty bright."

"Well, good luck with choosing a college you like," Sasha told him. "You can't go wrong with any of those."

He shrugged shyly again.

"Hey," Alex said, "would you mind watching the eggs for a bit while we go grab some dinner?"

Jerome glanced over at the nests. "No problem!"

"Great!" Alex told him. They watched as he plunked down in Alex's beach chair, beginning his vigil.

Alex and Sasha piled into Alex's Jeep, and they drove to Ānuenue, where they tried to get a table at Keola's place. It was absolutely slammed, with a wait time of two hours. So instead they chose the other restaurant in town, a Thai place at the end of the main street. They were seated in the window with a view of the quaint street, a few tourists nipping in and out of the two trinket shops. An old movie theater stood across the street, though it was boarded up and in disrepair.

A TV mounted on one wall in the restaurant was tuned to a news station. A meteorologist reported that a big storm was brewing to the east, with a chance that it might develop into a hurricane, and Doppler radar showed the mass of precipitation churning out at sea.

A waiter greeted them and handed them menus. While they waited for him to pour ice water into their glasses, another news report drew Alex's attention back to the TV. "No news yet on the missing cargo ship *Sunfish,* which disappeared off the coast of Los Angeles and is thought to have sunk, taking with it thousands of pounds of vegetables, fruits, and pharmaceuticals. Rescue craft in the area have failed to locate any debris from the vessel, and searches by air have also come up empty. It is thought that the vessel might have struck an underwater reef or been caught in the storm that hit Baja over the weekend."

Sasha pivoted in her seat to take in the images on the television, showing security footage of the small cargo ship when it was last in harbor.

"That's scary," she said, turning back to Alex. "Can you imagine being out at sea and just vanishing? I wonder what happened to them."

"It's spooky. Brings to mind tales of the Bermuda Triangle, ships disappearing without a trace." Alex imagined being out there on the gray sea, waves tossing any survivors who ended up in a lifeboat or floating in life jackets. "Don't ships have some kind of automatic locator signal that lets other ships know where they are?"

Sasha nodded. "The AIS. Automatic identification system. It sends out all kinds of information, like where a ship is located, what its call number is, type of vessel, cargo."

"Can't they use that to find it?"

"It depends on if they *have* AIS. Ships are *supposed* to have it, but not all of them do. And then it depends on if the ship has sunk or if the system has malfunctioned somehow." Sasha took a sip of her water and leaned forward. "There was this intense case of when AIS worked really well. This fishing vessel, the *Hallgrímur,* was sailing between Norway and Iceland when it got hit by this massive storm. We're talking sixty-foot waves and eighty-mile-an-hour winds."

"Whoa."

"The ship started to fill up with water, and the four men on board were forced to evacuate. They sent out a distress signal. Two managed to get on survival suits, but the other two didn't have time."

Alex was familiar with survival suits; she had worn one herself in the Canadian Arctic. They were suits designed to keep a person dry, warm, and afloat even in frigid conditions like the North Sea.

"They tried to launch the lifeboat, but the men got separated from it in the water. The *Hallgrímur* sank. As soon as Norway's Joint Rescue Coordination Centre received the distress call, they looked to see if any other ships fitted with AIS were in the area and could aid in a rescue. But once you're over forty miles offshore, you can't be located by terrestrial AIS. But a couple years before, the International Space Station had installed an AIS receiver that allowed them to see vessels anywhere on the planet. The ISS was able to see that a ship was in the area, and its crew was asked to investigate and pick up any survivors. They searched, along with some helicopters, and managed to locate one of the men who had been floating for four hours in his survival suit in these crazy conditions. He was rushed to a hospital, and he survived."

"And the other three?"

"Unfortunately, they were never found. The lifeboat was located, but no one was in it."

Alex shook her head. She could just imagine the rough waves, the immense blackness of the sea around her, the fear of knowing that her shipmates had drowned. "That's really sad. And sixty-foot waves! That's insane!"

Sasha glanced over her shoulder again at the TV, but the news anchor had moved on to a different story. "So who knows what might have gone wrong if that vessel had AIS but they still can't find it. Hopefully they'll figure it out and retrieve any survivors."

Alex considered her friend. "Have you ever been afraid of that? Of getting stranded out at sea somehow?"

Sasha raised her eyebrows and took a deep breath. "Yes. It's a total nightmare of mine, to be out there and something going wrong with my equipment or communications system. Probably everyone who sails alone worries about that." She went quiet and bit her lip.

She hadn't always sailed alone, Alex knew. She'd had a diving partner, Rex Tildesen, who had been murdered in the Canadian Arctic. It was that murder and the circumstances around it that had led to Alex and Sasha's strong bond.

"I'm so sorry about Rex," Alex said, reaching across the table to give her friend's hand a warm squeeze.

Sasha looked up, tears glistening at the rims of her eyes. "I think about him every day. What adventures we had. He was one of a kind."

"He sounds amazing. I can't imagine losing a kindred spirit like that."

"I wonder if I'll keep working alone. It's tough. You really shouldn't do solo dives. That can be dangerous."

"Have you looked into teaming up with another marine archaeologist?"

Sasha stared wistfully out the window. "I don't know. I've thought about it, but right now I can't imagine it. And my interests are so niche that it would be hard to find someone else willing to investigate the kinds of things that interest me."

Alex knew that Sasha and Rex had gone to Hudson Bay in the Canadian Arctic specifically to find evidence that Vikings had sailed that far west from Newfoundland. It was just the kind of fringe theory that Sasha loved to dig into.

The waiter returned, and they ordered a delicious meal of pad see ew jay, sweet flat noodles, and yellow curry. Sasha caught Alex up on her last expedition, searching for the *Independence Turtle,* an American Revolution–era submarine that had been built in 1775, along with another called the *American Turtle.*

"The Americans tried to use them to attach bombs on to the underside of British ships," Sasha explained. "But things went wrong with the *American Turtle* when the pilot tried to use it. He couldn't get the mine to attach, and it ended up floating away and blowing up harmlessly downstream. There were a couple more attempts by the *American Turtle,* but then the ship that was transporting it was sunk. They salvaged the sub but didn't have the time to repair it.

"But people know hardly anything about the *Independence Turtle,* including what became of it. The pilot paddled it out into New York Harbor, and it just vanished from history."

"Did you find it?"

Sasha gave a rueful laugh. "If only! I found some promising shapes on the seabed, but no luck. But I haven't given up yet."

"Fascinating! I didn't know submarines were in use that early on."

"It was just a little egg-shaped, one-person affair, propelled by a treadle and a hand crank. And it had only thirty minutes of air."

"Sounds challenging!"

Sasha gave a small chuckle. "Probably why they weren't too successful. And you? What have you been up to?"

She'd talked to Sasha after the mountain caribou study in Washington State, but she hadn't yet told her about searching for jaguars in New Mexico. She related what she'd gone through out there in the desert, and Sasha leaned back in her chair, eyebrows raised. "Are you okay?" she asked when Alex finished the story.

"I am now. But it was pretty intense for a while there."

"And Casey? How is he?"

Casey MacCrae was the helicopter pilot who had ferried Alex and her team around the Canadian Arctic while she tagged and studied polar bears. They'd grown close during their time out on the ice. "I haven't heard from him in a while," Alex told her. "I'm not sure where he is."

At the very thought of him, Alex felt a knot tighten in her stomach. She and Casey had each other's backs; they had fought side by side and been through some truly harrowing experiences together. But he was still largely an enigma to her. He worked for justice, sometimes taking things to extreme measures and operating outside the law. As close as they were, even she didn't know the full extent of acts he'd committed over the years.

And she also didn't know if she'd ever see him again.

She and Sasha fell into a comfortable silence for a few moments, both of them sipping on cool glasses of Thai iced tea. "I'm serious, by the way," Sasha said.

"About what?"

"Volunteering to help you with the turtle eggs."

"Really?"

"Yep."

"That'd be great! Thank you." This trip just kept getting better and better. Alex got to be in gorgeous Hawai'i helping turtles, and now she got to hang out with her friend.

"So tell me about them. What is their situation?" Sasha asked.

"It's pretty dire. Hawksbills are the most critically endangered sea turtle on the planet. Their population has really plummeted. All the sea turtle species have. It's crazy. Hawksbills have been around for a hundred million years, but in just the last couple hundred, they've lost ninety percent of their population."

Sasha grimaced. "Due to humans, I take it?"

Alex nodded, suddenly not feeling hungry. "And this Hawaiian population is particularly small, and therefore extra precarious. There are populations in other parts of the world bigger than this one. Most of them nest in Australia and the Great Barrier Reef. Others lay eggs in places like Indonesia, Mexico, and islands in the Caribbean. But the Hawaiian hawksbill population is a lot smaller, with maybe only twenty-five females laying eggs on a few beaches on the Big Island and on Moloka'i. And living to be old enough to lay eggs is pretty much a miracle," she added. "Current research says that they probably aren't old enough to mate until they're somewhere between twenty and thirty-five years old."

"How long do they live for?"

"Even that isn't really known. Probably around fifty to sixty years. Much more research is needed."

"So what is threatening them?" Sasha asked, taking a bite of noodles.

Alex described the bekko trade and how global warming was decimating their numbers.

"The fishing industry is a huge threat, too," Alex continued. "Turtles get killed in staggering numbers when they get caught in fishing nets. They're also crushed by dredges used in shellfish hunting, and when new shipping channels are dredged to accommodate bigger ships. They're even sucked up by nuclear power plants that use seawater to cool their reactors."

Sasha paused mid-bite. "Seriously?"

"Yep. Plus building resorts and housing developments lead to noise and light pollution, which drastically affects their nesting. Flooding prevention measures like seawalls rob the turtles of their egg-laying beaches. Climate change causes these unprecedented storms that erode beach habitat and inundate nests, drowning the eggs."

Sasha put her fork down. "Sheesh. I think I've lost my appetite. How many hawksbills are left?"

"We're not certain. It might be around seventy thousand, but only twenty thousand or so of that population are egg-laying females." Alex thought of one of the towns she'd lived in as a kid that had a population of seventy thousand people. It had felt big when she was little, riding her bike around the neighborhoods and going down to the little corner store to buy candy. But then she imagined if those seventy thousand people were the only people in the entire world, instead of eight billion, and that population felt tiny indeed.

Alex felt bad for bringing the mood down so much. "Sorry to be a downer. The good news is that we still have all seven sea turtle species on the planet." There were still hawksbills, green turtles, olive ridleys, Kemp's ridleys, leatherbacks, loggerheads, and flatback sea turtles. Then she thought, but didn't voice, the very real possibility that if nothing was done, all seven species could disappear by the next century.

"It's got to feel good to be making a difference here," Sasha observed.

Alex shifted uncomfortably in her seat and moved the pad see ew jay around on her plate with her fork. "I don't know. I'm honored to work with them, of course. But to be honest, I wonder if the work I do moves the needle at all. But I don't know what else to do except keep trying. Even though the U.S. Fish and Wildlife Service has listed the hawksbill as critically endangered under the Endangered Species Act, its marine counterpart, the National Marine Fisheries Service, has been really slow to enact changes that could keep the hawksbill from extinction."

"What do you mean?"

"Well, one of the biggest threats to sea turtles is longlines."

Sasha nodded. "I've seen those suckers when I'm out diving. Huge!"

Longlines were many-miles-long monofilament lines with thousands of baited hooks tied all along their length. Sometimes in addition to bait, light sticks were attached. Turtles got caught in the hooks, and even if a conscientious fisherman freed them, the turtles could still die from the wounds. They could also drown if they got hung up on a deep hook. One study estimated that half the leatherback and loggerhead turtle population got caught up in these longlines per year. Longlines also killed and injured whales, dolphins, endangered shorebirds, and more.

But most fishermen didn't want to do anything differently, and most governments hadn't responded to the threat. In the United States, Alex knew that the NMFS had been very slow to act, almost always choosing special interests over upholding the Endangered Species Act. The NMFS had been sued numerous times by various conservation organizations.

Longline fishing had been banned off the coast of California since 2004 in order to protect sea turtles. But Alex had read that NOAA Fisheries recently announced that it was considering allowing longline fishing again in federal waters off the western coast of the United States to target swordfish and other species.

"Have you heard about maybe using circle hooks instead of J hooks?" Sasha asked.

"I did read about that. It does less damage, right?"

"That's what I've heard when I've talked to fishermen." Sasha shrugged. "But that still doesn't solve the problem of getting tangled in the line."

"The NMFS has been sued by a few conservation nonprofits because they have refused to require seasonal or area closures of longlining in areas with a high turtle density. A judge ordered them to close them, but the NMFS fought it and still issues longlining permits."

"It's bad," Sasha agreed. "And a lot of governments around the world don't offer any turtle protections at all, do they?"

"Unfortunately, no."

"We'll just have to keep the pressure up," Sasha said. She lifted her glass of tea. "To saving the turtles!"

Alex laughed, then clinked glasses with her. "To saving the turtles."

When they finished dinner, night had fallen. Alex drove them back to the beach where Sasha's car waited. They hugged again, and Sasha opened her car door. "Call when you need me. I'm looking forward to seeing some baby turtles."

"I'll do that," Alex told her.

"And hey," Sasha added, "you are making a difference. Whether you know it or not."

Alex exhaled. "I hope so." Then she watched as her friend drove away.

When Alex got back to the beach, Jerome stood up, stretching. "Anything exciting happen?" she asked him.

"Nope. I hoped one might come to shore and lay eggs, but no luck."

"Thanks for watching the nests. I really appreciate it."

He gazed out at the waves. "Watched some surfers for a while. Looks relaxing. Maybe I'll try that out. Give my pitching arm a rest."

"Sounds like a great idea."

"You good for now?" he asked.

"Yep."

"I'll get home to my aunt. She keeps wanting me to play some card game with her. Cribbage or something."

"I used to play it with my dad. It's fun."

"Well, see you later," he said, and started down the beach. "Hit me up if the eggs start hatching," he called back.

"I will."

After he left, Alex returned to her Jeep. Rummaging around by moonlight, she retrieved the Bluetti power station and lugged it over to her tent. She set out its solar panels so it would start charging up as soon as the sun rose in the morning. Then she went back for her laptop.

The waxing moon hadn't quite set yet, and it bathed the beach in a magical silvery glow. The white of the waves rolling in flashed silver, the gentle susurration lending a peaceful rhythm to the night. Some crickets chirped from the nearby bushes, and wind stirred the palms above her. In the glow of the moonlight, she could see a number of crabs scuttling down the beach as waves receded, grabbing little nibbles to eat, then racing back up shore as the next surge of waves rolled in.

She checked the hawksbill nests, finding them undisturbed, then scanned the beach for any predators, be they humans or dogs.

When she found the beach just peaceful and quiet, Alex crawled into her tent and changed into her PJs. But she didn't feel sleepy. Her mind was a tangle of thoughts. She kept thinking back on her dinner conversation with Sasha and about the National Marine Fisheries Service.

She often felt conflicted about its actions. The agency's two main jobs were at odds with each other. On one hand, it was tasked with protecting wildlife that was listed under the Endangered Species Act. But on the other, it served to promote fisheries. Too often the money side of things won out, with marine life such as sea turtles, whales, dolphins, coral reefs, and endangered fish taking a back seat to the fishing industry. Regulations that could be put in place to protect marine wildlife from fisheries were often put off or delayed just so that extra buck could be made. Alex often wondered if this was because the NMFS reported to the U.S. Department of Commerce rather than to an arm of the government whose main focus was conservation. She hoped for some kind of marine protection agency to be formed.

One compromise that could help would be the use of pound nets, which posed the least threat to turtles. It basically created a series of boxes, like a big maze, that eventually led fish to an area with a small opening. Often this opening was at the top, so if a turtle was caught in a pound net, it could swim to the surface to breathe. When the fishermen arrived to check the net, they could scoop up any turtles and free them, along with any unwanted species of fish, and keep only the fish most valuable to them. It would be wonderful if the NMFS began encouraging the use of such less harmful nets.

And sometimes arms of the government did help, such as

Operation Green Turtle, in which the U.S. Navy spread hatchlings all over the Caribbean and the Gulf of Mexico. The thought made her feel a little better. Sometimes good things did happen.

She made sure the camera alarm was set on her phone and tucked it in next to her shoulder inside the sleeping bag. Now the vibration would wake her up should anyone approach the eggs. Then she drifted off to the gentle sounds of the surf. *I could get used to this,* she thought.

EIGHT

The next morning Alex climbed out of her tent and stretched, emerging to a serene scene. A few surfers were out, bobbing on the waves, but no one had yet arrived on the beach itself.

The sound of a car pulling into the small parking area caught her attention, and she recognized Sasha's compact red rental car. Her friend stepped out. "Have you heard?" she asked before she'd even shut the car door.

Alex walked over to her. "Heard what?"

"A hurricane. And it might be a bad one."

"What?"

Sasha held out her phone. She'd pulled up the National Oceanic and Atmospheric Administration's weather page for the area. "NOAA says there's a good chance it'll make landfall here." She handed Alex the phone.

On the screen, Alex watched a time-lapse satellite image of a churning hurricane off the coast of the Big Island. If it kept on its current trajectory, it would hit in the southeast, right where this beach was. The turtle eggs would drown in the storm surge.

Alex scrolled around the page. "Does it say when it'll hit?"

"Six days, they think."

"Including today?"

"Yes."

"Oh boy. I better get a contingency plan in place. If I have to move these eggs, I'll need containers, a place to store them..." Alex trailed off as she watched the churning monster of clouds in the image. She handed Sasha's phone back. "What about your boat?"

"It'll be okay, I think. If it keeps on its current track, I'm going to move it to the west side of the island near Kailua-Kona. If that happens, I'll just have to hold off on my dive till this thing passes over. I can help you move eggs if you need it."

Alex felt a flush of gratitude. "Yes, please." She looked over at her Jeep. "Any chance you could hang out here for a few hours? I'd like to drive to the center and get some egg containers. They have special padded ones for just this kind of emergency."

"You want me to hang out on a tropical beach?" She laughed. "Twist my arm."

"There's good cell reception over by that tree. Great for streaming."

Sasha stared out at the ocean. "I think I'll just hang out here."

"Thanks, Sasha."

Alex grabbed her keys and drove her Jeep to Kealakekua, on the west side of the Big Island, where the center was located. She could store the eggs here temporarily if the storm hit, as this area would be safe from the brunt of the incoming hurricane.

News of the storm had reached the center when Alex arrived. The director emerged from her office and set Alex up with a number of egg containers, which they carried out to Alex's Jeep.

Returning to the southeast side of the island, Alex found Sasha sitting at the water's edge in Alex's beach chair, letting the waves splash up over her feet.

"I really appreciate your doing this."

"No problem. And Jerome stopped by. He had a boogie board and had a great time out there. Said he's definitely going to learn how to surf now."

"Maybe he'll become a champion pitcher *and* surfer."

"And astronomer," Sasha added.

"He seems determined enough," Alex agreed. "I like that kid."

"Me, too."

They hung out a little longer, catching up. Sasha described more of what led her to become fascinated in Revolutionary War–era subs and the vanishing of the Wasp. Alex went into more detail about some of the more harrowing events in New Mexico.

"I'm glad you're okay," Sasha told her.

"Me, too!" Alex gave a small chuckle.

"Well, I'd better be getting back," Sasha said, standing up. "I've got a lot of prep work before my dive. Maybe the hurricane will veer away from the island."

"We can hope."

Alex walked Sasha to her car and watched her friend pull away, giving a wave.

Then she returned to the beach and checked the thermocouples. She listened to the two nests with her microphone, but the older nest was likely still a few days away from hatching.

She powered up her laptop and checked the location of the two tagged turtles. Both were swimming just offshore, with some satellite passes missing them and others pinging. It all looked normal to her. No one caught in a gillnet. She sighed with relief.

Sitting down on the beach, Alex stared out at the waves, watching the same trio of surfers from before floating on their boards, conversing. She heard the sweet chatter of a yellow-fronted canary and looked around until she spotted its beautiful golden plumage in a nearby gigantic koa tree.

It felt good to be back in Hawai'i. When Alex's mom had been stationed on Hickam Air Force Base in Honolulu when Alex was a kid, Alex had loved it. Summers were the best. While she was on vacation from school, she'd travel around the islands with her father. They'd hiked the Nā Pali Coast, those dramatic peaks fronting the ocean on the island of Kaua'i. Many movies had been filmed there, including *Jurassic Park, Pirates of the Caribbean: On Stranger Tides,* and the 1976 version of *King Kong*. Alex had grown up watching reruns of *Magnum P.I.*, seeing the detective solve crimes on glorious beaches.

When she was a kid, accompanying her dad while he was out finding new vistas to paint, Alex would take along a little sketchbook and make notes on the wildlife and flowers she saw, write down what the weather was like, and draw visual representations of the soundscape around her—from which direction this or that bird sang or which direction insects droned.

And when her mother was home, she'd make up inventive games for Alex to play, games that required skills like orienteering, mechanical or electrical know-how, route finding, code breaking. While her friends played Frisbee and went on picnics with their families, Alex's mom was teaching her combat training, mechanical repair, gun safety, and how to use any objects at her disposal to defend herself. She'd dropped Alex off in the woods countless times, and Alex had to find her way back on her own using clues from the trees, landscape, or stars. She'd loved it all. It was only when she was an adult, talking to other people, that she realized what an odd upbringing it had been. But she and her mom had bonded over the experiences, and more than once that training had saved Alex's life.

Alex fought back the sudden sting of tears when she thought about how they'd lost her mom.

A car pulling into the small parking area brought Alex's gaze in that direction. She spotted Dora's well-loved station wagon and hurriedly wiped away her tears and stood up. Dora got out of her car and started scanning the ground. Then the retired teacher spotted Alex out on the beach and waved.

Alex joined her. "Nice to see you."

"And you." She frowned, glancing around on the ground. "I don't suppose you've seen a pair of glasses out here, have you?"

Alex cast around. "Sorry, I haven't."

Dora giggled a bit ruefully. "I'm afraid I was so distracted when I ran into Nakoa that I've completely misplaced them. I remember I hooked them onto my shirt, and then . . . nothing! I might have dropped them in the sand."

"I'll help you look," Alex offered.

Together they scanned all around the parking area, then retraced their steps down onto the beach. Near where she had first met Nakoa, Alex spotted the arm of a pair of eyeglasses sticking out of the sand. She pointed it out.

"There they are!" Dora cried happily. She hurried and retrieved them, shaking them off.

As they walked back to her station wagon, Dora glanced at her a few times, studying her face. Finally she said, "I don't mean to pry, but you look like you've been crying."

Alex sniffed, feeling embarrassed. "I think I'm allergic to some of the flowers here," she lied, not wanting the woman to feel uncomfortable.

"I'm not buying that for a second. I'm a teacher, you know. That means I'm good at reading people."

Alex looked up at her, meeting the kind woman's gaze. "I was just thinking about my mom," Alex confessed, surprised she'd said it out loud. Dora was pretty much a stranger, after all. But something about her sympathetic nature invited confidence. "I lost her when I was twelve."

Dora touched her shoulder. "I understand. I lost my own mother when I was young. The pain never really goes away when you lose someone like that." She gazed off into the horizon. "Important dates come and go—marriages, graduations—and you want your mother there to share them with you."

"Yes," Alex said, feeling a painful lump growing in her throat. The tears came back, stinging her eyes.

"Tell me about her," Dora said.

With most people uncomfortable when the subject of grief came up, Alex had grown used to never mentioning her mother. She had become a taboo subject the moment she died. For Dora to ask about her showed Alex just how rare and lovely the woman was.

"You sure? You have time? I don't want to keep you."

"Not at all. It would be my honor to hear about what kind of woman raised a daughter like you."

Alex smiled. They walked beside the surf, Alex's mind drifting to a long-ago time, when her family had still been intact. "She was a pilot for the Air Force."

"Oh, wow. A trailblazer!"

"Her plane went down during a mission. My dad and I were devastated. Our whole lives changed." Alex gazed out over the surf. Even after all these years, it was still hard to believe she was gone. "We moved around a lot because of her job. It's weird, but we lived in so many different places that part of me illogically believes that maybe my mom is still in one of those places I haven't been back to. Like maybe I'll find her whenever I return."

Dora put a comforting hand on Alex's arm.

"It feels more like we just haven't talked in a long time for some strange reason, rather than the seemingly impossible idea that she's simply gone." She met Dora's eyes. "Is that crazy?"

"Not at all, honey."

The wind sighed in the palms around them. "We lived in Hawai'i when my mom was stationed at Hickam. Being here makes me feel closer to her. Like a part of me is home because I lived here with her."

"Where is your home now?" Dora asked.

Alex had to shake her head. "I guess you can say I really don't have one. I go wherever my work takes me." She gestured toward her little tent. "I've got a backcountry pack full of the necessities. Some clothes and novels. A first aid kit. Toiletries. Not much."

"And that's all you have in the world?"

"Well, the last place I lived anywhere full-time was in Boston. I moved out there to be with my boyfriend from grad school. It didn't work out. But I've got a storage unit there with stuff like this great emerald-green velvet rocking chair that had belonged to my mom's mom, and this antique mahogany secretary from the Victorian period that has been passed down on the paternal side."

Alex smiled at the thought of that secretary. When she had been little and her grandmother had still been with them, she'd sat at that secretary and pulled antique volumes off its shelves, reveling in tales from Robert Louis Stevenson and Edgar Rice Burroughs and Baroness Orczy. She especially loved the latter's tales of the Scarlet Pimpernel.

That storage unit also held papers from her grad and undergrad days, a desktop computer and monitor, rock climbing equipment, and some research books.

But for now, she traveled light, bringing only what she'd need for each assignment in the wilds.

"So you've got nowhere to go after this?" Dora asked.

"I can always go stay with my dad if I need a place before my next gig comes up. He lives in Berkeley and is a professional painter. He's coming out in a few weeks, actually." She couldn't wait for her father's visit. It would be their first time together in Hawaiʻi since they lived here. They could visit some of their old haunts, reminisce about her mother.

"I'd love to meet him."

"That would be great. I'd love to get him out here with all the volunteers, spend some time with the turtles. And I'm sure he'd love to paint the view from this beach."

Dora stared out at the scenery, contemplating. "I've always believed that home is where your soul feels most at peace. For me, that's here, returning to this island. Where is that for you?"

Without hesitating, Alex said, "Anywhere in nature. It's where

I feel true comfort and solace." Alex suddenly felt self-conscious. She'd totally been dominating the conversation. "What was your mom like?"

Dora grinned. "An absolute firecracker. Powerhouse of a woman. She never stopped. She was involved with everything. I swear she volunteered for every charity in town. She was a teacher, too. Really inspired me. I was lucky enough to have her through my teens. I'm sorry you lost your mom so much earlier."

"Thanks. And I'm sorry you lost your mom, too."

"Thank you."

Both of them went quiet then, and they strode for a while along the beach in companionable silence.

"How are you settling in, now that you're back?" Alex said at last.

Dora beamed. "It's a dream. An absolute dream!" She grinned mischievously. "And I'm having dinner with Nakoa tonight. I can't wait!" She glanced down at her watch. "In fact, I better get cracking if I'm going to get dolled up beforehand."

"Don't let me keep you," Alex said, delighted at the woman's excitement.

She walked Dora back to her car, and Dora held up her glasses. "Eagle eye! Thanks for spotting them."

"My pleasure."

"And call me if those little darlings are about to hatch and you need a hand!"

"I definitely will."

Dora got in her station wagon and drove off down the dirt road, around the corner and out of sight. Alex felt a sudden pang of loneliness, a bone- and soul-deep sense of loss. She thought again of her mom and how her dad had suffered, how the vivid and living spark of his spirit had dimmed after her loss.

Her whole childhood felt so distant at times. Alex hadn't stayed in touch with many of her friends from back then, a product of moving around so much. She'd tried—written letters, found a few on social media, and gotten back in contact. But she found that most people didn't have the bandwidth to really connect with anyone outside their daily lives. If they didn't work with you or live with you, or at least nearby, and you weren't family, most people just let friendships fall away.

One thing Alex struggled with in the life she'd chosen was isolation. She moved to a new place for each job. She was close to Zoe and her father, but she didn't have any daily friends she could hang out with, spend time with, and just get in some social time. So she was always grateful when she could get together with someone like Sasha while out on these gigs. And this visit with Dora had been a welcome spot of social contact.

When she was on a job, her head deep in the research of it, Alex didn't notice the loneliness so much. But whenever she had to drive into a town for food or to pick up her forwarded mail, she'd see friends getting dinner or couples out on dates. There was a keen sense of awkwardness, she'd found, in sitting by herself in a restaurant. Maybe she imagined the look of pity that hosts gave her when she confirmed that yes, she just needed a table for one. Then she'd have to repeat that same thing to the server, that no, she wasn't expecting anyone else to join her and could go ahead and order.

She'd never been a very gregarious or social person, never had a huge group of casual friends or was into going out every night, even when she was a teenager or later in college. But she was comfortable talking to a lot of different kinds of people. Her few true friends had run the spectrum of social groups when she was growing up: introverts, extroverts, band geeks, jocks, quiet studious types, theater folks, mathletes.

Alex's interests ran so wide that in college she'd taken a number of courses outside her required curriculum. Mythology, climatology, history. And she'd played the oboe in her college orchestra. She sighed, thinking of her oboe. It was in her storage unit in Boston.

That was one thing she really did miss. And it was so portable—she should have brought it. *Next job,* she told herself, imagining the oboe's dulcet tones flowing out through the swaying trees and over the sparkling water.

Alex stood up, stretching. The surfers rode a small wave into shore and toweled off. She watched as they loaded their boards into an old VW bus and headed off.

She checked the transmitter data again and then fired up her Sterno stove. She made herself a dinner of chickpeas with curry sauce, which she ate while sitting on the sand outside her tent.

The sun dipped below the horizon, and soon, Alex grew sleepy. She crawled into her tent, made sure the motion cameras' alarms were active, and was soon asleep.

ALEX AWOKE THE NEXT DAY to the crowing of a red junglefowl. They'd been brought to the islands centuries ago and had proliferated and gone feral. The chickens crowed at all hours of the day and drove some people crazy.

As the morning wore on, wind began pulling at her tent. Her rain fly came loose and flapped against the door. She secured it and pulled out her phone, checking NOAA's site again. The hurricane had moved closer to the islands. They expected landfall in five days if it stayed on its current path.

She called her volunteers, asking if any of them would be willing to move the eggs and drive them to the main facility if the hurricane continued to churn toward them and an evacuation order came down. She wanted to give them enough time to safely move the eggs. She was relieved when all of them agreed.

They might have to deal with some pattering of rain and a bit of wind, but enough time prior to landfall would mean they wouldn't have to deal with downed trees, palm fronds littering the roadways, heavy winds, or dangerous traffic if people were forced to evacuate.

Moving the turtle eggs under those circumstances would be a far more hazardous prospect.

She was loath to move them at all, but it was better to risk transporting them than to have them all drown.

That task finished, she checked the thermocouples, making sure neither of the nests had been disturbed. Then she showered and retrieved her laptop from her car.

She sat out on the beach as she checked where the two turtles currently were, wondering when they might come to shore to lay eggs again. The time was getting close for one of them. She pulled up the emailed results of the GPS trackers.

The one she'd freed from the gillnet hung out close to shore, likely feeding on sponges in the coral reefs. The satellite had recorded its location only five out of the last twenty passes, so it was definitely spending the majority of its time underwater.

She pulled up data on the second hawksbill. It, too, had been hanging out close to shore in the coral reefs. She scanned down the passes, then frowned. The last four pings had all been in a totally different latitude and longitude. She pulled up a topographical map on her geographic information software and entered the last four x,y coordinates to see where the turtle was. And she stared down in disbelief. Those coordinates weren't even in the water. They were on land. She quickly entered the rest of the turtle's most recent coordinates.

Now she saw a clear path of the turtle. It had been hanging out close to shore about two miles north of her location. But then it had moved to land. But not up onto a beach. It was too far inland, miles from shore. The next satellite pass clocked it even farther down the coast, about five miles inland. This turtle had not come to shore to lay eggs. It would never travel that far from a beach. The next two satellite passes hadn't recorded anything. Had the transmitter been covered? Had the turtle been inside something? Then the most recent pass, taken twenty minutes ago, showed it at a small private airfield. She sucked in a breath.

Wildlife traffickers. That had to be it.

And now they were going to load it onto a plane, if they hadn't already. There could be other imperiled species, too: green turtles, nēnē hatchlings, hoary bats, and birds with brilliant plumage like the ʻiʻiwi, all in demand on the black market. She thought of the men with the gillnet and wondered if they were still out there, not caught yet and trapping additional wildlife.

Alex knew that poachers often removed transmitters when they spotted them. She was lucky they'd grabbed a turtle with the new flat kind of transmitter developed by the center. They were a lot less noticeable than the old kind.

Alex closed her laptop, grabbed her phone, and raced for her Jeep.

NINE

Alex climbed into her Jeep and roared out of the small grassy parking area, then bounced down the long, pitted dirt road that led away from the beach. Progress felt too slow. Finally she reached pavement, passing the Museum of Vertebrate Paleontology, which lay on the outskirts of Ānuenue. She turned down the quiet residential streets that led into the small town.

Jerome lived the closest to the beach, and she hated to ask him again so soon after he'd watched the nests, but she needed someone who could get to the beach quickly. She called him and explained the immediacy of the situation.

"I'll call someone to relieve you if it looks like I'm going to be gone for too long," she assured him.

"Okay. No problem."

Alex thanked him, then hurriedly hung up.

She drove quickly but carefully, watching for pedestrians and bicyclists along the less-traveled roads, relieved when she hit the larger road that led out of Ānuenue. She joined a swarm of cars heading south on the Hawai'i Belt Road.

Then she voice dialed Special Agent Jason Coles, who was with the Department of Justice's Task Force on Wildlife Trafficking. She'd worked with him before, and while he was headquartered in Washington, D.C., she hoped he might know someone on the island.

Alex passed a car as he came on the line.

"Agent Coles."

"Hi, Jason. It's Alex Carter."

"Wow. A voice from the past! How are you?"

"I'm good, but I've got a situation."

"Tell me."

She blurted out the predicament in one go.

Coles was all business. He wrote down the turtle's location. "Where are you now?"

"Heading south on the Hawai'i Belt Road. But I'm still twenty miles away from the airfield. They could be gone by now."

"We've been following a group of smugglers in that area. I have two agents on the ground in Hilo."

"How soon can they get there?"

He paused, calculating. "About an hour and twenty minutes."

"That might be too late. Can you call the local police?" she asked.

"I can. But if it's a private airfield, then there will be a lot of red tape involved. They might not be able to move in right away."

"This is terrible," Alex said, passing a slow-moving sedan and pulling ahead of it. She was speeding now. "What can I do?"

"Nothing for now. Get as close to the airfield as you can and wait for my agents. Keep an eye on the turtle's tracker."

"I don't know if the satellite will make another pass before they leave. They may already be gone." *Or the poachers might have noticed the tracker and removed it,* she thought. "I can't just stand by."

"Don't do anything rash, Alex. I know you like to throw yourself into the thick of things, and as you know, I'm personally grateful to you for that, but these smugglers are no one to mess around with. Let me put you on hold for just a minute while I contact my agents."

"Okay."

Alex had been forced to deal with dangerous people in the past, including what led her to meet Coles in the first place. But she knew how to fight—had studied the martial art Jeet Kune Do since she was a kid. And she had her mom to thank for other survival skills.

But Alex wasn't armed, and these smugglers probably were. But she couldn't just stand by. People who trafficked wildlife made her sick. And the trade in turtles could be especially cruel. She couldn't stand the thought of turtles who'd been happily enjoying the ocean being crated up and shipped, with little chance of surviving the voyage, to be abused in the illegal pet trade or killed for use in cruel practices. Or a beautiful hawksbill, a species that was barely hanging on as it was, being made into an ashtray or a plate or a comb. Some traffickers even encased baby sea turtles inside liquid-filled plastic key chains, where they died and were sold as cheap trinkets.

She waited for Coles to come back on the line, hearing only silence and the occasional click. Just as she started to wonder if they'd been disconnected, he returned. "We're in luck. My agents were following up on a lead. They're in Mountain View. That's twenty minutes closer."

Alex glanced at the Jeep's clock and her speed and did a quick calculation. She'd arrive at the airfield about thirty minutes before them. If the traffickers were getting ready to leave, maybe she could stall their plane somehow or create a distraction.

"What are you thinking, Dr. Carter? Nothing foolish, I hope."

"Of course not. I'll drive to the airfield and wait for your agents."

"Dr. Carter?" he asked, suspicious.

She could handle herself. "Don't worry about me."

And then she hung up.

She did some quick addition. The satellite wouldn't make another pass for an hour and forty minutes after the last one. Maybe they were still loading the plane. Who knows what else they were smuggling, including body parts from animals that had already been killed, like shark fins, monk seal pelts, and whale teeth. Not to mention things these traffickers might be bringing *into* this airfield from other places. Alex knew that Hawai'i was one of the top U.S. markets for the illegal wildlife trade, bringing in animal parts from whales, tigers, walruses, and elephants, including ivory.

She passed a few more cars, driving carefully but quickly, and her Jeep's GPS nav screen showed that she was approaching the turnoff for the private airfield. It lay down a small dirt road lined with koa trees. She turned onto the road, slowing. About a hundred yards down the lane, she spotted the airfield. It was small, with a grass runway. An orange sock gauging wind direction and speed flapped on a pole near a small hangar. A chain-link fence surrounded the airfield, a red-and-white-striped gate blocking its entry drive, with a sign reading "No Trespassing."

She saw a small jet parked off to one side, but no one moved around it. Grass grew taller around its wheels, giving her the impression it hadn't been used in a while. A cargo plane stood by the hangar, and several men milled around it. She pulled her binoculars out of her pack and focused on the men.

She sucked in a breath. She knew it. Two were the same men who had put out the gillnet, the scrawny one who had tried to stab her with the barbed pole and the burly, sunburned one who had driven their boat. They probably had at least one other net out there somewhere or had previously gleaned some rare fish or other turtles in the one she'd discovered.

They were arguing with a man wearing a sidearm in a holster on his hip, gesticulating angrily at him. Finally the man frowned and shelled out a large wad of cash from an envelope stuffed in his back pocket. He handed it over.

Then the man with the gun joined a chubby, short man at the rear of a larger truck. He, too, wore a sidearm, and she didn't recognize either one. They started loading crates from the truck into the back of the cargo plane. The two gillnet men divvied up the cash between them and then lit up cigarettes, milling around, talking by the hangar.

Alex counted four total men and probably at least one more in the hangar, likely an airfield manager who directed air traffic. Only the two by the plane looked armed.

She pulled over onto the grassy shoulder behind a screen of trees and glanced into the rearview mirror. No sign of any other cars. She checked the clock. She'd made good time, but that meant the agents wouldn't be here for another fifteen minutes at the earliest.

She pulled out her Canon PowerShot camera with its 60x zoom lens and took photos of all the men, including close-ups of their faces. Then she took images of the two planes and jotted down their registration numbers. She wondered whose jet it was, who owned the airfield, and if they knew that it was being used like this.

The two men doing the loading stretched, then walked over to the smoking men. They passed around a flask, stopping to talk. Alex saw that several more crates waited inside the truck, but it looked almost empty. Time ticked by at an agonizing pace.

After a few sips from the flask, the armed man who'd shelled out the cash pulled out his phone and frowned. He slid it into his back pocket, eyed the plane, and pointed at the load inside, gesturing hurriedly. He seemed to be running the operation. Two of the men climbed inside and started shifting boxes around. Then the other two unloaded the remaining crates from the truck but just placed them on the ground while the cargo was shifted around in the plane.

The man glanced at his phone again and waved for the two gillnet men to get in the truck.

They all spoke together for another few minutes, and then the two gillnet men climbed into the truck and turned it around. They started to head down the drive toward the gate, so Alex moved her

Jeep, pulling farther away down the road. The men entered a code at the gate, and the red-and-white bar rose up. They drove through, turning toward the main road. Alex took note of their license plate. When they were well down the road, heading back toward the main drag, she turned around and parked again on the side of the road behind the screen of trees, close to the chain-link fence that surrounded the airfield.

She pulled out her binoculars again, peering through the branches and trunks. A man emerged from the hangar and waved the two remaining men over. They strolled toward him, taking the time to light another cigarette, and then disappeared inside the building, probably to make last-minute preparations or check their flight path.

Through her binoculars, she spotted a single security camera, mounted on the front of the hangar, pointed down by the door.

The cargo ramp of the plane was still open, the few remaining crates piled at the bottom of it. Alex's gut twisted. Any second now they'd emerge and finish loading everything. She glanced down the street but saw no sign of the agents. She thought of the hawksbill and all the other animals they could have on board that plane right now stuffed in those crates, probably struggling to move or breathe. She had to do something.

Just then her phone rang. She saw Jason Coles's name flash on the screen. She picked up.

"My guys are stuck in traffic," he said. "Some bridge construction has the road closed on one side, so they're alternating traffic."

"How long will it take them?"

"They're thinking twenty more minutes."

"I'm here outside the airfield. They're getting ready to leave."

"Don't do anything crazy," he warned her. "You stay put till my guys get there."

"I will," she told him, knowing even then she was lying. "I'm just taking photos of their faces."

"That better be all you're doing," he admonished her. "Because if you do anything illegal and I know about it, that puts me in an awkward position." He paused, then added, "Especially if my agents or I know anything about it. Capisce?"

"Capisce. Just keep me posted on their ETA."

"I will."

Alex hung up. Then she climbed out of the Jeep, glancing up and down the deserted road. She didn't know where it led and didn't see any houses. It probably belonged to whoever owned the private airfield, some billionaire or corporation far down the lane.

She walked to the chain-link fence, still under the cover of the trees. The road was empty.

She made the decision and curled her fingers around the chain-link, then stuck the toe of one boot into the metal. She hefted herself up and over the fence, the sharp metal at the top catching on the sleeve of her shirt. She jumped down, now on the other side of the fence, still in the cover of the trees. She eyed the hangar but saw no movement outside it or by either plane.

She checked for signs of cameras or motion detectors along the fence but saw none. The side of the hangar facing her had no windows. Now was her chance. She took off, sprinting toward the building. As she approached, she studied it again for signs of additional cameras but didn't see any. She reached the building and pressed herself against it.

She could hear voices now, men talking about a flight path to an island in Micronesia and using it as a stopping-off point before continuing on to China.

She darted a look around the corner of the building, then skirted around it, taking care to avoid the front of the building with its windows and camera.

As she rounded the hangar, she broke into a run again, sprinting to the front of the cargo plane. She crept around the far side, eyeing the wooden crates that stood at the bottom of the loading ramp. She pulled out her multitool and slunk over to one of them. Making sure the men were still inside, she opened the flathead screwdriver and jabbed it into the small space beneath the lid. She wriggled it back and forth, hearing a nail loosen. When the gap was wide enough for her fingers to fit, she grabbed the lid and wrenched upward. The crate was poorly made and part of a side came loose, too, the box rickety and weak.

What she saw inside made her sick. Hundreds of squirming little green sea turtle hatchlings were enclosed in a sharp wire cage, many cut and bleeding. An adult hawksbill struggled underneath them, the one she'd tagged. Severed shark fins stood crammed against one wall of the crate, and a brilliantly scarlet 'i'iwi honeycreeper stood in a tiny wire enclosure that was too small for it, its feathers jutting sharply out of the mesh. Two little eggs rolled loose beside it.

A powerful anger welled up in her, and for a second she just saw red. Her body temperature shot up and she felt her face flush. Then she forced her breathing to still.

She had to think this out. She replaced the lid and moved back, crouching down by the landing gear. Staring over one of the tires, she mentally went over her options. Any second now the men would be done inside. She had only minutes and couldn't count on the agents getting here in time.

She pulled out her multitool. Extending a blade, she drove it into the side of the tire. Its point stuck into the exterior of the rubber but didn't penetrate the tire. She thrust it again with the same effect. It wouldn't push through. She leaned on it hard, putting her full weight behind it, then pounded it with her fist. Finally the blade slowly slid through the rubber. With a violent hiss, the tire expelled its air. She pressed harder, widening the hole.

Glancing up, she made sure the men were still inside the hangar, then she crawled under the plane and punctured the second rear tire. After considerable force, air erupted from it, and she pulled out her blade, then ran to the front wheel.

But movement just inside the door of the hangar snapped her attention up. Two men stood in the doorway, their backs turned to her, still talking to the man inside. The two rear wheels would have to be enough.

She turned and sprinted for the little jet parked some distance away, glancing back over her shoulder fearfully as she ran. But they hadn't emerged, still standing by the door.

She reached the safety of the jet and lay down in the tall grass by its landing gear, out of sight.

Her gut flip-flopped as the two armed men emerged, striding toward the plane. The third man stayed behind, leaning against the hangar's doorframe. He was probably the manager for the airfield.

The two men didn't notice the flattened landing gear at first. They moved to the back of the plane and hefted up one of the crates. But as they moved up the ramp, the short one pointed at the flattened rear wheels. They slammed the crate down.

"What the fuck?!" the one who seemed to be the boss yelled.

The other stared down, scratching his head. "Did we hit something when we landed?"

"We must have." He turned toward the hangar. "Don't you believe in runway maintenance?" he boomed. "Our landing gear is shot! What the fuck are you doing out here?"

The airfield manager appeared nonplussed, still leaning on the doorframe. "There's nothing wrong with this runway. Maybe you assholes just don't know how to land a plane."

"Get on the goddamn phone and get us a repair team pronto," the leader shouted.

The manager flipped him off and then turned back into the hangar.

The shorter man gestured at the crates. "We'll have to load these before anyone gets here. Don't want anyone seeing them."

"Goddamn it," cursed the leader, resting his hand on the butt of his handgun. "Let's go in there and make sure that asshole is actually calling for a repair."

He stormed back toward the hangar, his compatriot close on his heels.

Now was Alex's chance to get back to her Jeep. She took the same path back, racing to the back of the hangar, pressing against it, and then sprinting to the cover of the trees. She scaled the chain-link fence again and jumped down on the other side.

Just then a black SUV turned onto the small lane and headed toward her. Two people sat in the front seat. Her heart started thumping again. They could be with the smugglers. She climbed into her Jeep.

But then the passenger gave her a small wave.

The SUV pulled up alongside her, behind the screen of trees. Alex rolled down her window as the driver did the same. She came face-to-face with him—a chiseled, russet face beneath a short crop of black hair, black aviator sunglasses reflecting the golden light of the afternoon sky. In the passenger seat sat a petite woman with blond hair and a tanned, freckled face.

"Dr. Carter?" the man asked.

"Yes."

"I'm Agent Carlos Santiago." He nodded at his partner. "This is Agent Juliet Grant."

"Thank you for coming out." She pointed toward the cargo plane. "They're loading crates onto that plane and only have a few more to go."

"And they are transporting endangered species?" Grant asked.

"Yes."

Santiago frowned. "Are you sure?"

"I'm positive. A hawksbill tracker is pinging at this location." She didn't want to admit that she'd also seen the contents of one of the crates. She wanted to heed Agent Coles's advice. She'd broken the law and didn't want to put them in the uncomfortable position of knowing that.

He stared out at the cargo plane. "Unfortunately, we need to see illegal activity in progress in order to move in there without a warrant."

Alex's stomach flopped. She pulled out her binoculars again and focused on the cargo plane. The men were out of the hangar now. They'd already stashed the crate that they'd set down on the ramp and now shifted to move the final ones.

"They're loading the last of the crates," Alex told the agents.

Grant pulled out a pair of binoculars and joined her partner in watching the men. As they hefted another crate into the plane, one man's foot slipped off the ramp and he fell backward, dropping his end of the crate. It was the one that Alex had pried open, with the loose side. It struck the ramp and then crashed onto the tarmac, spilling its heartbreaking contents.

She heard Grant gasp in horror at the sight.

"That's good enough for us," Santiago said immediately. He tossed his binoculars into the back seat of the SUV and whipped the vehicle around. He turned on the flashers, and the siren wailed to life.

The SUV tore through the red-and-white bar, splintering it and sending it flying. They roared onto the airfield, closing in on the plane.

The two men at the plane scattered like cockroaches, both headed in different directions. The boss sprinted toward one section of fence.

The SUV slammed to a halt, a spray of dirt billowing up around the car. The agents jumped out. "Department of Justice! Halt and drop your weapons!" Grant shouted at the shorter smuggler. The man continued to run, so she took off in pursuit.

The airfield manager emerged at the ruckus and took off when he saw the SUV. Santiago shouted for him to stop. He made it to the chain-link fence, and the agent ran up behind him, yanking him down, wrestling him to the ground, and cuffing him.

Grant had now reached a different section of fence, the shorter smuggler readying to climb over it. He whirled, seeing her feet firmly planted, her gun aimed at his chest. He didn't touch the pistol in his holster. "Get on your knees!" she shouted. He did. "Lie face down and lace your fingers behind your head!" He flopped onto his stomach.

She raced over to him and cuffed him, then removed his pistol from its holster and stowed her own weapon.

Santiago had taken off after the smuggler who'd been giving the orders. The trafficker had almost reached another section of fence. Santiago shouted again for him to freeze, but the man turned and reached for his firearm.

"Don't do it," Santiago warned him, pulling his own gun and taking aim. The smuggler thought the better of it and dropped his weapon. Santiago ordered him to lie down on his stomach and cuffed him.

Grant escorted her prisoner to the back of the SUV, then helped her partner wrangle the other two inside.

Alex watched from the fence, relief flooding through her.

The agents climbed into the SUV, and Alex could hear Grant on the radio.

Alex got out of her Jeep and walked to the shattered gate. Grant spotted her and headed over.

"There were two other men," Alex told her. "They'd put out an illegal gillnet that NOAA Fisheries Enforcement removed. But they were here at the airfield."

"Do you have a description?"

"Better than that. I took photos of them and got their license plate."

"Can you send me that info?" Grant pulled out a card with her contact info from a slim metal case and handed it to Alex.

"Of course. So what happens now?" Alex asked.

"We'll need to do a thorough check on the health of the trafficked wildlife. They'll have to quarantine before they can be released."

Alex fished her own card from the wallet in her back pocket. "Will you call me when you release the hawksbill? She might be about to lay some more eggs."

Grant took the card. "Of course."

"Thank you," Alex said, shaking the agent's hand. "Thank you so much."

"We'll have to ask you to remain here for a time. We need you to give us a detailed statement."

"Okay. No problem."

The woman nodded and then returned to her partner.

Alex breathed a sigh of relief and walked back to her Jeep. Her heart was still beating hard, and she took a few deep breaths to slow it down.

She sat down in the driver's seat and pulled out her phone, first calling Dora to see if she could go relieve Jerome. She explained the situation, and Dora said she was happy to help. Alex then phoned Jerome, who said that all was well on the beach and that he'd wait for Dora to arrive. Alex thanked him profusely.

Then she pulled up the photos of the gillnet poachers on her camera, connected it to her iPad, and emailed those images to Grant.

Alex waited a few more minutes, and then Grant returned to her and took her detailed statement. She started back to the beach, hoping that neither Jerome nor Dora would run into any issues while guarding the eggs.

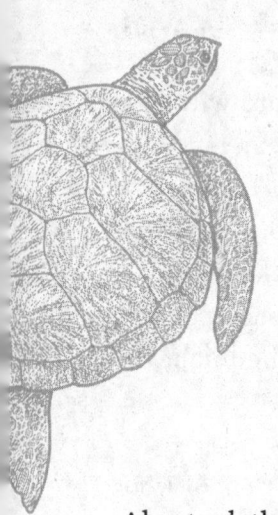

TEN

Alex took the drive back more slowly, at first feeling fumingly mad about the traffickers. She gripped the steering wheel, her stomach knotted up. She'd spent a lot of her years angry like this, or disillusioned. Seeing the challenges wildlife faced could make her feel utterly hopeless. Recently she'd come to the realization that despair and cynicism were detriments to her health, so she'd been trying to focus on positive things.

Her mind turned to the kind volunteers she'd found, to the hawksbills laying new eggs, to the beauty of the island. She tried to remind herself that good things could happen. These turtles could hatch and make it safely out to sea.

She pulled up at Honu Beach and parked her Jeep. As she walked out onto the sand, Dora stood up from a beach chair. "I was worried. Did you find the turtle?"

"I did. And three of the traffickers have been arrested. They're on the lookout for the remaining two."

Dora frowned. "This is just awful."

The image of the crate's contents flashed into Alex's mind, and she took a sharp intake of breath and fought down another white-hot flash of rage.

"I hope they catch the bastards," Dora added, and it made Alex chuckle to hear that kind of language coming out of a retired grade school teacher.

"Me, too." She gazed around at the beach. The only other people out were two surfers just carrying their boards to shore. "Any issues here?"

"None. It was altogether an extremely pleasant afternoon." She folded up her beach chair, and Alex walked with her to her car.

"I appreciate your coming out on such short notice," Alex told her.

"My pleasure!" Dora turned and gazed wistfully back at the waves. "It's so peaceful out here."

"It sure is." Alex watched as Dora climbed into her car and tucked her colorful broom skirt in so it wouldn't catch in the door. "You seeing Nakoa again soon?"

Dora grinned broadly. "Tonight, actually!"

"That's great!"

The teacher looked a little sheepish. "I think so, too. And I'm glad you rescued the turtle," Dora added, then started up the engine.

When she drove away, Alex felt strangely alone, a different feeling from her usual loneliness. She felt lonely in a bigger sense. Lonely that so few people cared about the welfare of the natural world, that they would exploit it and abuse it and not realize that their very survival depended upon it being healthy and intact. She felt lonely that greed held such powerful sway and that her ideals were shared by so few others. Her fight felt monumental and endless, a battle she worried she'd be fighting and losing for the rest of her life.

As the sun set, Alex sat out in her beach chair, watching the clouds shift from white to gold to purple. A quiet wind sighed through the palms above her. The air got a bit chilly, so she donned her fleece jacket. She loved these quiet moments out in nature. All she could hear was the wind and susurration of the waves. A yellow-billed cardinal sang from a nearby tree. She couldn't hear traffic, or yelling, or car horns honking, or any noises of human habitation. She could only smell the sweet and salty breeze. No hint of car exhaust or toxic spew from factories. She reveled in these moments and felt far more at home in them than she did in a bustling city packed shoulder to shoulder with other people.

She worried over the trafficked wildlife and hoped they were still in good health and uninjured, though she knew that was unlikely.

Soon the sun dipped below the horizon and night spilled over the beach. Alex made a dinner of pasta with pesto sauce on her little Sterno stove, then settled into her beach chair to read the mystery novel she'd brought with her. She clicked on her headlamp and got comfortable.

She glanced up as several party boats cruised by, colorful lights strung up on their decks, speeding carelessly over the coral reefs. People on deck lifted beers and shouted to each other over the engine noise. Alex winced. Boat propellers could slice right through turtles, and hulls could crush them. She hated to see people being negligent like this. An eternal war seem to wage between people who came to beautiful places like this to enjoy nature and people who came to use the landscape as a recreational spot to party.

The boats passed into the distance, and Alex returned to her book. But then a splashing noise in the darkness caught her attention, and she watched with amazement as a hawksbill emerged from the waves and waddled up onto the beach. Quickly Alex switched her headlamp to the red light so as not to disturb the turtle.

It trudged up the sand above the tide line and entered the trees. Hawksbills preferred areas with vegetation where the nest would have cover. It started to dig a hole in the sand.

Alex grabbed her small field notebook and pencil and approached quietly. While the turtle fell into the single-minded job of digging a nest, Alex measured the length and width of its carapace. It had no tags or transmitters, so she knew she had to fit it with one.

Then she dug an angled hole through to the turtle's nesting hole, big enough that she could see into it and count the eggs as they dropped into the nest. As the turtle began laying, Alex smiled with each new egg.

Thirty minutes went by, and Alex began to cramp up in her uncomfortable position. So she lay down on the sand, which was still a little warm from the day's sun. She continued to peer into the hole. Another thirty minutes passed by, eggs plopping into the nest. Her headlamp's red light began to dim, and she asked it to please hold on a little longer. Her neck had developed a serious crick. She rubbed it, trying to adjust her position. When an hour and a half had passed, Alex had counted 156 eggs, which was healthy and average, Alex was happy to note. The hawksbill then stopped laying and sat on top of the nest, resting.

After a while, the turtle began moving her flippers, burying the eggs, so Alex quickly covered the hole she'd dug and stepped back.

She wondered when it might be back to lay more eggs. Hawksbills typically waited two to three weeks between each clutch of eggs they laid and could lay as many as four or five on the same beach. Alex wasn't sure which number clutch this was for the turtle, but she hadn't found any more nests on the beach when she'd arrived, so she suspected this was her first. She wondered if this was also the female's first year laying eggs. Usually they nested every one to five years after reaching maturity.

After the nest was buried, the turtle took more minutes to rest, and Alex used the opportunity to affix a transmitter on her shell.

As Alex worked, the turtle moved its flippers against her hands and arms. Given its girth—nearly three feet long and weighing close to two hundred pounds—Alex wasn't surprised at the muscular strength of the creature. It was a struggle to keep her in place.

Then Alex held a small balloon to collect a number of breaths expelled by the turtle, then sealed up the balloon. She'd use a rudimentary setup to calculate the turtle's metabolic rate from the contents.

She collected a few more breaths in a second balloon. This one she'd send to the center's more sophisticated lab. There they'd be able to use a gas analyzer to determine what the turtle had been eating.

She took in the turtle's prefrontal scales, two on each side, that lay between her eyes and her nose. These helped her move more aerodynamically through the water.

When she was finished and the epoxy had dried on the transmitter, Alex got out of the hawksbill's way. Instantly the turtle waddled toward the water, and Alex watched the turtle's head disappear into the darkened waves.

She wondered how far it would go to its feeding grounds after it finished the nesting season and where those feeding grounds might be. It was a total mystery why sea turtles traveled so far between their feeding grounds and their nesting grounds. One theory was that because young hawksbills couldn't dive yet, they were carried at the whim of currents and ended up in whatever foraging ground the sea took them to, which could be quite far away.

One aspect of this turtle journey back and forth that fascinated Alex was how they found their way back to their natal beaches. Current theories included navigating using Earth's magnetic field, the stars, the position of the sun or landmarks, the chemical composition of different waters, or even their sense of smell. If it was the latter, Alex was seriously impressed. She couldn't imagine traveling up to a thousand miles merely by scent.

But then again, she was often astounded by the talents of such creatures. When she watched a dog sticking its nose out of a car window, she imagined all the information it was picking up: who had passed by earlier; what they were feeling at the time, be it fear or happiness or stress; what other dogs had been in the area; whether rabbits or squirrels were present. Too many times while out in nature, Alex had wished for those very same skills. She could only imagine how much easier it would be to track wildlife with that kind of sense of smell—no longer would she have to use clunky methods such as radio collars and telemetry, carrying around some bulky antenna and listening through headphones. She could merely sniff the air.

Gathering up her gear and the balloons, she walked to her Jeep and opened up the back end. Inside lay a rudimentary lab with O_2 and CO_2 meters. She used it to test the contents of the first balloon. After determining the O_2 to CO_2 ratio, she double-checked the Keeling Curve. This was a measurement of how much CO_2 was currently in the atmosphere. Scientist Charles Keeling had taken the first measurement at the Mauna Loa Observatory in 1958, when it was 315 parts per million. Using ice core records, climate scientists had been able to determine the ppm going back to 1700, before the Industrial Revolution. Back then it had been 275 ppm.

She frowned, seeing how high it was now, 428.4 ppm. A feeling of despair crept over her. CO_2 had been increasing ever more rapidly in the atmosphere, and humans needed to reduce it down to 350 ppm if we were going to stave off the worst of the anthropogenic climate change effects, many of which we were already seeing, such as sea level rise, disastrous hurricanes and forest fires, flooding, and more.

She bit her lip, returning to the task at hand. Taking into account the current level of CO_2 in the atmosphere, she calculated the turtle's metabolic rate as being healthy. At least that was some good news.

Sudden movement down the beach swung her gaze in that direction. A black dog streaked across the sand, heading right for the nest. For a second Alex thought it would dash right by it, but it picked up on the scent at the last minute and spun around, nose to the sand, snuffling right up to the hidden eggs.

"Hey!" Alex called, hurrying over. It was a black Lab with a huge grin, and Alex knelt down beside it, ruffling its fur. "I don't think so, mister," she told it. She led it away from the nest and gazed up and down the beach for its human. An older woman was walking a few hundred yards down beach, a dog leash dangling from one hand. Alex continued to ruffle the dog's ears and play with it until the woman was within earshot.

"Is this your dog?" Alex called.

"Yes," the woman said. "I'm sorry—is he bothering you?"

"Not me, but there are endangered turtle eggs on this stretch of the beach. Could you keep him on his leash if you're in the area?"

The woman rushed forward. "I'm so sorry. I had no idea." She clipped the leash on, and the dog jumped around playfully at her legs.

"No problem," Alex said, standing up.

She watched as the pair walked away and wondered if she should have some signs made up in addition to the yellow caution tape, maybe place the signs beside the nests. The problem was that the same signs that would keep well-meaning people and their dogs away would also be a blaring sign for poachers, letting them know exactly where to dig.

Alex folded up her beach chair and carried it over to her tent, then unzipped the door and crawled inside, her arms and back aching as she longed for sleep. She was just about to climb into her pajamas and lie down when the proximity alarm on her phone buzzed.

ELEVEN

Alex checked her security cameras but didn't see what was setting off the motion sensors. She unzipped the tent and stepped out barefoot onto the beach. She donned her headlamp, switching on the red light.

It didn't take long to spot the source of movement: another hawksbill waddling up the beach into a different section of trees. Alex grabbed her gear and field notebook and walked quietly over to it.

She was happy to see another hawksbill, and in such a short period of time. The Hawaiian hawksbill population was considerably smaller than other hawksbill populations around the globe. And while loggerheads could gather by the tens of thousands—more than a hundred thousand nested on Florida beaches each year—hawksbills nested in very small numbers, with only a few coming to shore to lay eggs at a particular destination. So she was lucky to see this second one so soon after the last.

After the nest was completely dug, the turtle prepared to lay eggs. Alex lay down in the sand and again dug an adjacent hole so she could count the eggs. She waited.

Minutes went by, but no eggs dropped into the nest. Then *too many* minutes went by. Alex frowned, watching through the hole. The turtle strained and strained. She shifted around, flippers working in the sand. Still, no eggs emerged. She continued to struggle, and Alex realized something was wrong. Tentatively she stood up, not wanting to scare the turtle back into the waves.

She gently dug a slightly bigger hole behind the turtle so she could see what was going on, then lay down behind it. She could see the turtle's cloaca now, the multiuse body part that served as a way to breathe, lay eggs, urinate, and defecate.

The rib cages of turtles were rigid and affixed to their shells. They didn't expand as turtles breathed like the rib cages of mammals. So turtles supplemented their oxygen intake while in the water by drawing water into their cloaca. Tissues there then extracted the needed oxygen from the water. In a nutshell, they breathed through their butts.

The turtle kept straining over the hole. Alex's red beam revealed something wet and white sticking out from the turtle's cloaca, but it wasn't an egg. It was wrinkled and rustling and had some kind of red lettering on it. Alex peered closer. It was a plastic bag.

Alex realized the turtle must have ingested the bag at some point. This happened all too often. Plastic bags drifting in the ocean often looked like jellyfish, and turtles would swallow them, thinking they were food. And then the bag clogged their insides, resulting in malnutrition and even death.

This bag had clearly started to pass through the turtle's system but was lodged in the cloaca, blocking the eggs from coming out.

Alex dug a slightly deeper trench, wide enough for her arm, and reached under the turtle. She grasped the slimy bag and gave a gentle pull. At first it didn't budge, and she had a hard time maintaining a grip on the slippery object. But then she gathered a bit more of it, pinching it between her fingers, and gave another light tug. The bag started to come out. Alex shifted her position to get a better hold and continued to pull. Soon she managed to free several inches, then a full foot.

An unbelievably vile stench blossomed up from the plastic and Alex gagged, shutting her eyes against the assault. Then she opened her eyes and resumed pulling, reading "Thank You for Shopping with Us!" on the bag as it slithered out.

The bag now free, Alex pulled it out from under the turtle as a stream of eggs plunked out into the soft sand. The hole started to fill up, and Alex crawled away, filling in the trench she'd made.

She resumed her position at the egg-watching hole, counting 142 eggs in total. The turtle rested, and Alex continued to lie there, waiting for more eggs to drop. So she was shocked when the turtle suddenly flew into action, flinging a plume of sand right back into her face. Alex wiped the grains away, startled, and stifled a chuckle as the turtle moved forward and started covering the eggs with sand, throwing up huge sprays with its hind flippers. Alex filled up her own two holes and backed out of the way, shielding her face now with her arm.

When the turtle had covered the nest, she scuffed up the surface with her fins until it was completely disguised. Her task done, the turtle rested, and Alex repeated the process of affixing a transmitter, gathering turtle breath, measuring its carapace, and estimating its weight.

Having recovered from egg laying, the hawksbill then waddled off toward the sea. Alex stood up, brushed herself off, and watched the turtle vanish into the darkened waves. She was glad both turtles had made their nests above the high tide line, as eggs could drown.

She looked forward to gaining more information from the transmitter. As more and more data came in, she'd be able to learn specific routes the turtles took to their feeding grounds and how long it took them to get there. And by learning this, she could see if there were spots along the way that could be improved for their survival, such as seasonal fishing closures or boat patrols by the center to remove illegal gillnets.

Alex wondered where this hawksbill would go when it was done nesting and hoped it would survive long enough to come back.

ALEX AWOKE THE NEXT DAY, showered and dressed, and sat out on the beach eating a quick breakfast of fruit, tea, and an energy bar.

The wind had picked up, and she saw gray clouds on the eastern horizon. The storm was getting closer.

She noticed a man sitting down beach from her, playing music on his radio. He pulled it closer to himself and switched to a news station. Alex listened in case it was about the storm. There was a brief update, giving the same information she'd gotten from NOAA's website, that residents should be prepared in case an evacuation order came down. Estimates of when it could make landfall still put it a few days off, and there was some thought that it might die down in intensity before then. But with climate change, storms were getting harder and harder to predict.

Then the reporter switched to a new topic: "This just in. A crew member from the missing cargo ship *Sunfish* has just been picked up by a passing freighter off the coast of Baja. He told a harrowing tale of high seas piracy, in which an armed crew forcibly boarded and took over the ship, killing all hands except him. He managed to make it to the bridge to radio for help, only to find that the communications panel with VHF, medium frequency, and satellite communications had been completely destroyed. In a daring attempt to save his fellow crew members, he overpowered one of the pirates and managed to lower a lifeboat. But after gunmen opened fire on the crew, he alone survived. He donned a life jacket and swam away, where he was picked up two days later by the freighter *Królik*. The current location of the cargo ship *Sunfish* is unknown, and its automatic identification system has been deactivated."

Frowning, the man switched the channel again, moving to a rock station.

A few early-morning surfers were out, clearly enjoying the bigger waves the wind brought in to shore. On previous days, when the sea had been calmer, they'd mostly just hung out together, talking amiably and enjoying the gentle rocking of the sea. But now they rode waves in every few minutes, whooping with excitement and then paddling out to do it again.

Alex needed to go into town to restock her food supply and wanted to take advantage of the trip to also visit the museum. But she needed a volunteer to come watch over the nests, so she started to make calls, her first one to Keola. He was more than happy to come out with his daughter.

Before they arrived, Alex checked the thermocouples and saw that the temperature in the first nest had started to fluctuate. As soon as it began to drop, she knew the hatchlings would emerge, probably the next day. She grinned, excited, but also felt nervous about the approaching storm. It would make the seas rough and difficult to navigate even for ships, let alone baby turtles. But before the storm landed, these turtles would be off and into the surf. She'd have to call all her volunteers out to the beach so they could witness the magic of the little hatchlings scrambling for the waves. And she'd need their help, too, to keep them safe on their short journey across the beach.

Keola and Lupesina arrived, and Alex told them the good news—that soon, possibly tomorrow night, the little hatchlings would come out of the nest. Lupesina's face glowed at the news. She plopped down to diligently guard the nests.

"I don't even think you need me here," Keola said, shaking his head and smiling. "You've got the perfect guardian right there."

She thanked them both and got into her rental Jeep, pulling out of the grassy parking area and driving the seven miles to Ānuenue. In the center of town stood a small but lively park where musicians gathered and played to the delight of tourists and locals alike. As Alex drove past the park, she saw three musicians just setting up, a few people in lawn chairs waiting for them to begin. She also spotted a couple of businesses boarding up their windows, but most places remained open. Clearly people were hoping the storm would miss the island or weaken considerably.

Alex arrived at the grocery store and found that to be the case there, too. Part of her expected the store to be cleaned out, but most items were still in stock. She gathered up pasta, rice, beans, camp stove fuel, nuts, fruits, tea, and a few spices. She didn't have a way to refrigerate food, so everything had to be nonperishable.

At the checkout stand, a teenager with purple hair and a nose ring rang her up.

"Have people been stocking up with evacuation supplies?" Alex asked her.

"A few people came in and hoarded stuff, but only a couple. I think we're all hoping it'll pass us by."

"Me, too," Alex told her. She paid and carried the groceries out to her Jeep and stowed them inside.

That task finished, she looked forward to seeing Nakoa at his work.

Alex followed her Jeep's GPS directions to the Museum of Vertebrate Paleontology. The building was larger than she'd expected, and the parking lot was nearly full. The silvery metal building gleamed in the sun, a multistory affair with large glass windows that reflected the emerald-green mountainous landscape around them. Images of the storm clouds in the east were cast back in the windows high above.

She and Nakoa had exchanged a few texts about her upcoming visit, so as he had directed, Alex parked her Jeep and walked around the side of the museum to the employee entrance. Nakoa waited for her there, standing out in the sun with his face uplifted, his eyes closed. He took a few deep breaths as she approached, then noticed her there and looked a little embarrassed. "I just love the air here, don't you?" he asked sheepishly. "I think I missed that part most of all when I was at Harvard. That and all the colorful flowers." He pointed to a brilliantly gold patch of hibiscus growing along the edge of a nearby cluster of koa trees.

Alex took several deep breaths herself. The tropical air felt so different from the drier air of the mountain, desert, and Arctic areas where she'd worked recently. "I agree. And it's so cool to hear such different birdsong from what I'm used to, too." As if on cue, a bird called out from the trees, a buzzy, determined note.

"Ah!" Nakoa exclaimed. "An 'amakihi!" They both glanced around until they spotted the little yellow honeycreeper. Then he turned toward the door. "Shall we?"

"Of course!"

He punched a series of numbers into a keypad beside the door, then scanned his palm on a biometric reader. Alex heard a lock disengage inside the thick metal door. He pulled it open and held it there for her to enter. Cold immediately greeted her, and she wondered if she should have brought her fleece jacket.

"Feel that chill?" he asked.

She nodded.

He gestured for her to follow. "Come look at this!"

They walked down a short corridor and came to a large window mounted in the wall.

And inside Alex saw something that made her jaw drop. A gigantic mammoth mummy lay in the center of the room, its curved tusks resting on the floor, which was covered with a protective tarp.

Alex couldn't believe the condition of it. Other than a large gash in its side, the rest of it was nearly pristine. The face was perfectly preserved, the eyes closed, the mouth slightly open and a few teeth visible. It looked like it was just sleeping there. Its huge curved back rose far above the head, and its legs were tucked up under the bulk of its body, all covered in thick, woolly brown fur.

"Isn't she amazing?" Nakoa asked. "We got her from a dig in Alaska."

"She looks alive," Alex gasped.

"She's thirty-two thousand years old."

Alex turned to him, amazed, her eyes wide.

"She was extracted from a gold field, which is where she got that damage to her midsection, from their digging equipment. The miners didn't notice her until she had tumbled out of the permafrost. Right now we're running a series of tests on her, but eventually she'll be displayed outside in the gallery."

"How does she look so . . . lifelike still?"

"She's basically been freeze-dried by the permafrost. And we're keeping her in this cold environment while we run tests."

Inside she saw a lab tech milling about with a clipboard. She was fully suited up as if for surgery, with an apron, gloves, and mask.

"That's my lab assistant, Nia."

Alex could feel the chill radiating out through the window.

"Then we'll freeze-dry the mammoth even more. Eventually we'll be able to put her out in the open. Won't need a glass enclosure or anything."

"That's amazing!" Alex stared at the magnificent woolly mammoth. "What kinds of tests are you running?"

"We're testing her mitochondrial DNA to see if she's distantly related to other mammoths that have been excavated. That way we can determine where her family group migrated from."

Alex pictured a herd of mammoths with little frolicking babies, meandering across Beringia, the land bridge that existed between Russia and Alaska and was at its widest twenty-one thousand years ago, when sea levels were much lower because of water being locked up in massive continental glaciers.

"We'll also run isotopic analysis on her fur."

Alex had done isotopic analysis herself, most recently when she was working with polar bears in the Canadian Arctic. The isotopes of elements such as oxygen, nitrogen, and carbon could reveal what the animal had been eating.

"And it was radiocarbon dating we used to determine that she died about thirty-two thousand years ago."

Alex still couldn't get over the age of this mammoth. It looked like it had died a week ago.

A few years ago, on a trip to the Yukon, she'd visited the Yukon Beringia Interpretive Centre in Whitehorse and seen Zhùr, a stunningly well-preserved wolf pup that was fifty-seven thousand years old. And she'd seen Blue Babe, who was on display in Alaska, a magnificent steppe bison that had died thirty-six thousand years ago. Its skin had turned a brilliant blue from a reaction with the mineral vivianite in the silt where the body lay.

Nakoa took in Alex's fascinated gaze. "You want to see the museum proper?"

She nodded but struggled to tear her eyes away from the mammoth. "Yes, but it's hard to leave this right here!"

He chuckled, then looked back at the mammoth affectionately. "I know what you mean." He gestured for her to follow and led her farther down the employee hallway. They passed the door to the lab they'd just been gazing in, fitted with not only another keypad but a biometric palm reader and a retinal scanner.

"Impressive security," Alex commented.

"We've got a lot of expensive equipment in there. Kalino Noelani spent millions of dollars building this facility and wanted every security protocol observed."

She'd heard of Noelani, an elusive billionaire. He'd grown up on the Big Island but moved to the West Coast of the United States to attend college. Eventually, he'd amassed a considerable fortune with a tech start-up in San Francisco. But he missed his home. He had a lifelong interest in paleontology and a massive collection of fossils himself. Eventually he paid to have this state-of-the-art museum built in his hometown and donated all his fossils to the collection.

"What's Noelani like?" Alex asked.

"Quite nice, quite nice," Nakoa told her. "Very down-to-earth and generous with his time and money. Gives to an inordinate number of charities."

Alex smiled, happy to hear that.

Then Nakoa came to another door with a keypad and biometric palm reader and unlocked it. He held the door open, and Alex was admitted into a huge, open hall of magnificent fossils. The space echoed with the chatter of visitors and some children squealing with excitement. She could hear the narration from an educational film playing somewhere nearby.

She stepped fully into the gallery and stared up at a massive, mounted *Apatosaurus* skeleton, its neck and tail gracefully curving and soaring above the visiting patrons. Next to it stood a menacing *Tyrannosaurus rex* skeleton, and beyond that she saw many more mounted skeletons: an *Ankylosaurus*, a *Stegosaurus*, a *Mosasaurus*, a *Triceratops*. The bones of an *Indricotherium*, which was an ancient relative of the rhinoceros, towered eighteen feet high at the shoulder.

They started to walk around the room, Nakoa telling her details of each creature. They examined displays with smaller fossils along the walls: a winged *Archaeopteryx*, the gaping jaws of a megalodon, countless smaller dinosaurs and fishes, some examples of where dinosaur skin, scales, and feathers had made impressions in rock. A collection of amber held small insects.

From one wall hung two incredibly large arm bones ending in vicious claws. They were eight feet long, just the arms alone. Alex stared up in fascination.

"Aren't they amazing? And you want to hear something creepy?" he asked.

Alex nodded.

"We don't know what creature they belonged to."

Alex could only imagine what kind of lanky nightmare sported those terrifying-looking arms.

Then they passed a skull in a display case, and Alex felt a primal shiver go down her back. It was at least three feet long, bristling with teeth, and clearly carnivorous and mammalian. "What is *that*?" she asked breathlessly.

He followed her gaze. "That's the skull of an *Andrewsarchus*. Only a few have ever been found, and even then only their skulls. It's the largest mammalian predator to have ever roamed the earth. It was actually a relative of the whale and lived on land around forty million years ago."

Alex breathed out, taking it in. How big would the body have been if the skull alone was three feet long? She imagined it hunting ancient forests, this gigantic, carnivorous land whale. "Wow," she managed to say.

He toured her through the rest of the museum, and they ended up in a large research library with a stunning stained-glass dome overhead. Multiple stories of books soared up to the ceiling, with ladders that slid along the shelves to reach books higher up.

It was the kind of library Alex had dreamed about since she was a kid. "Wow," she murmured again, finding herself speechless once more.

"Pretty beautiful, isn't it?" Nakoa said with admiration. "And it's open to the public. Anyone can come in here and do research—students, librarians, or anyone at all who's curious about the ancient earth."

"This is amazing!" She walked around the shelves, perusing titles on continental drift, paleoclimatology, fossil preservation, paleoecology, asteroid strikes, volcanic eruptions, paleobotany. Some titles were aimed toward beginners, while others were extremely technical. It was a rich resource.

Nakoa gestured toward a bank of computers in the center of the room. "Users can also tap into numerous databases around the world. All the latest research going on worldwide."

A group of polished antique wooden desks stood against another wall, each one fitted with a green glass study lamp, creating a welcoming environment for research.

"Shall we grab a cup of tea?" he asked. "Perhaps a bite to eat? The commissary is just down the hall."

Alex nodded. "I'd love to."

They walked out of the library, passed again through the gallery, then a small gift shop, and entered a large cafeteria. It was tastefully decorated and offered a variety of vegetarian options, each with clever paleontology-themed names, like Taro-saur salad, and desserts like Tricerapops cake pops and Archaeoptermint ice cream. Alex ordered the salad, which featured slices of cut and peeled taro that had been simmered in coconut milk and sugar. Nakoa opted for a sweet potato burger, and they ate in one corner of the room, sipping hot tea.

She liked Nakoa. He was kind and knowledgeable, and she felt blessed that he was going to volunteer on her project. He'd be a competent, valuable asset.

"I still can't believe you got a mammoth mummy in such great condition!" she told him.

He took a bite of his burger and finished chewing it. "The story of how this mammoth got to us is kind of crazy. Maybe you heard about it on the news? Some gold miners found it in Alaska. One of my dearest friends from grad school was alerted and traveled out there. He managed to get it safely crated up and shipped out to us here. But then he returned to the site and actually found an additional mummy buried in the permafrost there. This mammoth's baby."

"Wow! What an incredible find! Are you going to get the baby, too?"

Nakoa shook his head, his mouth twisting at the corner. He went silent, then started fiddling with his napkin. "No," he said at last. Then he looked up. "A finance guy from the gold company failed to reach the miners after several days, so they sent someone out there. My friend and his colleagues had been killed, along with all of the gold miners at the site." He paused. "Apparently it was a brutal scene. Whoever did it shot them and burned the bodies."

Alex's mouth came open. "What?"

"I know. It was very extreme. The baby mammoth had been stolen. I guess word got out about the find, and someone really wanted it."

"That's awful!"

"I know." He shook his head. "Caleb was a good friend. We had each other's backs in grad school. He was one of those people you know you're lucky to meet, someone who's going to be a lifelong friend. Someone who feels like they're part of your tribe, you know?" He twisted the napkin more. "I miss him." After a self-conscious moment he added, "I'm so sorry. I don't know why I told you all that."

She reached across the table and touched his arm. "Please don't be sorry. There's no need."

Alex believed that someone should never say sorry for expressing sorrow or loss. Too often people were expected to bury those emotions for the comfort of others, while the grieving person had little understanding or support. Of course, she understood feeling uncomfortable. She herself had felt that way on the beach when Dora found her crying about her mother.

"I'm so sorry you lost your friend," Alex told him.

"Thanks," he said, and looked up at her sheepishly.

When they'd finished eating, he walked her out the main doors of the museum and then to her car. "I hope you enjoyed the tour," he said as she climbed into her Jeep.

"I loved it. Thank you so much!"

"And do call when you need assistance with the hawksbill eggs."

"You know I will."

She closed the door and pulled out of the parking lot, giving a wave to him as she did so. It had been a fascinating afternoon, and it was good to connect with another researcher. Even though their fields of expertise were different, they both specialized in biology. It had also felt good to have some social contact.

As she drove away, she thought about the man's loss of his friend and the insanity of what had happened at the mammoth dig site. Sure, she knew such paleontological finds were valuable, but to kill everyone at the site and burn the bodies? She couldn't even comprehend that. Had it been some crazy collector? All just to get the mummy of a baby mammoth?

Her mind then shifted to Nakoa's awkwardness on bringing

up the murder of his friend. It was hard when you couldn't really openly talk about how much someone's loss had affected you. Alex remembered that after her mother died, when Alex was only twelve, the people around her didn't want to hear about it. Teachers, her friends, other adults, grew uncomfortable and changed the subject if her mother came up. Some even asked her why she wasn't "over it" yet. Alex thought as she got older that her friends would mature and she'd be able to talk about her mom and how difficult that loss was for her and her father. But that didn't prove to be the case. No matter how old she got, even now, in her early thirties, people withdrew awkwardly if Alex brought up the subject.

It made her conversation with Dora on the beach that much more appreciated and unexpected.

Usually these days she resisted the urge to talk about her mom at all, but sometimes she had moments, like on her mother's birthday or on holidays, when it was particularly tough, and she wanted to share how much she missed her. But it seemed that no one wanted to hear it. People looked around uncomfortably, shifted in their seats, changed the subject. But her mother had been such an amazing person—dynamic, lively, and an incredible combat pilot for the Air Force. She'd not only taught Alex those survival and mechanical skills, but she had been playful and goofy and fun-loving. To act as if she'd never existed for the benefit of other people's comfort was something Alex could never get used to.

Alex sighed, gazing out at the swaying trees. The storm clouds out to the east had grown darker, gray and brooding.

She returned to the beach and relieved Keola and Lupesina, thanking them for watching over the eggs. When they'd gone, she sat for a while by the nests.

She wondered how many hatchlings would be male and how many female. One fact about turtles that Alex had always found fascinating was that temperature determined gender in hatchlings. Warmer nest temperatures meant more females. Cooler ones resulted in more males. But because of global warming, more and more nests were resulting in predominantly females, which presented a real problem for sea turtles to recover their numbers if fewer males were born. For hawksbills in particular, Alex knew that any nest measuring a temperature above eighty-five degrees would result in predominately or all female hatchlings. During a warm El Niño cycle, the percentage of females was even higher, but during a cool La Niña, hatchlings could skew more male.

Alex also knew that temperature fluctuations due to these cycles of El Niño and La Niña affected turtle reproduction in general, not just the gender of the hatchlings. During an El Niño year, the surface waters of the Pacific warmed up. This prevented cold bottom water from cycling upward, which would normally bring nutrients to the surface and encourage algal growth. This growth served as the base for the food chain. But without this growth, there was less food, which meant turtles didn't get as much nutrition and therefore couldn't produce eggs. And the warmer waters during an El Niño reduced migration, too.

She looked forward to seeing how this particular nest would turn out.

After sunset, Alex made a quick dinner of corkscrew pasta in marinara sauce. Then she cleaned up and climbed into her tent. She didn't realize she'd dozed off until a vibration on her chest stirred her from a strange dream. She'd shown up at her high school reunion, only it was in a bowling alley and she realized she wasn't wearing any pants. She spotted Casey across the room and was trying to reach him, but a classmate kept intercepting her, telling her that Alex had missed the calculus final and that she had to organize a tray of asparagus to make up for it.

She opened her eyes, suddenly alert. Her phone's alarm buzzed again, telling her something was outside. At first she thought it might be another turtle, but then she heard voices whispering outside her tent.

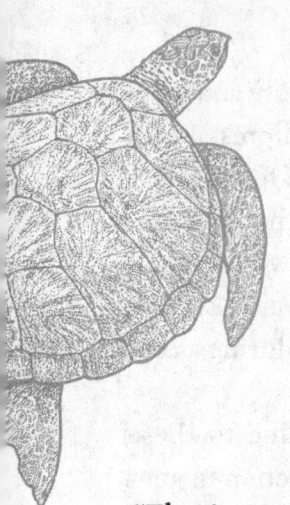

TWELVE

"They've got to be around here somewhere," Alex heard a male voice say, low and almost at a whisper.

She hurriedly climbed out of her sleeping bag, grabbed her flashlight, and unzipped the tent door.

"What was that?" said a lower, raspier voice, different from the first one.

Alex slid on her boots and stood up, switching on the flashlight. The beam pinpointed two men standing near the newest of the turtle nests. One had a shovel and was digging a hole in the sand, dangerously near where the eggs were hidden.

They were the same two men who had placed the gillnet and later been at the airfield.

"Found 'em!" the man with the shovel declared. He was the burly one who had driven the boat.

"Hey!" Alex shouted. "What are you doing?"

Both whirled to face her.

"You cut into our profits," the portly one snapped. "You know how much we got off that net before you had it taken down? Almost nothing. But we'll fetch a nice profit with these eggs."

The skinny man who had tried to stab her with the barbed pole out at sea turned toward Alex. "Just go back to whatever you were doing," he warned her, taking a step forward. Then to his compatriot he urged, "Dig 'em up. I'll hold her off."

Alex dialed 911 on her phone. "I've called the police," she told them. "And they already know about you from earlier." She put the phone on speaker, and when the operator came on, Alex began to explain hurriedly: "I'm the biologist stationed at Honu Beach, and two men are attempting to steal the endangered turtle eggs here." As she talked, the skinny man advanced on her.

She set her phone down, leaving the connection open, and braced herself to face him, grateful she could call on her Jeet Kune Do training. But she loathed fighting—abhorred the sick feeling she got in the pit of her stomach, the way her mouth suddenly went dry, the fluttering of her heart in her chest. But she had no choice. Even if she turned and ran, this guy could chase her down before she reached her car. And besides, she wasn't about to leave the turtle eggs at the mercy of these poachers.

The man looked a little nonplussed when Alex moved into a fighting stance. But after only a second's hesitation, he closed in, fist swinging toward her in a large haymaker. She easily ducked under it, then grabbed his arm, using his own momentum to shove him forward. He stumbled and pitched down onto his hands and knees. She came down hard on his back, a knee in his spine, thrusting him down face-first into the sand. Grabbing one of his wrists, she pulled his arm back, then slammed her other hand down on his elbow to hyperextend the joint. He cried out in surprise and pain and managed to buck her off.

She fell backward onto the sand and sprang to her feet, then moved some distance away, facing off with him again. He staggered to his feet, rubbing his elbow. He didn't look that eager to reengage with her.

"You got them yet?" he called to the other man.

"Not yet."

Alex glanced over. The bulky man was still digging, but she saw that he'd cast aside the shovel and was on his hands and knees, scooping turtle eggs out of the sand and putting them in a large duffel bag.

"I'm gettin' 'em," he called out.

Alex couldn't let this happen. She didn't know if the cops were on their way or not. If she spent too much time fighting this man, the other could just take off with the eggs.

The gawky man came forward again, approaching her more cautiously this time. He threw another punch, which she dodged, then brought a fist up into his solar plexus. He grunted, momentarily stunned, and she brought a rain of fists pummeling into his chest, a move in Jeet Kune Do called a "straight blast." He staggered backward, and she delivered a powerful blow to the soft underside of his chin. His head snapped back, and he fell into the sand. He tried to get up, so she raced forward, stomping down hard on his chest. She grabbed his wrist, extending his arm upward, then slammed the palm of her hand into his damaged elbow, breaking it. He screamed in pain.

She pivoted and left him there, running toward the hefty man on the beach. He spun, taking in his fallen comrade, and stood up. The duffel bag full of eggs lay on the sand.

He faced her, his face furrowed with anger.

"Just go and leave the eggs," she told him.

"Damned if I will!" he shouted back at her, then to his friend, "Get up!"

But the other man just lay there, cradling his broken arm.

The man picked up his shovel, wielding it like a club, and Alex kept her distance. He swung at her once, twice, and she dodged. But after the third swipe, she stepped into his space and used his own momentum from the swing of the shovel to propel him off balance. He fell forward, landing hard in the sand. She stepped down on the shovel's handle and delivered a vicious kick to the man's face. His nose erupted in blood.

"Alex!" cried a voice.

Alex whirled, trying to find the source. Jerome stood about twenty feet away, eyes wide, panting.

"What's going on?"

Just then blue and red lights streaked through the trees. A police cruiser pulled in behind Alex's car in the small grassy parking area. She heard the car door open, and then a powerful flashlight beam clicked on.

"Go get help!" Alex called to Jerome. In her distraction, the stocky poacher with the broken nose got up and landed a solid punch to her jaw. She staggered back, momentarily stunned by the powerful blow.

Jerome sprinted to the parking area, holding his arms up to get the attention of the officer.

"What's going on?" boomed a familiar voice. It was the same cop who'd harassed Jerome earlier, and Alex's heart sank. She squared off against the poacher with the broken nose, dodging another blow aimed at her head.

"Those guys are attacking Dr. Carter!" she heard Jerome yell.

"Stay here," commanded the cop, and Alex saw him approaching cautiously. "Everybody freeze!" he yelled.

The rail-thin poacher with the broken arm continued to just lie on the sand, but the other poacher took no notice of the officer. He lunged toward Alex, trying to grab her. She parried, slapping his hand away, keeping her feet moving.

"I said freeze!" the cop yelled again, his hand going down to a taser stowed on his belt.

Alex darted a brief glance at Jerome, who stood back by the cruiser, looking scared and uncertain.

Just as the cop began to pull out the taser, the poacher lunged down toward the satchel and pulled out a handgun from one of the pockets.

He whirled, aiming it at the cop, and Alex saw a look of fear bloom on the officer's face. He was too far away to hit the man with his taser and didn't have time now to go for his sidearm. Everything slowed. The officer started to move out of the way, his hand going down to the butt of his gun. Alex pivoted, wondering if she could reach the poacher in time to strike his gun hand, and knowing at the same time there was no way. He was about to fire, and the cop was a wide-open target.

Then something streaked through the air and struck the poacher's hand, sending the gun sprawling into the sand. A large rock landed in the sand beside him, and immediately he cradled his injured hand.

She spotted Jerome still up by the cruiser, arm poised to launch another rock in the attacker's direction.

Alex kicked the gun into the surf where neither poacher could reach it.

Then both men took off, running into the trees. The cop gave chase, sliding in the deep sand, struggling to keep up. The men vanished into the darkness, the officer close behind.

Jerome ran up to her on the beach. "That was close!"

"Damn! You *do* have a great pitching arm!" she said, clasping him on the shoulder.

He broke into a laugh. "I didn't know what else to do."

"That was amazing!"

She got a stick and retrieved the gun from the surf, hooking the wood through the revolver's trigger guard. She laid the weapon down above the water line.

Jerome stared into the trees where the officer had disappeared. "Do you think he'll catch them?"

"I don't know."

They waited there in the darkness of the beach, Alex trying to catch her breath, Jerome shifting nervously from foot to foot.

Then they heard someone crashing back through the underbrush and braced themselves. The cop emerged from the trees. "Lost 'em. But don't worry, I recognized them."

"I've dealt with them before," Alex told him. "And the Department of Justice is after them, too."

"We'll get them."

"Thanks for showing up when you did," Alex told him.

He hesitated, staring at Jerome, looking awkward. "Quite an arm you got there, son."

"He's the star pitcher of his team back home," Alex told him.

"I can see that." He set his jaw stubbornly, still looking at Jerome, and then finally muttered, "Thanks, kid."

Jerome nodded in return. "No problem."

"Either of you need medical attention?"

Alex rubbed her jaw where she'd been punched. It was sore but not too bad. "Not me."

Jerome held up his hands. "I'm good."

"Pulled that out of the surf for you," Alex said, pointing out where the gun lay in the sand.

The officer retrieved an evidence bag from the trunk of his cruiser and collected the gun. "Thanks." He was about to grab the satchel, too, and Alex stopped him.

"I need to put those eggs back in the nest," she told him.

He crossed his arms, looking gruff. But finally he shrugged. "Okay. But glove up." He went to his cruiser and returned with two pairs of latex gloves.

Together, Alex and Jerome lifted them out one by one and replaced them in the nest. The man had only managed to scoop out about fifty of the more than a hundred eggs in the nest. When they finished, Alex gently replaced the sand, using a small fallen branch with some leaves on it to scrape over the top of the nest, hiding it just as the mother turtle would do with her hind flippers.

The cop took down brief statements from both of them. "I'll let you know when there are further questions."

Alex was still shaking with adrenaline. "Okay."

He drove away then, leaving Alex and Jerome still standing on the beach in the quiet aftermath.

"Think those guys will come back?" he asked.

"Not tonight. And hopefully they'll be arrested soon."

"You going to be okay?"

Alex nodded.

"Well, I better get going, then. My aunt's going to wonder why I'm not home yet."

"Thanks for showing up when you did."

"No problem." He turned and walked down the beach, but then looked back over his shoulder. "You'll still call me when those eggs hatch, right?"

"Of course I will. In fact, I think they're going to hatch tomorrow night. I'll text you the details of when we're all going to meet up."

"Great!" He walked off, and the quiet returned to her little haven.

Alex stood on the beach for a long time. The adrenaline slowly faded, leaving her shaky and a bit queasy. She'd studied Jeet Kune Do for this very reason, to defend herself and others, but fights always left her feeling tarnished and grubby, like she'd somehow polluted her soul.

Deciding to take a quick shower, she grabbed her towel from her tent and rinsed off in the public shower house. Returning to her tent, she changed into clean PJs and lay down in the darkness, listening to the rushing in and out of the surf. It sounded more intense than normal—a sign of the approaching storm. She breathed with it. In. Out. In. Out. She let her body still. She closed her tired eyes, and soon sleep took her again.

THE NEXT DAY ALEX AWOKE to another crowing fest of feral chickens. She changed into fresh clothes and climbed out of the tent. After checking on the nests, she sat down in her beach chair and gazed out over the sea, feeling part hopeful and part worried. She wondered if the poachers had been caught yet.

The turtles faced so many threats. She glanced over at the halted hotel construction site and wondered how long this beach would remain relatively undeveloped. If the hotel got built, this could present a number of problems for any turtles returning to nest.

Too many beaches around the world simply couldn't support a turtle population anymore. Some of this was because of development, some of it because of global warming.

Before anthropogenic climate change, Earth cooled and warmed very gradually, which allowed wildlife time to evolve accordingly. Back then, as ocean levels rose slowly, new beaches formed, just as they did as ocean levels gradually dropped.

But now human-caused warming was happening dangerously rapidly, not allowing wildlife the time it needed to adjust. And as sea levels rose now, new beaches did not open up in developed areas, where seawalls and other human barricades prevented them from forming.

Understandably, people loved the ocean and beaches, where many wanted to live and visit. Unfortunately, development along beaches had become a serious impediment to sea turtle survival, as it often led to the problem of beach recognition. Years passed between the time a hatchling broke out of her shell and waddled into the sea and when she returned later to lay her own eggs on that same beach. By the time she returned, the beach could be unrecognizable.

Even if the beach was still there, and rising sea levels hadn't drowned it, human structures could make it inaccessible. Seawalls presented a staggering barrier, as did structures such as rock revetments and large tubes that some communities placed along the beach to prevent erosion. These all kept turtles from reaching areas above the high tide line where it was safe to lay eggs.

It made her particularly sad that in Florida, where she'd spotted her first hawksbill, hardly any nested now. Though they'd always nested on beaches on the Big Island, a few years ago, they'd started to show up on Hawaiian beaches they'd never been known to nest on before.

In some places, though, like on Jekyll Island off the coast of Georgia, great strides were being made to mitigate these factors. For years, lights and barriers had affected the island's loggerhead nesting population, so the island's inhabitants started prohibiting lights from shining out onto the beach during nesting times and started keeping areas open on the beach for turtles to come ashore.

Alex hoped that more places would start taking these steps to help nesting turtles and that maybe some sea turtle populations could start to recover from the devastating population losses they'd suffered in recent years.

She smiled, thinking of that first time she'd seen a hawksbill. She'd been snorkeling as a kid in a mangrove bay in Florida. She'd been out with her dad, drifting along in the warm water, taking in the short, vividly green trees with their exposed tan roots snaking down into the water. Her mom was on a mission overseas and hadn't been able to join them. That day, as the sun grew low on the horizon, several manatees, algae growing on their backs, had drifted by, passing within a couple feet of her. Then the hawksbill had swum by, its colorful shell catching the fading sunlight in the shallow water. Her father had pointed to it excitedly, giving her the thumbs-up. They followed it for a little bit, and it seemed to be heading somewhere specific.

That night, back at their campsite, they'd read all they could find in their field guides about hawksbills and learned that they sleep in the same spot for many nights in a row. So the next day, as roseate spoonbills gathered to sleep for the night, they'd returned to that same place at dusk and slipped into the warm waters. The hawksbill swum by them again, presumably on its way to its sleeping spot. She and her dad followed at a distance until it grew too dark to see it in the water. They hadn't wanted to use a light in case it would disturb it. But Alex had never forgotten that amazing experience of seeing one in the wild.

Feeling a little nostalgic, she called her dad, but it went to voicemail. She knew he was probably perched on some seaside cliff in Point Reyes National Seashore in California, in an area without reception.

She glanced at the time and realized she might actually be able to talk to her friend Zoe Lindquist. They hadn't spoken in a few weeks because Zoe had been working extremely long hours shooting a horror film in London in which she played a vampire queen. The time difference had made it hard to find a time to chat. But now Alex realized the hour would be just when Zoe was finishing for the day. She decided to take the chance and see if she was available.

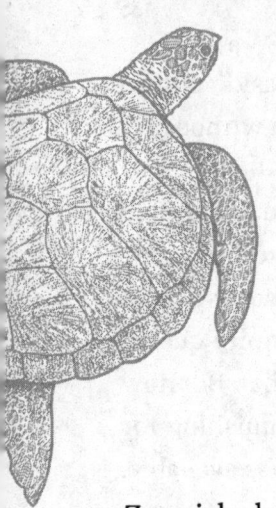

THIRTEEN

Zoe picked up on the second ring. "Alex!"

Alex grinned at the sound of her voice. "How's my favorite overworked actor?"

"Overworked. And how are the turtles? And Hawai'i? You must be livin' the dream!"

"I am! It's gorgeous here. Hawksbills have been coming to shore to lay eggs, and I get to lounge around on a beach looking after the nests. So for the most part, it's been amazing!"

"Sounds like heaven." She hesitated. "But 'for the most part'? Why do I hear some reluctance?"

Alex told her about the wildlife traffickers and the events at the airfield.

"That's awful! And scary! Why the hell did you go to the airfield alone?"

"I couldn't wait. I was worried they'd get away."

"You're crazy, Alex. You know that? You're going to give me a heart attack one of these days."

"That's why I only tell you about these things *after* I do them."

"Oh, shut up."

"And there's something else."

"Oh no, don't even tell me."

"This side of the island might have to be evacuated."

"What?"

"A hurricane is heading this way. But they're not sure yet if it's going to make landfall, or if it does, how powerful it will be by then. It might veer off or weaken."

"*Might* veer off or weaken? What is the deal with these gigs you keep taking? Can't you just find a nice, peaceful one? Like watching harmless pikas collect wildflowers or something? I thought for sure when they offered you a gig in Hawai'i that you'd just be chilling on a beach with your toes in the water. Maybe meet a cute surfer guy. Hell, I was thinking I could come visit you when we wrap. Maybe *I* could meet a cute surfer guy."

"I'm sure you could." Zoe was gorgeous, and being an A-lister, people recognized her wherever she went. But she was also extremely amiable with people. She never acted entitled or rude. She always thanked waitstaff and left big tips, and if fans recognized her, even when she was trying to be incognito and just get some grocery shopping done, she was always kind and gracious to them. It was one of the things Alex really admired about her. She was a people person—unlike Alex, who was more than ever in danger of becoming a serious misanthrope.

"But I don't think I'll risk it now," Zoe said. "A hurricane? No thanks. I'll just stick to the insanity of this shoot. You going to be okay?"

"Sure," Alex told her. "If it comes to it, I've got a group of volunteers who seem pretty great. We'll just move the turtle eggs into protected containers and get them to safety."

"I don't mean the *turtles*," Zoe said with exasperation. "I mean my best friend. Are *you* going to be okay if a hurricane makes landfall?"

"Definitely," Alex assured her. "I'll just hunker down somewhere inland until it passes. Take the opportunity to see more of the island."

"Okay. That doesn't sound so bad. I worry about you, you know."

"I know, and I appreciate it."

She and Zoe were so different, and Alex was continually grateful that they'd remained friends after college. Zoe had gone on to be a hugely successful actor, and Alex had continued on her rather solitary path of studying wildlife. Zoe was an extrovert, gregarious and fun, loving the club scene and the latest fashions and clothing trends. The only thought Alex gave to the clothes she wore was if they'd keep her warm and dry, or how durable or versatile they'd be in the field. Zoe was all Prada and Jimmy Choo and Gucci, and Alex was all Patagonia, Columbia, and Mammut. Zoe bought the latest Manolo Blahnik shoes, while Alex researched the latest hiking boots and which ones had Vibram soles and waterproof uppers. Zoe chose tops based on how well they flattered her figure; Alex, if they offered SPF protection while she was out in the wilds and if they had wicking qualities to keep the sweat off her while she hiked.

So they were an odd pair. Instead of being like two peas in a pod, they were more like a bean and a carrot that had been stuffed inside a chili relleno. Hardly alike at all, yet they could talk. Really talk meaningfully. They'd been there for each other through hardships, disappointments, triumphs, breakups. Zoe was a solid, loving friend—the one constant friend in her life since college—and Alex was incredibly grateful and hoped she offered her the same in return, especially since Zoe was famous and had her pick of people. Zoe, though, had told her most of the people who entered her life were fake and just wanted an introduction to a director or producer, or were men who wanted to use her for how good they'd look with her on their arm. Others just wanted to sponge off her considerable fortune. But Zoe could count on Alex and knew that Alex truly loved her for who she was, not what she could do for her.

"So you mentioned insanity on set. What's going on with you?" Alex asked.

Zoe took a deep breath. "Well, for one, I've been spending six hours a day in makeup. Can you believe it? Six hours! It's not easy to look like a terrifying vampire queen, let me tell you. I've got full-face prosthetics, including these deep brow ridges and sunken cheeks, and these creepy, fleshy finger extensions and weird, crepey skin coverings for my arms. Not to mention red color contacts and leathery bat wings."

"Sounds extensive."

"Tell me about it. I have to get up at the crack of doom, come onto the set before any of the other actors, and then just sit there in a chair for six whole hours while they slather me in cold foam latex prosthetics and paint almost my entire body with a special airbrush. But damn, I look good when they're done. I give myself nightmares! You don't know how many times I've accidentally spotted myself in a mirror or window and almost gave out a shriek. Can't believe it's me in there!"

"I can't wait to see it!"

"Today was pretty brutal. I'm afraid I fell asleep a couple times in the makeup chair. Luckily I didn't have a nightmare and jerk myself awake, or I might have ended up with a prosthetic nose glued to my forehead."

"Oh, the struggles you face. I feel for you."

"I'm serious!" Zoe laughed. "So check this out. We shot one of the big fight scenes today. It's this epic battle where I go after this group of five friends who have infiltrated my lair. I'm supposed to completely eviscerate three of them. Like just rip them apart. Blood gushes everywhere, totally drenching me, them, the set. I mean, it's a bloody mess, no pun intended. But get this—the special FX guy is new, and he thinks he has this great idea for a new blood recipe."

"Blood recipe?" Alex asked.

"Yeah . . . you know, like corn syrup and red dye, maybe some little oatmeal chunks mixed in there to imitate brain tissue . . ."

"Okay. Gross. But I got you." Alex began to regret the lumpy rice she'd eaten earlier that day for breakfast.

"So the FX guy mixes up a batch of this stuff that's supposed to be super realistic looking when it comes to color and consistency. Then comes the shot where I tear these actors apart. Of course I don't *really* tear them apart. They all have green screen stuff on their limbs. I mean, I'm not really going to rip their arms and legs off, but it'll look like it in post."

"Gotcha."

"But the blood is not going to be done in post. It's done live, and this FX guy just starts spraying us with it. The stuff gets everywhere: in my mouth, in my hair, in the crack of my butt. There is no escaping it. We're all absolutely drenched in it, and the first thing I notice that's wrong about it is that it smells like ten-day-old roadkill that someone tried to clean up with gasoline."

"Seriously?"

"Seriously. So one of the actors, the so-called final girl, you know, is supposed to leap on my back and reach around with a stake to stab me in the heart. At first they were going to use my stunt double. But I'm all like, 'Hey, no problem. She weighs next to nothing, and you can get a close-up. I can take it.' I mean, it wouldn't have been a big deal under normal circumstances."

"Uh-oh. I feel a disaster coming."

"So she jumps on my back, and we're whirling around, and she's trying to bring the stake in to drive through my chest by wrapping her arm around my neck. And this is when her friends dive in and I rip their arms off.

"But by then the smell is *really* getting to me. My eyes are streaming. We're all stifling gags, and I'm standing there with this actor on my back, wondering if this FX guy's 'special recipe' is actually real blood. Like maybe he's some sick jerk who butchered a deer for it or something. I mean, the stuff looks and feels real. And the director is all excited because damn, the stuff looks convincing.

"Then one of the actors can't hold it in anymore and starts

retching, and that sets off another one, and soon all three victims I've eviscerated start puking their guts out, contributing to the mess. I'm gagging, but I manage to hold it in. I mean," she added, "I *am* a professional."

Alex laughed. "Of course."

"But not so the woman on my back. And this stuff is *vile*. Next thing I know, I'm shucking her off my back while she's projectile vomiting across the soundstage."

"Yuck!"

"Yeah, it was a total disaster."

"And what about the guy and his brilliant new blood recipe?"

"Normally he'd be fired on the spot. But I think he's the producer's nephew, so they just sent him home. Probably straight to bed without dinner."

Alex laughed. "Oh no! What if he comes up with another brilliant concoction?"

"Well, they banned him from the blood work. From now on he's just going to be getting sandwiches for the FX team."

"That's a relief, anyhow."

"But my skin itches now. And everywhere that stuff touched is dyed deep, deep scarlet like I'm a boiled lobster or something. So now I have to sit in the makeup chair for an extra hour just to cover up even more of my skin."

"Oh, wow. Sure you don't want to come out and face this hurricane with me instead?"

Zoe laughed. "Maybe I do." Then she asked after Alex's dad. "I know you guys used to live there when your mom was still alive, right?"

"Yes."

"You doing okay with that? Are you feeling sad?"

"No, it's actually comforting in a lot of ways to be back. It's like I can feel her spirit here."

"That's awesome. That makes me happy. I know how much you miss her. I'm just sorry I never got the chance to meet her. She sounds amazing."

"She really was."

"So what's next for you?"

"Waiting for more turtles to come ashore. I got some great volunteers to help me when the eggs hatch. And you?"

"Home to bed and then back to the set to do it all over again."

"It's a hard life."

"It is."

They talked for a few more minutes and then hung up, Alex feeling buoyed. She always felt cheered up whenever she talked to her old friend.

She spent the rest of the day keeping an eye on the eggs and reading through the latest data other researchers had been publishing about hawksbills. Then she checked the thermocouples again, excited that yes, indeed, the turtles would likely hatch the next day.

Finally, long after the sun set, she made a dinner of spaghetti with the rest of her marinara sauce and crawled into her tent.

FOURTEEN

The next day, Alex checked the thermocouples, then hooked up the mic and put in her earbuds. She stilled her breath, listening to the nest that was about to hatch. Inside she could hear shifting and squirming, a sure sign that the hatchlings had emerged from their eggs and were crawling upward, scrabbling their way through the sand.

She grinned. It was time to call her volunteers. The hatchlings would emerge that night.

Her calls were greeted with enthusiastic excitement. Unfortunately, she wasn't able to reach Sasha. She knew that her friend had been planning to dive that day and take advantage of the small window before the hurricane drew closer, and could well be beyond cell range.

But the others all answered, and at dusk the small grassy parking area was filled with the cars of Dora, Nakoa, and Keola. Jerome jogged down the beach from his aunt's house, not wanting to miss a moment.

They gathered around the nest, each person donning a handlamp with a red light. The moonlight reflected off the waves, lending an extra touch of magic to the moment.

Alex bent and sniffed at the sand, then encouraged everyone to do the same. When it got to Lupesina, the little girl broke into a grin. "It smells like dirt from our garden after we've watered it."

"You're right. That means they're on their way out!"

Next Alex placed the microphone beside the nest and put out a small speaker. "Hear that?" Alex asked them. "That squirming?"

Everyone nodded.

"What are they doing in there?" Lupesina asked.

Alex sat down cross-legged on the sand, inviting everyone to do the same while they waited. "Well, they each have a little egg tooth that allows them to break out of their shells. This whole time they've been scrunched up in their eggs, so they need to stretch out. Once they break through their shell, they'll eat the egg yolk to bulk up for their journey out to sea. Then they start crawling upward, so the hatchlings on the bottom tamp down the sand. As the ones on top bump their heads on the ceiling of the nest, they knock sand down to the bottom and it gets stomped flat. That makes the floor higher, so they're all that much closer to the top. They keep repeating this process, climbing higher and higher." Suddenly a different strong scent reached Alex. She wrinkled her nose. "Smell that?" she asked everyone.

They leaned in close, sniffing.

"Egg yolk," Keola said.

"And dirt and something else. Like mushrooms," Dora commented.

At the top of the nest, the sand sank a couple inches, then started shifting around.

Alex checked her thermocouple. The temp had dropped a little bit. It was about to happen.

A little head poked out, followed by two tiny flippers.

The first little hatchling crawled out, its back flippers struggling in the loose sand. When it fully emerged, it rested there for a couple minutes, its little eyes taking in the new scene around it.

"Look at that!" Dora exclaimed, finger pointing at its carapace. "Its shell is heart-shaped!"

Everyone gathered around, and Keola bent over the tiny creature. "How about that?"

"Does it stay that way?" Lupesina asked.

"Slowly it'll grow into an oval shape," Alex told the girl.

Nakoa knelt down beside it. "I'm so glad we're here to see this. I haven't seen hawksbill hatchlings since I was a kid." He made a few notes in his field journal, doing a quick sketch as the turtle got its bearings. Alex was seriously impressed with his talent. With just a few quick strokes, he was able to capture its movement and character.

This first little one was only two inches long, but Alex knew others would be as big as three. Though they couldn't currently tell under the red light, Alex knew their shells would mostly be brown at this stage, as they had yet to develop the colorful mix of ambers, reds, blacks, and oranges that decorated the carapaces of adults.

"How does it know where to go?" Lupesina asked.

"It'll use several clues." Alex pointed out to sea. "See how the sky looks lighter over the ocean than it does over the land?"

The girl looked back and forth, then nodded.

"And right now, we've got the moon shining on the water, so that makes it even brighter." Alex pointed along the beach. "See how dark it is here on the beach? That's really important. If that hotel had gone up, the lights from it would have confused the hatchling. It might have crawled toward it instead, and been picked off by predators or died of heat if it was still lost when the sun came up."

"That's awful," Lupesina said.

Alex nodded. "I agree. These little guys got lucky." She returned to the original question. "They'll also use the sound of the surf to orient themselves."

"What about noise pollution?" Dora asked. "Does that get in the way of them hearing the surf?"

"It does. Hatchlings can sense the vibration of the waves. But if there are things nearby like generators, air conditioners, power plants, or car engines, they can throw them off and make them crawl inland."

"This is depressing," Lupesina lamented.

Alex had to agree. Silence overtook the group.

As they watched, the little hatchling recovered from its ordeal of crawling up out of the nest. It spotted the moon on the ocean waves and scampered in that direction. Another followed, and another, each resting outside of the nest before waddling off toward the surf. Keola and Nakoa escorted these early emergers all the way to the surf line, watching as they dipped into the cool water and swam away.

"Three away!" Keola called happily.

Alex gave him the thumbs-up.

Then more and more emerged, much to the delight of everyone. Dora and Lupesina took turns with Nakoa and Keola, the group walking up and down the beach with the turtles, their red headlamps illuminating the sand. Alex and Jerome stayed by the nest, keeping a tally of how many had emerged. The biologist who originally witnessed the laying of this initial nest had counted 135 eggs.

"They're drinking!" called Dora, excitement evident in her voice. "What a bunch of cuties!" At this comment, Nakoa wrapped an affectionate arm around Dora's waist and pressed his head against hers, sharing in the moment.

Unlike humans, sea turtles had the amazing ability to process seawater into drinking water. They drank down the salty brew, then excreted the salt via their tear ducts.

As the evening wore on, Alex continued to count and her volunteers worked diligently, smiles of pure enchantment on their faces. Alex loved this. Too often she was confronted with people who sought to harm wildlife. It felt like a relief to be around other people who cared. She felt her shoulders relax and she exhaled a huge, grateful breath of air.

Nakoa approached her and gripped her hand. "You're these turtles' kahu."

From his kind smile, she knew it was a compliment, but she was unfamiliar with the word. "What does that mean?"

"It means 'guardian.' 'Protector.'"

She smiled, looking down at the little hatchlings. "We all are."

"In Hawaiian, we don't say we own our pets," he went on. "We are their kahu, their steward, their protector. It's all about the safekeeping of something cherished." He watched more hatchlings waddle toward the sea, the moonlight reflecting off their heart-shaped carapaces. "Like these little turtles."

"The little guys are all making their way out to sea," Keola called from the surf, where Jerome had joined him.

Alex knew that hawksbills would orient themselves by continuing to swim into the breakers until they were beyond them and at sea. Hawksbills had magnetite in their brains, which allowed them to sense the earth's magnetic field and use it as a compass. These little hatchlings' compasses would be set as soon as they hit the water, and they'd use that directional aid to continue to go out deeper into the sea. Other turtle species like loggerheads used the inclination of the earth's magnetic field to navigate toward the north Atlantic or to the Gulf Stream.

And their coloration would help. By being lighter on their underside, they blended with the bright sky when viewed from below. And with a darker color on their upper shell, they blended with the dark color of the ocean when viewed above by predators such as birds.

These baby turtles couldn't yet dive to great depths and would often be at the mercy of strong currents. So they'd seek out calm waters where they could just float and eat. This usually meant they'd swim to a drift line. Wherever two different ocean currents met each other, drift lines formed and provided a cornucopia of food for turtles, a floating smorgasbord of delicious creatures such as plankton, small crustaceans, algae, clams, jellyfish, shrimp, and more.

However, drift lines could also be dangerous, as loads of human trash also collected there: plastic bottles, party balloons, Styrofoam, fishing line, plastic ties from six-packs—all manner of garbage. Plastic bags could appear as jellyfish when floating underwater and be gobbled up by turtles, just like what happened with the mother turtle Alex had helped. This trash constituted a serious threat to turtles through poison and suffocation.

But if they managed to find a good source of food, these little hawksbills would mature out at sea. They'd hang out for at least three years, bulking up until they were big enough to leave that area and seek out their favorite adult food, sponges, which grew on coral reefs. An adult hawksbill could eat more than a thousand pounds of sponges a year.

Just the fact that adult hawksbills survived on sponges was amazing. Many sponges contained silicates—basically glass needles—and also accumulated cyanobacterial toxins and heavy metals like molybdenum that were deadly to other animals, making hawksbill meat inedible. So the turtles benefited from filling this rare diet niche.

Alex had read recent DNA studies that indicated hawksbills were closely related to Kemp's ridley and olive ridley sea turtles, both of which had a very different diet. She wondered how long ago they had branched apart and hoped future studies would reveal such information.

After living off sponges as adults, eventually they'd return to this same beach to lay their own eggs.

When the hatchlings stopped emerging, Alex and Jerome tallied up the count. One was missing. She knew it could be hard if you were the last little turtle out of the nest. Hatchlings climbed one another like a ladder, but if you were the last one, you didn't have anyone to climb. Gently, Alex dug down into the nest and located the final hatchling. Feeling its little flippers on her fingers, she lifted it out. It rested, exhausted. Then she carried it down the beach and set it in front of the waves. It waddled out, swimming away.

Lupesina jumped up and down on the beach. "We saved them!"

"We certainly did!" Alex agreed. She rechecked her tally and let everyone know.

Keola smiled. "Every single one of them survived. I'm amazed!"

Alex was, too. Usually, when left unguarded, the mortality rate could be high because of poachers and predators.

The little girl scanned the beach. "When do the next ones emerge?" she asked eagerly.

"Let's find out." Alex moved to the thermocouples at the other nests. While the others looked on, Lupesina took readings at each of the nests, then she and Alex compared them with the results from the day before. The nest temperatures hadn't started to go up yet.

"Looks like it'll still be a while before they're ready to hatch," Alex concluded.

Lupesina's eyes went wide. "You'll call us, right?"

"Of course."

She looked to her dad. "Because we can come out and help, right?"

Keola nodded. "You got it, kid."

With all the tiny turtles disappearing into the surf, a mood of celebration took over the small group. Alex ordered them all pizza, beer, and soda, having a DoorDash driver deliver everything right to the beach. They gathered around on beach chairs and dug into the food.

Dora finished a slice of pizza and suddenly looked thoughtful. "You know, I taught my kids about species extinction and climate change, and while I always maintained a tone of hope with them, inside I felt pretty helpless and bleak about it all." She gazed out at the ocean. "To actually do something hands-on really makes me feel better."

"Yeah, I got to admit," Keola put in, "when we first signed up to do this, I kind of thought it would be just like work. A job to do. I wasn't expecting to feel such satisfaction seeing those little guys waddle out to sea."

Nakoa held up his journal, which he'd been sketching in while they ate, the pages washed in red light from his headlamp. "And it's nice to draw another generation of honu'ea in my sketchbook here."

Lupesina leaned over to peer at the book. "I want to see!" He angled it so she could take in the page he was drawing. "That's really good!"

Nakoa flushed with pride. "Thanks!"

"Pass it around!" Dora encouraged him.

Looking rather shy, he handed the book to Lupesina, who thumbed through the rest of the pages, then handed it to her dad.

Keola paused on a page with detailed drawings of a coral reef. "These *are* good. You had art lessons?"

"A few," Nakoa told him. "Mostly it's just decades of practice."

"It shows!" Keola handed the journal to Jerome.

The teenager took the sketchbook, flipping through pages, turning it this way and that. "Damn, dude!" he exclaimed admiringly. "I can draw stick figures and that's about it. These are fire!" He stopped on the last page, and Alex could see it depicted the hawksbill hatchlings scrabbling toward the surf. "I'd love to draw like this."

"I could teach you, if you like," Nakoa answered.

"Seriously?" Jerome asked.

Nakoa nodded. "Seriously. Journals like that are not just fun, but they're a great way to show how an area is changing. If you keep the journal for multiple years, you can see if biodiversity is plummeting or increasing."

"Way to suck all the fun out of it," Keola said, laughing.

"No, I think that sounds cool," Jerome countered.

"So do I!" Lupesina agreed. "I want to start a journal like that.

Maybe I could document other species, like honeycreepers or something."

Nakoa gazed at her appreciatively. "There you go!"

"And I could document . . ." Jerome trailed off. "Wildlife of Detroit?"

"Yes!" Nakoa exclaimed. "Record what you see in the city and county parks. Those are areas where biodiversity is particularly at risk. Or you could record what you see here each summer when you come out to stay with your aunt."

"You guys!" Keola exclaimed good-naturedly. "Sheesh! Don't you ever just want to do something for fun?"

Jerome handed the journal to Alex, and once again she flipped through the pages, admiring the paleontologist's talent. She passed it at last to Dora, who eagerly took it. She examined the book thoughtfully. "Wow, Nakoa. I remember you drawing when we were kids. You've really kept at it. These are amazing!"

Nakoa grinned with pleasure. "Thank you, Dora."

"Let's all make a wish for the baby turtles," Lupesina suggested. "We can send the wishes out on the wind!"

Alex loved this idea.

"You go first, Dad!" Lupesina urged.

"Way to put me on the spot, kid!" The huge Samoan contemplated for a moment. "I hope that they have more than their share of delectable goodies to eat, like whatever the baby turtle equivalent of panikeke would be."

"Yum! My favorite!" She beamed.

He ruffled her hair. "I know."

"And your wish?" she asked Jerome.

The teenager tossed his baseball into the air. "That they hit it out of the park!"

"Yeah!" Keola called out, imitating swinging a bat.

Lupesina turned to Dora. "What's your wish for them?"

Dora thought for a moment, then suddenly brightened. "Oh my god. Remember that weird puppet show that used to be in the town park every summer?" she asked Nakoa.

Nakoa burst into laughter. "How could I forget?"

"What puppet show?" Jerome asked.

"It was about these two baby turtles who find out that aliens have landed on the island and are planning to take over the Earth," Dora told him.

Nakoa nodded. "Yes! Didn't they end up getting caught by the aliens, who tried to cook them in a stew?"

"What?!" Jerome exclaimed, amazed.

"Yeah," Dora went on. "And then they escape, only to crash-land in the middle of a volcano. And wasn't there, like, lava people who—"

"Save them, yes!" Nakoa cut in. "And the baby turtles join forces with the lava people to fight the aliens!"

Dora was cracking up now and wiped away a tear. "And the lava people always talked in rhyme, if I'm remembering right."

Nakoa lit up. "Yes! Oh, wow. I haven't thought about that play in years. It became a tradition with all our friends to watch it. We knew the whole thing by heart!"

"And this thing was put on every summer?" Keola asked, incredulous.

"Every summer, without fail. Multiple times," Dora told him. "The puppeteer was kind of a weird guy. He wrote the play himself."

"You'd never have guessed," Nakoa added.

"But what happened to the two baby turtles?" Lupesina asked, clearly upset at the animals' plight.

"Oh, they make it back home to their parents," Nakoa assured her.

Jerome shook his head, amused. "That is just too weird."

"So my wish," Dora said, "is that none of these turtles end up falling into a volcano and having to fight aliens."

"A fine wish," Nakoa told her, chuckling. "A fine wish indeed. And my wish is that they live long lives and end up preserved in the fossil record so that future paleontologists learn vital things from them."

Keola looked at his daughter. "You haven't told us what your wish is, kiddo."

Lupesina closed her eyes and took a deep breath. "I wish that they never get eaten by sharks and live to a ripe old age getting fat on sponges, and that they all get together at night and sing turtle lullabies in the coral reef."

It brought a vivid image to Alex's mind, and she felt a real affection for the kid.

"And what's your wish, Alex?" Lupesina asked.

Alex looked around at this warm, gregarious bunch, feeling grateful for them and their dedication. "That in the future, the only humans they run into are wonderful, caring folks like you all."

"Oh, hush," Dora said, smiling shyly.

"Yeah, don't get all mushy on us," Keola added.

Jerome gave her a playful punch on the arm, and Nakoa lifted his beer. "To the honuʻea!"

"To the honuʻea!" everyone chimed in, clinking bottles of soda and beer.

As the evening began to wind down, Nakoa stood up, clasping his hands together. "In a week's time, my friends, I invite you all over to my cousin's house. He's having a luau to celebrate my niece's graduation, and we can regale everyone with our tales of the hawksbills."

Everyone agreed with gusto, and Nakoa gave out the address. Then slowly each person said their good nights and returned to their cars. Jerome left to walk home.

Nakoa was the last to leave. He and Alex finished their beers together, sitting side by side, gazing up at the moon and listening to the quiet whispering of the waves.

"I'd love to see more turtles come back here," he said. "I think the work we're doing here is going to make a difference."

"Hear! Hear!" Alex said, and she clinked her beer bottle to his.

THE NEXT MORNING, ALEX AWOKE to winds buffeting her tent. She dressed quickly and stepped outside, seeing dark storm clouds churning in the east. Her hair tossed around her face and she pulled it back. A slight rain pattered down on the sand. She spotted a few people on the beach all pulling out their phones and frowning.

The same man she'd noticed just the other day listening to his radio sat up suddenly out of his beach chair as the unmistakable tones of an emergency broadcast cut in. Alex listened intently.

"The National Weather Service has issued a mandatory evacuation order for the towns of Ānuenue, Pāhala, Nāʻālehu, and Discovery Harbor near the southeast coast of Hawaiʻi. All residents are urged to secure their homes as best as possible and move inland. Be sure to take with you any prescription medications, important contact information, plenty of water and food, and necessary clothing, as return to the area might not be possible for several days. Be prepared for power outages, downed trees and power lines, torrential rain, and wind gusts up to two hundred and fifty miles per hour. Do not attempt to stay in the area. Repeat—"

The message went on to repeat itself, followed by the emergency tones again.

Alex felt a small flutter of fear inside her chest. The storm must have picked up speed. She watched beachgoers pack up in a hurry and rush to their cars. Soon she was the only one on the beach.

Alex took down her tent and stowed her Bluetti power station inside her Jeep, along with her laptop, sleeping bag, and pad.

It was time to move the turtle eggs. She couldn't wait any longer.

FIFTEEN

Alex turned as a car pulled into the small parking area. Sasha stepped out, giving a small wave. She joined Alex down on the beach.

"Look at that choppy sea," Sasha gasped. "I've never seen Hawaiian waters look like this before."

Alex followed her gaze, seeing the eastern horizon piled high with dark, stormy clouds. "Hurricanes have been getting worse and more frequent, and hitting places that normally don't experience them too often."

Alex knew that climate change had affected the strength, frequency, and duration of storms. And not just hurricanes, but thunderstorms, tornados, and tropical cyclones.

Hurricanes were becoming more frequent and intense because ocean temperatures had been warming dangerously. The oceans absorbed 90 percent of the excess heat that humans produced and 25 percent of carbon pollution. But warmer waters are less efficient at absorbing carbon, so in the future, more of that heat will stay trapped in the atmosphere, warming the planet even more. All of this was a closed system, and heat had to be released somewhere, so it was unleashed in the form of devastating storm systems.

The oceans were far warmer than they were fifty years ago, and she knew that hurricanes were becoming more and more destructive. So-called hundred-year storms were now happening every other year. Though the power of such storms was measured by wind speed, what was also incredibly damaging was the water released by the systems. Heavy rain and storm surges caused fatalities and billions of dollars of damage. Warming oceans supercharged hurricanes because warmer air held more water vapor. Alex had read a study that human-caused climate change had caused the 2020 hurricane season to deliver up to 11 percent more rainfall, and this percentage was expected to keep going up.

She also knew that the effects of these storms were reaching farther and farther inland, to places like Tennessee, Missouri, Illinois, and New Mexico. During hurricanes such as Helene in 2024, places hundreds of miles inland in North Carolina suffered devastating losses and destruction. But in the future, places a thousand miles or more inland would be affected.

And on top of that, the ocean was warming farther and farther north, so areas like Rhode Island, Maine, and Nova Scotia would be hit with hurricane weather in the future. These places would suffer all the more, as they didn't have the infrastructure to deal with such storms, such as levees, evacuation routes, advance warning systems, and more.

The cataclysmic hurricanes in recent years had already maxed out the Saffir-Simpson hurricane wind scale, which placed hurricanes into five categories based on the strength of their sustained winds. Soon, a new, more intense category would be needed.

As Alex and Sasha watched, a small cargo ship hove into view, fighting against the tossing waves. It came to a halt and dropped anchor.

Sasha stared out at it. "What are they doing? They're not seriously going to leave their boat out there during the hurricane. It'll get dashed to bits."

"Maybe they're waiting for something," Alex suggested.

Sasha turned to Alex. "You have binoculars?"

"Sure thing."

Alex jogged to her Jeep and returned with them. Sasha took

them and studied the hull. "Check out this slapdash effort," she said, handing the binocs back.

Alex took them and focused on the ship. Rust streamed down the sides of the vessel, the paint chipped and worn in myriad places. The ship's name, written with scrawled white paint, read *The Mary Sue*. Uneven letters varying in thickness gave it a disreputable look. "I think they hired someone's cousin to paint that name on it instead of going with a pro."

Sasha stared at it. "The whole tub looks a bit worse for wear. And it's towing a pocket trawler," Sasha pointed out. "That's kind of a weird combo."

"What about your boat?" Alex asked.

"I moved it last night over to Kailua-Kona," Sasha said. "It'll be safe on the west side of the island."

"I'll have to move all the turtle eggs to safety now."

Sasha looked over her shoulder at the nests. "I'll help you."

"Thanks, Sasha."

Alex started making phone calls, wanting to catch her volunteers before they left town. Nakoa picked up immediately, as did Dora, and both offered to come within half an hour. Keola and Lupesina also responded to the call, saying they'd be there soon. Jerome's phone went to voicemail.

Sasha and Alex retrieved several of the egg storage containers from Alex's Jeep and began gently excavating one of the nests. Alex picked up the first turtle egg, finding it surprising light, around an ounce. They placed the turtle eggs inside the specially cushioned padding, making sure not to jostle them too much.

Keola and Lupesina were the first to arrive, and Alex handed a container to them and then dug through the sand to reveal the eggs in a second nest. She showed them how to gently handle the eggs and how to place them inside a container, then left them to it.

Moments later Dora's well-loved station wagon pulled into the parking area, and Alex set her to work on the third nest. Nakoa was the last to arrive, pulling up in his small Ford compact and joining them on the beach.

She directed him to help Dora load up the eggs from the third nest. Dora lit up when she saw him. They embraced and kissed, making Alex happy to see that their reunion was working out well.

Soon Keola and his daughter had finished the second nest, and he carried that batch of eggs to their SUV.

Alex and Sasha finished the first nest and hefted the eggs toward Alex's Jeep. "I can take those," Keola offered.

"Could you?"

"No problem."

She loaded the eggs into his SUV and dropped a pin on his phone with the center's location, where the eggs would safely ride out the storm. Then they could return them to the nests after the hurricane had passed.

After getting her voicemail, Jerome jogged down the beach from his aunt's house and helped them with the third nest, carrying the eggs up to Keola's car. There wasn't enough room for any more eggs inside.

"We can handle the last nest," Alex told the father-daughter team. "You get going to safety. You, too, Jerome. I'm sure your aunt needs you."

She watched as Jerome raced toward home, and Keola buckled in the egg containers and pulled out of the parking area.

Alex and the remaining volunteers returned to the final nest. "Once we finish loading the last of these eggs, if you could just help me carry them to my Jeep, you two should take off, too," she said to Dora and Nakoa. She turned to Sasha. "Then we should all get out of here."

As they knelt down beside the final nest, Alex's attention was momentarily pulled back out to sea. The small cargo ship anchored offshore still bobbed there on the water, and Alex watched as several people moved into the pocket trawler it was towing and detached its line.

Sasha stared out, brow furrowed in confusion. "What are they doing? Don't they know about the evacuation order? If they leave their ship there, it'll get wrecked for sure."

Alex hunched over the last turtle nest, gathering more and more eggs into the last container. Dora and Nakoa worked quickly and efficiently, and she was glad they'd stayed on the extra few minutes to help. She caught Dora and Nakoa sneaking glances at each other and smiled.

The sound of a boat engine drew Alex's attention to the pocket trawler. Five people now stood out on its deck. They revved the engine and powered toward shore.

"You don't think they're off-duty Coast Guard or something, do you? Maybe they saw us on the beach and are coming in to tell us to evacuate?" Alex ventured.

Sasha continued to stare out. "In a tub like that? I don't know. Maybe."

Alex agreed. The disreputable look of the ship made her doubt the idea. She bent down to help with the rest of the eggs. When they placed the last egg gently into the container, Dora and Nakoa sealed it up and stood.

The people in the trawler bounced chaotically on the rough waves, one of them stumbling and nearly pitching over. He gripped the boat's railing and held on. Alex noticed all of them were dressed in black, and as they got closer, she saw that they wore what looked like combat gear: utility vests, weapon belts, black caps on their heads. A primal chill went through her. Something felt wrong. She stood up, helping Dora and Nakoa lift the last container.

Sasha followed, glancing back over her shoulder. "Maybe they're police or something. Look at how they're dressed."

The trawler pulled up to the pier and breakwater that had been built to serve the now-halted hotel project. The people jumped out, tying up the small trawler and then jogging down the pier to the beach, which they started to cross, angling for the parking area.

Alex could see now that they each had earpieces with mics and carried sidearms and combat knives. One person, a slender man with long blond hair pulled back in a ponytail, held an M4 assault rifle, and another, who Alex saw was a woman, held a combat shotgun, her black eyes glittering. A long auburn braid hung down her back. A third sported long, greasy black hair and a snake tattoo on his arm, and another was a muscular hulk of a man with brown hair shorn very close to his scalp.

The last wore his long black hair pulled back in a ponytail, his beige face weathered. He paused at the parking area, staring out at Alex and the others. "What are you all still doing here?" he boomed. "Didn't you hear the evacuation order?" He had a distinct Australian accent.

"We did," Alex explained, wondering who the hell these people were. "We are just removing these turtle eggs before the storm hits."

The Aussie stepped forward, eyeing them all. And then his eyes fell on Dora and Nakoa. His expression changed, face screwing up in what looked like recognition. "Hey, you there." Dora and Nakoa turned to look over their shoulders but continued crossing the beach toward their cars. "Stop!" the man ordered. He turned to the woman. "Tatiana, is that him?"

The woman pulled her phone out of a Velcroed pocket in her vest and checked something. "Yeah," she said. "Damn right. It *is* him."

The Australian man, who acted like their leader, stepped up to Dora and Nakoa. "Put that down," he ordered.

"We're just carrying it up to our cars," Dora started to explain.

"Put it down," the man bellowed.

"Now look here," Nakoa started. "I hardly think that's any way to speak to—"

"I won't ask again," the man ordered. His tone was threatening and loud, and Dora flinched at his words.

Alex stormed up to him. "What is going on here? Who the hell are you?"

"That's none of your concern," he barked back. He turned to Nakoa. "You're coming with us, Dr. Kahananui."

"The hell I am!" the paleontologist barked back indignantly. "Answer the lady's question. Just who the hell are you?"

The leader hesitated, then gestured for his men to come forward. "Bring him," he ordered, and Snake Tattoo and the hulking man each grabbed an arm. Nakoa struggled, the egg container coming loose from his grasp. Alex rushed forward and grabbed the other side of it, and together she and Dora lowered it to the sand.

"What are you doing?" Sasha asked the strangers, striding up to join the others.

The two men muscled Nakoa away from Dora, dragging him up the beach toward the parking area. The Australian and Tatiana followed.

"Where are you taking him?" Alex demanded. "We need to see some identification now. Are you with the police? The Coast Guard?"

The men said nothing, just continued to force Nakoa along. They entered the trees, and suddenly Dora, who had been staring, mouth open, ran after them. "Wait just a second! You can't go hauling people off without cause!" Her imperious schoolteacher voice, designed to strike fear and discipline into the hearts of her students, carried through clearly. She rushed toward them, Alex and Sasha following close behind.

"Stop!" Alex yelled. "Let him go!"

Dora raced up to the man with the snake tattoo and grabbed his arm. "Stop!" she shouted. She dug her heels into the sand, leaning backward. The man jerked his arm back, trying to throw her off, but she clung on, determined.

Nakoa glanced back helplessly over his shoulder at Alex and Sasha, who stayed close. "I have no idea who these men are," he pleaded. "Please call the police."

With a forceful shove of his left arm, Snake Tattoo managed to dislodge Dora's grip. She crashed into the sand, landing on her back.

Alex rushed to her and helped her up. Now they were almost to the parking area. Dora broke away from Alex and rushed forward again, grabbing on to Snake Tattoo once more, trying to wrench his grip away from Nakoa. This time the man did let go of the paleontologist briefly. He turned to Dora, reaching down to his thigh and unsheathing the wicked-looking combat knife.

Before Alex could race forward to intervene, the blade came up so fast that Alex could barely track its movement. He jabbed it into Dora's throat with a vicious thrust. Blood spurted out, spraying his vest and the grass beneath them. He turned away, disinterested, and continued marching Nakoa toward the black SUV that had been left in the parking area for days.

The teacher reached up, grabbing at her neck, stumbling. Nakoa turned back, struggling, horror stealing over him when he saw Dora's crumpling body. His legs went limp beneath him, only the men's grip keeping him upright.

"Hey!" the blond man yelled. "I've had enough with killing people! You didn't say anything about that when I took this job! This is *not* what I signed up for!"

"Shut the fuck up and get in the car," the Aussie commanded.

Dora collapsed, and Sasha knelt beside her, pulling her phone out. She hurriedly dialed 911, listened, then looked up at Alex in dismay. "There's no service. It keeps saying that the network is busy!"

"People must be calling in like crazy during the evacuation," Alex said breathlessly, her mind struggling to process what was happening. "They must be slammed."

The strangers were almost at the SUV. Alex had to act now. She rushed forward, her Jeet Kune Do training flooding in. She kicked out, sweeping the legs of the huge man holding Nakoa's right arm. The man stumbled and fell backward onto his back. She delivered a powerful kick to his solar plexus, and the air exploded from his chest with a gasp. He rolled on the ground, struggling to get up.

The Aussie turned on her, pulling his sidearm out and aiming it at her head. "Don't." When Alex continued to move forward, he retrained the gun on Sasha. "I mean it."

Alex hesitated.

Nakoa struggled, almost breaking free before the woman with the combat shotgun strode over and harshly took hold of his neck, shoving him violently into the back seat of the SUV.

The Australian moved to the driver's-side door but briefly hesitated as he took in the three remaining cars in the small parking lot. Then he lifted his pistol and fired rounds into all their radiators. Alex flinched at the cacophonous thunder of each shot, slapping her hands to her ears.

He noticed Alex's little ruined Zodiac boat lying deflated in the trees then. He harrumphed, evidently satisfied that it was beyond use, and turned away.

Then he stepped into the SUV and started up the motor. Alex ran forward, but the car lurched and roared off, Nakoa inside. Alex watched as it tore out of the parking area, pluming up dirt and grass in huge clumps. It turned left out of the lane and disappeared through the trees.

Alex raced back to Dora's side. She lay in the sand, frantically clamping her hands to her neck. Sasha had stripped off her jacket and pressed the material to the wound.

Alex pulled out her phone, dialing 911. But the line just beeped and played an automated message: "We're sorry. All services are engaged right now. The network is busy. Please try your call again later."

"Damn it!" she cursed.

Blood pulsed from Dora's neck, a clear sign that the man had severed an artery. Alex's mind raced, thinking of the nearest hospital. "C'mon! We need to get her to my car."

They bent to grab her, but in just those few moments, Dora went limp, her hands sliding down to the ground, her eyes wide and staring, then going glassy. The blood stopped pumping.

Sasha continued to grip the woman's neck tightly, pressing down with her jacket. She glanced up at Alex. "Is she . . . is she gone?"

Alex listened for a breath, then felt for a pulse. She couldn't believe how much blood had pumped out of the woman's body. It pooled all around them, collecting in red rivulets in the sand, streaming down to fill one of the holes left by the eggs.

Alex could detect no breath and no pulse. She traded with Sasha, continuing to hold the jacket against Dora's throat while Sasha double-checked for vital signs. "She's gone," Sasha whispered.

Alex rocked back on her heels, shocked. What the hell had just happened?

"What should we do?" Sasha asked.

"We need to follow that SUV. Find out where they're taking Nakoa."

Sasha stared down at Dora's body. "But . . . do we just . . . leave her here?"

Alex jumped up, her gut churning. "I'm afraid we'll have to, just for now." At Sasha's pained expression, she added, "Believe me, I hate it, too." Dora had been such a sweet person, so willing to help, and her reconnection with Nakoa had been so touching to witness. No wonder Dora had fought so hard to protect him. That she'd been killed so violently and so suddenly, and just cast aside as if she were a mere nuisance, enraged Alex. She had to catch up with these guys.

Sasha stared toward the parking area. "What about the cars? Aren't they toast?"

"He only hit the radiators. Cross your fingers." She pulled out her keys and ran for her Jeep. Along the way, she hefted up the final egg container and stashed it in the back.

Sasha got up and raced after her. They climbed in, and Alex started up the engine, roaring out of the little parking area and racing toward the lane. She turned left, spraying up dirt in a plume behind them. They tore after the kidnappers.

SIXTEEN

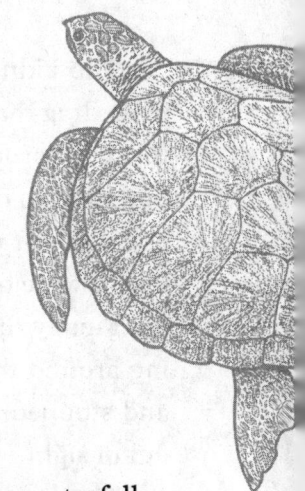

The road before Alex and Sasha was empty. Rain began to fall, a portent of the storm that loomed ever nearer. Alex switched on the wipers as the precipitation grew heavier.

"See if you can get through to anyone else," she asked Sasha.

Sasha lifted her phone, tried a couple other local numbers, then one of her friends on the mainland. She hung up and shook her head. "Nothing. It keeps saying that all networks are busy."

Alex pushed the speedometer past forty, bouncing and jostling over the dirt road that led away from the beach, speeding past the few homes along the route. They crested a small rise, and Alex spotted the SUV in the distance. "There!"

She jammed harder on the accelerator, their speed jumping to fifty miles an hour. The road wasn't meant for traffic anywhere near this speed, and they careened along, hitting potholes and ruts. Sasha gripped the dashboard. The rain slashed down, making it harder to see. So far the radiator was holding, probably because the car hadn't heated up yet. But once it did, it was going to start giving off steam like crazy.

The SUV made a right turn onto the paved section ahead. Alex slowed, still pursuing the car, but now that they were close enough to keep an eye on the armed group, she kept at a distance. "I don't want them to know we were able to follow them. If we can find out where they're taking Nakoa, we can get the police and tell them."

The kidnappers drove past the museum and pulled onto the main drag that led into Ānuenue. Soon they entered the town, Alex turning corners and following them from parallel streets, using buildings to obscure the line of sight. Houses all looked empty. No one was out milling around the gift shops or restaurants, most of which were boarded up. The place was deserted.

Finally the SUV pulled into the grocery store parking lot, driving around to the back of the store where deliveries were made, and stopped. Alex eased the Jeep up beside the building, staying out of sight.

The huge, muscular man with the shorn head got out of the SUV and jogged over to a refrigerated eighteen-wheeler. He walked up to one of the tires and felt along the wheelbase, coming up with something. He held it up and smiled.

"Well, don't just stand there grinning like an idiot, Jake," she heard the Australian bark from the SUV. "Get in it. Time's wasting."

It must have been the key, Alex guessed, because the man unlocked the driver's-side door and climbed up into the cab, but not before throwing a belligerent look back at the SUV. Jake started up the truck.

Alex craned her neck to try to catch any glimpse of Nakoa in the SUV. She could see five heads inside, but with the reflective glass and pouring rain, it was hard to tell which one was him. The SUV backed up, swinging out of the way of the eighteen-wheeler.

Then the semi pulled out and the SUV whipped around it, returning to the main drag. They drove through town, onto the main road, heading back the way they'd come.

"What in the world?" Sasha wondered aloud. "What the hell do they need an eighteen-wheeler for?"

Alex squinted at the rain-drenched scene. "I have no idea. This is getting weirder and weirder." Her stomach churned at the thought of Dora, lying back there dead on the beach. Anger flashed through her and she bit it back.

She resumed following them at a distance, using parallel streets again. They left the town behind. Then, to her amazement, both vehicles pulled into the parking lot of the Museum of Vertebrate Paleontology. The SUV and semi parked. Wanting to get a closer look, Alex pulled partly down the dirt section that led to the beach and parked amid some trees. She jumped out, and Sasha came with her. The museum sat up on a hill surrounded by trees, and they used them for cover. They crept to the top of the hill and lay down in some tall grass, watching.

The leader emerged from the SUV, then the woman, blond man, and Snake Tattoo, who dragged Nakoa out with him and shoved a gun into the paleontologist's ribs. Jake climbed out of the semi and joined them.

They forced Nakoa toward the side door of the museum, the same employee door where he'd met Alex before. Nakoa fished around in his pocket, Snake Tattoo jabbing him with the pistol, urging him to hurry. Nakoa nervously dropped his key card, and when he bent to retrieve it, the woman, Tatiana, slapped him hard across the face. Alex bristled. Tatiana grabbed his key card and swiped it. He struggled in Snake Tattoo's grasp, vehemently shaking his head no. But Tatiana grabbed his hand and forced it against the biometric scanner.

The leader wrenched open the door, shoving the paleontologist inside. They all marched in after him, the door closing behind.

"What could they want in the museum?" Sasha asked.

Alex considered. "Some of the fossils in there are worth bank. Sue, the tyrannosaur skeleton, sold for over eight million dollars."

Alex glanced around them, seeing only a deserted street and parking lot. She tried to call emergency services again, but once more got the automated message that the network was busy.

"This is crazy. What should we do?" Sasha asked.

Alex chastised herself for not getting a new satellite communicator. The one she'd been using in New Mexico had been destroyed, and she hadn't bothered to replace it because she knew she'd have cell service on this job, even when she was out on the beach. She wasn't expecting a storm to wipe out service.

Alex frowned. "One of us should stay here, make sure they don't move him again. The other can drive around, see if we can find a cop. There's got to be at least one still here, right? Don't they stay around to make stubborn people leave?"

Sasha nodded. "That's a good idea. Which one do you want?"

"I'll stay here and keep an eye out."

"Okay. I'll see if I can find a cop."

Alex handed the Jeep keys to Sasha and watched her friend jog back to the car.

Alex crept closer, keeping to the trees around the museum, trying to see if she could get a glimpse of the men through any of the windows.

She heard the Jeep's motor start up, then watched Sasha drive away.

Alex waited, tense, wondering what to do. She didn't know how long it would take Sasha to find help. She watched the employee entrance where they'd disappeared. The day she herself had gone through that door felt a million years away.

Just then Jake, the man with the shorn head, emerged from the side door and jogged over to the semi. He climbed into the driver's seat and drove the truck around the building toward the back, out of Alex's sight. Keeping to the trees, she followed it from a distance, watching as it backed up slowly to a loading dock. Two large metal sliding doors in the building raised up with a grating noise. Alex ducked down well out of sight as the leader and the woman appeared in the opening. The driver climbed out of the truck and hurried up a ramp to the loading dock. He swung open the back door of the semi.

Alex moved back to a middle spot where she could see both the truck and the side door where Nakoa might appear, and waited. The rain fell cold on her head and back. She checked her phone. It felt like Sasha had been gone a really long time, but it had only been twenty minutes.

She watched while the men started carrying out small bundled objects and stashing them in the semi. Then a forklift appeared, hefting something gigantic wrapped in a moving blanket. The forklift disappeared inside the truck and, after a few moments, backed out, now empty.

She checked her phone again. Sasha had been gone for forty-five minutes. Alex felt hopeful. Maybe that meant she'd found someone.

She watched the thieves continue to load up the truck.

A car's engine brought Alex's attention to the road. Sasha pulled into view. She parked the Jeep in the same hidden place and then emerged. She entered the trees, jogging up the hill at a crouch over to where Alex waited.

"No luck," Sasha told her. "I tried to drive back into town, but a bunch of trees were blown down on the road, and they're blocking the way through. I got out on foot and jogged the rest of the way, but the town's deserted. Didn't see a single person. And even over there, the cell towers weren't putting my call through. I think the emergency systems are completely tied up. When I couldn't get through, I didn't want to leave you for too long. I was worried they would just kill Nakoa."

"I'm worried about that, too."

A gust of wind kicked up, blowing Alex's hair into her eyes.

"What's happening here?" Sasha asked, taking in the building and the semi parked in the back.

"They're robbing the place. They've been loading items into the truck."

Two men appeared with something wrapped in a moving blanket with strips of duct tape keeping the covering in place. But Alex saw bones sticking out of a section of the bottom of the blanket.

"They're certainly not being careful with this stuff," Sasha commented. "That one's going to get scratched up."

Alex knew that the larger mounted skeletons were actually plaster cast replicas just because of the sheer weight of a huge creature like an *Apatosaurus*. But others in the museum had been real, like the *T. rex*, and she was sure these thieves knew the difference. Those fossils would go for a fortune.

Stan, another *T. rex*, sold for $31.8 million in 2020. Hector, a *Deinonychus*, went for $12.4 million in 2022, and Apex, a *Stegosaurus*, sold for $44.6 million in 2024.

As they waited and watched, wind tossed the palms around them, the trunks bending with each gust, fronds tearing free and crashing down in the parking lot. The wind tugged at Alex's hair, strands lashing at her eyes. She fished a ponytail holder out of her pocket and tied her hair back. She could imagine how much the waves must be surging up onto the shore now.

The rain continued pouring down, and it wasn't long before both she and Sasha were completely soaked.

Movement at the employee door drew her gaze in that direction. It opened, the wind catching it and banging it back on its hinges with a loud crack. The blond thief, who'd been holding on to it, was wrenched unexpectedly outward, and he stumbled. He righted himself, gripping his M4 assault rifle, and gestured for someone in the hallway to come out.

Seconds later Nakoa emerged, looking scared. Bruises marked his face, blood seeping from a tear in his upper lip. Alex's jaw muscles tightened. The brutes. The man with the gun shoved him forward, gesturing angrily. He looked to be the youngest of the group, maybe no more than twenty-five, his long blond hair coming loose from its ponytail, looking windblown and chaotic beneath his black skullcap.

Nakoa kept his gaze down. The man marched him toward the SUV. But just then a handheld radio clipped to the man's belt squawked. He lifted it up.

"Chet, where the fuck are you?" demanded the Australian over the radio.

"I'm taking Nakoa out. What do you expect, Garrett?"

"We still need him to get in and out of the lab! We can't just prop the door open, you idiot. You want this thing to start to thaw?" the radio squawked back. "We'll get rid of him later. Can't you follow simple directions?"

Chet rolled his eyes, flipping off the radio. But he marched Nakoa back toward the employee door.

So they still needed Nakoa. That was a good sign. Where had that man intended to take him? Back to the ship? Or to kill him somewhere along the way? Why not just shoot him there in the museum?

Panic gripped Alex's stomach. They didn't have much time. They could decide to shoot Nakoa right there in the museum parking lot.

She eyed the semi, thinking it must be nearly loaded by now. She pulled out her phone and tried 911 again, but still got only an automated message that the emergency system was busy. "Damn."

Sasha tried, too. No luck.

Alex turned to her friend. "I don't like this. I don't see why they won't just kill him when they're done."

Sasha's mouth turned down into a grim slit. "I think you're right."

"I don't think they're planning to leave by air. Not in this weather. They're probably just going to steal the most expensive fossils and then hightail it out of here via their boat."

Sasha nodded. "That's how I'd do it. But they're going to have a small window before waves get too large to manage."

"So they don't have a lot of time."

Alex pulled out her phone and checked the time. She guessed the hurricane would make landfall and turn into a tropical storm in two hours.

They heard static and voices over a radio. Tatiana, on the loading dock, stopped and unclipped a radio from her belt. She spoke into it. "The truck's getting pretty full. We'll need to make a run out to the boat and come back for the final load."

The reply crackled through the radio. "Okay. Do it."

Sasha spoke low to Alex. "Guess that answers our theory that they're going to leave via sea."

"They'll likely keep Nakoa alive until they've secured the last items. That buys us some time."

"What are you thinking?"

"We need leverage. Some kind of bargaining power." She eyed the truck again, then the SUV. "We disable their cars, then head out to the beach and steal their boat."

Sasha raised her eyebrows. "Excuse me?"

"We can use the ship-to-shore radio to call for help."

"And if that's busy, too? Or if we get through and they don't have anyone left to send in the midst of this hurricane?"

"They're using radios to communicate. If we can't raise the Coast Guard, then once we're on board their ship, we move it. Maybe they'll have another handheld radio on board. We get it and say we'll make an exchange. Their boat for Nakoa."

Sasha grimaced. "Ummm . . . what if one of their radios isn't on board? Or what if it is, but it's clipped on to the belt of a man armed with a grenade launcher?"

"We'll just have to take that risk. You think you could drive that kind of cargo ship?"

"I probably could, but . . ."

"You don't like this plan?"

Sasha stared toward the employee door. "It's crazy. They've got guns."

"I know. It's not good." But Alex powered on. "We ask them to drop off Nakoa unharmed at a specific location. Once we see that he's safe and alone, we say we'll radio them back with the ship's location. Only we pick up Nakoa and don't fulfill our end of the bargain."

Sasha winced.

"We arrange it so we never have direct contact with them."

"They've got handguns. And a rifle. And a shotgun. And you saw what that guy could do with a knife."

"Exactly. And they'll kill Nakoa if we don't do anything."

Sasha bit her lip. "Poor Dora."

Alex nodded. She couldn't let her mind dwell on Dora for too long or the pain would overwhelm her. She had to focus.

Sasha continued. "But seriously, what if there *is* a whole army waiting on that ship?"

Alex gave a rueful smile. "There'll probably only be one or two at the most. They'd need all hands on deck to pull off this heist in a timely manner. And they likely won't want to use a lot of men because that'd be a bigger split and a lot more moving parts and things that could go wrong."

"Okay . . ." Sasha said reluctantly. "So what if there is just one guy?"

"We take him out."

"*'Take him out'*?"

"Incapacitate him. Tie him up." After seeing Sasha's doubtful expression, she added, "It's nothing we haven't done before," thinking of the dangerous situation they'd found themselves in in the Canadian Arctic.

"And if there's more than one guy waiting on the ship?"

"We'll cross that bridge when we come to it."

Sasha smiled ruefully. "A solid plan." She paused. "Well, I'm no Jason Bourne, but I'm in," she said at last.

Alex felt a wave of relief wash over her. She didn't want Sasha to be in even more danger, but Alex didn't know how to pilot a cargo ship, even if it was a small one. She imagined the controls would be completely unfamiliar to her.

Beeping brought their attention to the loading dock. The fully laden truck drove away from the building and came to a halt out front, engine idling. The man with the shorn head, Jake, hopped out and jogged back toward the employee entrance, where the blond gunman Chet opened the door for him.

Now was her chance. She wouldn't get a better one.

"I'm going," she told Sasha.

Keeping low, Alex jogged toward the truck, staying in the trees as long as she could. Then, glancing back at the museum and seeing no movement, she raced out and reached the truck. Wrenching open the driver's-side door, she hit the hood release, then slammed the door closed again. She ran around to the hood and lifted it. She had to awkwardly crawl up on a tire to see the engine, but it took only a moment to locate the fuel pump. Out of financial necessity, when she was an undergrad, she'd learned how to repair her car and knew her way around engines.

She pulled out her multitool and used it to pop out the fuse from the fuel pump. She closed the hood.

Then she raced over to the SUV, once more checking the museum exterior. When it remained empty, she tried the handle of the SUV, but it was locked. She pulled out the glass-breaking tool on her multitool, but before she could strike the driver's-side window with it, the employee door thunked open again. She crouched down behind the SUV's grille, daring a look to see if the thieves were approaching.

Tatiana turned to yell at someone in the corridor. Alex had run out of time. She raced back to the cover of the trees. For now, disabling the truck would have to be enough of a delay. They'd have to find a replacement fuse somewhere and install it, either steal it from another suitable engine or break into an automotive supply store.

She and Sasha then slunk through the trees and jogged back to Alex's Jeep. She saw tendrils of steam curling up from the shot-up radiator. Not a lot, but enough to indicate the vehicle could start having problems by the time they returned to the beach.

They piled in and took off. She hated to just leave Nakoa at the museum, but they needed to gain some time if they were going to beat the thieves out to the shore and then move the boat far enough away that they wouldn't spot it. Alex raced through the streets back toward the beach, but when the radiator began to hiss and the temperature gauge pressed into the red, she was forced to let up a bit. She drove on, rain slashing at the window, too much for the wipers to contend with even at full blast. The windshield steamed up, and Alex cranked up the defrost, but it did little to help. She and Sasha wiped at it with their sleeves, trying to keep the view clear.

Torrential rain pooled and streamed along the dirt road, creating muddy rivulets of water. Wind buffeted the car in gusts, rocking it. After what felt like an interminable time, with the radiator hissing and issuing huge plumes of steam, they arrived at the beach.

She didn't want to leave her car where the thieves could again harm it or the turtle eggs, so she pulled into the driveway of one of the nearby evacuated houses. Alex grabbed her day pack from the back seat. It contained a flashlight, her GPS unit, a pair of two-way radios, some extra clothes and food, her water bottle, and her binoculars.

They jogged over to the beach, seeing Dora's body lying out in the downpour, her sightless eyes staring up. A painful lump swelled in Alex's throat, and she fought hard to swallow.

At the edge of the surf, Alex took out her binoculars and studied the deck and bridge of the small cargo ship. She didn't see any movement. But if someone was on board, they might be below. The wheelhouse was largely glassed in, and all she could make out was the reflection of the stormy gray sky.

"Now the pocket trawler makes sense," Sasha said. "They docked it at the hotel's pier to transfer the goods from the truck. They'll need the trawler's crane for that."

"We might have to think of a ruse in case we get close and someone is on board," Alex said.

"Like what?"

Alex saw a twinge of fear in her friend's eyes and felt bad that she'd gotten caught up in this. "A call for help," Alex told her.

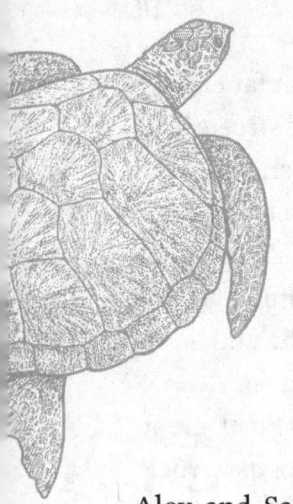

SEVENTEEN

Alex and Sasha jogged to the trawler and climbed in. Sasha did some quick hot-wiring and got the engine going. She pulled the boat away from the pier and wheeled the boat around, and then they were chugging out to the ship on rough water, the boat jolting and bouncing violently. They hit a particularly tall crest of waves, and Alex clung to the railing so she wouldn't go flying off.

Then they were past the breakers, powering toward the ship.

"Hopefully, with this limited visibility, they'll assume we're the thieves returning to the ship," Alex said, shivering a bit in her wet clothes.

Sasha shouted over the engine. "What if they see it's not them and start firing on us?"

"Let's hope that doesn't happen."

"Not a very comforting reply!"

They bounced on the waves, approaching the ship from the starboard side. The cargo ship rolled and rocked on the rough water, the anchor chain pulling tight and then going slack, then yanking tight again. Alex didn't see any movement on the deck, but if someone was on board, they could be in the wheelhouse.

Sasha deftly pulled up alongside the ship, and Alex grabbed the boarding ladder. She started climbing while Sasha tied the pocket trawler to a cleat. With the lurching waves and turbulent wind, she struggled to manage it.

Alex's heart hammered as she ascended. What if armed men *were* on the boat?

She reached the top of the ladder and cautiously scanned the deck. No one waited there. And they might not have heard the sound of the approaching boat over the rain and gusting wind. Or they might have watched their approach via radar and wouldn't have realized it wasn't their compatriots if they didn't have eyes on.

She glanced down the ladder, seeing Sasha at the foot, gazing up at her. She made a motion for Sasha to wait and then crested the ladder. She didn't want to endanger her friend if armed men were waiting. She'd do a quick recon first.

Keeping low, Alex slunk around the crane and foremast, moving toward the wheelhouse. An open toolbox lay on the deck, and Alex fished a wicked-looking pipe wrench out of it.

She gazed up at the wheelhouse, seeing a silhouetted figure up there, standing at the windshield. The figure moved, and a man emerged from the bridge. Alex saw that he wore the same black tactical gear as the other thieves. His right hand rested on the handle of a combat knife holstered on his thigh.

He startled when he saw her, then glowered. "Who the fuck are you?" he boomed, an Irish accent evident.

"Hi," she said, trying to sound innocuous. She dangled the pipe wrench down behind one of her legs, out of sight. "Could you help me?"

"What do you want?" he asked, his hand still down by his knife.

"My friend and I were trying to evacuate the island, but this massive tree fell down on the road and we're trapped. We can't walk out. Could you possibly radio the Coast Guard to come pick us up? We tried our phones, but all the emergency systems are busy."

He frowned, taking in Alex. She knew there was no way he was going to call the Coast Guard out to the boat in the middle of a heist.

He crossed his arms, frowning at her. "I tell you what. You bring that trawler back to shore, right where you left it, and I'll call the Coast Guard and have them pick you up on the beach."

"We can't stay here with you?" she pleaded, trying to sound helpless. "We don't know what to do."

"Clearly," he said condescendingly. "Stealing someone's boat is hardly the answer."

On top of all the other reasons not to like this guy, his pompous attitude wasn't doing him any favors.

"Could you call them real quick, then? Just so we know that you actually got through?" Alex added, making her eyes wide.

The man sighed in exasperation. She knew he'd have to fake a call to the Coast Guard to get them to leave.

As soon as he turned his back to return to the wheelhouse, Alex sprang. She brought the pipe wrench down hard on the back of his head. He staggered, falling, grabbing at his skull. Alex swept one leg out, knocking him to the deck, then fell on top of him, getting an arm around his neck. Blood seeped from the back of his skull as she tightened her grip. He struggled, concussed and disoriented, weakened from the blow. As she held on, he finally went limp, unconscious.

Alex unclipped the radio from his belt and turned up the volume.

She listened for a few minutes, hearing one of the men say that they'd found a replacement fuse for the fuel pump and were securing their fossil load in order to head to the beach in the semi.

The rain picked up even more, cold little needles on Alex's face, and she knew that as bad as it was, the full force of the storm had yet to arrive. For now, though, her wet hair tugged free of the ponytail holder in places, plastering onto her forehead and whipping into her eyes.

She dashed to the top of the ladder and motioned for Sasha to come up. As Sasha emerged, Alex clipped the radio on to her own belt and grabbed the man's feet. "Help me drag him below," she said to Sasha.

Sasha hefted up the man's shoulders, and together they carried him belowdecks. They found some nylon cording and trussed the man up in a small, windowless storage cabinet. They shut him in there, then locked the door. It opened outward, so Alex took the long pipe wrench and threaded it through the door handle so that it lay across the doorjamb. If he woke up and got untied, he'd have a heck of a time getting out.

Worrying there might be more crew members, Alex and Sasha swept through the ship, moving quietly from area to area. It was a small cargo ship, probably requiring a crew of fewer than ten. It sported only one lifeboat, plus the pocket trawler they'd taken from the shore. The amenities were minimal, just a few tiny crew cabins with cramped bunks, a small galley and canteen, and a washroom. They moved through the engine room, finding most of the equipment dating to the 1960s. The cargo hold itself seemed to be the only updated part of the ship—completely refrigerated and looking almost brand-new. They peered inside only to find it empty.

"Why use this old, outdated ship with an empty refrigerated hold?" Sasha wondered aloud.

Then it hit Alex. She snapped her fingers. "The woolly mammoth."

"Excuse me?"

"There's a woolly mammoth mummy at the museum. It's got to be the most valuable object they can steal from there. It's an entire woolly mammoth carcass, complete with tusks, that looks like it died only days ago but actually died thirty-two thousand years ago."

Sasha gave a long, low whistle.

"But the thieves would need a way to keep it preserved and stave off decay," Alex continued. "That's why they had a refrigerated truck waiting for them."

"Did you see them move the mummy?"

Alex shook her head. "And now we know the truck is full."

"Which means they'll *have* to make that second trip they mentioned. That buys us more time."

They went to the bridge after finding no more crew members.

"Okay," Alex said. "Let's raise some help on the ship-to-shore."

Sasha moved to a large panel with several handsets, dials, and buttons. "Here's the communications array." She frowned, examining it. "They've got VHF, MF, LF, even GMDSS, but none of the power indicator lights are on." She threw a few switches and picked up one of the handsets. Clicked the talk button. Nothing. Adjusted the dials. Still no noise. She leaned in, trying more switches, but everything remained dead.

Finally she bent to open a small utility door granting access to the insides of the console. Twisted, melted wires and smashed microchips met their gaze. Sasha's eyes went wide, peering closer. She lifted up a few of the wires, which had clearly been cut.

"The whole thing's shot," she said, straightening up with a frown. "Everything. Someone's totally sabotaged the communications. They even took out the automatic identification system."

Alex gazed over her friend's shoulder, thinking back. "Remember that report we saw on TV at the restaurant? About that cargo vessel that went missing? I wonder if this is the same ship."

Sasha gritted her teeth. "If so, the hijackers must have dumped its load into the sea. People make me so mad."

"You and me both," Alex concurred. "There was an earlier broadcast I heard, about a ship being seized by the government in that same area. It had a refrigerated hold, too. So maybe they stole this one out of necessity." She thought back. "I heard a radio report later about a lone survivor from a cargo ship that got hijacked. He said that the pirate crew had disabled the ship's communications in case he managed to reach the bridge and call for help. Eventually he dove overboard and was picked up later by a passing freighter." She glanced around. "This could be that ship, the *Sunfish*. They could have painted over the ship's original name and hull identification number. That could be why the paint job looks so unprofessional. It was a hasty job to cover up the real name."

Sasha put her hands on her hips, staring down at the communications panel. "The bad news is we're not going to raise anyone on this mess." With a degree of disgust, she shut the utility door. "What now?"

Alex lifted the radio she'd taken off the tied-up man. "We've still got this, and we know what frequency the thieves are using. Unless you've got a better idea, this is our only option if we want to save Nakoa. We have to negotiate with them."

"And say what?"

Alex glanced around. "We stick to the original plan. We move their boat. Tell them they have to deliver Nakoa unharmed, or we won't reveal its location."

"We could even threaten to scuttle it," Sasha agreed.

Alex took a deep breath. "Okay. Here goes." She readied to press the talk button, then thought the better of it. "They could be nearing the beach even now. Can you go lift the anchor? I want to be sure we can get under way immediately while I make this call."

"Of course."

Sasha moved to the helm and started up the engine. The whole ship thrummed with the vibration of it, humming through Alex's boot soles. Sasha moved to the anchor controls, and Alex heard the clanking sound of it retracting.

Sasha revved up the engine and moved them from their current location. The ship felt sluggish in the storm, and Alex could feel the minutes ticking by. But soon they began to cut through the waves, Alex holding on to the communications console for balance. In just the few minutes they'd been on board, the seas had gotten even rougher.

Alex glanced out the port window, seeing that the small trawler was being towed along behind them. She steadied herself and lifted the radio. She turned up the volume slightly and could hear the chatter of the thieves. They were just now pulling out of the museum parking lot.

Alex cut in. "I want to talk to whoever is in charge of your crew."

Silence came over the line as the conversation halted.

"Who the hell is this?" came a familiar Australian voice, the man the others had called Garrett.

Alex's heart hammered. Her mouth had gone dry, and she swallowed hard before going on. "We have taken your pocket trawler and cargo ship and refuse to return them unless you deliver Dr. Kahananui to Honu Beach unharmed."

Garrett didn't respond. Alex had expected him to say something, even to just spew bravado.

Sasha continued to take them along the shoreline, aiming for a point where she could move the ship around a bend and out of sight.

Finally she heard Garrett say, "Go check this out," to one of his crew.

By now Sasha had made good progress along the shore, fighting the waves the whole time. The ship bucked and lurched, Alex feeling a little bit green around the gills. Soon Alex needed her binoculars to make out the beach where her tent had been. She watched for movement there.

Then the large truck pulled up next to the construction equipment and pier by the halted hotel site. Sasha was right. They'd intended to use the pocket trawler and the pier to unload the goods from the truck. Alex saw a lone driver behind the wheel.

Snake Tattoo jumped out, then ran along the pier. Alex could see him lifting a surprised hand to his head. He spoke into the radio. "The trawler's been moved, and both it and the ship are heading out to sea!"

"What the fuck?" Garrett boomed over the radio. "We need to get that first load out of the truck. Like *now*."

"It ain't my fault," Snake Tattoo snapped back. "What do you expect me to do?"

Alex pressed the talk button. "Like I said, you'll get your boat back when you deliver Dr. Kahananui unharmed to the very location where you're currently standing."

Silence.

"Who the hell is this? What are you doing with our ship?" Garrett roared.

"If you have him with you now, just drop him off and leave the area," Alex instructed.

"And if we don't?" he barked back.

"Then say goodbye to your boat."

"We don't have him right now."

"Where is he?"

"At the museum."

"Then bring him back here. I'll be watching and waiting. And don't leave anyone else here except him, or I won't be returning your boat."

"Goddamn motherfucking son of a—" The radio clicked off midway through the Aussie's stream of invectives.

She watched Snake Tattoo get back in the truck, then reverse angrily, the vehicle lurching. He swung onto the dirt road, sending up plumes of mud.

When the truck had disappeared from the construction area parking lot, Alex considered her options. Though a space to hang a large lifeboat was evident, the vessel was no longer there. But there was a smaller one still on board, a Zodiac. A crane stood nearby to lower it into the water. She turned to Sasha. "I'm going to take their Zodiac down the beach from the rendezvous point, get there ahead of them. I want to be sure I can get Nakoa out of there quickly. But I don't trust these guys at all. Can you just keep moving the ship around this bend?" she asked, pointing out the window. A spit of land drew nearer, an excellent place to cause obstruction of sight from Honu Beach. "We can use their taking out the AIS against them."

She dug around in her backpack. "I got these in case I needed to use them with my volunteers," she said, producing the pair of small two-way Motorola radios. She dialed both into a specific frequency. She handed one to Sasha. "We can use these."

"What's the range?"

"I'm not sure. It can be anywhere from one to twenty-five miles depending on the terrain. I think it's about six miles in open water."

"Okay. Good luck. Be safe."

"You, too."

As Sasha temporarily powered down the engine, Alex exited the wheelhouse and used the crane to lower the Zodiac into the water. Then she climbed down and fired up the outboard motor, racing away as she heard the cargo ship's engine revving up again in rpms.

Alex bounced over the choppy waves back toward shore. She didn't want to leave the Zodiac where they could seize it to return to the ship, so she drove it far down beach and pulled it up on shore into a cluster of trees. There she used fallen palm fronds to disguise it even further, hefting the heavy branches over it.

She jogged through the trees then, moving closer to the construction site and the pier. When she was within a few hundred yards of it, she stopped to choose an observation point. She climbed up into the vast, spreading branches of a koa tree and waited, her binoculars at the ready. The leaves offered a small respite from the continuous rain.

She watched as Sasha piloted the ship far up beach, parallel to the shoreline. The wind tore at the sea, creating large crests and troughs, which the ship clearly fought against. At times, the troughs were so low and the waves so high that the ship vanished behind a wall of water, only to surge up again into view. Soon the ship rounded the spit of land and vanished out of sight, the pocket trawler whipping around chaotically behind it.

Alex moved to a more comfortable perch and continued to wait.

A painful lump swelled in her throat at the sight of Dora's lifeless body, still lying there on the beach in the rain.

She tried to still her breathing and the nervous roiling in her stomach. This was a long shot. She had serious doubts the thieves would comply with her demands. But she had to try. She wondered what was taking them so long. Probably devising some plan to keep Nakoa and take out whoever had stolen their boat.

About twenty minutes later, movement in the trees on the far side of where Dora's body lay drew Alex's attention. She spotted Snake Tattoo and Tatiana—him wielding an M4, and her, a combat shotgun—moving stealthily among the trunks, approaching the beach, obviously trying to get the drop on Alex. She hadn't heard or seen a vehicle pull up, and none was in sight.

When the pair didn't spot anyone, they moved more boldly, emerging into the open and scanning the beach. Alex waited. The woman signaled for the man to sweep the trees just down beach while she covered the area where Alex's tent had been. He did so, then returned to the woman. Neither spotted Alex in her hiding place. They were definitely alone and hadn't brought Nakoa. Apparently they still needed him, probably hoping to keep him as leverage to force her to reveal where the ship was.

Tatiana moved to Alex's destroyed Zodiac, noting the multitude of holes the gillnet poacher had pierced in it. "This thing's toast," she heard her say. The woman had to shout above the wind. "Goddamn it!"

Snake Tattoo joined her. "We couldn't use it to haul our stuff anyway."

Snake Tattoo walked to the water's edge and stared out at the sea, the rough surf crashing up around his boots. He cursed, stepping back. "It's totally out of sight now," Alex heard him yell. "What the fuck!"

The pair began to hunt around, stepping over Dora's body with disinterest and storming through the grassy parking area, peering inside Dora's and Nakoa's cars. The woman kicked Dora's station wagon in frustration. Alex was glad she'd parked the Jeep somewhere else.

"What do we do now?" she heard Snake Tattoo ask.

Tatiana turned into the wind, her tight auburn braid swinging. They discussed something, but Alex couldn't hear anything from so far away over the wind. The man gesticulated angrily, pointing out to sea, and the woman shook her head. Finally they returned the way they'd come, moving through the trees and then out of sight.

Alex's radio crackled and Tatiana's voice came through. "No one's here."

The Australian's voice came booming over the static. "Okay, whoever this is, you need to bring our boat back now."

Alex took a deep breath and pressed the push-to-talk button. "Not until you return Dr. Kahananui unharmed."

"I tell you what," he growled. "You bring back our ship, or I'll kill him on the spot."

Alex gripped the radio, unsure of her next move. She considered the options, then lifted her radio. "The way I see it, you need your ship or you're going nowhere with your haul."

A long silence followed, and Alex bit her lip. Had she made the wrong choice? But the man never came back on. Nervousness churned in Alex's stomach. She worried she'd just signed Nakoa's death warrant. She waited in the tree, gripping the bark, her unease mounting with every passing moment.

And they knew she was on this channel, so it wasn't like they'd discuss their plans with her listening in. She switched through a number of channels, hoping to hear their chatter, but was met with only static.

She thought about what she'd do in their position. They must still need Nakoa to get through the retinal and palm scanners. They could have cut his hand off to use the palm scanner, but if they'd cut his eye out for the retinal one, eventually it would cloud over and be useless. She looked out at the surging waves growing more and more chaotic by the hour. Time was running out fast for them to get out of here by ship.

Then a chilling thought hit her. What if they'd already killed Nakoa and had nothing to bargain with? Maybe that's why they hadn't brought him to the rendezvous point. They might even now be planning to steal another boat and take it out in the direction that Sasha had sailed. Then they'd just board the boat by force.

Maybe they'd already found a ship for pursuit. They could be catching up to Sasha soon. Alex had to do something.

EIGHTEEN

Alex gritted her teeth, determination stealing over her. She had to find out if Nakoa was alive, one way or another, and if the gunmen were still at the museum or had found another boat. She swept the trees with her binoculars for any sign of the woman or Snake Tattoo but didn't see anyone.

She dropped down from the tree, stowing her binoculars back in her pack. Pulling out her two-way radio, she hoped Sasha was still in range. She was.

"They didn't bring Nakoa," Alex told her.

"What happened?"

Alex described them arriving on foot, searching for her in the trees, then leaving again. "I'm worried they may have already killed him. I have to find out. And I'm worried they might steal another boat and seek out their cargo ship. Can you continue to move it?"

"You got it," Sasha said.

"I'm going to go take a look back at the museum."

"Be careful. Keep me posted."

Alex clicked off. Quickly she jogged to where she'd hidden the Jeep. She prayed it would still make the trip back to the museum. The radiator had had time to cool off. She started up the engine and swung onto the dirt road leading away from the beach and toward the museum. She parked where she had before, far back on the road, and raced up the hill through the trees to her vantage point by the museum.

At first she didn't see anyone. The thieves had propped open the employee door with a massive four-foot crystal-encrusted geode.

To Alex's immense relief, she spotted Nakoa standing in the corridor just outside the lab. A man stood beside him, an M4 rifle slung over one shoulder. But strangely, he was wearing a hazmat suit, kitted out from head to foot, the yellow of it vivid in the overhead corridor lights. Nakoa still wore the clothes he'd been abducted in: a pair of jeans and a button-down shirt.

Nakoa shifted nervously from foot to foot, biting his fingernails and staring in the direction of the lab window. Alex couldn't see what was going on.

The thief shoved him then, driving him outside, and Alex saw now through the window in his face mask that it was the blond thief, Chet. Alex clenched her teeth when she took in the state of Nakoa. One eye was completely swollen shut, his lip was split open and bleeding in a second location, and he was cradling one arm.

Chet placed a hand on the paleontologist's upper back and forced him outside. Nakoa was talking, pleading, but Alex couldn't quite make out his words. She crept closer until she could hear him.

"Please don't do this. I'm begging you," he said to Chet. "You don't have to do this. It's not worth a lousy paycheck. You can stop this right now."

"Shut up," Chet ordered, pushing harder on the paleontologist's back. "Just keep walking. To the edge of the lot."

Alex didn't like this. Chet stole a look back toward the hallway. Alex saw movement there, more of the thieves emerging from the lab, all of them dressed in hazmat suits.

What in the world? Alex thought.

Chet pushed Nakoa in her direction, the paleontologist still pleading with him. "Don't you see what could happen? You've got to stop this! He's crazy! You don't have to follow his orders!"

"He's not crazy," Chet said. "He's greedy. There's a difference," but his voice was softer now. He kept stealing worried glances back toward the others. When they reached the edge of the lot, he handed Nakoa his radio. "Take this," he said suddenly, shoving it into the paleontologist's hand. "Get in touch with that person trying to save you."

Alex startled. Chet looked back over his shoulder, his expression scared in the small window that revealed his face.

"What?" Nakoa said, but he took the radio. "What are you doing?"

"I didn't know this was the plan. I thought we were stealing some fossils. I had no idea that—"

The cacophonous crack of a handgun made Alex jump. She pressed flat behind a tree trunk. Daring a look out, she saw the leader Garrett framed in the doorway, holding up his sidearm. Chet crumpled, blood blossoming through a hole in his hazmat suit. He'd been shot in the neck. Another round rang out, and Nakoa cried out, falling down. Alex emerged from the trees, racing to where he lay. The leader fired off another shot, and Alex felt splinters from a palm trunk hit her in the cheek. She grabbed Nakoa's arms and dragged him toward the tree line as another shot went off. She felt something sting her deltoid muscle and glanced down to see red seeping through her shirt.

She got him into the shelter of the trees just as Garrett marched out into the parking lot. Alex stared down, seeing that Nakoa had been hit in the right side of his lower torso. Blood wept through his shirt there. "Can you run?" she asked him.

He grimaced. "I don't think I have a choice."

"Then let's go!" She grabbed him under the arm, and he leaned on her as they ran down the embankment. Alex heard another shot and saw a clod of dirt explode just to their left. She steered Nakoa to the right, then to the left, veering back and forth. Another shot rang out, and Alex felt a weird tug on her leg. She looked down to see a bullet had gone through the hem of her jeans. Fear erupted inside her like fire. How many shots did that make? What kind of gun did he have?

They reached the bottom of the hill, now out of sight. Nakoa stopped running, grabbing her shoulder for support. He gasped, blood pouring out of his side.

"We can't stop yet," she urged him, pulling him toward the Jeep. They reached it, and she wheeled him around to the passenger side. She hefted him in, feeling pain erupt in her shoulder as she did so. Then she ran around to the driver's side and jumped in, firing up the car.

Steam issued from the hood almost immediately, but Alex stomped on the gas. They tore down the road. She couldn't see the museum now because of the embankment, didn't know if even now Garrett was standing at the edge, ready to fire down on them. She sped away, making sharp turns, heading toward the town.

But as she approached the turnoff, she saw what Sasha had described. Three huge trees had toppled over in the high winds and now sprawled across the road. And it was the only access to the town.

She whipped the car around, speeding back past the museum. Their only hope for shelter now were the handful of houses along the beach.

The loud pattering of rain on the hood of the car let Alex know that the storm was fast approaching. The windshield wipers couldn't keep up with it, and rain washed in torrents across the street, carrying with it palm fronds, mud, small tree branches, and other debris.

The radiator started to tick loudly, steam now pouring out in such profusion that it obstructed Alex's vision. Nakoa moaned in the seat beside her, leaning over and gripping his side. "Where exactly are you hit?" she asked.

He lifted his shirt and cried out as the material dragged against his wound. "Looks like in my oblique."

"Is there an exit wound?"

He craned his body around, suddenly screaming in pain. Beads of sweat sprang up on his forehead. "I can't tell. Oh god."

"That's okay, that's okay," she assured him as she took another turn. The radiator started to clank violently, the Jeep's temperature gauge pushing all the way into the red. Alex switched the car's heater on to full blast, hoping to draw some heat away from the radiator. It worked for a few minutes, but then the Jeep gave a loud gasp and the engine just died.

She reached into the back, grabbing her beach towel, and pressed it tightly to his side.

Nakoa groaned. "They'll catch up to us for sure now."

Alex thought a moment. "I don't think they'll bother. They don't know where we are, and their attention will be focused on getting their haul out safely. I think we're good." But she thought of Sasha and called her on the two-way radio.

"Alex! You okay?"

"Yes, for now. I've got Nakoa. But there's a good chance they're going to steal a boat and try to overtake you. So be on the lookout."

"My head's already on a swivel, believe me."

"That guy still unconscious?"

"So far. But I'm listening for when he starts banging around in that closet."

"Be careful and keep me posted."

"You, too."

They signed off, and Alex looked out at the downpour. "We just need to find a place to ride out the storm."

Nakoa reached out and gripped her arm, so tightly she sucked in a breath.

"No," he gasped. "We can't let them leave. Everyone will die if they do."

NINETEEN

"Why?" Alex asked Nakoa. "What do you mean?"

The paleontologist gripped her arm harder. "They're not just after the fossils to sell. They're after a pathogen."

Her eyebrows shot up. The hazmat suits. "What?"

He struggled to speak. "The mammoth. We just discovered that she might have died from an ancient virus. We extracted it from her body, and it was still viable." He winced, groaning. "Modern humans would have no defense against it."

Alex leaned back in her seat, shocked. She knew that scientists had been successful in resurrecting Ice Age viruses in recent years. One was *Pandoravirus yedoma,* a 48,500-year-old virus that was revitalized from the permafrost and found to still be infectious.

"And this virus could infect humans?" she asked.

He nodded. "We wondered if it could be zoonotic. We didn't know it was there at first. But we always wore masks and gloves and suited up whenever we ran tests, just so there wouldn't be any cross-contamination from our own DNA." He winced, the words coming with difficulty. "But in the end, this was lucky, because it kept us from contracting the virus ourselves. Then later when I thought about it, my friend Caleb said people on his team were getting sick while on the dig. It could have been this ancient virus." He looked at her pleadingly. "But you must believe I never willingly let them into the lab! They physically forced my hand onto the biometric scanner and shoved my face to it so it could read my retina. The woman . . . forced my eyelid open." Alex could see where it was bruised there, that eye not quite as swollen as his other, where he'd clearly been punched.

"What are they planning to do with it?"

He coughed, gritting his teeth as she continued to press the towel tightly to his wound. The bleeding had slowed a little bit, she saw with relief.

"I knew they were planning to kill me because they talked freely in front of me. From what I gathered, they were hired by the CEO of some big pharma company." He squeezed his eyes shut in pain. "Apparently they've been searching for a zombie virus just like this one to resurrect and spread."

Zombie virus. Alex had heard the term before. It was what researchers called a virus that had gone dormant through environmental conditions but was able to be resurrected and become infectious again.

"They want to genetically modify it to be worse," Nakoa went on. "Then they can come up with a vaccine and make billions. They had an inside man—some zoologist they bought off. He was at the dig site with Caleb. Apparently when some of the team and the miners started getting sick, this zoologist tested the mammoth carcass for the presence of a virus and found one. The guy stayed well away from the others.

"He alerted the CEO, but by the time they organized a recovery effort and hired these mercenaries, the mammoth had been shipped here. Then they heard about the discovery of the baby mammoth and sent the mercenaries to steal it. Only something happened. I'm not sure what. But this CEO never got the baby. So she wanted them to go after the mother." He swallowed hard, closing his eyes. "They . . . burned the bodies because some of the team had contracted the contagion. They didn't want anyone else to have samples of the virus that they could develop a vaccine for."

Alex shook her head in disbelief. "This is crazy."

Recent history had shown that pharma companies could make a killing off developing vaccines and antiviral treatments. And if they were unscrupulous and obtained some rare pathogen, something only they had access to . . .

Alex hesitated. She thought of just hiding out with Nakoa. He was safe now. But her heart felt sick at the thought of how they'd murdered Dora, snuffing out her life like a mere afterthought. She didn't want them to leave the island, to never pay for what they'd done. And now, if Nakoa was right, and she had no reason to think he wasn't, the thieves could get off the island and deliver a pathogen to the world, creating a deadly pandemic.

She gritted her teeth. With this storm raging and police and emergency crews tied up, and with only her and Nakoa knowing the true aim of the thieves, the possibility of their escape was too great. Nakoa was too injured to go on. It was up to Alex. If she didn't act, the consequences could be catastrophic.

She turned to Nakoa. "We need another car."

"There's mine," he groaned. "But it got shot up just as much as this one."

They also needed a hospital. But the nearest one was in Hilo, and no medevac chopper would be flying in this weather, even if they could raise one.

Nakoa leaned over in his seat, writhing in pain. Alex eyed the nearby houses, looking for another car. All those hours of working on her car through her undergrad and grad school days could pay off. She'd replaced the transmission, the fuel injectors, even welded in new floor pans and rocker panels on that car. Older cars were easy to work on. Everything was manual—no need to use a diagnostic computer on the car, just a set of wrenches and screwdrivers.

So now she just needed to find an older car. Then she spotted it: a tarp covering a vehicle parked on the side of someone's driveway.

"Hang tight," she told Nakoa, and jumped out of the Jeep. She ran up to the house, banging on the door. She didn't expect anyone to be home, but she wanted to be sure she wasn't about to steal anyone's mode of evacuation. No answer came. Then Alex spotted a note taped to the window beside the door: *Gone to Sue's to ride out the storm. Meet us there.* Relief swept through Alex. She jogged back to the Jeep, rummaged through her small toolkit, and grabbed the screwdriver she'd been using to build the thermocouples. Then she lifted the tarp off the car. It was a green 1976 Triumph TR6. Perfect. This trick would only work on an older car. She tried the door, finding it blissfully unlocked. Yay for small towns.

Then she slid into the driver's seat and jammed the screwdriver into the ignition. She rotated the screwdriver, and the car started right up. She'd learned the trick once when she'd lost her keys while hiking in Yosemite. She'd come back to her car, unable to leave, but she'd had her multitool with her and used it to start the ignition.

Unfortunately, the trick ruined the ignition, so Alex made note of the house's address. She'd return the car when all this was over, give them money to fix the ignition, and just hope they didn't press charges.

She hurried back to the Jeep, opening the passenger-side door. Nakoa spilled out, and Alex caught him, struggling to keep hold of him. "I think I'm dying," he told her, gripping her shoulder. It was where she'd been hit, and she cried out herself, shocked at the sudden pain. In her desperation for a new car, she'd blocked out the wound.

Now she peeled her shirt collar back and looked at her shoulder. A bullet had grazed her deltoid, leaving a furrow about two inches long and a quarter of an inch deep. It stung like a mother.

She helped Nakoa over to the TR6 and opened the passenger-side door, readying to ease him in there. But first she propped him up against the side of the car.

"I'm going to look at your wound," she told him.

"No!" he cried. "I can't do it. I can't stand the pain."

"It'll just be for a second," she assured him. She lifted the material of his shirt up, and he cried out, squeezing his eyes shut. The bullet had entered his oblique muscle. "I don't think it would have hit any organs," she assured him.

The wind tore at her hair, trees tossing violently around them, wood creaking, palm fronds cascading down. The storm was getting worse by the second.

She bent down to look at his back. But the bullet hadn't exited. Damn it. That wasn't good. She couldn't drive him to a hospital with the trees down, blocking the road out to the main drag. And she couldn't keep moving him around. She needed to treat his wound and stash him somewhere, then radio Sasha with his location so they could get a medevac chopper out there as soon as the storm cleared. But she didn't know if he'd make it that long, and doubtless other people would be in need of such a rescue. But all she could do for now was stop the bleeding and get him somewhere where he'd be comfortable.

Just then a tree crashed down behind them, barely missing the TR6.

"We can't stay out here. But we can't keep moving you around. Should we break into one of these houses?" she asked.

"We can go to my cousin's house. It's not too far, just a little more down this road. I've got a key, and he's a nurse. I know he's got some medical supplies there."

She eased him into the car, then ran back to her Jeep and retrieved the container of turtle eggs. She jogged back to the driver's side of the Triumph. Once they pulled out in the new car, Nakoa directed her down the pitted road, each bump making him cry out in pain. Alex's shoulder throbbed where it had been grazed.

But then they reached the house. She helped Nakoa inside and laid him down on a bed. She worried Sasha might already be out of range by now, so she pulled the two-way radio out of her pack, making sure it was still on her and Sasha's channel. "Sasha."

"I'm here," came the response.

Relief washed over her. "Nakoa's not doing so well. He's been shot. We need a medevac. I've stashed him at his cousin's house." She gave Sasha the address. "When you reach help, can you send a helicopter to this location?"

"Of course."

"Where are you now?" Alex asked.

"About four miles away from where you left me. I've had to stick inland. Trying to find a place to stash this boat and get help. The waves are really getting rough. A few times they've swamped the deck."

"You be careful. I'll check back in when I get him settled."

"Okay."

They signed off, and Alex went in search of a first aid kit. Tree branches scratched against the windows, the howling wind rattling the glass panes.

Nakoa was right about his cousin—in the bathroom she found supplies to clean and suture the wound. She did her best, pulling on years of first aid training she'd taken after she'd started working in remote places.

Then she tended to her own wounds, cleaning a few cuts and scrapes and examining her deltoid where the bullet had grazed it. Thankfully the furrow wasn't that deep. It wouldn't need stitches. She cleaned it and bandaged it.

She raided the kitchen next, bringing food and bottles of water over to the bedside table. She placed them down for Nakoa. When he was settled, Alex tried to reach Sasha on the radio again but got only static. "Damn."

"What is it?"

"She must be out of range now."

Alex weighed her options. She couldn't let the thieves leave with the mammoth. But what would they do, now that they didn't have a boat to get off the island? And they'd need a big one to accommodate the mummy.

She thought about where the nearest boats would be. It would have to be in Ānuenue, at the rental place where she'd gotten her scuba and snorkeling gear. It also rented boats, including one she remembered would definitely be big enough. But the thieves would have to drive the truck down there, and the road was blocked.

They could still steal a smaller boat somewhere, drive around the island, and come back with a larger one. But she saw no boats at the few houses she'd passed, and the scrawny poacher had destroyed her Zodiac. They might be able to find the one she'd stolen from their cargo ship if they looked hard enough. She'd covered it with palm fronds, but the wind may well have blown them off.

"Did they mention any kind of a backup plan after we took their boat?"

Nakoa shook his head. "Not that I heard. The leader was furious, though." He managed to crack a small smile.

"Okay. Do you think you'll be okay here for a little bit? I'm going to check on a Zodiac I have stashed."

He bit his lip but nodded. As she started to get up, he gripped her hand. "Alex?" he asked.

"Yes?"

"I'm scared."

She squeezed his hand reassuringly.

"Not just for myself," Nakoa said, "though this is no picnic. We've got to stop them."

"I'll do my best." She released his hand and stood up.

Not knowing when she'd have the chance to eat again, she grabbed a couple of energy bars from his cousin's cabinet and gulped one down, pocketing another two.

Returning to the Triumph, she grabbed the container of turtle eggs and brought them inside the house, hoping they'd be safer there. Then she climbed into the TR6 and headed back on the dirt road. When she reached the beach where she'd stashed the Zodiac, her heart sank. Water had surged ashore, inundating that part of the beach. The area where she'd stashed the launch craft was completely underwater now, and the boat was nowhere in sight. It must have washed out to sea. Or maybe the thieves had found it.

And she noticed, with a stab of grief, that Dora's body was gone, too, taken by the sea.

Alex ran back to the car and drove on toward the museum, wanting to see if they were still there. The drive was harrowing, with trees swaying dangerously overhead. Any second she expected another to come crashing down, either blocking her way or crushing the car. Huge mud puddles had formed on the dirt road, and in some places she splashed through a foot of standing water. But finally she arrived. She parked the car again slightly down the street, out of sight.

Then she climbed out, grabbing her pack in case she needed any supplies, and headed for the embankment by the museum. After running up the hill, she took up a position in the cluster of trees. To her relief, she saw that both the SUV and the truck were still parked in the lot.

The dead thief still lay where he'd been shot, a bloody hole in the neck of his hazmat suit. Blood ran in red rivulets down the parking lot, mixing with the rain. At first she saw no movement inside the museum, though the door was still propped open.

Then the leader appeared, carrying a silver briefcase with a biohazard insignia on it. He still wore his hazmat suit. Walking to the back of the SUV, he placed the case down and started shucking off the suit. She could see he'd sweated inside it, and he took a minute to retie his long black hair in a fresh ponytail, perspiration dripping down his face.

Moments later the other three thieves appeared, still wearing their hazmat suits. They, too, stripped them off at the back of the SUV, where Garrett stowed them away in a large lockbox.

Garrett's phone rang. He glanced down at the screen and frowned in distaste. "Goddamn it!" He angrily punched the button to answer it and put it on speaker. "What is it, Ms. Cromwell? We're busy."

"Why haven't you reported in?" came a woman's voice. She spoke with an English accent. "You should have secured the mammoth by now on the ship. What's going on?"

"Change of plans. We had to use the sample case instead of getting the entire carcass."

"What do you mean 'change of plans'? What the hell happened?"

Garrett grimaced. "We . . . uh . . . lost access to the boat."

"You *what*?" the woman shouted.

"But we got samples for you."

"That sample case was only to be used in the most extreme circumstances," she bellowed.

He wiped several strands of rain-soaked hair out of his eyes. "Believe me, it's extreme. We're in the middle of a damn hurricane here."

"Which we planned *on purpose*. You knew you were going to land in the middle of that storm."

"There have been extenuating circumstances," Garrett told her.

"This is going to result in a cut of pay. I warned you."

"We can talk about *that* when we see you. This job is a lot trickier than you let on. We had no other choice but to only take samples."

"I want no other part of that mammoth remaining, then. None. Only the samples you take with you. You understand me?"

"We've already planned for that. We've got it all under control," Garrett assured her, gritting his teeth impatiently.

"It doesn't sound like you have *anything* under control," she snapped.

"I have to go," Garrett told her, and stabbed at the button to end the call. Then he turned to Snake Tattoo. "Let's torch the place."

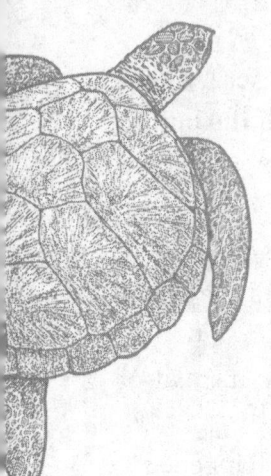

TWENTY

Alex's mouth dropped open as she struggled to comprehend his words. They were going to burn down the museum?

Clearly they'd given up on moving the entire mammoth mummy. She thought of the biohazard case Garrett had been carrying. They must have retrieved samples that carried the virus, which a lab would be able to replicate. And now they were going to burn down the museum and destroy the remains of the mammoth so that no one else would have access to the pathogen and be able to develop a cure.

The thieves disappeared back into the museum, presumably to set the fire. Alex knew she had only minutes. She needed to somehow get a sample of the mammoth herself before it was destroyed or stop them from torching the place.

She dragged Chet's body into the trees, stashing it in a patch of tall grass. She took in the state of his hazmat suit. It looked new, pristine, except for the hole where the bullet had entered his neck. She pulled off the hood and neck and fished some duct tape out of her pack. Wincing at the coagulating blood around the hole, she did her best to wipe it off in the grass. Then she pulled off several strips of tape and patched the hole. Struggling with the man's deadweight, she stripped off the rest of his suit. Checking the door, she saw that all four thieves were still inside. She moved back out of sight, ducking behind several trunks, and shimmied into the suit, securing the sleeves and pants with duct tape around her wrists and ankles.

The suit instantly weighed her down, muggy and hot, smelling of plastic and the sharp copper scent of blood. She grimaced, then returned to her hidden post closer to the museum, stashing her day pack behind a tree.

She couldn't enter through the employee door. She'd have to go in a different way—perhaps through the loading dock. Hoping they left it open, she lumbered awkwardly in the suit through the trees, rounding the museum. There, to her relief, she saw the metal doors rolled up, revealing the inside of the museum. She scanned this section of the back lot and, not seeing anyone else, started toward the dock.

She hated the limited sight in the hood but knew she had no choice, and just hoped no one spotted her. She reached the dock and hurried as fast as she could up the cement stairs, then pressed against the exterior wall there. She darted a look inside the museum, fighting with the hazmat hood, which repeatedly shifted down to cover her eyes. She adjusted it, then saw a utilitarian corridor beyond the roll-up door. Empty.

She hoped the thieves were elsewhere in the building, wrapping up their preparations to burn it down. Straining to hear their movement, she couldn't make out anything inside the hood except her own breathing and heartbeat thrumming in her ears. Beyond an open loading bay lay a corridor and a series of doors. The lab would be down that hall and around a corner to the left. If the thieves stayed out of sight in that one corridor by the lab, she could make her way farther inside.

She waited, sneaking a peek every few seconds, and when she still didn't see any movement, she ducked inside and ran to the first open door. She hurried inside, finding an employee break room with tables, chairs, and coffee and vending machines. She pressed against the inside wall, then dared another look back into the corridor. Empty.

She darted out and ran to the next open door, a small administrative office with stacks of papers on the desk. A desktop computer drew her attention, and she hurried to it, wondering if the internet was still up. Maybe she could get help that way. She moved farther inside the office, leaving the door propped open in case the thieves noticed it being closed. She leaned over and jostled the mouse to wake up the computer. Nothing. Then she noticed the light was out on the surge protector the computer was plugged into. She toggled it. Again, nothing. The power was out.

As she straightened back up, she drew up short.

Plastic explosives were taped to the desk and bookshelves behind her. C-4 from the looks of it, all kitted out with detonators. She didn't see any timers—it would be a remote detonation then. But Alex had no idea how to disarm such a setup and worried any attempt would set off the explosives immediately. And now she truly wondered how much time she had left.

Returning to the door, she dared a look into the corridor and then exited the office, moving to the next room. This was a side room off the lab, a supply room full of cleaning supplies, extra microscopes, lab coats, masks, and gloves. C-4 had been wired to the shelves here, too, a detonator buried in the thick beige putty.

Sweat trickled down her neck and back. She wanted to move on to the lab, figure out some way to secure a sample, but she knew she didn't have the time. They could be outside even now, readying to detonate the explosives.

If Alex was going to stop them, she couldn't die now, here in the museum. She hated it, but she had to get out of there. She turned and lumbered out of the room, down the corridor, across the loading bay, and into the parking lot just as an earsplitting explosion and concussion wave hit her. The force of the blast lifted her off her feet, flinging her ten feet forward, where she skidded across the asphalt, tearing the biohazard suit. Her elbow came down hard on the pavement, sending a sharp spear of pain shooting up to her wounded shoulder. Her ears rang, head throbbing.

Then a wave of heat hit her, and she craned her neck back to see the museum completely engulfed in a cloud of acrid black smoke, flames licking up from the ground. Gasping for air, she ripped off the hood, heat sweeping over her body.

The fire roared, then a series of smaller, secondary explosions rocked the air, Alex guessed from all the cleaning supplies and other flammable materials going up with the fire. The high winds caught the fire, curling it up into the sky.

She crawled back on her heels and elbows, staring up at the destruction. Black smoke billowed up into the sky, mixing with the rain, bringing down ash and pieces of building material. Larger chunks started to cascade down, and Alex backed away farther, still reeling from the power of the explosion.

She hoped the thieves wouldn't spot her, there in the open in the ridiculously bright yellow hazmat suit. Eyes tearing from the heat and smoke, she scanned the parking lot. For a second her heart crawled up into her throat. Both the truck and SUV were gone.

But then as her ears began to hear better again, she could make out the idling sound of the truck's engine nearby. It must be on the other side of the building.

She managed to get to her feet, her head spinning, then staggered in the direction of the engine sound. Without the safety of the building as cover, she opted to angle back into the trees. As the front portion of the parking lot came into view, she saw with relief that both the truck and SUV were still there. The thieves had pulled them away to a safe distance and now stood beside the vehicles.

Garrett was moving the silver metal biohazard case to the back seat of the SUV. He leaned in, and she watched him fasten the seat belt around it.

Since none of them wore a hazmat suit any longer, Alex followed their lead and stripped out of hers, glad to be free of the suffocating material and obvious bright color. She stashed it in the tall grass behind a tree trunk and retrieved her day pack.

For several minutes, the group stared at the burning building, obviously making sure the lab was sufficiently destroyed.

Finally Garrett turned away. "Let's go." He started toward the SUV.

But the hulking thief with the closely shorn hair didn't move. He pointed at the body of their fallen comrade, lying crumpled near the trees. "What about Chet?" he demanded. "We just going to leave his body there?"

"What the hell else do you want to do with it, Jake? Carry it around with us?" Garrett snapped.

"Now wait just a goddamn minute," Jake shot back. "This is getting worse and worse. I don't see why you had to kill that cargo ship crew. We could have let them just take the lifeboat. And why did Mitchell have to kill that woman on the beach? And then you kill Chet? You know how many jobs he and I have pulled off together?"

"He'd gone soft," sneered Garrett.

"Soft! You never said a damn thing about murdering anyone, let alone releasing some fucking plague."

"*We're* not going to be the ones releasing a plague," Garrett snapped impatiently.

"Yeah, but *someone* will. You told us we were hired to rob a museum, not cause another pandemic."

Garrett marched up to Jake and jabbed an angry finger in his chest. "You listen here, you fucking meathead. You'll get your cash from this heist. Now shut up and find us another way off this goddamn island before we're all blown away by this fucking hurricane!"

Jake held up his hands. "I won't be a party to this. I'm here for the fossils, and I'll get my take from that."

"We're not taking that truck," boomed Garrett.

"What the hell are you on about now?" shot back Jake.

"We're leaving the damn truck! We don't have time to drive that lumbering thing around to find another boat." Garrett stared up at the rain, which was hammering down, plastering his long black hair to his scalp and neck. "And soon these streets are going to be flooded with storm surge. You really want to be weighed down by that thing?"

Tatiana joined Jake by his side and gestured at the SUV. "Oh, and you think we'll have a better chance in a lightweight car like that?"

"It's more maneuverable," Garrett snapped.

Tatiana crossed her arms. "I'm with Jake. We take the truck. I'm not leaving that behind. You know how much that load is worth? The *T. rex* skeleton alone is worth millions. If we get additional money from some evil pharma company, so be it. But we're still keeping the truck."

She turned then to the man with the snake tattoo, who Alex now knew was named Mitchell. He had been standing to one side, watching the argument.

"Well? Whose side are you on?" she demanded.

"My own," he growled. "Whichever way makes me more money. If I have to see that this plague thing makes it safely into the hands of our client, then so be it."

Jake glared at them all. "You're all such unbelievable assholes!"

"Look," yelled Garrett, "I don't care who does what. Let's just get the hell out of here and find another boat."

For a moment everyone stared angrily at one another. Then Tatiana turned to Garrett. "When I did my original recon of the island, I noticed a boat rental place in that town down the street."

Garrett made an exaggerated sweeping gesture toward her. "Thank you! See? That's helpful. Let's go."

"But we're taking the goddamn truck," hissed Jake.

"It's your funeral," snapped Garrett. "I'm taking the SUV."

They started making their way toward the vehicles, and then Tatiana paused and turned to stare at Chet's body. "Wasn't he wearing a hazmat suit?" she asked the others.

Jake followed her gaze. "Yeah . . . I think he must have been."

"And wasn't he in the parking lot and not in the trees?" she added.

Alex's stomach froze and suddenly she felt sick.

Garrett wheeled on his comrades. "Maybe he was, maybe he'd already taken it off! Maybe he continued to crawl away after he'd been shot. He's dead now, and who the fuck cares! We need to go now! This storm's getting worse by the minute!"

Just then a violent gust of wind hit the stand of trees off to the thieves' left. One tree teetered and bent, then came crashing down into the parking lot. They all flinched, turning in surprise.

But then Tatiana stared back at Chet's body. "Didn't you notice if he was wearing one?" she pressed.

"All I noticed was that the fucker was betraying us," Garrett snapped. "Now are we going, or are we going to just stand here like idiots until we get crushed by a tree?"

Alex watched while Jake and Tatiana reluctantly turned and piled into the cab of the truck. Mitchell looked back and forth between the SUV and the semi, then finally jogged toward the truck. He jumped up into the passenger side of the cab. "I think you're right about the weight of this thing helping us plow through any rising waters," she heard him say as he climbed in.

"Always out for your own skin," Tatiana quipped as he shut the door.

Garrett climbed into the SUV and pulled out, the truck following close behind. This was Alex's chance. Before they could pull far enough away that they'd be able to see her in the truck's side mirrors, Alex ran toward the back of the semi. She grabbed one of the handles beside the rear double doors and swung herself up on the bumper.

She clung there awkwardly, wondering what in the hell she was going to do next. She struggled to maintain a grip on the cold metal of the door handle, and her toes were in danger of sliding off the rain-slicked bumper. The truck went over a speed bump and then another, and one of her feet slipped free. She scrambled to get it back in place, her knuckles going white with the effort of clinging to the truck. Her grazed shoulder burned with pain.

They trundled down the street. All the while Alex hoped that the SUV wouldn't for some reason pull over and let the truck pass. Garrett would spot her in a second.

They motored toward town, Alex's arms starting to ache, then suddenly braked so hard she jerked forward, banging her head and elbow on the back of the truck. The resulting opposite tug of inertia almost threw her off completely, but she managed to hold on.

She heard the truck doors opening and then the SUV's.

"What the hell do we do now?" she heard Mitchell yell in his gruff voice.

"Cut through it!" yelled Garrett. "You're the one who insisted the truck be stocked with all those tools."

"Thought we might have to cut through the museum loading bay doors," Mitchell shot back.

Worried they'd come around the side of the semi, Alex jumped off and shimmied under the massive vehicle, crawling on her knees and elbows toward the front to see what was happening. She peered out from between the two front tires and saw that they'd reached the section of road that was completely blocked by three huge palms that had toppled over in the gale. More trees stood off the left side of the road, so they couldn't go around that way. And the right dropped off in a steep embankment. That was out. They'd have to go through the trees somehow.

Holding her breath, she watched the thieves' feet walk around toward the back of the truck, thankful she'd hidden beneath. She heard the double doors creak open and muffled voices as they climbed inside.

"Told that jerk we might need this stuff," she heard Mitchell grumble.

"Where's the . . . Hey, need a blowtorch?" Alex recognized the voice as Jake's, the one who'd been having second thoughts.

"Why would I need a goddamn blowtorch?" Mitchell snapped.

"Who brought a handheld Mattel football game?" Tatiana asked.

"Oh, that's mine. Been looking all over for that thing!" Jake said.

"Here's the chain saw," Alex heard Tatiana say.

"See? I told you this thing would come in handy," Mitchell

crowed. "Believe me. I grew up in Georgia, and I can't tell you how many downed trees we had to deal with in hurricane weather. You don't go anywhere without a chain saw. Everyone knows that."

"Yeah?" Tatiana shot back. "Even to a hoedown? Everyone needs a chain saw at a hoedown."

"Why the hell did you include a 3-D printer?" Jake asked.

"In case I needed to make a tool I didn't have," Mitchell retorted.

"Like what?" Jake asked. "You have everything back here already."

"Like a retro encabulator."

"A what?" she heard the woman say, echoing Alex's thought.

But Mitchell didn't answer. The truck shook slightly as they jumped out the back. The double doors slammed shut.

"You know, to prevent side fumbling..." His voice trailed off as she watched three pairs of boots make their way toward the fallen trees.

"I'm waiting in the goddamn car," Garrett complained. "I'm soaked."

"We're all soaked," Tatiana shot back. Then she heard the woman mumble to her comrades: "Guy's always bragging that he's some big outdoor guide. What a joke. Can't even stand a little rain."

Garrett climbed back in the SUV and shut the door. The other three moved to the fallen trees, and she saw now that they carried pry bars, an axe, and a chain saw. Mitchell ripped the cord on the chain saw, starting it up. The engine overpowered the noise of the cascading rain. They all bent over their work. Mitchell began cutting through the first trunk. He sliced through one section, then moved to the next as Tatiana and Jake dragged that section of tree to the side of the road.

With those three busy, focused on the job at hand, and the chain saw muffling any noises, Alex realized she had a chance here. Garrett sat in the car alone with the case. He would be staring at their progress, being impatient.

She crawled to the front of the truck. It was idling just six feet from the end of the SUV.

She flattened herself, made sure the thieves were still over by the trees, and then shimmied out from under the truck and straight under the SUV. A large branch lay under the car, and she grabbed it.

The chain saw roared and whined, cutting through another section of tree. More of the wood was dragged out of the road. They were making quick work of it, having nearly removed half of the first tree already.

Alex had to time this just right. Even if she managed to get the case, she couldn't escape on foot. Not when they were armed with guns.

She waited, her heart pounding, while they removed the first tree and went to work on the second. The SUV would be able to make it through a narrower space than the truck.

As soon as they began sawing through the first section of the second palm, Alex rolled out from under the SUV, using the vehicle to block their line of sight. She sat up and crouched, gripping the branch. Garrett sat still, eyes fixed on the progress with the trees. Quickly she opened the back door of the driver's side and slipped in. She instantly spotted the case buckled into the back seat on the passenger side.

"What the fuck?" Garrett cried out, whirling in surprise. Alex swung the branch up, connecting violently with his right temple. His head jerked back, banging against the car window. He slumped down in the seat. She hit him again, this time driving the end of the branch into the side of his head. He went limp.

Her heart hammering, Alex looked up. The other three still labored by the trees, the roaring of the chain saw muffling what had just happened. Adrenaline flooded her body, bringing with it a flash of heat.

She crawled forward, squeezing between the two front seats, and lowered herself into the passenger seat. She shrugged out of her pack and laid it on the passenger seat. Glancing forward at the thieves, she found them still at work. Mitchell had sawed through a section of the third tree, and the other two readied to pull it aside. Alex judged that she'd be able to squeeze through the space it would free up. As Mitchell brought the chain saw down on the next section, Alex used the noise to cover the sound of her opening the driver's-side door. She hoped they wouldn't notice or, if they did, just think Garrett was getting out to bark orders at them again.

The door swung open just wide enough for Alex to push Garrett out onto the ground. His limp body tumbled out and sprawled on the side of the road.

Alex slid into the driver's seat, keeping her head low. The other three bent over the next section of tree.

Alex started the engine and stomped on the accelerator, the SUV surging forward. The thieves spun, surprised, Tatiana and Jake jumping out of the way as she roared through the narrow, freed section. Mitchell lunged forward with the chain saw as she passed, and Alex heard the screaming of metal as the saw raked along the side of the SUV. She winced against the squealing, high-pitched whine. Then she was past them, cramming the SUV between the sawed end of the final tree and the steep embankment at the edge of the road.

She had to swerve onto the soft shoulder to get completely around the last tree, and for a second she thought the SUV might slide down the slope. But its tires gripped the pavement on the left side, and she whipped back onto the road.

Her heart pounding, her mouth gone dry, she looked into the rearview mirror to see Jake and Tatiana scurrying back to where Garrett lay. Mitchell still stood by the tree, chain saw in hand, his face a mask of rage.

Alex sped on, heading for the boat rental place where she'd rented her scuba gear. It was only then that she realized the car was acting sluggish. Her heart sank. Mitchell had done more than tear at the side of the SUV with the chain saw. He'd nicked one of the tires, and it was losing air fast.

TWENTY-ONE

Nervously Alex checked the rearview mirror but saw no sign of the thieves. It would take them a while to saw through enough of the last tree to get the truck through. They wouldn't be able to drive it partly off the embankment as she had, not unless they wanted to overturn it.

Then she felt the tire go completely flat, but she kept on. As she drew nearer to the coast, she saw that the storm surge had begun. Her car hit the incoming water, growing even more sluggish. As she got closer to the sea, the surge grew stronger, and a few times its power pushed the car to the side of the road and Alex had to force the steering wheel back on course. She fought against the standing water, which sent up plumes as she drove.

Alex didn't think she could make it all the way to town now. The car had slowed considerably, the flat tire thump-thumping on the road, steering growing increasingly difficult. She knew she'd pass the town's tiny marina before she reached the town proper. There might still be a boat there. If not, she'd head on to the boat and Jet Ski rental place in town.

When the sign for the marina came into sight, Alex's hope swelled. She started to pull into the parking lot, but her heart sank when she didn't spot any boats. Everyone must have evacuated with theirs. But then she pulled fully into the parking lot and couldn't believe her luck when she spotted a small fishing vessel still there, tied to the pier and bobbing in the surge. She drove the limping car to the edge of the dock.

She was about to jump out and race to the boat, and then she froze. She recognized this vessel. It was the small fishing boat used by the men who had set out the gillnet. She paused, not sure what to do, but saw no movement on deck. No lights were on, either, and in the gloom from the storm, they'd be necessary.

Her mind ran through the possibilities. All the other boats had been moved. It was possible the men had already been arrested and therefore weren't there to move their boat. She waited another two minutes, feeling anxious and continually checking the entrance to the parking lot, worried the truck would catch up with her.

She eyed the case in the back seat, wondering how to proceed. It had a handcuff and chain on it, but she didn't want to attach it to herself if she didn't have the key. And she would need both of her hands and arms free to survive this anyway. She thought of her belt.

Grabbing the case from the back seat, she examined it. It felt solid, completely sealed, and extremely cold to the touch. It was refrigerated, she realized. A digital clock on the exterior of one side read eighty hours. She guessed this was how long the refrigerant would last and hoped she'd be well away to safety by the time it counted off its last minute.

She closed the handcuff around her belt. If she needed to, she could strip off her belt, but for now, the case would be attached to her.

After a few more minutes of watching the boat and seeing no signs of life, Alex donned her day pack and jumped out of the SUV. Jogging toward the pier, she glanced back at the SUV, seeing the rake of the chain saw against the metal, the deep gouge in the flattened tire.

Once on the dock, she listened for voices above the roar of the wind. Her wet hair was plastered to her face, and the rain fell so hard it stung her skin. The storm had really picked up now, and she struggled to balance on her way down the pier as the wind buffeted her in powerful gusts.

She looked out at the storm-tossed sea. It was rough, to be sure. But she thought she could probably power out away from shore and sail the boat around the southern end of the island to the much calmer western shores, which would be protected from the storm.

She reached the boat where it banged violently against the pier and struggled to get aboard it as it surged violently up and down against the wooden dock. Finally she just made a jump for it, landing on board. She grabbed on to the railing of the rocking boat, making a circuit around the deck.

She saw no one in the wheelhouse and decided to check below-decks to be sure the men weren't on board. Then she'd go up to the bridge, radio for help, and start up the boat. She crept around the mast and reached the stairs that presumably led down to the galley and bunks.

Tossed side to side and barely able to keep her balance, Alex banged against one wall and then the other as she descended the stairs, gripping the railing to keep from pitching forward. It was hard going with her other hand holding tightly on to the case.

At the bottom of the stairs lay a small galley and head, and beyond that, a tiny room with four bunks. Crumpled bedding lay strewn over them, along with coffee cans full of cigarette butts, some old magazines, and dirty laundry tossed on the floor.

The boat seemed empty, but she wanted to quickly check the fish hold. She ascended the stairs and crossed the heaving deck. A sudden wave hit the side of the ship, causing her to lose her balance and pitch forward. She caught herself on the mast, waited for the wave to roll through, and then stumbled the rest of the way to the hold.

When she reached it, she saw that it was already open about a foot and a half. She bent down and peered inside. It was empty except for a ladder that descended into it on her side. The stench of death overwhelmed her, issuing up from a vile layer of watery slime and blood that sloshed around below. Gagging, she swallowed back the urge to throw up.

She was just pulling her head back out when she heard voices.

Alex listened, tensed, not daring to straighten up and make her presence known. She heard men aboard the vessel, shouting above the storm. She lay down and slid through the open foot and a half of the hold, grabbing on to the ladder and descending a few feet. She kept her head at the level of the deck, peering out.

The two poachers who had strung out the gillnet came into view, fighting against the wind. They walked along the pier toward the boat, their jackets glistening with rain. They boarded the boat, the portly one shouting at the scrawny one above the storm. "We've *got* to retrieve the last one, or we'll lose everything in the storm!"

"You're crazy," the scrawny one shouted back. "I'm not going out there in this." She noticed that his arm was in a cast and sling where she'd broken it.

The bigger man waved off his friend's concern. "The storm is the perfect cover. The Coast Guard isn't going to be out in this."

"*No one* should be out in this!"

"You want to miss out on whatever we caught? You know how much money that could be?"

"Yeah, it could be nothing. We only caught that one adult turtle and some tiny hatchlings last time. I'm not risking my life for that."

"Suit yourself. I'm going out there," the big man shot back.

Alex gritted her teeth. The boat wasn't here because the men had been arrested; it was here because they still had a gillnet out there somewhere and wanted to retrieve it.

She glanced around, looking for a place to hide in the hold. But it was just a single, open square. If they looked inside it, she was toast. She considered shinnying out and finding somewhere to hide on deck, but they would spot her easily.

She decided to stay put. If she could wait them out, see if they went straight to the wheelhouse, then she could sneak off the boat before they took off.

Damn. She needed this boat. The sea was really heaving now,

the boat straining against its moorings. Maybe taking it out at this point was a bad idea anyway. But at the very least she'd wanted to use the radio.

Alex heard something else then and strained her ears to make it out over the pounding of the rain. A thrumming sound. A diesel engine. But not the boat's. That was still silent. This was outside. She froze. The truck. The thieves had caught up to her. She cursed herself for not hiding the SUV, but then realized there had been nowhere for her *to* hide it.

Moments later, she heard the thieves board the boat, saw them come around the corner by the stern. She stayed put, hoping no one would look in the hold.

The Australian spotted the two poachers as they made their way up to the wheelhouse. "You!" he shouted. "Come down from there."

"Who the fuck are you?" she heard the portly one shout back.

"Get off our fucking boat!" snapped the other.

"We're taking your boat," Garrett shot back.

"Fat chance!" the bigger poacher shouted.

Silence fell, and Alex strained her neck to get a glimpse of what was going on. She heard the clang of boots on metal and watched as the poachers descended the stairs. Then Mitchell came into view, raising an M4 at the two men.

"Okay, okay," the skinny poacher said, and both came into Alex's view, hands raised.

Mitchell gestured with his rifle to the pier. "Get out."

She watched as the two men stepped over the gunwale and out onto the rocking pier. The boat ground against the wood there.

"Untie the lines," Mitchell ordered, again pointing with his rifle. The men did so, casting the lines up onto the ship's deck.

"Now get out of here," she heard Jake say.

But Mitchell stepped forward, extending his M4. "No." Alex could see the snake tattoo on his arm, and images of Dora's death flashed in her mind. An eruption of gunfire ripped through the noise of the storm, and Alex watched bullets tear into the two poachers. They collapsed, blood mixing with the rain. They fell out of sight on the other side of the boat's rail.

But she could hear one of the poachers screaming. Mitchell leaned over the gunwale and fired another burst of shots. Then just the downpour of rain filled the ensuing quiet. Mitchell turned away, his face a mask of disinterest.

"You didn't have to do that!" Jake yelled at him.

Alex had fought those two poachers repeatedly, but to see them gunned down like that, with as little concern as Mitchell had when he'd murdered Dora, was shocking. She clenched her teeth, staring out, feeling cold steal over her.

Mitchell shook his head. "We've taken enough chances. No more witnesses."

Jake stared over the rail, his mouth a thin, pursed slash.

Garrett spun now, facing Tatiana. "Get up there and drive this rusty tub to the western side of the island so we can get the hell out of this storm. We'll meet you there with the truck after we've found the case."

"What about our cargo ship?" Jake asked.

"We'll worry about that after we recover the case," Garrett snapped. "In case you haven't noticed, we don't need a whole refrigerated vessel anymore, you idiot, just a small fridge for when the case's coolant runs out. Besides, for all we know, the ship's already been dashed to pieces in this storm."

"Yet you think nothing of asking me to go out in this?" Tatiana said, incredulous. "Are you crazy?"

"It's the only boat we've seen. You want to get off this island or not?"

"I'd prefer to get off it alive," she retorted.

"You want to see your money, you'll do it," Garrett shot back.

The boat rocked again as the three men stepped off. They filed past the bodies of the poachers. Only Jake looked down at them, his expression miserable.

Their voices faded, becoming indistinct, farther away. She heard the woman cursing as she climbed up the stairs to the bridge. The boat's engine started up.

Knowing she was out of sight from the bridge, Alex climbed back up the ladder and slid out from the hold. On the pier lay the crumpled, dead bodies of the two poachers, waves splashing over them, blood running red off the dock.

The truck pulled out of the parking lot, its tires sending up plumes of water. The storm surge had grown in intensity, and a good six inches of water lay on the roadway. The truck turned onto the street, heading for the main part of Ānuenue.

Alex weighed her options. If she could stay out of sight, she could just ride with the woman to the sheltered west side of the island. Then she could sneak off the boat and get help after it docked. Landlines would be functioning there. People would be milling about. She could get help. She just needed a place to hide.

But before she could formulate a plan, the boat surged away from the dock, heavy on the engine, nearly causing Alex to topple backward into the hold. She gripped the railing and held on as the boat motored away from the pier.

Moving out into the stormy seas, the boat surged chaotically. Alex clung to the railing, her knuckles going white. A huge wave splashed over the deck, engulfing her in cold water.

Another wave hit, this one so powerful that it slapped Alex in the face like a physical blow. Cold seawater drenched her again. She could feel the squish of it in her socks inside her boots, feel how cold her feet were getting. Her fingers were freezing and claw-like where they gripped the railing. She couldn't stay out here and couldn't risk hiding below where the bunks were, either. If the woman reached smoother waters and came down there to use the head, there was nowhere for Alex to hide.

Then another wave surged over the deck, ripping Alex free from the railing. She slid across the deck, grabbing at anything, her fingers finding the mast and clinging to it. The boat rocked violently, Alex's legs sliding first to port and then to starboard. She felt tossed like a rag doll. Another wave hit, slamming into her back. But it wasn't as strong as the previous three. She held on, belly down on the deck, clinging desperately to the round base of the mast.

The boat surged up a crest then plunged down into a trough, Alex's stomach going with it, and she fought the urge to throw up. Then she was thrust upward again, and for a second her body went nearly vertical. Her feet flailed to find something to brace against but found only empty air. Then the boat heaved downward again, and Alex slid forward, banging her head painfully on the base of the mast. With each wave, the case whipped around her, slamming into her legs and the small of her back, tugging against her belt.

The boat surged sickeningly upward, and Alex felt her grip start to loosen as once again the ship went nearly vertical. Just then the biggest wave yet crashed over the deck. It tore Alex free from the mast, sending her sliding backward across the deck. She felt her feet hit the lip of the hold, and the impact spun her violently to one side. She crashed into the side of the hold just as the boat lurched upward again. Her body left the deck, and for a moment she was weightless. Then it slammed down again and she rolled straight into the hold, falling the eight feet onto the slimy, gut-strewn floor.

Vile slime coated her body, some of it getting into her mouth. She spat it out and struggled to get to her feet, but instead just got tossed around, sliding on her hands and knees. The case repeatedly collided with her legs, and she tried to grab it and right herself.

As a surge of the boat carried her toward the ladder, Alex reached for it but came up short. She slid across the entire floor of the hold, hitting the opposite wall with her feet. Then she careened back on the next wave crest and this time managed to seize the bottom rung. She clung to it, hauling herself up and climbing partway up the ladder, the case dangling off her belt. The boat continued to surge and plummet.

Alex's feet slipped off repeatedly as she tried to climb higher. She leaned down and reeled in the case's handcuff chain, then gripped the handle. Waves continued to crash in, sending torrents of seawater down into the hold, cascading over her. She struggled to get any higher.

Then something struck the side of the boat, jarring her off her perch. She landed hard on her back. The boat spun, turning 180 degrees, throwing Alex around as she flailed in the bottom of the hold, arms and legs spread out, trying to catch herself as she banged against one wall and then another.

A second violent collision struck the boat, spinning it again. Alex gaped in horror as the hull collapsed inward, a tremendous rock suddenly bursting through one side of the hold. She heard a tremendous crash up above and then a jarring impact as something fell across the deck.

Crashing waves tore the boat away from the rock, and water poured in through the breach. Alex swam for the ladder, hauling the case after her, and grabbed one of the rungs. She struggled to climb upward. Waves seized the boat again, slamming it once more into the sharp black volcanic rocks, more of the hull crumpling inward, almost reaching the ladder.

Alex climbed desperately now, but the large gap that had once been at the top of the hold was gone. Alex braced herself for the next impact and pushed on the hold door. It opened just a few inches now, and by peering through the crack, she saw what was wrong.

The mast had collapsed and fallen across the hold door, pinning it nearly closed. Alex braced her shoulder against the hatch, pushing upward. But it didn't move at all. Another impact threw her off the ladder into the flooding seawater below. She surged up against a rough rock breaking through the hull as the boat swung to the left and then spun in the surf like a toy.

Alex struggled back to the ladder and clung to it. She couldn't get out the way she'd come in, and the boat was sinking fast.

TWENTY-TWO

A retreating wave tore the boat off the sharp rocks, sucking it deeper out to sea, water pouring in now through the gaping holes so quickly that in no time the hold was almost completely flooded.

She continued to cling to the ladder, keeping her head above the water. She had to get clear of the boat or she was going to drown in it. She let go and swam for one of the holes, but the power of incoming water was too strong for her to swim through. The weight of the water dragged the boat downward. The diffused light from the stormy sky faded, and Alex knew the trawler was sinking, and fast. She fought against the inflow of water, but it was no use. It kept pushing her back.

She realized with a sense of fear that she'd have to wait until the pressure had equalized, when the hold was completely filled with water, before she'd be able to swim out.

So she returned to the ladder, holding on to keep from being tossed against the walls. The boat descended, then landed with a dull thump on the seabed. Alex had no idea how deep she was, but it hadn't taken too long to land.

As she stood at the top of the ladder, the water reached her knees, then her waist, then her chest. When it reached her chin, she hyperventilated, saturating her lungs with as much oxygen as possible. Then it went up past her lips and nose, enveloping her head. The flow of water ceased. Now was her chance.

She kicked out from the ladder, eyes able to make out the dim light coming through the holes in the hull. She grabbed the edges of one and pulled herself through, making sure the case was still attached to her belt. She needed both hands to swim.

Free of the boat, she glanced upward, seeing light on the surface of the water. She wasn't that deep, maybe only thirty feet. But her day pack pulled her down, the relentless surge of the waves tearing at it, jerking her back and forth. Then a downward torrent of water ripped it violently off her back. She struggled to grab at the pack, reluctant to lose its contents: the radios, her phone, her water bottle. It whipped away from her and she could feel the last of her breath burning in her chest. She had to let it go or drown. She swam upward, but as she got closer to the surface, the current picked up, sucking her down and then pushing her up. She struggled against it, kicking and pumping her arms, but it was too strong. She realized she had to use the movement of the waves to her advantage.

She broke the surface of the wild, wind-tossed sea and gulped in air. She spotted land not too far away. She let the ocean pull her out, and when the next wave came, she kicked and paddled like crazy to make headway. As the water retreated, she relaxed, but was dismayed to see her backward progress. Then it moved forward again, Alex swimming as fast as she could.

She heard a cry and looked back across the choppy gray water to see Tatiana flailing and struggling in the water, managing to keep her head up but not doing well.

Alex powered on toward the shore. She could see that they'd been carried toward the town, and the place where she'd rented her scuba equipment was ahead of her. She swam for the shore—two lengths forward, one length back, two lengths forward, one length back—slowly making her way to land. The case surged ahead of her and then dragged behind her, constantly banging her legs as it shot back and forth. She hoped it was a sturdy as it looked.

Wave-tossed sand scraped at her arms and legs as she went, and her teeth started to chatter. She swallowed so much seawater, she started to feel sick.

The small dock by the rental place stood empty. Though she'd seen three boats here when she'd first rented her scuba gear, they'd obviously been moved when the evacuation order came down. So Alex would have to think of a new plan. And she now knew that the storm was so bad that taking a boat out was unrealistic.

At last her feet could touch the bottom, and she struggled to stand, but was knocked over by the next wave. She just let it carry her to shore, sliding in on her stomach. She gasped for breath, feeling rough sand beneath her. She managed to get to her feet and grab the handle of the case, then staggered out of the surf. But the storm surge was truly deep now.

Alex checked the integrity of the case, thankfully finding it scratched but not dented. She didn't even want to think about it coming open or the refrigerant element getting damaged.

But she'd lost everything else. Her pack. Her phone. The radios. She checked her pockets, finding her beloved multitool still tucked deeply into her jeans, and was grateful for that.

Kayaks had been stacked beside the building, along with paddleboards, oars, and several older-model Jet Skis. Around her, huge waves crashed against the shore, palms bent violently back and forth. The roar of the surf was almost deafening, and she struggled to remain upright as ferocious winds buffeted her body.

Instinctively she reached for her phone in her back pocket, wanting to try emergency services again, before remembering that it was gone, likely smashed to pieces somewhere out on the rocks.

She spotted a thick wire going from a telephone pole into the rental building. A landline. And it might still work.

She splashed forward through knee-deep water and waded across the parking lot, fighting the intense winds, her arm raised to shield her face against the onslaught. She held the case up, keeping it above the water.

She reached the main building and its three stairs up to the front door. Thankfully she found it unlocked and ducked inside, shaking the rain out of her hair and jacket.

The water inside the raised building was up to her ankles, and she sloshed across the floor. Inside she found the place much as it was the day she rented scuba gear.

A show-model Sea-Doo stood as the centerpiece of the room. Racks of clothing for sale stood on either side of it—life jackets, rash guards, wet suits. A floor-to-ceiling window looked out over the churning gray sea, but it had been boarded up. Shelves behind the reservation desk held scuba and snorkeling gear. Posters depicted beautiful beaches at sunset and colorful coral reefs teeming with fish.

She spotted the landline sitting on top of the reservation desk and hurried to it. She picked it up, then her heart sank. No dial tone. She pressed down on the receiver, waited a minute, then lifted her finger again. Nothing. *There must be lines down all over the coast,* she thought.

A sudden loud bang made her jump, and she whirled around as a huge wave crashed against the main window. Boards came loose, washing away with the water. Another wave came in with a crash, carrying away more boards, revealing large sections of open glass. Water receded in a swirling white froth. She felt cold seeping up her calves and looked down to see that the water now reached her knees, even inside the building.

Then another wave hit the window, and Alex watched as the glass flexed and shimmied. She thought surely it would break. But it held.

She looked around in desperation. She needed a way out of the storm, toward the west side of the island. A mode of transportation. She glanced out the window facing the parking lot, and to her horror saw the truck plowing through the high water, leaving a huge wake. Then it slowed as a massive surge hit it. The water shoved the truck to one side of the street. Then another surge struck it, spinning the truck. Alex watched as it teetered, leaning, and saw the panicked faces of the thieves inside. Then a third surge collided with the truck and sent it crashing over on its side.

It splashed into the water, briefly going afloat, then sank down, water gushing against its underbelly. The thieves scrambled out of it, crawling through the window and standing on top of the truck's side. One of them pointed toward the building, and they all scrambled in her direction. She had minutes before they'd know she was here.

Alex was just turning back around to weigh her options when a tremendous crash struck the oceanside window. She watched in horror as the entire pane shattered, seawater surging inside. Instantly the level of water shot up to her waist, cold and swirling.

Her gaze shot to the Sea-Doo. The key hung from its ignition. She grabbed a scuba diving mask, pulling it on to keep out the wind and rain.

As the water rose quickly, up to her chest, the Sea-Doo became buoyant, floating out of its display stand. She jumped on it. Tucking the case onto her lap, she started up the engine.

The surge had momentarily subsided now, leaving an opening between the water and the top of the huge window frame. Alex revved the engine, wheeling the Sea-Doo in a circle, and drove out through the window.

As she cleared the building, she looked back, seeing the abandoned truck had been pushed even farther down the street on its side. She spotted the thieves struggling through the storm surge near the boat rental building, half walking, half swimming. Then she saw Tatiana crawl out of the surf. She'd survived the boat crash, too. She shouted something at her comrades, but it was lost in the wind and noise from Alex's Sea-Doo.

Mitchell was the closest to Alex and pointed her out as she fled on the machine. A wave hit Jake, sweeping him over to the rental building and right into the jumbled pile of kayaks, paddleboards, and older Jet Skis. He floundered for a moment, trying to grab on to something, and swung himself up onto a Jet Ski, then fiddled with its ignition, pulling out a multitool. Damn it. If he knew how to hotwire that thing...

Her thought was cut off as she heard the whine of the Jet Ski's engine over the pounding rain.

She gunned her Sea-Doo, thudding out over the incoming waves, the wind and rain tearing at her hair and jacket. She had to keep heading west. Break free from the worst of the storm.

But already she saw Jake wheeling his Jet Ski around in her direction. She couldn't risk going back out to sea. That would be suicide. Instead, she'd have to ride the storm surge through the more sheltered streets of the town.

Behind her, Jake revved his engine. She had to lose him somehow.

Tossed by the powerful surge coming in from the sea, Alex sped into town. She veered onto the main street, racing past Keola's restaurant, the grocery store, the Thai place where she'd had dinner with Sasha. Everything was flooded with at least six feet of water, and she felt sorry for Keola and the cleanup that he was facing. His restaurant would have to be closed for quite a while. Many businesses had boarded up their windows, but she could see in more than one place that those protective boards had been torn free by the violent winds and surge.

But her thoughts of sympathy were cut off by the sound of a Jet Ski close behind her. She glanced over her shoulder to see Jake closing in, roaring around a corner by a shaved ice establishment. He swung an M4 around from a strap on his back and aimed it. Alex weaved the Sea-Doo across the road, making herself a difficult target. She heard the crack of the weapon and saw water splash up to her right. She dared another look back and saw that he was aiming low, likely trying to hit the Sea-Doo and not her. She recalled his protest at the museum, mad at Garrett for having murdered people and angry at the plan in general. She didn't think he wanted to kill her. But she couldn't risk him hitting the Sea-Doo and disabling it, then getting the case.

She guessed that even if he hadn't signed up for Garrett's plan, now that the truck had been washed away, it was his only payday left.

She swerved around a corner, then heard a round ping off the back of her Sea-Doo. She looked back, seeing a hole in the rear deck, the plastic cracked around it. Then another round hit the handlebars in front of her.

This shot had not come from behind her. She wheeled the Sea-Doo into an abrupt turn, just as another bullet struck the water beside her. Movement above her caught her eye, and she glanced up to see Garrett on the roof of the old theater, handgun pointed down at her, fighting against the intense winds. She knew he wouldn't have the best aim in conditions like these, so she gunned it and swept around another corner.

She sped down the street, taking another turn away from the theater, and almost crashed into another Jet Ski barreling straight for her.

Mitchell drove it, with Tatiana riding behind him, holding on with one arm and wielding an M4 with the other. The semiautomatic weapon pivoted in Alex's direction, and she swung the Sea-Doo around, heading back the other way.

As Alex sped around the corner, back by the drugstore, she nearly collided with Jake taking a turn too fast in an effort to catch up with her. Another round from Garrett pinged off her Sea-Doo, this time next to her foot. He was still far away, but she felt like her luck was going to run out soon. She also guessed that, for now, they would only fire low at her Sea-Doo, as they wouldn't want to risk hitting the case tucked against her torso.

She sped past Jake, and he reached out to grab her, lunging too far and falling off his Jet Ski. She powered by, spraying him in her wake. She took another corner, obstructing Garrett's line of sight, trying to figure out where she should go. She needed to go west, out of the town, try to see if the storm surge was less powerful in that direction. If she could just start veering around the southern tip of the island . . .

A flurry of bullets hit the Sea-Doo then, this time in the fuel tank. The unmistakable stench of gasoline bloomed up around her, and she turned to see Mitchell and Tatiana closing in on her. She gunned it as gasoline poured out into the water.

She didn't know how long her fuel would last. She revved the engine, taking another corner way too fast, and almost rammed into a building on the far side of the street. She brought the Sea-Doo back under control, almost falling off it, gripping the handlebars so tightly that for a second her arm almost felt wrenched out of its socket.

She sped around one corner, then another. She raced down the next street. She'd nearly circled back to the rental place, and here the water was much deeper. The corner hardware store where she'd ordered the materials for her thermocouples had floor-to-ceiling windows, and the waves had torn away its protective boards. The large pieces of plywood tossed in the water beside the storefront, being dragged in and out with the surge. Both windows had been smashed out completely.

As Mitchell and Tatiana sped up behind her, Alex saw Tatiana raise the barrel of the M4 again. Alex suddenly turned, veering straight through the broken windows of the hardware store. Then she jerked the handlebar, steering out a shattered window opposite.

But Mitchell wasn't fast enough. He tried to jerk the Jet Ski to follow her, but he was too late. He collided with the stone outer wall in a crunch of plastic and metal. Alex watched over her shoulder as both riders flew off the Jet Ski, hurtling through the air and smashing into metal shelving inside the store.

Alex gunned it, once more turning the Sea-Doo to head west.

The fuel gauge's needle dipped down into the red. She didn't know what she'd do when she ran out of gas.

She glanced around at the rooftops, trying to spot Garrett, but didn't see anyone up there now. For a brief moment, the street behind and ahead of her was empty. She took the opportunity to gain some ground, revving the engine into max rpms and leaning forward as the Sea-Doo sped on. She crossed an intersection, then another, and as she passed the third, she spotted Jake racing toward her, trying to cut her off. She bounced along in the water, the cold sea splashing her face. He wheeled around the corner and fell in behind her, once more bringing his gun to bear.

And then a powerful wave hit her, and she almost slipped off the seat. The case came off her lap, hitting the water and dragging heavily through it. She reached down and grabbed it up out of the waves.

She tried to tuck it onto her lap again, but it kept sliding off her legs with the sharp turns she took. Jake was close behind. She dared a look back, seeing him bent forward at the handlebars, determined.

Then a solid, powerful wave collided with her right side, the pain sudden as the cold water slapped her face and body, and she realized suddenly she was off the Sea-Doo, flailing in surging water. The case dragged her downward, and she windmilled her arms, trying to catch a breath.

For a moment the waves parted, and she sucked in air, and then she was underwater again, not sure which way was up, struggling and thrashing. She fought her way toward light and air, and for a second her head came up above the waves and she caught sight of Keola's restaurant, the tiles getting ripped right off the roof by the wind. And then a violent sucking force pulled her down, down, spiraling and flailing, into a narrow opening. She caught for a second on concrete, then went down more, down, down, into darkness.

TWENTY-THREE

Alex stuck her hands out, fingertips trailing along rough concrete, and she realized she'd been sucked into a storm drain. She heard a sharp cry behind her and glanced back, seeing Jake perfectly framed in a dim rectangle of light as he, too, was sucked down after her.

Disorientation swamped Alex's world. She didn't know which way was up and was forced along in a powerful current of water, trying desperately to keep her head above the surface, gasping for air whenever she could. A surge of water splashed up into her mouth, and she tasted cold salt. Her hands continued to drag along the sides of the tunnel, scraping at her skin, and she could feel the pull of the case, yanking on her belt, tugging her forward into the darkness.

At first she was only able to graze the sides of the tunnel with her fingertips, but then her knuckles could touch, and then the backs of her hands, and now her forearms. It was getting narrower.

Alex's face suddenly hit air, and she gulped in a breath, and then she was underwater again, grappling for what felt like the ceiling of the tunnel. Pure, cold fear gripped her.

She remembered exploring such storm drains when she was younger with her friend Becky, another Air Force kid who moved all over the world with her parents. One tunnel they'd explored had started out wide enough for them to walk through at full height. Then it had gotten smaller and smaller and smaller until they were stooped over. Soon enough, they'd had to crawl through the narrow tunnel, their skinny shoulders touching each side. And finally it was too tiny, and they'd had to back out awkwardly in the dark, scaring each other with stories of rabid sewer clowns and starving alligators that someone had released as small pets but that had grown to gigantic sizes down in the storm drains, eating kids just like them.

Alex realized with horror that this tunnel could get narrower and narrower until her body wouldn't pass through. And then she'd drown.

Suddenly light spilled into her world, and she realized too late that she'd passed a storm drain inlet above, with a ladder stretching down. She reached out with grasping fingers, but water forced her past the opening. But now she just had to wait. There would be others. *Had* to be others. She just had to keep her head above the surging current, getting breaths any chance she could. Behind her she heard a yell, Jake cursing as he hurtled past the ladder as well.

She tried to straighten herself, to go feetfirst, to keep her face up so that she could spot any sign of light coming from a place of egress.

She could do this. She flexed her cold fingers, readying to grab on to the next ladder. She wouldn't drown down here.

But then all the air disappeared. She involuntarily swallowed seawater and struggled to spit it out, fighting her way to oxygen. Her lungs burned in her chest, and her vision started to tunnel. Then suddenly she was pushed up, up, and her hand collided with the ceiling of the tunnel as her head burst into air. She gasped in long, grateful breaths.

She slammed into something solid, something metal. Pain racked her body. Water surged up and over her head, and she struggled to find air. She felt along the obstruction, finding rough metal bars blocking her way. A grate of some sort. And she was pinned against it, the water pounding at her back with such force that it compressed her chest. She struggled to breathe, craning her neck toward the ceiling of the tunnel to gasp in any of the air she could from that tiny space.

Dim light filtered down from the storm drain opening she'd passed. She felt between the bars, realizing that she could squeeze through them. But the case was trapped sideways in front of her. She braced her feet against two of the bars and pulled against the case, the force of the water keeping it pinned. Her fingers slipped on the handle. She tried again, hoping to budge it just enough that it would slip sideways. She felt it move a little, then a little more, and then it was through the bars in a rush, and the pull of it on her belt made her hip slam painfully against the bars. Now she just needed to slip through herself.

She started to turn to the side, forcing her left shoulder out against the pulverizing water, but suddenly a heavy weight slammed into her back, a dozen sharp edges jabbing into her. Hands flew up on either side of her, gripping the bars. She heard a man gasp for breath. It was Jake, trapped against her back.

She shoved against him, hearing him gasping and scared, panicking. She couldn't move. They were going to die down here. "Push off the bars!" she yelled. "Or we'll both drown!"

He strained—she could see that in the white of his knuckles—and managed to lift some of his weight off her, enough that she was able to turn slightly to the side. Her slim frame passed through two of the bars, catching only for a moment on the buckle of her belt. Then she was through, still holding on to one of the bars.

"Help me!" Jake gasped, spitting out seawater. She clung there, just on the other side of the gate, and hesitated. She could let him drown here. Just swim away. Find a way out.

But then his words in the museum parking lot came back to her, that he didn't want to be part of releasing another pandemic. He hadn't known what he was getting into, hadn't known anyone would be killed.

Alex held on to the bars, fighting against the slippery metal and deciding what to do.

"Slide through!" she yelled at him above the roar of the water.

"I can't!" He coughed, trying to gasp for air when the surges of water would allow it. "Something's jammed in front of me."

Alex felt down beneath the water, her fingers coming into contact with a length of cold metal just on the other side of the grate. It was the man's M4, lodged sideways against the bars.

She kicked to stay up above the waterline. "It's your rifle! Unstrap it from your neck!"

He reached up and unhooked the strap.

"Push off the bars so I can turn the gun!"

He braced his hands against the metal and pushed off, water streaming up and over his back, hitting Alex in the face. For a moment she couldn't breathe. She struggled upward, caught a breath, then reached through the bars to grip the M4's stock. But the force of the water was just too strong against it, and she couldn't get enough room beneath the man's body to turn it. So instead she shoved it to the side until it was clear of his torso.

"Okay! Got it! Now slide through!"

He released his hands, slamming against the grate again. With considerable effort, he managed to turn to the side, but he still didn't slip through. "I'm still jammed!" he yelled.

The water level grew higher in the drain. The top of Alex's head banged against the ceiling, and soon the water rushed by so powerfully that she had to turn her chin up to get a breath against the roof.

She felt along the man's body, feeling numerous bulky objects in the pockets of his combat vest. "It's your vest! Take it off!" she urged him.

The water lifted him all the way to the roof, and for a second Alex couldn't see anything in the dim, filtered light except the rush of water. She lifted her chin again, gasping for breath, and heard the man crying out in alarm, choking and gasping.

She started unfastening the Velcro on his vest, pulling out numerous objects: a handheld radio, multiple ammo magazines, a multitool, and a voltmeter. In his front vest he'd tucked away two grenades, and he flailed at these pockets, trying to unstrap the explosives. His hands fluttered over the vest, tossing out a bulky set of what looked like lockpicking tools, a silver flask, and a Maglite.

"Just take the whole vest off!" she urged him. She pressed her face against the bars, trying to feel for the fasteners, her fingers going numb in the cold water. She found one and undid it, but realized the other fastener must be on the opposite side. "Undo the vest!" she shouted again, involuntarily swallowing a gulp of seawater. But he was too panicked to think clearly and just kept trying to empty his pockets.

The water surged higher, and Alex almost lost hold of the grate. She tried to lift her chin up to breathe and found there was no longer a pocket of air. Panic bloomed through her.

She felt the man's arms flailing, grabbing at her, yanking her toward him against the metal grate, spasming, then going still. She tried to wrench his fingers off her jacket.

A pocket of air opened up, and she gulped in a grateful breath, momentarily seeing his face, unseeing eyes wide open, mouth parted and slack. His fingers loosened on her jacket, and she watched his other hand drift down, down, the thumb hitting the ring on one of the grenades.

"No, no, no . . ." Alex said, and then his dead thumb went right through the ring and pulled it.

Alex shoved off from the grate, banging her knee on the case underwater, and kicked as hard as she could into the current. She pumped her arms in powerful strokes, trying to get as much distance as possible.

The storm surge thrust her down the drain, which suddenly took a downward dip, and her back scraped along the cement bottom. Then it angled to the left, and her right side hit the tunnel, dragging along it before being swept up again in the current.

Complete darkness enveloped her. And then a concussive wave hit. She felt an extra-powerful pulse of forward movement, and seawater went up her nose. She flailed in the current, feeling the tug of the case against her belt, and worried it might get hung up on something. The drain took another turn, a momentary swirl of air opening up above her, and she sucked in air.

And then her face plunged back into water. Her lungs burned in her chest, and she fought an almost overwhelming urge to breathe in, even if that meant gulping in water. She shut her eyes and decided to just go with the flow and not try to fight it, to plummet through this drain feetfirst and hope another pocket of air would open up or it would dump her out somewhere soon, hopefully not into the surging sea.

And then she felt a violent backward tug on her hips. The case. It had gotten caught on something. She reached back for it, the urge to gulp in air now almost uncontrollable. She felt thick, slimy branches along the bottom of the tunnel. The case had gotten hung up in them. She fought against the current, managing to force her way back to the case.

She tugged at it, but it refused to come free. She pulled on the chain until she could bring her feet down on the branches and brace herself. Then she used one hand to start snapping branches. She couldn't see what she was doing in the pitch-dark. Suddenly the case came free, flinging her backward in the water, and she was tumbling again, flailing, out of control and at the mercy of the storm surge.

She ran her hands along the ceiling and walls of the tunnel, hoping for a manhole opening or a ladder. The tunnel got so narrow it barely accommodated her, and she started to feel claustrophobic, trapped, panic rising up within her.

It felt like she'd been plunging through this drain for an hour, but she knew it had been only a few brief minutes.

The tunnel constricted more, Alex's knees banging on the ceiling. Her boots scraped along the tunnel walls on both sides. Her vision narrowed, black creeping in at the edges.

And then suddenly the tunnel opened up. She rushed upward, and her head broke through into air. Her grasping fingers felt a flat ceiling. She couldn't touch the bottom with her feet and began to swim.

But soon she could be plunged back into a tight, airless space, which could quite possibly end in a small grate wherever the storm drain let out. She could be trapped against it.

She let go of the case, reaching her hands out, wanting to find something to grab on to so she could stay in this larger space for a few minutes longer. Maybe she could ride out this surge and the water would lower. Her grasping hand touched a bar of cold, vertical metal. She grabbed on to it, pulling her body in against the wall. She pulled on the bar, feeling along it, finding it curved and welded to flat metal at both ends. Her fingers found a long crack, then a latch. It was a door.

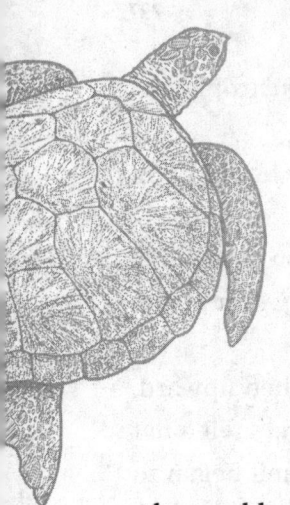

TWENTY-FOUR

Alex grabbed at the latch, finding it embedded in the doorjamb, which meant the door opened inward. Alex couldn't see what she was doing, struggling to keep her head above the water. Finally she took a deep breath and dove down, still holding on to the door handle. She worked at the latch, which felt rusted shut. Her fingers, cold from the seawater, could barely detect any details. She wriggled the latch and tried to force it open. Finally it gave way, pinching her fingers in the process.

The force of the water pushed the door open. Still holding on to the handle, Alex went with it, streaming into a dark room beyond. She got her feet on the floor and leaned against the door with everything in her, trying to shut it. She felt up along the doorjamb, finding a latch on this side, too. But the water pushed powerfully against her, the room quickly flooding more and more. The water rose to her ankles, then mid-calf, but with every moment she managed to close the door a little more. It finally slammed shut when the water had reached her knees. She drove the latch home, locking it.

Alex gasped, catching her breath, leaning against the door, water streaming off her body. She felt absolutely chilled and shivered there in the complete darkness.

Blood rushed in her ears, the sound of her own pounding heart. Finally her breathing slowed. She could hear the water surging past the closed door.

Slowly she stepped away from the door, flexing her fingers in an effort to warm them up. The darkness was absolute. If only she still had her phone, she could have used its light. But it was gone, somewhere out there in the sea.

The place smelled musty and damp, disused. She reached her hand up above her head, trying to feel if she was in another tunnel. She couldn't reach the ceiling. She felt along one wall. It ended in a right angle and she turned with it, groping along it. Then her shoulder struck something high up. She felt for it, finding metal there—long, cold slats of it—and then a railing.

A staircase, she realized, going up. She ran her fingers along it, finding the entrance. Then she checked the rest of the walls, feeling for doors or another way out. Her legs sloshed through the standing water, the salt stinging the scrapes she'd suffered along the cement walls of the storm drain. The rest of the room was just a solid little square, so she turned back to the stairs.

Grasping the railing at the bottom, she took a tentative step up, feeling the metal grating of the stair beneath her feet. The smell of rust bloomed up when she ran her hand along the railing, and it felt rough, peeling paint and bare metal beneath her skin. She climbed upward, eyes wide in the dark, but seeing nothing, feeling ahead of her as she went.

She took each step slowly, counting them. When she got to twelve, her hand touched a metal wall in front of her. She took the remaining steps and felt along the metal surface until she found another long, attached vertical handle like the one she'd felt in the storm drain. Her searching fingers reached another latch, and she tried to pry it open. It was rusted shut. Her cold fingers worked at it tirelessly, relieved when it finally started to budge a little. With a screech it finally came open, and then she pushed against the door. It wouldn't move even an inch. She pressed her shoulder against it and shoved. Nothing.

Finally she moved down a couple of steps and kicked out. The door groaned. She'd felt it shift. But her fingers discovered it had opened only a couple inches, so she kicked again. Another screech of rusted metal. Then she moved back to the top and shoved again with her shoulder. The door wrenched open with a deafening squeal, and Alex almost fell into the pitch-black room beyond.

She regained her balance and stood there, listening and sniffing the air. She could still only hear the rush of water in the storm drain. The place smelled musty and disused, mildew and something else—kerosene and wet cement and some unidentifiable industrial smell.

Putting her hands out in front of her, she took tentative steps forward, finding herself in a large, open space. She'd gone a few feet when the toes of her boots bumped against something. She bent down, finding an oddly textured metal surface. She felt along it, and her hands closed on a cylindrical metal object. She felt up along its base to find a glass globe, then a metal hood.

It was a lantern. Feeling buoyed, she groped along next to the lantern, her hands coming across a small metal box. She picked it up and opened it, feeling inside. Small wooden sticks. Matches. She reached out, finding the cement wall, and struck the match, hoping it would still work. It flared to life, giving brief, bright illumination to the room.

Quickly Alex lowered the match to study the lantern. It was an old mantle-style kind that ran off white gas. She stuck the match into the hole by the mantle and turned the dial to let out a little fuel. It caught, the mantle glowing to bright, cheerful life. Alex smiled and exhaled. She had light.

Now she could see that the lantern sat on top of a long ammo box. A series of spray-painted, stenciled letters marked the outside, reading "MK 6-50 CAL."

Beside the lantern sat several rusted cans of Spam and two small tins of sardines. A box of saltines stood propped up at the end of the ammo box. Judging from the style of the packaging and lettering, Alex could tell it was old.

Alex lifted the lantern by its handle, pocketed the matches, and then shone the light around the room. A metal chair stood along one wall beneath a series of hooks holding old-fashioned-looking hazmat suits and gas masks, their rubber still looking new. Another door stood in the far wall. Other than that, the room was empty.

Alex moved to this other door, finding the hinges red and rusty in the warm light. Alex set the lantern down on the floor, its hissing sounding loud in the small confines of the room. This door opened toward her and had no latch.

She grasped the metal handle and pulled. This door came open more easily, groaning and screeching on its hinges. When she'd opened it enough to slip through, she picked up the lantern, carrying the refrigerated containment case in her other hand, and slid through the dark opening.

Alex looked around in wonder. The walls of the space beyond weren't cinder block or cement. They curved up and around her. She was in a gigantic lava tube, formed when the outer surface of a lava flow cooled and hardened, but the interior remained molten until it drained out, leaving a large tunnel behind. Alex knew that some lava tubes on the island ran for miles and miles.

In front of her lay a barracks, metal cots in neat rows, woolen blankets folded at the bottom of each bed as if they'd just been placed there yesterday. Steamer trunks sat at the foot of each bed. She opened a few of them, finding them full of extra blankets, pillows, and sheets. Several lockers lined the walls. These held beige woolen shirts and pants, folded white undershirts and socks.

She moved from room to room, following the different branches of the lava tube. One room held a small clinic with metal-and-glass cabinets full of medications. She saw vials of dried-up crystalline penicillin G potassium and morphine, bottles of aspirin and chloroform, packs of sulfa powder. Splints, bandages, scissors, needles, and blood transfusion kits rested on shelves.

She paused here and used the supplies to clean and rebandage her shoulder. She also sterilized the numerous scrapes and cuts she'd suffered in the storm drain. Then she resumed her search of the bunker.

Another branch of the lava tube led her to a kitchen with a stainless steel cooking area, larders full of Spam, canned beans, packages of saltine crackers, even some boxes of Cracker Jack. The packaging still looked pristine but appeared to date from the 1940s.

Still another large room in the lava tube served as a maintenance bay. Small and large hydraulic jacks, old leaking car batteries, decayed timing belts, battery cables, mechanic skids, drawers upon drawers of tools with socket wrenches and screwdrivers. An engine sat on a block, tools beside it as if someone had just stepped away for the moment.

This had to be a World War II bunker. She knew that bunkers like this had been built on Oʻahu, but she had never heard of one on the Big Island. This one was old, disused, perhaps forgotten. She knew that at least one on Oʻahu allowed tours and had been converted into a museum about movies like *Jurassic Park,* which had been filmed in the Hawaiian Islands. But some bunkers still had classified locations. This could be another such secret place. She wondered if she was the first person to step inside here in eighty years.

Alex's body ached with exhaustion. She lifted the case, checking the timer on it. She had seventy-five hours before the refrigerant ran out. But she had no idea how she was going to get the case to safety. If she didn't have this ticking clock, she'd hide out down here for several days until the storm passed over, but she didn't have that luxury.

But she did need sleep. Her mind felt fuzzy and unfocused, and she didn't trust that she could make good decisions in her current battered state. Her body ached for a good long drink of fresh water, and her stomach growled. She hadn't eaten since she left Nakoa at his cousin's house.

She walked back to the barracks room, wanting to lie down for just an hour or two and get some rest. She stripped out of her soaking wet clothes, hanging them up to dry in one of the lockers, and slipped into a pair of clean long johns she found inside it. She set the case down under one of the bunks where it wouldn't get jostled.

Then she lay down and extinguished the lantern, wanting to conserve its fuel. She thought about this pharma CEO whom Nakoa had described. How could someone be so greedy that they'd kill likely millions of people just to make more money off a vaccine? And why was it that the richest people seemed to be the most obsessed with acquiring more wealth, even turning to unethical means to get it? When was enough money enough?

She thought of other epidemics that had killed millions of people worldwide and lingered on for years, disrupting life, spreading grief throughout families, communities, and countries. It was beyond her ability to comprehend how someone would cause that kind of trauma intentionally.

Finally she closed her eyes, sleep taking her exhausted body.

TWENTY-FIVE

London, England
Early the Next Day

Advantageous Pharmaceuticals Inc. CEO Agatha Cromwell paced angrily around her living room. Her heels clicked on the expensive hardwood floor, pattering out a rhythm as she strode from one end of the room to the other. Finally she stopped before one of her floor-to-ceiling windows and gazed out over London from her penthouse on the seventy-sixth floor of the exclusive, brand-new Landmark Building.

The sun dazzled over the city, light flashing off the Thames. She watched the crawl of traffic, tiny toy cars far below, and little dots of people hurrying to and from their pointless little errands—scurrying about to the laundromats, the cheap restaurants, then home—minuscule ants busy in their meaningless lives. She stared down at the seething mass of humanity, imagining their little squirrel brains whirring away like tiny, ineffective machines, their suffocating little lives full of children's pointless football games, cheap peasant foods like macaroni and cheese, carpools, and disgusting sausage barbecues with the in-laws. It made her shudder to think of it.

And once the pandemic hit, they'd all be trapped in those houses in those asphyxiating existences. For now they complained about traffic, and not being paid enough, and working hours that were too long, and not being able to afford groceries or university. They scraped by, relying on people like her to pay the lion's share to the government to support them.

But soon, when the world was forced to withdraw because of the virus, they'd long for those outings. Long to be stuck in traffic just to simply be outside the house. They'd beg to be saved from the tedium and suffocation.

And Agatha would come along with the vaccine, produced in record time, and she'd make absolute *billions*. No waiting for months on end for a vaccine, companies competing with one another to get theirs out first. Hers would be ready and waiting. The only one on the market. And she'd become truly, obscenely wealthy.

She'd inherited wealth from her parents' oil company and started a multibillion-euro pharma company. She'd always been interested in pharmaceuticals. When she was a child, her nanny had given her a peanut butter sandwich, and Agatha had nearly died from an allergic reaction. The nanny rushed her to the hospital. She'd been saved and from then on carried an EpiPen. Even as a child, she realized the enormous wealth that could be built on medicinal drugs. So she'd shifted her parents' wealth from oil into pharmaceuticals. But it was never enough. The board of her company had been angry with her after some recent losses, damn them. Okay, so a couple of her drugs were a little bit misrepresented and didn't quite work the way she'd claimed. And maybe that had cost them a few billion. It was nothing compared to the profits they'd enjoyed over the years. Those greedy bastards on the board didn't care about the hours and effort she put in. All they cared about was their own selfish little profit.

They'd even tried to vote her out. She fumed at the memory. She'd only just scraped by and survived the vote. The next time she wouldn't be so lucky. And those ingrates didn't care at all that *she* was the one who had made them rich. It was always *her* brilliant plans, not theirs. Her genius at work. All they did was sit on their fat arses and rake in the money. And they had the audacity to want *her* out?

Agatha smiled. She'd make sure those bastards were the first to get the virus. A tiny puff of contagion in the executive elevator. And unfortunately, the vaccine would just be a little too late in coming and wouldn't be able to save them in time. Such a shame. And Agatha would be free of them forever.

For the tenth time in as many minutes, she glared at her silent burner phone. Nothing. Why the hell hadn't Garrett reported in? She dialed his number, but just as it had for the last day, it went straight to voicemail. She hadn't heard from him since he was leaving the museum.

She pressed one hand against the glass, staring out at the disordered chaos below, all those little ants. She liked the view from up here. Even better than the view from her secluded mansion in the Cotswolds, where a hundred acres of manicured lawns and elaborate flower gardens provided her space to walk and think and plan, and be away from the grime and vulgarity of London.

She clicked her nails on the window, then pivoted on one heel and strode into her private library, resuming pacing again, this time on the ornate Persian carpet that had been handwoven in 1727 and cost her twenty-five million euros.

She paced restlessly, stopping at a window here, her desk there, then back to the doorway to the living room. She was irate that they'd carved up the mammoth. She needed the entire carcass. Had to have as big of a sample as possible. Garrett was supposed to take a smaller section only if the operation went irretrievably wrong. And what had he meant that he'd "lost the boat"? He'd already lost the state-of-the-art ship she'd provided him when it was seized at the Port of Los Angeles. Now he'd lost a second boat, too? He'd hung up on her before she could demand what his backup plan was. Were they planning to steal yet another boat? Or fly out of there? In a hurricane? She didn't think so. They'd have to wait for the storm to die down, and by then the authorities could have caught up to them.

She hoped the samples he'd taken were enough. This whole operation to seize a mammoth had already gone sideways once before. She thought of the disaster that resulted after the retrieval of the baby mammoth at the Alaska dig site.

For seven years, she'd been on the lookout for a zombie virus she could resurrect. She'd paid off a zoologist, Nigel Miller, to visit different digs in Siberia and Alaska, hoping he'd find a suitable candidate. He'd found two viruses prior to this one. One she was unable to revive, and the other had proven barely infectious, something that would take far too much time and effort to cultivate and genetically engineer to be much of a threat.

Then he ran tests on the mammoth found in the Alaskan gold field and reported back to her that it had a suitable virus. But she was disgusted to learn that the carcass had been shipped off to Hawai'i before she had the chance to claim it. Then she got the news that it had a baby, also a carrier of the virus, and she was ecstatic.

Immediately she'd ordered a hit team to grab the baby and kill the gold field workers and researchers out there, burning their bodies so there'd be no evidence of the pathogen. The last thing she needed was some health worker with access to the virus—a disastrous leak that might result in some other company developing a vaccine to rival her own.

She'd given strict instructions to the hit team to glove up and wear respirators under their helmets. They were told to lock the infant in a special airtight case. They'd done so, stowing the baby mammoth on their helicopter. And she'd told them not to leave any loose ends. She could always pay off another zoologist if she needed to in the future. No sense leaving Miller around to talk.

The hit team had then flown to Anchorage but had to wait for an available rental plane to fly to New York. There they'd rented a second, bigger plane to carry them to London and to her waiting hands. But they'd gotten careless. Stopped wearing their respirators. Maybe even opened the case. She wasn't sure. All she knew is that the pilot got sick first, and the contagion was fast and virulent. He passed out at the controls, and the rest of the crew hadn't known how to fly. The plane had gone down somewhere east of Greenland, crashing into the Atlantic Ocean, where it was lost forever—along with the baby mammoth and the virus.

After that, she'd had no choice but to go after the adult mammoth, which was already locked away in a museum's lab. When she learned of the incoming hurricane, she cobbled together another team and provided them with a state-of-the-art refrigerated vessel, not wanting to risk another plane trip. But the idiots had filed their papers wrong and pissed off some port authority officials, and the ship ended up getting seized.

She should have canceled the operation even then, at the first sign of incompetence, but the hurricane was such a great cover, and in the end she couldn't pass up the opportunity. She knew that law enforcement on that side of the island would be tied up. Emergency systems like 911 would be jammed from overuse. It was just too perfect. So the mission had gone forward.

But who knew what else had gone wrong? Garrett certainly hadn't gone into specifics. But the fools had managed to lose a second boat? What was wrong with them? She gripped her phone tightly, staring at the black screen, willing it to ring.

But it didn't, and she was left, pacing and seething, completely in the dark.

TWENTY-SIX

Alex woke with a start, sitting bolt upright in the darkness, momentarily forgetting where she was and wondering why she couldn't see anything.

Then it came back to her. The bunker. The case. The storm. She reached for the lantern, her injured arm screaming in protest. She found the metal handle in the darkness and relit the lantern from the little tin of matches.

As the warm glow suffused the room, Alex swung her feet off the cot. She had no watch, and with her phone missing, she had no idea what time it was. She looked at the timer on the case. Seventy hours. So she'd slept for about five hours. She hadn't meant to sleep for that long. She moved to the locker, feeling her clothes.

She was desperately thirsty and her stomach growled from lack of food. She thought of the energy bars she'd taken from Nakoa's cousin's house. She reached into her jeans pocket, finding a single remaining energy bar still tucked inside. It was crushed into crumbles, but no water had gotten into the packaging, so she ate it. Also still in her pocket, Alex was relieved to find, was her beloved multitool her father had given her.

Her boots and clothes were still damp, so she changed into a woolen shirt, socks, and pants from one of the lockers. She even found a pair of combat boots that fit her. She put her belt back on and handcuffed the case to it again so she could have her hands free if needed. For now, case in one hand and the lantern in the other, she resumed her exploration of the bunker, wanting to find another way out, preferably somewhere that would lead her far away from the thieves and hopefully farther inland, away from the storm. She walked and walked, hours passing by, finding that the lava tube extended for many miles underground. She knew that one lava tube, Kazumura Cave, on the eastern slope of Kīlauea, stretched for nearly forty-one miles, and wondered how big this one could be.

Movement on the ceiling pulled her gaze upward, and she spotted a small cluster of Hawaiian hoary bats resting on the ceiling. Their golden-brown fur frosted with white and charming little faces made her break into a grin. It was a welcome sight in this cold, dark place. Habitat loss, use of pesticides, and roost disturbance were only some of the threats that had caused this bat to become endangered. She was thrilled to see that some were roosting down here. She moved on quickly and quietly so as not to disturb them further.

In one room she found a water filtration setup with canteens hanging from hooks on the wall. She took in the setup, finding that it seemed to collect rainwater from above, filtering it down into a tank. She chose one of the canteens and turned the spigot on the tank, pouring out a little bit. She sniffed at it, then sipped it, finding it surprisingly fresh and good, so she filled the canteen, drank down the entire thing, then refilled it. If she got a bug from it, she could deal with that later when she was back in civilization.

She draped the canteen's strap over her shoulder and continued her exploration. She reached a narrower section she hadn't seen the night before. One room off to the side served as a supply room. She found canvas satchels, matches, mess kits, collapsible shovels, rain slickers, and mini sewing kits. She cast around for a compass or map but found none.

She returned to the corridor, walking along its labyrinthine length for an indeterminable amount of time. It dead-ended at a flight of metal stairs that led up to the lava tube's ceiling, where a set of angled double doors was mounted, closing off the top of the steps. A locking mechanism composed of a sliding bar operated by a lever had been engaged.

Alex lifted the lantern high, peering up at the blocked staircase. She'd had to take shelter in a storm cellar once in Arkansas, and the style of doors reminded her of this. Water dripped through them, the smell of rust strong.

She walked up the slippery steps and placed the hissing lantern down on the top stair. She let the case hang down off her belt and pulled on the lock. It stubbornly refused to move, so she tugged harder. Then it came free in a rain of rust.

She tentatively pressed against the doors. They didn't budge. She pushed harder, then braced her shoulder against one of them. It felt slimy and cold, covered with algae and moss seeping through the center crack. Pushing upward, she strained with everything in her, but the door wouldn't move.

She stepped back, considering. The only other way out that she was aware of was through the storm drain, and she wasn't about to go down there again. Just the thought of that airless, confined space whirling with water made her heart thump a little faster.

Then she remembered the car jacks she'd seen earlier. She picked up the lantern and case and headed back that way. In the mechanic's bay, she chose a portable jack and picked it up, finding it surprisingly heavy. She found the jack handle and let the case hang off her belt in order to carry everything.

For the hundredth time she checked the case for any signs of damage, but to her relief she found none. It was a tough enclosure.

She returned to the slanted doors and set the jack down on the top stair. She inserted the handle and raised the jack until it was flush with the center seam between the doors. Then things got tough. She cranked it as much as she could but came to another impasse. So she stood on the top step, too, awkwardly hunched over beneath the slanted doors, and stepped on the jack with her foot, then raised it with her hand, then stepped down on it with her foot, over and over again.

Suddenly the metal screeched and made a loud *prang* noise. Muted sunlight streamed in through the center seam where the two doors met. Alex pumped the jack a few more times with her foot, and the work came more easily now. She bent over and used her arms to raise the jack a little farther. More dim sunlight cascaded in, along with trickles of water. Fragrant moss and soil spilled inside, along with the delicate fronds of an uluhe fern.

Now Alex used her uninjured shoulder and pushed up one of the doors all the way, taking in the dawn light of the overcast sky.

But what she saw astounded her. Jungle, as far as she could see. No beach in sight. Rain from the storm still battered down. And she had no idea where she was.

TWENTY-SEVEN

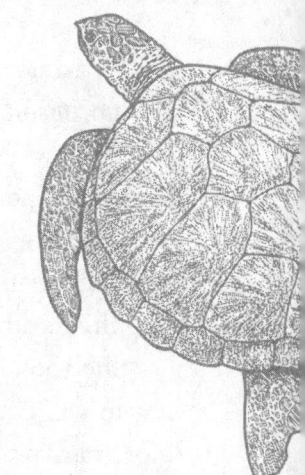

Thick, dense trees grew overhead, their canopy blocking out what little light cascaded through the branches from the stormy sky.

Alex squeezed through the door, moving aside roots and branches. The jungle floor lay thick with vegetation and vines, choking any path forward. She imagined trying to make her way through it. And she had no map, no GPS unit, no way to determine where she was. Tens of thousands of square acres of jungle occupied parts of the island, and she knew she could become irretrievably lost. She'd read and listened to enough survival podcasts to know that people had wandered for days and weeks, lost in Hawai'i, some never making it out alive.

One woman had gone missing for seventeen days, surviving on stream water and fruit she found along the way, hobbling along on a wounded knee and fractured tibia.

She couldn't risk getting lost and the timer running out on the case. Before she took this route out, she had to exhaust all other options.

Letting the door close, Alex made a mental note of the location of this jungle exit and returned to the heart of the bunker. She passed through the clinic and kitchen again, into other barracks areas, and found a small spiral notebook sitting on one of the beds, a Parker fountain pen, and a small bottle of ink beside it. She picked up the notebook, flipping through the contents. Only the first page had writing, a list of names: *Aunt Carol, Jennifer, Gordon, Aunt Norma, Jason.* She wondered if the soldier had been making a list of letters to write or maybe a gift list. She flipped to a clean page and loaded the pen with ink. She drew a rudimentary map of the layout of the bunker so far. Then she tucked the small notebook and pen in her pocket and set off again, arriving at another tunnel that led off into the darkness.

She took this other tunnel, walking for what felt like another few miles. The lava tube meandered left and right, getting more and more narrow. Finally she came to another dead end. A metal ladder stood anchored to the wall here, leading up to a rusted hatch with a locking wheel.

Alex set down the lantern and canteen, detached the case from her belt, and climbed up the ladder. The hiss from the lantern filled the confines of the small space. She tried to turn the hatch, but it refused to shift. She could smell the overwhelming scent of rust. She put all her strength into it, but the wheel wouldn't spin.

Grabbing the lantern, she hurried back to the supply room, locating a pry bar and an ancient can of lubricating oil. She returned to the stubborn hatch and applied the oil liberally. Then, after waiting a few minutes, she crammed the pry bar into the spokes on the wheel and pushed with everything in her. It creaked, moving a few inches. Then with a shower of rust that cascaded down onto her face, it spun free.

She pushed upward on the hatch, rainwater spilling down onto her forehead and cheeks. She welcomed the rinse and brushed the last of the rust off her face. Stepping up to the top of the ladder, she peered out into a green world.

All around her grew ʻōhiʻa trees with their light green leaves and feathery red blooms. For a moment she thought it was another jungle exit, but then she spied brown jumbles of rock beyond the vegetation. She pulled herself all the way out, stepping into dense greenery. Above her, the gray sky roiled with clouds. She carefully made her way through the dense undergrowth of ferns and emerged at the edge of what she realized was a small oasis.

Her mouth came open at the sight before her. Volcanic rock stretched as far as she could see, and in the distance she could see a fresh lava flow issuing from Kīlauea, steaming in the weak sunlight, making its way to the sea. She had emerged into a vast lava field. She wondered how old the rocks around the oasis were and, given the tall height of the 'ōhi'a trees above her, figured this oasis had established itself many years in the past. In the distance she could see other small oases, their green leaves tossed by the stormy winds.

The jumbled landscape before her was sharp 'a'ā lava, rocks that could cut through her boots and flesh. The going would be arduous and dangerous, and she knew people had gotten just as hopelessly lost out in these very same fields as they had in the dense jungles. One man had come out to look at Kīlauea glowing in the dark, had gotten turned around on his way back to his car, and been lost for days. It was only when a tourist spotted him from a sightseeing helicopter that he was finally rescued. Alex couldn't risk that kind of delay. Not with the case ticking down the hours.

Reluctantly she returned to the hatch and climbed down the ladder, locking the wheel behind her. She marked this exit on her map. She reattached the case and draped the canteen across her chest, then grabbed the lantern.

Returning down the long, narrow corridor, she took a different side path, finding a small brig with a couple of jail cells, more racks of coats, gas masks, and ammo boxes. This tunnel led off for another indeterminable distance, Alex's legs starting to tire. The tunnel dead-ended at a set of large doors. These were affixed perpendicular to the floor and were big enough for a jeep to drive through. They had been mounted on metal runners so they could be pushed apart. In front of them, on a cracked cement slab, she noticed mounting places for two guns, likely something big like eight-inch Mk. VI Navy guns. The weapons themselves had long since been removed.

She tugged on the door handles, knowing there was no way they'd slide open easily but wanting to try anyway. After several minutes of tugging with no effect, she slid the edge of the pry bar between the doors and pulled. The doors shifted just a few millimeters, and she was able to jam more of the pry bar into the crack. Muted sunlight spilled into the tunnel. She pulled again, the doors sliding apart even more. Sea air gusted in, howling through the gap in the doors, blasting her in the face. Dirt and thick vegetation cascaded down through the opening, water dripping off it onto her head.

Now the opening was wide enough that she could get her fingers in there and push the doors apart. They shrieked in their metal treads but obliged, creating a space wide enough for her to slip through.

Wind hit her hard, whipping into the bunker, tugging at her hair and clothes. For a second she thought it was another opening into the jungle, but then she heard the crash of surf not far away.

She extinguished the lantern and left it beside the door, then let her case hang down from her belt. She pushed her way through the thick vegetation blocking the door. Her feet and arms caught in vines and leaves as she tried to squeeze her way out. The going was difficult, and it took her several minutes to crawl through the dense blockage. But finally she emerged. She turned, seeing that the rusted metal doors were set in a steep hillside, with soil, vegetation, roots, and vines completely covering their existence.

She stood just inside the tree line on a beach, the branches swaying violently above her, caught in the winds roaring in from the tropical storm. The lighthouse she'd been planning to visit when she first arrived stood just a short distance down the beach. It was a historical one, built in 1912. A small lighthouse keeper's residence stood beside it, a modest affair painted white with a red roof. But the lighthouse had been automated in 2017, so she knew that no one would be home, even if the area hadn't been under an evacuation order.

She scanned the beach for any sign of the thieves but saw only the lighthouse and an empty, storm-tossed beach with huge crashing waves. The lighthouse might have a radio or landline. It would be a risk going there, though. If the thieves had continued along the shore in the hopes of finding another boat, this would be the next spot of civilization they would reach. In fact, they might already be there. They could be in the lighthouse even now, maybe even using it as a place to wait out the storm. But it was also possible they'd been and gone or had gotten hung up somewhere and hadn't reached it yet.

And the lighthouse was a better option than venturing into the jungle. She also knew where it was on the island, finally allowing her to pinpoint her location. She was on the very southeastern edge of the island. Making up her mind, she dashed for the caretaker's house. She hoped there'd be a working landline.

She scanned the beach as she ran, finding it almost entirely open, just a few small breadfruit trees and areas of cooled lava with fronds of fishbone fern growing out of the cracks.

Kīlauea had been erupting over the last few weeks, oozing out fresh streams of cooling lava on the far side of the lighthouse. When she first arrived, Alex had driven out to look at the volcano glowing at night, delighting at the incredible gold and red of the mesmerizing moving lava mixing with the black rock as it cooled.

She still didn't see any sign of the thieves, so she made it the rest of the way to the house, the roar of the surf and wind making it impossible to hear anything else. She noticed the building was now being used as a small office for the Hawaiian Historical Society. Wind had shattered the windows. After pausing outside one of the broken panes, she peered inside for any hint of the thieves but found the place empty. She tried the door, but it was locked. So instead she crawled through one of the broken windows. Inside she saw a welcome desk, several displays about the lighthouse's history on the walls, and a small table with a coffeemaker, cups, spoons, and a clear Plexiglas box that read "Help yourself. Donations welcome." Several folded one-dollar bills lay inside.

Alex spotted the landline at the welcome desk and hurried to it. But when she picked it up, she frowned. No dial tone.

"Damn it." She wondered how many telephone and power lines were down around the south end of the island.

Then she thought of the lighthouse itself. Though it was automated, maybe a radio was still in there.

She cast around for a set of keys and found a ring of them in a drawer in the welcome desk. All were labeled: *Backup Generator Room, Supply Room, Lighthouse Main, Keeper House*. She also grabbed a small flashlight and a headlamp from one of the drawers and stuffed them into her pockets.

In another drawer she found a stash of granola bars and bags of peanuts and pocketed those, too. She'd make a point to come back and make a large donation into that Plexiglas box.

Then she let herself out of the house, locking it behind her. Scanning around quickly, she still saw no sign of the thieves. She ran at a crouch to the door of the lighthouse and used the key to get inside. The winds pressed at her back, jerking the door open as soon as she turned the handle.

She slipped inside, then pushed her weight against the door to shut it. She threw the dead bolt home.

With the roar of the storm suddenly muted, it took Alex a moment to adjust. She could hear her blood thrumming in her ears. Relief flooded over her at the break from the wind. She listened intently in case the thieves were inside, but she didn't hear any movement. Sudden shattering glass made her duck for cover, and the window to the right of the door blew inward, glass scattering across the floor. Wind howled through the fresh opening.

After her heart slowed from the startle, and she was sure she didn't hear any voices, she started searching for a radio. The bottom floor of the lighthouse had been converted into a museum. Displays stood on stands around the room, describing different kinds of lights installed in lighthouses around the world. Other displays described how lighthouses had their own unique flashing patterns and painted colors so sailors could distinguish them from one another. She saw facsimiles of weather records that keepers had kept. Display cases held historical gear: a well-used logbook, a clock, a lantern, an old fountain pen, a pair of binoculars.

Different glass cases held more than just lighthouse memorabilia. One contained a display about fishing and held an old fishing net, a rusted harpoon with a length of rope attached, and a Hawaiian sling—a spear shaft threaded through a hole in a wooden block with some rubber tubing used to propel the spear forward.

Alex searched the rooms on the bottom floor and a small storage closet but found no radio or phone. She ascended the circular staircase to the second level, finding two small bunk areas where the lighthouse keepers had originally slept. On the third level, she found a scarred wooden desk beneath a window facing out to sea. A logbook sat open on it, a fountain pen likely dating to the 1940s resting beside it.

One more flight of spiral stairs took her up to the top of the lighthouse, where the brilliant light spun on its axis. An exterior door opened onto a walkway that encircled the entire structure.

In none of the areas did she find a radio or other means of communication. She returned to the ground floor to figure out her next move.

But as she passed by one of the windows, movement outside drew her attention. She spotted the three remaining thieves rounding the lightkeeper's house. Alex froze, her heart instantly thumping. They were heading straight for the lighthouse.

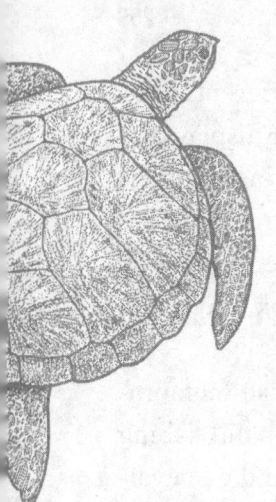

TWENTY-EIGHT

Alex glanced around, suddenly panicked. They must have known she'd end up here and been lying in wait, possibly patrolling along the beach and tree line, searching for her. And now she was trapped in here. She wondered if they'd seen her enter the lighthouse or the lightkeeper's residence. She imagined they would have grabbed her right away if they had. That bought her a few minutes.

She'd locked the lighthouse door, but it was old, wooden, and weathered. If they suspected she had taken refuge there, it wouldn't be hard at all for them to get in through the broken window, and if she were them, she'd certainly search this place.

On the ground floor, waves crashed against the side of the lighthouse, spray coming in through the broken window. She dared another look out, seeing them almost at the lighthouse door. Alex could jump out the window, but they'd easily spot her. And she had nowhere else to go even if she did. The coast out there was treacherous, huge waves and rocks, and she was only a short distance from the fresher lava flows that had been spewing out of Kīlauea. They could overtake her out there, three of them to one.

She thought of hiding, perhaps on one of the higher levels, but she hadn't seen any good places to conceal herself. They'd find her in no time.

But maybe she could slow them down.

She raced back to the fishing display case and lifted the glass lid.

She grabbed the Hawaiian sling, hoping the rubber tubing wasn't so degraded with time that it had lost its elasticity. She found that it was still quite stretchy. Then she grabbed the lead-weighted fishing net and the length of natural fiber rope.

The door handle rattled, the thieves trying to get in. She heard them slamming against it, trying to break it open, but the wood held.

Alex hurried up the first flight of stairs, fishing net and rope draped over her shoulder and the Hawaiian sling in one hand. She let the case hang down from her belt as she placed the spear through the hole in the wooden block and drew back on the tubing. The door was now out of sight, around a turn in the staircase.

And then she heard the thieves grunting as they climbed in through the shattered window. She waited, tensed.

"See if there's a phone," she heard Garrett bark. "I'll check the upper floors."

After a moment, she heard Mitchell say in a lower voice to someone, "You going to ditch?"

Tatiana answered. "I was thinking about it. But after all this shit? After we lost the truck? This is our only payday left now, and I sure as hell didn't go through all this for free."

Garrett started to climb. Alex turned and headed higher, hearing how close he was behind her, taking the stairs quickly. Then he came around the bend and spotted her. Their eyes met and Garrett's gaze drifted down to the case. He reached for his holstered sidearm, and she spun toward him, pulling back on the tubing and firing.

The spear flew free, rocketing toward Garrett and lodging in his thigh muscle. He cried out, reaching down to grab at his leg, and almost toppled backward down the stairs. He caught himself at the last second on the railing.

Tatiana appeared, following close on his heels, stepping around him on the narrow staircase as he bent over in pain.

Alex hurled the lead-weighted net, and it caught the woman

around the legs, tripping her. She fell backward, arms grabbing unsuccessfully for the railing, and she tumbled away out of sight.

She heard an "Oof" as the woman collided with someone below. Mitchell. But Alex knew it wouldn't slow him down for long. She reached the first landing and hurried up the stairs. She hoped maybe he'd think she stepped off there but couldn't hide the sound of her own thudding boots.

So she sprinted up as fast as she could, now holding only the case, canteen, and old length of rope, its rough fiber jabbing into her hand. She passed the third floor and kept climbing, hearing him on the staircase below. He was close.

Then she was at the top by the rotating light. It swung around in her direction, and she turned her head away, squeezing her eyes shut. She couldn't afford to lose even a moment to temporary blindness. When it swept past her, she opened the glass door leading to the exterior catwalk and climbed out. She tugged on the metal railing there, finding it secure, and so she knelt down, hastily tying the old rope to it.

Just as she saw Mitchell reach the top of the stairs and swing his head, searching for her, the light hit him in a dazzling flash. He swung his arm up, masking the brilliance, and she took advantage of the moment and swung down off the lighthouse, gripping the rope tightly.

She'd rappelled plenty of times before when she was studying at Berkeley. She'd belonged to a local rock-climbing group that made regular trips out to Yosemite to scale the granite cliffs there.

But she'd never rappelled off a lighthouse before, let alone on a natural fiber rope that was who knew how old. As she swung out over open air, she hoped it would hold her.

Alex began her descent, pulling her sleeves down over her palms in an attempt to protect them from friction burns. She moved hand over hand, lower and lower, her feet braced against the lighthouse exterior. Despite the protection of her cuffs, the rough rope jabbed through to her palms and fingers, bristly fibers piercing her skin. When she was about twenty feet down, she heard someone curse and looked up to see Mitchell staring down at her.

He traced the rope to where she'd secured it. He bent, working the knot, trying to untie it. But with her weight on it, the rope was too tightly wound. He gave up and reached for his wicked-looking combat knife and began sawing away.

Alex descended faster, the rope whipping through her hands, the pain sharp and immediate. She went another twenty feet and another. She dared a look up, seeing the rope starting to fray and snap where he cut it, and when she was ten feet above the ground, it came free. She careened downward, landing flat on her back. Air erupted from her lungs, leaving her stunned and breathless. The case had fallen to her side, a welcome miracle that she hadn't landed on it awkwardly.

For a few seconds, her whole body hurt. She wondered what she'd broken and couldn't get a breath. Then finally she managed to suck in some air. She wiggled her toes, then her fingers, staring up at Mitchell's angry face. He turned away from the railing in a hurry, and she realized he was on his way down the stairs.

Alex had to move, and now.

She quickly assessed her arms and legs, finding nothing broken, and heaved herself to her feet. She expected both Mitchell and Tatiana to come barging out of the lighthouse at any moment. Garrett would likely be seriously delayed, given the wound to his leg.

Alex ran through her options. She thought of retreating to the World War II bunker. She knew a lot of its twists and turns now, and the thieves wouldn't. She could get ahead of them, maybe enter one way and leave another.

She glanced over to the far side of the lighthouse, where the recent eruptions from Kīlauea had spilled out lava into the sea. The lava was cooled and black now in many sections. She could cross it quickly, get close to the bunker entrance she'd discovered near the lava field.

But she'd have to be careful. While the lava looked black and cool, she remembered from her visit to another volcanic flow that it could be deceptive. The cooled crust might feel hard but still be hot enough to melt the soles of her boots. Or she could break through an area with a very thin crust.

The thought made her cringe. Maybe instead she could make it to the main entrance of the bunker. But Mitchell ran out just then, catching sight of her. He stood directly in her way if she wanted to return to the bunker the way she'd come out. He started lumbering toward her. He was huge, muscled, face angry and mottled, the snake tattoo on his arm rippling with engorged veins.

She had little choice now. She had to race out onto the volcanic field. Clutching the case, she jogged toward the flow.

If she could lose him out there or outrun him, she could retreat to the bunker, and he might not see her doing it. She knew that the exit by the lava was completely covered by the dense oasis, and he wouldn't spot the hatch if he didn't know it was there.

But first she had to get far enough ahead of him. She bolted to the edge of the lava flow. It didn't look that different from the one she hiked on when she first arrived. She reached down, hovering over it with the palm of her hand to sense any heat. Nothing. So she touched it. Cool. She stepped up onto it, the lava hard, smooth, and ropey beneath her feet. She began to pick her way across it, gaining speed. She kept to the edges, testing for hardness beneath her feet before putting her weight on anything, moving quickly.

She dared a glance back, seeing Mitchell at the edge of the lava field, frowning, gazing down uncertainly. He definitely didn't look like he wanted to cross it.

She glanced back toward the lighthouse but didn't see the

woman yet, and she wondered if she'd been injured seriously in her tumble down the stairs.

Then Mitchell stepped up onto the lava. He locked in on her position and started to move rapidly, following in Alex's footsteps.

But he had an advantage. While she had to check every step, Mitchell merely had to follow her, using her as a guinea pig to find the more stable areas.

She stepped over the long, ropey pieces of pahoehoe lava, the terrain uneven and difficult. Mitchell was gaining on her, and Alex suddenly knew there was no way she was going to reach the bunker, let alone with enough lead time to lose him. With her leading the way, it was just too easy for him to catch up. Then suddenly that gave her an idea. If she could find a place with a thinner crust, perhaps it would be able to hold her weight but not his.

Winds thrust at her back and side, and she struggled to maintain her balance. Rain slashed at her face, obscuring her vision at times.

She headed closer to the center of the flow, where the lava would be deeper and take a longer time to cool. She stepped down carefully, testing each step before she put her weight down. Mitchell followed. He was now only about fifty feet behind her.

And then she stepped down on a section that squished a little beneath her foot, depressing just ever so slightly. She took another step and another, finding the lava here slightly soft. An acrid odor bloomed up, and she glanced down to see the soles of her boots smoking. As she moved, the rubber there became so slippery that she almost pitched backward at one point. Rain hissed as it struck the hot surface.

Mitchell was now only about thirty feet behind her.

Then she stepped on a section of black lava that was still so hot she could feel the heat radiating up through her soles. She winced but kept going, the lava getting mushier by the minute. She was pushing it and knew it.

Mitchell picked up his pace, following in her footsteps. He hit the area that was more spongy and stopped briefly, looking down. The soles of his boots smoked, and for the first time, she saw fear bloom on his face. He took another step forward, then another, continually glancing up to check her progress and follow her route, but moving more slowly now.

And then he cried out, and she turned again to look back at him. His foot had broken through the top crust, plunging into hot, burning lava. He screamed as his leg sank deeper, up to his knee, and then his other foot broke through. He teetered, arms windmilling, and pitched forward, his hands coming out to catch him. But they cracked through the crust, sending up splashes of lava as he sank deeper and deeper. She watched his agonized face, all panic and terror now, and then he was gone, swallowed up by the molten rock.

Alex's feet were really hurting now, and she lifted one foot, seeing that her sole had almost completely melted. As she pulled her boots off the lava, thick strands of melted rubber came with them. She needed to get off this flow, and fast.

She darted to the edge of the twisted black mass, then wondered if she should go back the way she came and not risk going any farther. But when she turned to scan a possible route, she spotted Tatiana deftly crossing the lava flow, keeping to the cooler parts, heading straight for Alex, her face a mask of rage.

TWENTY-NINE

Alex had to press on. She hurried forward on the lava, now at a jog, moving along the very edge of the flow where it abutted the length of a steep rock outcropping. The lava had flowed around it. Alex thought of trying to climb the outcropping to get off the lava, but it was too steep and would take too much time. So she kept forward, moving in the direction of the lava field bunker entrance.

She rounded the rock outcropping, Tatiana temporarily out of sight as the fin of rock stood between them. Here the new flow crossed over an older, long-cooled flow. Alex moved onto this older one, running now. Picturing the map she'd drawn of the bunker, she knew that the lava field entrance was still quite distant, and Alex had to speed up considerably if she was going to reach it before Tatiana caught up with her. She just hoped she'd be able to find it.

Keeping the rock outcropping between them, Alex navigated the rough terrain. The rocks here weren't smooth pahoehoe. They were rough and jagged ʻaʻā lava, slicing at Alex's legs and hands as she climbed through the jumbled mess. Here some of the rocks stood six to ten feet tall, and she struggled to move between them. Rain battered her face, wind whipping over the open landscape with considerable force and tugging at her hair. A few times gusts slammed into her back, driving her forward, almost making her trip.

She left the rock outcropping behind, glancing back for any sign of the woman. But she didn't see her. Maybe she'd given up. She'd sounded a little bit reluctant back at the museum.

Alex sprinted all the way to where the bunker entrance lay hidden in the small oasis in the heart of an older flow. She darted into the thick mass of 'ōhi'a trees with their vividly red lehua blossoms, scanning for the hatch, hoping she was in the right oasis. But she wasn't completely sure and couldn't find the opening.

She plunged deeper into the dense greenery, pushing past ferns and moss-covered trunks. Though she was slightly sheltered from the rain here, cold water dripped on her from the leaves above, sliding down the back of her shirt.

The oasis wasn't that big—maybe only a hundred feet wide and long—but Alex still couldn't find the entrance. She stumbled through the thick vegetation, arms out, moving aside fronds and branches, searching the ground.

But it just wasn't there. She stood up, suddenly panicked. Was this the wrong oasis? There was a better than good chance it was. She knew how easy that would be out on a lava flow, a featureless landscape without a lot of points to navigate by. She pulled out her rudimentary map and tried to pinpoint where she stood in relation to it, but she just couldn't be sure.

She was just about to poke her head out of the oasis, to see if another lay nearby, when her foot hit something metallic. She looked down. It was the metal wheel on the bunker hatch. Alex let out a breath of relief and bent down. She turned the wheel and tugged upward on the hatch, swinging it open, and descended the ladder quickly into the darkness beyond.

She pulled the hatch closed above her and spun the locking wheel. Then she waited, tensed. She hadn't seen Tatiana catch up with her, hadn't seen even a hint of her entering the oasis. But the vegetation there was so dense that she could have. Then when she discovered Alex wasn't there, and looked around at the surrounding lava fields and found them empty, too, she'd return to the oasis. Maybe feel around and find the hatch.

Alex switched on the headlamp she'd taken from the lighthouse keeper's residence and descended the rusty metal ladder to the lava tube's floor. She checked the timer on the case: sixty-one hours. Somehow she had to get out of the bunker and get this case to safety, and soon. The hurricane was still raging, though, even on this more southerly part of the island.

The exit by the lighthouse hadn't offered help. She would have to try to hike out via the jungle.

She had just started down the lava tube back toward the main part of the bunker when a clanking metallic sound rang out and light flooded into Alex's world.

Tatiana had found the hatch. She may have been reluctant about cashing in on the pathogen before, but now she was clearly committed, wanting her payout.

Alex briefly thought of trying to fight the woman. But she very likely could have picked up a gun from one of the others, her shotgun probably having been lost in the boat wreck.

Alex sprinted down the lava tube. She heard the woman descending the ladder and then giving chase. And Alex was an obvious target with the headlamp beam bouncing crazily over the walls. She reached up and turned it off and then was racing through the dark, trailing one hand against the side of the tube so she wouldn't run headlong into it.

A beam of light penetrated the darkness. Tatiana had a flashlight. She shone it over the walls, then Alex heard her footsteps pick up into a run.

Alex mentally ran over her options. Maybe she could lose her down here. Get out through one of the other exits without the woman noticing.

But even now, hearing her feet stomp along the lava tube behind her, the sound echoing, she didn't know if she could get enough of a head start to leave her behind.

From this direction, the first room Alex would come to would be the infirmary. Her trailing hand glided along a rack of coats and gas masks, and she had an idea. Grabbing one of the gas masks, she cinched it on, awkwardly trying to tighten the straps with the case in one hand. The mask was old and smelled stiflingly of rubber and some kind of industrial compound. As Alex ran, breathing in gulps of air, she started to feel a little dizzy and sick. But then she reached the infirmary.

She switched on her headlamp and raced to the shelves, scanning the bottles until she found what she was looking for: chloroform. She grabbed a wad of gauze and soaked it in the liquid, then held tightly on to the bottle.

Tatiana closed the distance, the beam of her flashlight darting chaotically down the tube. Then she was at the open clinic door. To her relief, Alex saw she didn't have a gun after all.

In that brief moment, the woman's eyes shifted from Alex's gas mask to the bottle in her hand, her expression one of confusion. Then Alex hurled the bottle, smashing it on the woman's chest and neck, the liquid splashing up over her face and running down her torso. Tatiana turned away and pushed back into the hallway, then started to sway.

The woman teetered, staggering. Alex took advantage of the moment and raced forward, jumping on the woman's back and pressing the chloroform-soaked gauze over her nose and mouth. In moments Tatiana crumpled, Alex going down with her, until the woman lay immobile on the floor.

Alex thought about trying to lock her in the infirmary, but then had a better idea. She jogged down the corridor to the maintenance bay and grabbed one of the mechanic skids.

She returned and hefted the woman onto the skid and rolled her down to the small brig. She dumped her off the skid, dragged her inert form inside, and then returned with a stack of Spam cans, crackers, and several canteens full of water.

Then Alex turned the key, locking her inside, and checked the timer on the case: sixty hours. This wasn't looking good. Stress clutched at Alex's stomach, and she felt a flutter of panic. She removed the gas mask, wondering if she should just leave the case down here and go get help. If the refrigerant ran out and the pathogen escaped, at least it would be down in this bunker. But then she imagined some innocent person discovering this place, especially now that three of its entrances had been opened and would be more noticeable now.

If Alex was delayed getting help . . .

No, she had to press on.

She wondered where Sasha was now, if she'd made it to the sheltered west side of the island. Alex would have given anything to talk to her dad right then, to hear his reassuring voice. Thinking back just a few days ago, when she was so excited about his visit and all the fun things they were going to do together—snorkel, visit a local brewery, see Waimea Canyon on Kaua'i—now felt like another life.

She was just deciding her next move when she heard a strange shuffling sound. She stopped, listening, but heard nothing. She started walking and heard it again. Like a scraping noise. She halted, headlamp beam barely piercing the darkness in the long tunnel before her. It hadn't been Tatiana—it was coming from somewhere in front of her, not behind.

She listened intently, all too aware of the sound of her own heart pounding in her ears, but she didn't hear anything else. She let out a breath.

And then a rending, scraping noise echoed down the tunnel, followed by the echoing sound of footsteps.

Someone else was down here with her.

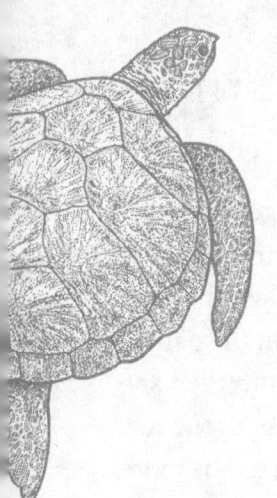

THIRTY

Alex realized the sound was coming from the exit by the lighthouse. For a moment, a glimmer of hope ignited inside her. Maybe it was help. The police. The Coast Guard.

But there had been no one out there before, and she'd been unable to find a radio. Sasha didn't know where she was. No. It had to be Garrett. He'd probably wandered around, searching for where the rest of his team had gone, and discovered the entrance. She wondered how bad his leg wound was.

She thought of waiting him out, hiding somewhere with the case, but if he started to explore, he'd discover the brig and Tatiana, and then Alex would be back to contending with two of them.

She had to lead him out the way that gave her the most advantage.

The lava fields had been treacherous and difficult to navigate. All the jumbled rock made progress slow going, and what Alex needed most now was distance. Distance between her and Garrett. But she couldn't head back that way now, not with him in the main corridor. And the lava entrance would let him pass right by Tatiana.

She had to take the most inland exit—the one that led into the jungle. And she likely had only minutes before he'd stumble across her.

Alex ran to the supply room and began shoving items into a canvas satchel. She grabbed matches, a rain slicker, and a first aid kit, and stowed them alongside the flashlight from the lighthouse keeper's residence. From the barracks room she grabbed a dry woolen shirt, a pair of pants, and a couple pairs of fresh socks. She stuffed her jeans and cotton shirt, now dry, into the satchel. She switched out the combat boots in favor of her own waterproof hikers.

She returned to the main tunnel, listening for a hint of Garrett. Then she heard him, still making his way down the long stretch that led from the lighthouse. He was moving slowly—slower than she'd expected—and again she wondered how seriously she'd hurt his leg with the spear. She could hear him limping—step, shuffle, step, shuffle—down in the darkness. Then a light flashed on the far wall, and she knew he was getting close.

She had to lead him out of the lava tube in a circuitous route that wouldn't take him past where she'd locked up Tatiana.

So Alex braced herself, watching the light get closer and closer. And then the beam fell on her. She let Garrett see her clearly, see the case clutched in her hand.

"Hey!" he shouted. "Stop!"

He wore his gun on his hip and drew it, aiming it at her. She lifted the case in front of her chest to dissuade him from taking any shots. She was sure he wouldn't want to risk hitting it.

Alex let him limp a little closer.

He holstered his weapon. "Look. Let's make a deal. I can cut you in." When she didn't answer, he added, "We're talking millions of dollars here. I don't know who you are or what you do for a living, but I'm guessing you could use that kind of money. Am I right? Hell, we all could."

Alex stayed put as he drew nearer. She thought of fighting him but couldn't risk it. If he got the better of her and grabbed the case, this would all be over. Her best bet was to evade him.

"What do you think? Say . . . two million dollars?"

Alex didn't answer. Then she turned and began walking at a brisk clip away from him.

"Hey!" he shouted. "Where the hell are you going? Okay. How about five million?"

How much was this pharma CEO willing to pay him for the case if he could spare that much for her? Of course, he'd likely just kill her at the first chance and save the entire take for himself.

"Stop." Garrett's deadpan tone made Alex look back over her shoulder. Now his gun was drawn again, aimed at her head. "I'll kill you. Just hand over the case."

Alex ran. She kept turns in the tunnel between her and Garrett but didn't get so far ahead of him that she'd lose him. She needed him to follow. She couldn't risk him finding and freeing Tatiana and having to face both of them again. She had to lead him away.

Every now and then she'd slow and listen, hearing him laboring behind her, seeing the flash of his beam playing over the rough walls of the lava tube. Then she'd pick up the pace again, always staying ahead of him.

Referring to her rudimentary map, she reached the long, narrow section that led out to the jungle. Here she had to be careful not to bump her head, as the ceiling was much lower. This was a long stretch, nearly two miles long, and she didn't want him tiring and giving up. But it was also a straight shot at the end, and she couldn't risk him shooting her when he had that clear line of sight.

So she ran ahead but continually glanced back, letting the beam of her headlamp play over the walls to alert him to her location. She spotted him rounding the last corner, seeing her, and assuming a firing stance, taking aim at her. She flicked off her headlamp and dropped. But the gun didn't go off. Doubtless he'd had second thoughts of firing when he couldn't make her out in the gloom. He might hit the case.

Alex continued down the tube, flicking her light on every few feet and then shutting it off again.

He followed, his light piercing the darkness behind her.

Alex reached the steps that led up to the jungle exit. She switched off her light and climbed up, then pulled the handle on the locking mechanism. She pushed the doors open. Muted daylight spilled in, making her look away from its brilliance. She squinted up into the late-afternoon sky, just small pieces of it visible through the dense jungle canopy, and climbed out.

She dared one look back, sticking her head through a crack in the door to be sure he was still coming. He was about a hundred feet away now. Alex swung the doors shut, finding an identical locking mechanism on the top side. She knew he could undo it from the other side, but it bought her a few seconds. She took off through the trees, stepping through thick uluhe ferns. Behind her she heard the squeal of the rusty doors opening, saw Garrett climb out of the exit, cursing.

He spotted her and lumbered in her direction.

Now she just needed to put distance between them.

The rain continued to drum down, and Alex donned the rain slicker she'd gotten from the bunker and that helped. She began a meandering route in the hopes of disorienting him. She didn't want him to give up and head back to the bunker and find Tatiana, so she left an obvious trail. When they were several miles away from the bunker and had taken enough turns that she hoped he was lost, she picked up her pace.

But as she powered on, she struggled to lose the determined Australian. Whenever she could, she stepped on rocks instead of soil, moving from stone to stone where she'd leave no trace. If she came to a streambed, she walked in the center of it, grateful for her waterproof boots. In areas of dense vegetation, she moved gently, careful not to snap branches.

In some places, though, leaving a trail couldn't be helped. Her boots stepped down on vegetation in the dense areas, leaving impressions in the greenery. Other places she crossed were muddy or had loose dirt. In these, she picked up palm fronds and dragged them behind her, trying to mask her path.

For the first few hours, she caught glimpses of him behind her, cresting a hill or moving between distant trees. But as the day wore into early evening, she lost sight of him and guessed she'd left him far behind with his injury. Or maybe he'd lost her trail entirely.

But she had to be careful to not lose the way herself. It could be more than a day before she reached civilization. Normally at night she could use the stars to determine her position and heading for the next day. She'd star hop from Polaris, the North Star, and pick out a constellation on the western horizon. She'd done this numerous times while hiking in the backcountry.

But if this storm held, the night skies would be too cloudy to use the stars. So instead she'd have to use the muted sunlight and mark any mountains, hills, or landmarks in the west and be sure to keep heading in that direction.

Because everyone had one leg that was slightly stronger than the other, one could end up walking in circles, so she continually tried to check for the position of the sun. But the cloud cover was so thick that the most she could make out was a slightly brighter patch in the skies, which could be the actual sun or could just be a place where the cloud cover was a little thinner.

So she had to rely on other clues to keep on her westerly course and was so grateful for her time on the island with her mother. More than once they'd done route-finding games in the jungles here. She knew to look for white terns and black noddies, who flew toward the ocean in the morning and inland in the evenings. She could use them to orient herself. And she knew how to backsight, where she chose two landmarks that lined up behind her. As long as they remained lined up, she knew she was still walking in a straight line.

As the sun dipped below the horizon, Alex continued on in the gloaming, that magical time when day and night existed at the same time. It had always been her favorite time of day, and as she moved forward on exhausted legs, she found a little comfort in it.

But she knew she'd have to rest soon. Her stomach growled. She ate some peanuts and a granola bar that she'd raided from the snack drawer at the lighthouse keeper's cottage.

The rain slicker did a good job of keeping her dry, but it was also almost intolerably hot, and she sweated under it. She switched to her cooler cotton shirt and jeans.

As the evening wore on, she stumbled on a protruding tree root and almost came crashing down, but she caught herself on another trunk at the last second. She marched on, but tripped on a rock, then another root. It was getting too dark to see, and she was getting too tired to be careful. She had to stop to rest.

Casting around, she found a sheltered space beneath a huge koa tree and laid out her things. She hoped its vast spreading branches would offer respite from some of the rain. The night would be chilly, so she donned one of the warm wool shirts and stretched out beneath the sheltering branches. A little rain still hit her here, but just a small drizzle. She turned on her side so that any water would cascade off her hood and opened her canteen to collect more water.

She checked the timer on the case: fifty-one hours. Fear flooded into her. She worried she'd oversleep somehow and the hours would tick away to zero. But she had to rest or she could make a critical error out here. Get lost or injured.

Soon a fitful sleep overcame her.

ALEX AWOKE TO THE SHORT, warbling trill of a Hawai'i 'ākepa singing in the tree above her. She couldn't believe her luck—they were extremely rare and imperiled. She spotted it then in the branches above her, its plumage a brilliant orange against the green of the leaves. It flitted there for a few moments, head moving quickly, then darted off.

The rain was heavier now, dripping off the branches, but she'd stayed relatively dry in her slicker. She stared up at a completely overcast sky and tried to find the bright spot that would be the sun.

A slightly lighter patch in the sky made her think that was probably it, and she made note of the direction and a distant ridge that lay that way. She'd keep that ridge in sight as she continued her westward journey.

She stood up, checking the timer on the case. Forty-five hours. She drank more water and resealed the canteen. She scanned the area for any sign of Garrett but didn't see even a hint of him. She listened for sounds of traffic or machinery, or anything that might signal she was nearing civilization, but heard only the soft sigh of the wind in the leaves.

After changing back into her cooler shirt, she draped the canteen and her satchel across her shoulder, wincing as she moved her bullet-grazed arm. She reattached the case's handcuff to her belt and marched on. She ate the last granola bar and bag of peanuts, but she'd exerted so much energy that they did little to assuage her hunger. Her stomach was cramping at this point from lack of food, but at least now she'd eaten a little and felt refreshed from her sleep.

She continued west, and soon the sound of trickling water beckoned her and she came to a small stream that ran nearly due west. She followed it for a short time, then came to an abrupt cliff face and had to stop. It dropped precipitously in front of her, stretching for hundreds of yards to her left and right. The stream picked up speed and careened over the edge here, becoming a roaring waterfall that plunged over the steep rock face, sending up a welcome spray of mist that enveloped her. She let her body drink in the cool moisture, resting for just a moment there.

To climb down would be the fastest way to keep heading west, but she didn't want to risk slipping on the moss-covered rocks and falling. If she broke a bone out here, she'd really be in trouble. So instead she backed away from the edge and scrambled through a patch of sharp uluhe ferns and shrubby 'ōhi'a trees. She found a place where the cliff tapered off into a gentler hill and took that route down to the base of the waterfall.

Her arms and legs trembled with exhaustion. She hadn't slept too soundly and had been pushing her body with such little food. Her canteen was almost empty again. If she was going to make it out of here, she needed to find some food and refill her canteen.

She walked to the edge of the stream, stepping over rocks and delicate bellflowers and purple blooms of liua shrubs. She sat down in the shadow of a large volcanic boulder, stretching out her tired legs. Then she took off her boots and socks and dipped her feet into the cool water.

After a few moments, she leaned forward and drank deeply from the stream, then refilled her canteen. The water was cool and fresh. Normally she would have filtered her water in the backcountry, but she didn't have that luxury now.

She sat on the stream bank, resting, letting her feet cool off in the flowing water. Several hot spots had developed on her feet, places that would become blisters. But she had no moleskin to place over the raw areas to keep them from getting worse. It was all a small price to pay if she could get this case to safety.

Above her, an 'alawī, a Hawai'i creeper, sang out. It was another endangered bird, and Alex felt incredibly lucky to be hearing it. She cast around, spotting the small olive-green bird with its little black eye mask in the branches above her. It rested a moment, then flew off, Alex watching it disappear. She leaned back on the big rock, closing her eyes, face to the sky, and just spent a few moments drinking in the scents and sounds around her. In the distance, she could hear the lyrical tones of a 'akiapōlā'au honeycreeper. She was just wishing for her binoculars when she spotted its bright yellow plumage as it flitted overhead. It landed in a nearby tree, and Alex took in its unique curved upper bill that was so useful for fishing insects out of holes drilled in trees. Above her the wind sighed through the koa trees, bringing a gentle susurration. If it weren't for the ticking clock on the case and her banged-up state, this could have been a pleasant place to stay. But as it was, her shoulder throbbed where the bullet had struck it, and all the bruises and scrapes from the storm drain made even resting uncomfortable.

After letting her feet dry in the wind, she tugged on her socks and then laced up her boots. She got to her feet and once again checked her direction. The cloud cover had lessened a bit, and she was able to pinpoint the location of the sun with a greater degree of certainty.

She checked the timer on the case: thirty-nine hours.

She stood and pressed on.

She continued along the stream for a while, drinking a little more and topping off her canteen, hoping she wouldn't get sick later from drinking the unfiltered water. The stream began to veer away from the west, so reluctantly Alex left it behind. She crossed through a dense grove of koa and 'ōhi'a trees and came to the bottom of a steep hill covered in uluhe ferns and dotted with 'ōhi'a trees.

She trudged up the hill and continued on, but the underbrush was so thick here that her progress slowed considerably. By the time she reached the next hill, she was spent. She checked the time on the case. Thirty-five hours. She'd been hiking for ten hours.

But she had to keep going.

She started tripping again on roots and rocks, plodding on like a zombie.

Taking a swig of water, she began to climb the next hill, her feet heavy. Sharp bushes cut her jeans. The going was slow, and Alex could feel every minute ticking by on the case. She wondered if Sasha was safe and if a medevac had been sent yet to retrieve Nakoa. She wondered how bad the hurricane had hit and about the businesses in Ānuenue.

More and more she thought of her mother, of the survival games they'd played here on the Hawaiian Islands and other places. She'd always enjoyed playing them with her mom just because she missed her mother so much when she was away on missions and reveled in the time they got to spend together when she was back.

As a kid, Alex never dreamed that she'd be in such situations in real life, and she was immeasurably grateful to her mom for teaching her so many vital skills at a young age. Not only was it helping her now, but it had started a lifelong passion to learn new things, to never feel daunted at the complexity of a subject or situation. It was that can-do mindset that drove her to learn how to fix her own car as an undergrad and to continue to gain survival skills as she worked in the field.

Right now she wished her mother could be there with her. But then, as she paused and looked around at the trees above her, a light breeze lifted her hair and suddenly Alex could feel her here, out in this amazing setting, not just the memory of her but her spirit, as if part of her were still here, on the wind, in the trees, and far above the clouds, in the jewels of the star-encrusted sky at night.

The thought gave Alex an extra burst of energy, and she crested the hill, almost falling to her knees in gratitude at what stood on top: a stand of strawberry guava trees, their branches dripping with fruit. She rushed forward, selecting the first ripe one she spotted, and pulled out her multitool.

She plucked the fruit and pressed it to her face, breathing in the sweet scent. Then she opened up the knife tool and sliced into the guava, devouring it hungrily. She'd never tasted anything so good in her entire life.

She ate one, then another, then a third. She gathered several more and stowed them in her canvas satchel. This was exactly what she needed to continue pressing on.

Feeling revitalized, she continued her westward journey, hope now blooming within her. She'd make it out of here. She had to.

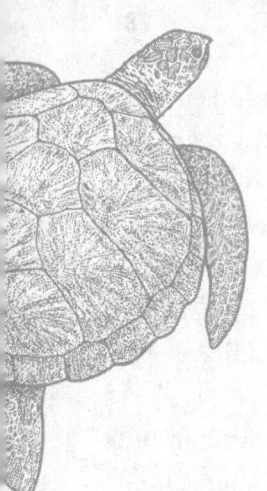

THIRTY-ONE

Garrett was not doing well and cursed himself. He should have been smarter about this, should have grabbed supplies from that bunker. But he thought he'd lose that damn woman if he wasted time searching around. He wondered now if there had been food in there. Maybe some medical supplies, MREs, matches, a compass. Maybe even a map. He'd continued to head west. Had to be where she was heading, to the lee side of the island. But how far away was that? How long to the coast? Were there any towns along the way?

His phone had been smashed to bits earlier when he'd been hit by the storm surge and careened backward into a rock. He had such a great app on there, too—a location-finding app that worked offline in areas with no cell reception. It was a rookie mistake to have only his phone for navigation and he knew it. To have only a digital guide—just a phone or GPS unit—was suicide. Batteries died. Things got smashed. But he didn't even have his phone now.

He was an outdoor guide back home in Australia. Had led people into the heart of the Outback, for god's sake. How many times had he told his clients that one always hiked with a paper map and an analog compass? Countless times. And yet here he was—no food, no map, no compass, no GPS.

Of course, he hadn't expected to find himself in this kind of situation. But wasn't that the point he drilled home to his clients? Always be prepared for whatever you might encounter?

It was this damn leg. It hurt like hell. He was tired, bashed up, and not thinking clearly.

Besides, he told himself, trying to feel better, he knew how to find direction without those things, knew how to navigate by the stars and to look at tree branches for the direction of prevailing winds. He didn't need a compass. And he'd catch up to her.

He'd hunted saltwater crocodiles and tracked dingoes and razorbacks through the bush. He could track a human wearing boots. Only he now found that it was a little harder than he'd expected. She'd clearly walked on hard rock or along streambeds as often as she could, and he'd lost her trail several times already, relieved when he managed to pick it up again on the far side of a group of rocks or farther along on a riverbank.

And who the hell *was* this woman, anyway? A guide herself? A tracker? He found places where she'd purposefully masked her tracks, though she was moving quickly and doing a hasty job.

He'd lost all sense of time and wondered how many hours were left on the refrigerant. If he could just catch up to her, blow her away, get the case, and hike out of here, he'd be set. Plus who knows what had happened to the others, if they were dead or had bailed. At least now he didn't have to split the haul with them. All that money would be his.

Night fell, and he continued to stumble forward, his mind on autopilot.

He knew he shouldn't be moving in the dark. He could barely make out the terrain in front of him, let alone follow her trail. Plus he could stumble and break his leg or go off a cliff. But he couldn't let her get too far ahead. She'd probably be resting in the dark, and it was his one chance to catch up with her.

He limped forward, his leg throbbing in agony where he'd been shot with the spear. He'd also lost a lot of blood. He probably shouldn't have pulled the spear out. Knew better than to do that. But he couldn't very well hike with that thing jabbed in his thigh muscle. So he'd removed it and patched up his leg as best he could back at the lighthouse, slowed the bleeding. It was clotted now, no longer seeping blood, but he knew he'd lost enough already that he was dizzy and unsteady on his feet.

But finally he just couldn't press on and knew he had to sleep. He lay curled beneath a tree to get some cover, but water collected on its branches and leaves, dripping on him continuously. He shivered the entire time, soaked with rain. He could barely sleep. His leg throbbed and had started bleeding again.

All the next day he followed the woman's tracks, sometimes going long stints of time without any trace of her and almost losing hope. But then he'd find a boot print, and he'd be back on her tail. He wondered how far ahead she was of him. But she had to be moving west. Had to be. He'd catch up with her. He knew it.

During the day the rain continued, winds high, tearing at his sodden clothes. He would have given anything for a rain jacket with a hood. Cold water trickled down the back of his neck and back, chilling him. Each gust of wind plastered his cold shirt against his skin, freezing him even more. This was the tropics, for god's sake. Why was it so damn cold?

He trailed her doggedly, nearly losing sight of any trace of her but finding more boot prints as early evening set in. He spent another miserable night beneath a tree, shivering in the rain. The rain! The rain! When was this storm going to end? Wasn't he far enough on the western side of the island by now to at least have a little shelter?

He thought of how warm the Outback was, of the sun beating down on his back. At one point he drifted off to sleep, and his dreams brought him to Australia, in the aridly hot Outback, sweat trickling down from beneath his wide-brimmed hat, the welcome, dry air filling his lungs. Then he jolted awake to realize it wasn't sweat dripping down his back but more miserable rain, ever the rain rain rain.

He tried to lie in a fetal position, left knee tucked up toward his chin, but found he couldn't lift his injured right leg up very high at all, and he had to always lie on his left side or the pressure on the wound was just too much.

So instead he lay on his back, staring up. A section of the tree above his head resembled the grim reaper, a mass of leaves making up the hood and cloak, and a long, curved branch forming the scythe. He turned back on his side, refusing to look at it any longer.

The next morning he awoke to a bad smell. He wrinkled his nose, trying to pinpoint it. Decay. He sat up, crying out in surprise at the blast of pain that came from his thigh. He cast his gaze around for a dead deer or pig but saw nothing. But the stench was close. Had he lain down in the darkness on a carcass? He forced himself to his feet, finding only guinea grass beneath him, and another plume of the bad smell issued up to him.

He stared down in horror at his leg. It was coming from his thigh. He peeled off the makeshift bandage he'd made from one sleeve of his shirt, and the smell of decay intensified. The wound was filled with infected, oozing pus. He hadn't realized it was so bad. The adrenaline of chasing after her had overtaken everything else. He'd managed to largely block the pain and keep going, but suddenly now a pang of fear shot through him.

He needed antibiotics. He wondered how much blood he'd lost. He didn't think it could be a lot. He'd managed to stanch the flow early on, and the wound hadn't seemed that bad, just pierced a little of his muscle.

But all this trekking through the jungle had worsened the injury. If he'd stayed put, given it proper medical attention, things would be different. But he hadn't. He had a single-minded focus on acquiring that case, of getting his payday.

He needed help.

THIRTY-TWO

After becoming too exhausted to hike safely, Alex had spent more chilly hours pressed against the trunk of an 'ōhi'a tree, trying to grab a few hours of much-needed sleep. She'd awoken to the dark of night and checked the timer on the case: twenty-six hours.

She pressed on in spite of the gloom, using her headlamp sparingly to fight her way through dense ferns and jungle, scaling steep ridgelines and hills. After hours of slogging, dawn came, morning light streaming into her world. As the day wore on, she came into a clearing and nearly fell down in gratitude when she saw it. A grassy park stretched before her, a few palms swaying in the wind. A picnic area held a few tables, and a blue sedan was in a nearby parking lot. In spite of her exhaustion, Alex ran out into the open field. Sunlight created inviting shadows on the green expanse, the brightest sunlight she'd seen since days before the storm hit. The wind had died down, just a gentle breeze now, and she knew she was on the lee side of the island.

A couple ate lunch at one of the picnic tables, and she staggered over to them. They looked up, surprised at her sudden appearance, then took in her bedraggled, bloody state.

Alex looked down at the counter on the case. Fourteen hours.

"Do you have a phone?" she asked them.

THIRTY-THREE

Garrett set out again, limping, the stench of decay from his leg even worse. He headed west, but the sky was so overcast that he had a difficult time seeing the sun. He thought he was *probably* heading west, was somewhat certain of it, but he couldn't be sure. He stumbled on, his leg really hurting now.

He drank deeply from a stream and continued on. But this time he didn't see a single boot print left by the woman. He walked all day and didn't spot any sign of her. He'd lost track of her completely. As the day wore on, he started to stumble and trip over roots and rocks. Lack of food and sleep were taking a toll on him.

He'd managed to find a banana tree and ate several pieces of fruit, but the small burst of energy they had given him hadn't lasted long. He needed to find a place to rest for the night. Tomorrow he'd pick up her trail.

He came to a flattened place beneath a tree. Looked like a good place to sleep, but it seemed familiar. He frowned, staring down. Then he looked up into the branches. There it was. That crooked branch he'd stared at all night. The grim reaper with its scythe.

Hope fled out of him like a deflated balloon. Somehow he'd walked in a big circle. The entire day had been lost.

He collapsed beneath the tree, spending another night suffering in the rain and chilly wind.

The next day he arose, feeling dizzy and sick. He had a fever. He was pretty sure of it. His head throbbed like someone was running a jackhammer inside it.

He set off, his progress unsure, once again unable to see the sun. There was a slight bright patch he thought might be it, but when he followed it, stumbling and tripping over rocks and roots, he found himself once again in familiar territory. Or at least he thought it looked familiar. Hadn't he passed that tree before? And wasn't that boulder rather familiar? He didn't see the place where he'd bedded down for the night again, so at least he wasn't walking in circles.

He felt sick and feverish, and his leg hurt too much to walk any farther. The lack of food and sleep was preying on him now, making him incapable of good decisions. At this point, he knew he just had to get to safety, had to figure out where he was and get medical attention. That's all that mattered now if he was going to live.

Fuck this woman. Hell, fuck finding the case. Fuck the money. He just wanted to get the hell out of here. Why had he pushed so hard? Because the money had been so good. It would have been the biggest haul of his life. Enough he could have retired on. He could have moved back to Australia, to his beloved Outback, and just spent the rest of his days drinking beer, grilling dinner, sitting on his porch and staring out at the dramatic red-and-brown rock formations.

All he wanted to do was get to help. But he had no idea which way that lay. How had he not foreseen these factors when he left the bunker?

He couldn't be lost. No way. He was going to make it. This was Hawai'i, for fuck's sake. An easy paradise. He was from Australia, land of infinite backcountry and a million places to get lost and animals that could kill you. And he'd always found his way.

And this was the land of hotels and tourists. He'd be damned if he got lost here. It was ridiculous. No way. He'd find his way out. He'd always bragged about his skills. He wasn't some mollycoddle loser who couldn't tell north from south. He'd wait for it to get dark. Look at the stars.

He lay down, waking up hours later. Darkness had fallen. But it was cloudy. He couldn't make out any stars. How long could it stay this way? He was not lost. Damn it, he was *not lost.*

He waited for dawn. Waited and waited, shivering in the rain. Finally the world lightened. A brighter patch in the sky appeared, and he knew it must be the sun. He used it to pick a westerly direction.

He was going to make it! He stumbled on with renewed vigor. Now he'd find his way!

He walked all day. The sun set and the light dimmed, and the going got harder and harder. But there was no way he was going to stop now. No stars appeared. If he slept, he might lose which way was west again. Might walk in a big circle. No. He'd walk all night if he had to, even if it was dark. He wished he had a light, but his flashlight had died the day before. He just had to make do.

He plowed on into the murky twilight, realizing too late that in the darkness, he'd stumbled to the edge of a sheer cliff.

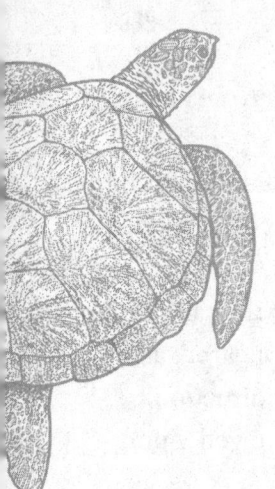

THIRTY-FOUR

After calling for help, Alex had traipsed over to the parking lot and sat down on the curb, cradling the case, and waited for the police. An ambulance arrived as well, but Alex refused to go in it to the hospital. Above all else, she had to make sure the case was secured.

She told the police to call the CDC, and soon after a van arrived with fully hazmat-kitted-out personnel who took custody of the case. Thankfully it was still intact, the refrigerant still working. As a precaution, they set up decontamination showers for Alex and the picnicking couple.

Then she'd ridden to the hospital, where she was treated for a bullet graze, malnutrition, and dehydration, and had her various cuts and scrapes cleaned and bandaged. After that, she'd called Sasha, who was relieved to hear from her. They kept Alex isolated for days until repeated tests for the pathogen came back negative. The CDC secured the virus in storage, in case it cropped up elsewhere in the world and a vaccine would need to be developed.

Sasha picked Alex up from the hospital, and they chatted on their way out to Sasha's new rental car.

"I was worried about you!" she told Alex as they exited the hospital. "All that time and no word."

"And I was so worried about you." It was a relief to see Sasha's face. "How'd you fare with the prisoner?"

"He kept trying to bust down that door. But we'd trussed him up pretty good. He did manage to break the door down by the time I got to Kailua-Kona. But he was just lying there, bound up, flopping around like a tuna fish."

"What did you do?"

"Called the cops as I approached Kailua-Kona. They were waiting for me when I anchored. Sent a skiff out to pick him up. And I told them to send a medevac out to Nakoa, but due to the storm, they weren't able to get out there till the next day. But I just checked on him, and he's stable."

"I'm so glad." Alex had been asking the nursing staff about him and knew he'd been Life Flight–ed to Hilo, where they'd removed the bullet and treated him for shock and blood loss. She was relieved to hear he was on the mend. "And the pathogen? Is he in the clear?"

Sasha nodded. "Yes. He was isolated and tested for it. He came up negative, and so did his lab assistant and her family. She'd hunkered down with them in Waikui to ride out the storm." Sasha frowned. "What about the thieves?"

The cops had been out to question Alex several times, and she'd received some updates. "They found Tatiana. I'd locked her in a brig inside an old World War II bunker."

Sasha's jaw dropped and she raised her eyebrows. "Seriously?"

"Yeah. The whole place was a lucky find. They tested her for the pathogen, and she's clear, too. She's under arrest for a whole slew of things: grand larceny, kidnapping, arson, assault, destruction of property, two counts of the unlawful taking of a vessel, and multiple counts of homicide. Apparently she's cooperating to have the murder charges reduced. She claims she didn't kill anyone herself—only Mitchell and Garrett had."

"And you believe that?"

"I don't know. They were a brutal bunch." She went on to tell Sasha about Mitchell dying in the lava and losing Garrett in the jungle. The cops had recovered the bodies of Dora and the thief Chet, who'd given his life trying to save Nakoa. Jake's body had been recovered from the storm drain. They'd found no remains of Mitchell, his body likely completely destroyed. A search had been ongoing for Garrett, but so far search and rescue had been unable to locate him in the wilds where Alex had eluded him.

"That's worrisome to think he's still out there."

"I know."

"And what about you? How are you?" Sasha asked.

Alex tried to rotate her wounded shoulder and winced. "The time in the jungle was harsh, especially with this shoulder. But it was also really beautiful."

Sasha shook her head, smiling ruefully. "Only you would think a wounded excursion through a jungle in a hurricane would be beautiful."

"Saw some endangered birds," Alex added, which made Sasha elbow her in the ribs. "Ow!"

"'Saw some endangered birds.' Sheesh. You are too much."

On the way back to Honu Beach, they stopped at the Center for Sea Turtle Restoration and picked up the eggs Keola had transported there before the hurricane hit. Then they stopped by Nakoa's cousin's house and got the rest. From her shot-up Jeep, they also retrieved Alex's computer and large backcountry pack where she kept most of her belongings. She was glad she'd gotten the additional insurance coverage for the Jeep. The rental car company told her they would send out a replacement vehicle.

From the hospital, Alex had also contacted the owners of the Triumph TR6 and paid to have its ignition replaced. Thankfully, the owners didn't press charges. She also checked on Keola, Lupesina, and Jerome, all of whom had ridden out the storm in safety.

When Sasha delivered Alex to storm-ravaged Honu Beach, she helped Alex set up her tent, then gazed about frowning. "You sure you want to stay here?"

"I'm sure. Got to rebury these eggs. And more turtles could show up."

"You can stay with me on my boat. I've got plenty of room."

Alex squeezed her friend's arm. "That's very kind of you, but I'll be okay here."

They stood for a moment in silence, staring at the spot where Dora's body had fallen. "I can't believe they just killed her like that," Sasha murmured.

"I know. It's just devastating. And imagine how Nakoa must feel. To be reunited with her after all that time, and then . . ."

"It's shattering," Sasha agreed.

When Alex was settled in, she walked Sasha back to her car.

"You sure you don't want to come stay on my boat?"

"No, thanks. I'm good."

"Call me when those little guys hatch. I'm bummed I missed it the first time."

"Will do."

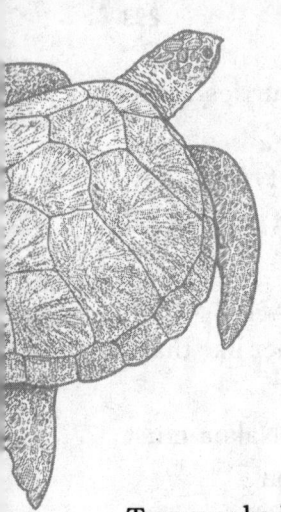

EPILOGUE

Two weeks later, Alex sat outside in a lawn chair at the house of Nakoa's cousin Khai. Nakoa had invited Alex to his family's luau as they celebrated his niece's graduation from the University of Hawai'i and Nakoa's release from the hospital. The luau had been postponed because of the storm, but now they were celebrating in style.

Alex sat beside Nakoa, a fire crackling before them. Khai's house had survived the hurricane with just minor damage, but many other houses hadn't, and businesses in Ānuenue had been flooded and many utterly destroyed.

Keola's restaurant had been completely inundated in the storm surge, and he'd been dealing with his insurance company, which had insured many of the businesses in Ānuenue. He thought he'd be able to repair and restore rather than completely rebuild, but it was going to be a long, hard road.

FEMA had arrived with food and medicine and set up temporary shelters for those who had lost their homes. Several people had been killed, and some were still missing. It was going to take a long time to recover and rebuild.

Alex was impressed with how much the community looked after its own, and though she'd seen her share of tears and grief in the last couple weeks, she'd also seen a lot of commitment, determination, and hope.

But she also knew that with climate change, these kinds of storms would only get worse, taking more lives and doing even more damage. She just hoped that communities and governments could come together and open more channels for solutions, like installing renewable energy, reducing emissions, and protecting vital forests that sequestered carbon. How many devastating storms, floods, and fires would it take before real, substantial change was enacted?

She looked across the fire to where her volunteers sat. Keola and Lupesina were playing a card game with Jerome, and Sasha was helping Khai bring out some more plates and utensils. Nakoa had invited them all, too, and they had toasted to Dora. Her volunteers who had left earlier on the day of the hurricane had been shocked to learn what had happened. Alex was just glad they were gone before the mercenaries had shown up.

Jerome's aunt's house had mostly survived the storm but suffered severe roof damage, so he and his aunt were flying back to Detroit in a few days to stay with their family there until the house could be repaired. It was going to be a while. Repair and construction companies would be swamped for months, and many families would have to wait an inordinately long time before they could return to their homes.

"How's your side?" Alex asked Nakoa.

"Hurts like the dickens. How's your shoulder?"

She rotated her arm. "Hurts like the dickens."

"But it could have been worse," he said with a rueful smile.

"It could have been a hell of a lot worse," she agreed. They clinked together their glasses of ʻōkolehao, a strong liquor made from the root of the ti plant.

A radio on a picnic table played '50s music.

Neither of them had told the others about the pathogen or how close they'd come to complete disaster. "What are you going to do now that the museum is gone?" she asked him.

Nakoa shook his head. "It makes me sick to think of all the

specimens that were destroyed. It was quite a collection. But Kalino is going to rebuild it. He's really committed to having a world-class museum in his hometown." He gave her a crooked grin. "So I guess I'll just go on a two-year vacation while that happens. I've always wanted to see Bali." He looked down then, a solemn expression coming over his face. He rotated the glass in his hand and bit his lip. Alex could see unshed tears shimmering in his eyes. "Still can't believe it about Dora. To meet up with her again after all this time and then lose her so quickly. It all just feels like a nightmare. I really thought we'd been brought together for a reason, like finally we were going to really be together."

"I'm so sorry, Nakoa. She was really someone special. So giving. And she wasn't about to let them take you."

"I feel so much guilt."

"Don't you dare," Alex told him. "Her death is one hundred percent on those assholes, not on you." Though inside, Alex herself felt her share of irrational guilt as well. If Dora hadn't been there on the beach at Alex's request, she wouldn't have been in danger. She would be sitting with them right now, sharing the 'ōkolehao, planning a future with Nakoa.

"I'm absolutely shattered," he said, then turned his face away, pursing his lips. When he'd taken a moment to recover, he faced her again. "I hadn't even gotten over the shock of losing Caleb. And now to think my sweet, sweet friend Dora . . ."

Alex reached over and gripped his hand, and they sat in silence together for several minutes. Alex felt wretched about Dora and couldn't get the image of her murder out of her mind. "I'm so sorry," she said again. She knew from experience that words did little to console. So often it was just company, camaraderie, and compassion that helped heal.

"We need to honor her somehow," Nakoa suggested.

Alex had already been thinking about placing a memorial on the beach for her, and she was sure Dora's students would want to pay tribute as well. "We'll put something on the beach for her. And then we'll get everyone together and hold a special tribute dinner to her. She'll be with us in spirit."

He sniffed and nodded, then swallowed hard.

The radio shifted to commercials, then a top-of-the-hour news report. "Authorities have just announced that the remains of Garrett Collins, who had been missing in the vicinity of the Kaʻū Forest Reserve for the last two weeks, have been discovered by two hikers who were backpacking through the area. An autopsy is forthcoming, but it is suspected that he tumbled off a steep cliff, where he died from his injuries."

Nakoa and Alex exchanged glances, then took another drink.

Alex's phone vibrated. She pulled it out, seeing a call from a blocked number. Normally she'd let such an unknown go to voicemail, but she had a strange feeling about this one, so she picked up.

"Excuse me a second," she said to Nakoa, and stepped away from the party. "Hello?"

"Alex."

At the sound of Casey's voice, Alex's stomach started doing flip-flops. "Casey?"

"Aye."

"How are you?"

"Wanting to check on you. Heard there was quite the storm where you are." His familiar Scottish accent lilted to her over the phone line, making a smile come unbidden to her face. How she loved his voice.

"There was," she told him. "Pretty intense."

"You okay?"

"I'm getting there."

"Anything I can do to help?"

"Want to come watch some turtle eggs in paradise with me?"

"More than anything."

Warmth suffused Alex suddenly, and the thought of seeing him made her heart suddenly pick up its pace.

"I'm calling because I heard you ran into some other trouble there, too."

"I did." She explained to him about the pathogen that was almost handed over to the CEO of a pharma company. "She would have made billions with the only vaccine."

"That's absolutely despicable. What's going to happen to her?"

"Probably nothing. From what I understand, she's unbelievably rich. The police questioned her but didn't make an arrest. She'll probably just pay off the right people or spend millions getting her case tied up indefinitely in court. Plus it'll be hard to prove. From what I've heard, she was very careful about not leaving a paper trail and only dealt with the mercenaries vocally through a burner phone. They haven't been able to find it or link anyone to its purchase." Alex went on to explain how Cromwell even ordered the murder of the gold miners and excavation team who found the mammoths. But all of it was hearsay and likely wouldn't lead to any kind of conviction. "She'll be free to try again."

"That's absolutely vile," he said, and she could hear the disgust in his voice. Casey had spent much of his adult life setting wrongs to right, sometimes using morally questionable methods. Some might call him a vigilante; others might think he was simply dangerous. But Alex had always felt safe with him. He'd had her back and she'd had his on more than one occasion.

"The mercenaries were pretty terrifying." She swallowed hard. "They killed one of my volunteers and came close to killing a second. But at least the second one is on the mend. In fact, I'm at a luau at his cousin's house tonight to celebrate his recovery."

They fell into a brief silence, and then he said, "And you? You're okay?"

"A little scraped and banged up, but I'll recover. Nothing serious."

"Alex . . . I don't know what I'd do if . . ." His voice suddenly choked with emotion.

Her heart felt like it skipped a beat. "I feel the same way about you," she said finally.

"I'm so glad to hear your voice," he told her.

"And I yours."

She wanted to ask when she'd see him again, where he was, what he'd been doing, but she knew better. As he would likely say, it was better that she didn't know. Plausible deniability and all that.

"And you?" she asked. "Are you . . . safe?"

"Aye. Hard at work on another case."

"Anything you want to talk about?" she asked, throwing caution to the wind.

"I'd better not. Don't want to involve you. But I will say that I myself am in the opposite of a tropical paradise. It's snowy as hell here, and I'm freezing my . . . my feet off."

"Sounds familiar," she said, thinking of their time out on the arctic ice.

He went silent for a few moments and then said, "I think about you."

"I think about you."

"And I'd like to see you."

Now her stomach really was doing somersaults. "I'd like that, too."

"Then soon."

"Yes."

And then the line went silent, Alex left clutching her phone, not realizing how hard she'd been gripping it or how tightly she'd been holding it against her ear until she lowered it.

Casey . . .

Her heart and mind swirled with emotion. They'd been through so much together. Their adventure out on the arctic ice, their fight for survival. She'd never met anyone like him and knew she never would again. He was absolutely singular, and a piece of her very soul longed for him like nothing else she'd ever felt, a fire burning inside her. But at the same time, she knew that he was deeply broken and unpredictable. He was good—good to the core of his being. She was certain of that. But his life was unpredictable and sometimes savage in his search for justice.

But then she thought of herself—her own life was unpredictable, moving from place to place, often finding danger out in the wilds, from natural forces like blizzards to humans who wanted to halt her research. But she deeply believed in her mission to help imperiled species, just as Casey deeply believed in his mission to stop injustice, even if that meant breaking the law. Even if that meant murder.

They weren't so different, but at the same time, they were. Vastly different. And they were both wanderers, going where causes called them.

The only thing she knew for certain, deep down within her, was that they were going to meet again.

A WEEK LATER, ALEX SAT on the beach by one of the nests, waiting for her volunteers. She listened with her microphone, hearing the hatchlings scrambling beneath, making their way toward the top. Alex couldn't wait to see them waddle off toward the surf. She'd reburied the eggs she'd stashed at Nakoa's cousin's house, as well as the ones that Keola had brought to the center. The turtles that had been taken by the traffickers had only a short time left in quarantine before they, too, would be released back into the sea, including the hawksbill she had tagged. So far, it was doing well and hadn't laid more eggs while in captivity. Alex hoped the eggs would come after it was back in the wild.

She pulled out her phone to check the current weather report, to see what they had in store for the night. It was going to be clear and mild. As she closed the window, the home page on her browser flashed the latest news headlines. Alex stopped, mouth coming open at one of the stories. She clicked on it.

> Advantageous Pharmaceuticals Inc. CEO Agatha Cromwell was found dead at her Cotswold estate earlier today, apparently of anaphylactic shock. While an autopsy is forthcoming, authorities found take-out food containing peanut oil, a known allergen for Ms. Cromwell. Ms. Cromwell had said in interviews that her interest in developing medications began when she was just six and suffered an allergic reaction to peanuts. An EpiPen saved her life that day and started her lifelong fascination with developing medications. However, no EpiPen was found on or near her person at the time of her death. While Ms. Cromwell ordered from that restaurant regularly and never had issues, the delivery driver that day reported that her order had been stolen out of his car while he was getting gas. When he arrived with her replacement order, he found her unresponsive and called emergency services. She was pronounced dead at the scene. Advantageous Pharmaceuticals Inc. stock plummeted today, with sources saying that it is unknown who will now head up the company.

Alex stared at the screen. She couldn't believe it.

A few minutes later, her phone buzzed, revealing a text from a blocked number: *Had takeout for lunch. Place had a varied menu, so people never have to worry about getting the same thing all over again.* Alex gripped her phone.

Casey.

Shock stole over her. *People never have to worry about getting the same thing all over again.* If Cromwell got off as expected, what would have stopped her from trying all this a second time? Nothing.

She lowered her phone, gazing out at the sea, thinking about Casey, about the threat of the CEO now being gone, about the terrible things Cromwell had done. About Dora. Her heart rate hitched up a notch, and Alex let the soothing sounds of the waves sweep over her and lowered her head, feeling the warmth of the sun on her back.

After several long moments, she lifted her gaze to the nests. She hoped the rest would hatch soon, that all of them had survived being jostled and transported. For now, all she could do was watch and wait and hope that soon the beach would be teeming with little hatchlings.

It was an important step to preserving the hawksbill turtle, but she knew that so much more needed to be done. The one way to really protect sea turtles was to establish marine reserves that were closed to fishing and whose beaches were safe from uncontrolled development and light and sound pollution. And that was going to be a long fight.

But for now, having survived the tropical storm and stopped the release of what could have been a devastating epidemic, Alex just felt grateful to be alive and grateful to be even a small part of nature's recovery.

She'd continue to fight, with everything in her.

AFTERWORD

In writing this afterword, I found that addressing the issues I mentioned in *Storm Warning* was incredibly distressing. Government agencies and legislation are being dismantled and altered so quickly that much may have changed already between the time I write this book and the time it is published. The very things that are in place to protect endangered species, habitats, and our air and water are in danger of being removed or have already been removed.

Species like the hawksbill are already in grave danger of extinction. Dismantling additional environmental protections, opening up federal waters to more oil and gas extraction, halting any effort to mitigate climate change, and circumventing the Endangered Species Act are all measures that will cause harm not just in the short term but in decades to come.

After the BP Deepwater Horizon oil spill, aerial surveys revealed that tens of thousands of sea turtles and other marine life had been exposed to oil, leading to the deaths of thousands of turtles from inhalation and consumption of oil and toxic chemicals. Still more turtles were killed when the gulf was set on fire to consume surface oil. Oil and wildlife simply do not mix, and if we double down on the production of fossil fuels and reduce or eliminate our efforts to move toward renewable energy sources, we are dooming many creatures both on land and at sea, including ourselves.

We need to rethink this idea that money always has to come

first, before conservation, before our health, before the health of the planet. Many people suffer from an epidemic of greed. Though they have plenty of money, they crave more and more, often to the detriment of humans, wildlife, and the environment. Developers and corporations have enormous economic power to do the wrong thing, while conservationists just keep losing out because of a lack of funds.

We really need to start thinking about what's important in the long term, not just cater to short-term financial gain. If we're going to survive, if the amazing creatures we share this planet with are going to survive, we need to value a healthy planet and a rich biodiversity of life.

So what can we do to help wildlife, the environment, and specifically, given the theme of this novel, sea turtles? Thankfully, we can do a number of things, including making beaches safer for turtles, reducing our plastic use and carbon footprints, even volunteering in the field to help nesting turtles. I have listed a number of specific actions we can all take in the following section, "To Help and to Learn More About Sea Turtles." I hope you will read it and feel inspired to take action.

And most important, especially today, don't give up. The challenges facing wildlife conservation and the environment may seem daunting, but we're not alone. We have each other. We have voices and our pens. We can speak out. We can protest. We can make meaningful local changes.

We're not separate from nature. We breathe its air. We drink its water. We eat the food grown in its soil. We live *in* nature, not apart from it. When we work to save the Earth, we work to save not just nature and the myriad animals we share this planet with, but ourselves as well.

TO HELP AND TO LEARN MORE ABOUT SEA TURTLES

Books:

Spotila, James R. *Saving Sea Turtles: Extraordinary Stories from the Battle Against Extinction*. Baltimore, MD: Johns Hopkins University Press, 2011.

Spotila, James R. *Sea Turtles: A Complete Guide to Their Biology, Behavior, and Conservation*. Baltimore, MD: Johns Hopkins University Press, 2004.

Documentaries:

"Hawaiian Hawksbill Turtles: One of the World's Most Endangered Sea Turtle Populations." Produced by NOAA Fisheries, 4 min., 23 sec., https://videos.fisheries.noaa.gov/detail/videos/sea-turtles/video/5797754468001/hawaiian-hawksbill-turtles:-one-of-the-world-s-most-endangered-sea-turtle-populations.

"Hawksbills: A Path to Recovery." Directed by Koaliʻi Puʻu, Dylan Falces, and Lily Katz, produced by Maui Huliau Foundation, posted June 21, 2013, mauihuliau, YouTube, 7 min., 1 sec., https://www.youtube.com/watch?v=hwWqNi8UURQ.

Open Season: Saving Grenada's Last Sea Turtles. Directed and produced by Nicolas Winkler with Ocean Spirits, posted March 19, 2025, Nicolas Winkler, YouTube, 44 min., 53 sec., https://www.youtube.com/watch?v=RZdb6fn9qqg.

"Sea Turtles: The Lost Years." Episode of *Changing Seas*. Produced by Julie Hollenbeck and Veronique Koch, Community Television Foundation of South Florida, posted June 17, 2015, ChangingSeasTV, 26 min., 43 sec., https://www.youtube.com/watch?v=stoZlVAj5e4.

Websites that offer facts about hawksbills:

World Wildlife Fund: https://www.worldwildlife.org/species/hawksbill-turtle

Ocean Conservancy: https://oceanconservancy.org/wildlife-factsheet/hawksbill-sea-turtle

NOAA Fisheries: https://www.fisheries.noaa.gov/species/hawksbill-turtle

Wildlife Informer: https://wildlifeinformer.com/facts-about-hawksbill-sea-turtles

You can support various nonprofit organizations that help sea turtles, such as these:

1. Turtle Island Restoration Network: https://seaturtles.org. This charity works to safeguard marine species, protect and restore critical habitat, combat climate change and plastic pollution, and expose seafood hazards.
2. Ocean Conservancy: https://oceanconservancy.org. This nonprofit organization works to protect oceans through plastic pollution reduction, promoting sustainable fishing practices, combating climate change, and more.
3. World Wildlife Fund: https://www.worldwildlife.org. This nonprofit works globally to protect turtles by eliminating turtle bycatch, preventing illegal wildlife trade, strengthening beach protections, raising awareness, and more. You can even adopt a turtle to support the organization's work and receive a certificate and plush turtle.
4. Conservation International: https://www.conservation.org. This nonprofit is a global effort to protect land and sea, reduce climate change effects, and communicate the crucial benefits nature provides to humanity.

5. The Leatherback Trust: https://leatherback.org. This organization helps the world's most imperiled populations of sea turtles through research, habitat protection, education, and advocacy.
6. Georgia Sea Turtle Center: https://www.jekyllisland.com/activities/georgia-sea-turtle-center. This is an education and rehabilitation facility with exhibits and indoor and outdoor programs.
7. Coastal Discovery Museum (a Smithsonian affiliate): https://www.coastaldiscovery.org. The museum relocates nests in danger of being washed away by tides and protects them during incubation.
8. ARCHELON (The Sea Turtle Protection Society of Greece): https://archelon.gr/en. This nonprofit combines scientific research with volunteer work. Its Sea Turtle Rescue Centre receives and treats injured sea turtles and carries out educational activities for students and visitors.

Things we can all do to help sea turtles, regardless of where we live:

1. Join or donate to nonprofits that are helping with turtle conservation.
2. Reduce your intake of food harvested from the ocean. If you do eat marine species, make sure they were taken responsibly and sustainably.
3. Don't eat turtle eggs or meat.
4. Don't make or buy jewelry or other accessories made from turtle parts.
5. Speak out against dangerous ocean drilling projects, unsustainable fishing practices, and the use of nets that kill turtles.
6. Write to your local, state, and federal government representatives about adopting environmentally friendly practices.
7. Share your love of nature and turtles with adults and children alike. Show them why such creatures should be valued and protected.
8. Protest the construction of beach obstructions such as seawalls, riprap, geotextile tubes, and other devices that prevent turtles from accessing nesting areas.
9. Start a movement yourself. Historically, it often takes only one person or a small group of people to stand up for a species or a location and get it protected.

Things you can do if you live near or routinely visit a turtle beach:

1. Adopt your local turtle beach. Keep it turtle friendly. Eliminate any light pollution coming from your property that can affect nesting turtles, and talk to local businesses and other homeowners about doing the same. Help restore the beach if it has obstructions that prevent turtles from coming to shore.
2. Don't build resorts or housing on turtle beaches, and protest any developments that aim to.
3. Engage in community science. Record locations of turtle nests and keep track of population trends and reproductive success. Use this data to see where and how things can be improved for turtles.
4. When boating, be very careful about boat strikes.
5. After a day at the beach, fill in any holes in the sand that you or your kids may have dug that might affect turtle movement.
6. Don't drive on turtle beaches. You could damage incubating nests beneath the sand, create tracks that inhibit movement, and drive females away who were wanting to nest there.
7. Check for and stop any pollution that is seeping into the groundwater.

Things we can do to reduce global warming:

There's a lot we can do about climate change to address rising sea levels and temperatures that are negatively affecting turtles. As I mentioned in the book, the warmer the temperature, the higher the likelihood of female hatchlings. As more and more nests result in largely female offspring, this greatly reduces the chances of rebuilding endangered turtle populations. But we can take steps to reduce the level of CO_2 in the atmosphere and therefore counteract global warming:

1. Drive a hybrid or electric vehicle.
2. Find out where your bank is investing its money to be sure your money is not supporting destructive practices.
3. Install solar or wind on your property.
4. Turn off electrical devices and lighting when you're not using them, including any lights that may burn all night at your place of business. When not in use, unplug devices that use power in standby mode when turned off, such as TVs and gaming consoles.
5. Improve the insulation of your home and business.

6. Encourage local, state, and federal governments to adopt more renewable energy sources.
7. Talk to your neighbors, friends, family, and coworkers about adopting these practices.

Things we can do to make the ocean safer for sea turtles:

We can also encourage our government to adopt and maintain practices that aid in the protection and conservation of sea turtles.

1. Urge the government to adopt and enforce better fishing gear practices, such as the widespread use of turtle excluder devices (TEDs), and limit or exclude fishing access to particularly sensitive areas.
2. Demand the establishment of protected, critical habitat for turtles and other marine life.
3. Encourage governments to crack down on the illegal wildlife trade.

Things we can do to reduce plastic pollution:

Microplastics and ocean garbage greatly impact wildlife in terrible ways, but we can address these issues, too.

1. Take part in beach cleanups.
2. Reduce your plastic use, especially nonrecyclable single-use items such as straws, utensils, and take-out food containers.
3. Do not have balloon releases and discourage others from having them at parties and other functions. Balloons end up in the ocean, entangling and killing marine life. Turtles swallow them, mistaking them for jellyfish.
4. Discard fishing line in a responsible way, and pick up any you find and dispose of it properly.
5. Employ reusable items as much as possible, such as refillable water bottles and reusable grocery and shopping bags.

If you would like to adopt a nest, check out these opportunities:

1. Coastal Discovery Museum: https://www.coastaldiscovery.org/make-a-difference/. This program is run through the Coastal Discovery Museum on Hilton Head Island in South Carolina, where sea turtles come to shore to nest. In addition to receiving gifts like turtle T-shirts

and souvenirs, adopters will be sent updates on how their nests are doing, as well as final reports on how the hatchlings fared.
2. The Leatherback Trust allows you to help safeguard a nest from laying to hatching: https://donate.democracyengine.com/LeatherbackTrustOne-Time.

If you would like to volunteer to help sea turtles in the field, see these opportunities:

1. To protect turtles in Parque Nacional Marino Las Baulas and Playa Cabuyal in Costa Rica, you can volunteer to patrol beaches, relocate nests in danger of being washed away, and collect data for researchers during the turtle breeding season. This opportunity to help turtles in Costa Rica is offered through Earthwatch, in collaboration with the Leatherback Trust. https://earthwatch.org/expeditions/costa-rican-sea-turtles.
2. If you'd like to help sea turtles on a beach in Greece doing much of what Alex herself did in this novel, check out ARCHELON'S volunteer program and become part of a team that monitors nesting loggerhead turtles at night. You will take scientific measurements and tag the turtles that come to the beach to lay eggs. During the day, you have a chance to educate visitors. https://archelon.gr/en/news/become-a-guardian-of-the-night-volunteer-with-archelon.
3. If you live in or spend time in the Hawaiian Islands, you can help identify and track hawksbill turtles through Hawaiian Hawksbill Conservation. There you can submit photos of hawksbills to identify individuals and thereby significantly contribute to research. https://www.hihawksbills.org.

ACKNOWLEDGMENTS

Many thanks to my wonderful editors, Danielle Dieterich and Grace Vainisi, who provided invaluable feedback and who are a delight to work with. Huge thanks to my amazing agent, Alexander Slater, who is simply the best agent ever and for whom I am eternally grateful.

For the sake of the action and plot, I took some creative license with the geography of Hawai'i. I hope those familiar with the area will forgive me.

Many thanks to Grant Zazula, Valery Monahan, Dick Mol, and Jeffrey Bond, who were fonts of information about ice age mummy excavation and preservation.

A heartfelt thank-you to my friends who have encouraged my work over the years, reading my fiction and being supportive. I appreciate all of you, each and every one! So thank you to Lucy, Tina, Dawn, Jen, Alex, Penny, Carol, Kimberly, Jon, and Joel, among many other wonderful friends.

A huge thank-you to my dear friend Becky, who has been a stalwart ally throughout my life, sharing in deep talks, going on birdwatching hikes with me, and being there through thick and thin.

And to Jason, wildlife photographer extraordinaire and fellow wildlife activist, thank you for your solid support and encouragement, for your fabulous company, for making me laugh, for reading my work, giving me feedback, and letting me bounce ideas off you while we adventure in remote places to help wildlife, drink in the scenery, and delight in all the magnificent creatures we share this planet with.

ABOUT THE AUTHOR

In addition to being a writer, Alice Henderson is a dedicated wildlife researcher, geographic information systems specialist, and bioacoustician. She documents wildlife on specialized recording equipment, checks remote cameras, creates maps, and undertakes wildlife surveys to determine what species are present on preserves, while ensuring there are no signs of poaching. She has surveyed for the presence of grizzlies, wolves, wolverines, jaguars, endangered bats, and more. These experiences in remote corners of wilderness inspired her to create the Alex Carter thriller series, as well as her cli-fi trilogy The Skyfire Saga, which begins with the novel *Shattered Roads*. Please visit her at alicehenderson.com, where you can sign up for her author newsletter, which includes wildlife news, green tips, volunteer opportunities, and more.